Praise for *Snow Like Ashes*

"*Snow Like Ashes* is a thrilling story with
unforgettable characters set in a stunning fantasy world
that had me quickly turning pages. I want more!"
—Morgan Rhodes, *New York Times* bestselling author
of *Falling Kingdoms*

"The plot and writing are superlative. . . . Highly
recommended."—*SLJ*

"An enjoyable adventure-romance."—*Publishers Weekly*

Epic Reads EDITION

SNOW LIKE ASHES

SARA RAASCH

BALZER + BRAY
An Imprint of HarperCollinsPublishers

To everyone who read the first (horrible) draft of this story
and did not laugh when twelve-year-old me said,
"Someday, I'm going to get this published."

Balzer + Bray is an imprint of HarperCollins Publishers.

Snow Like Ashes
Copyright © 2014 by Sara Raasch
Map art © 2014 by Jordan Saia

Library of Congress Cataloging-in-Publication Data
Raasch, Sara.
Snow like ashes / Sara Raasch. — First edition.
    pages   cm
Summary: Orphaned Meira, a fierce chakram-wielding warrior from the
Kingdom of Winter, must struggle to free her people from the tyranny of an
opposing kingdom while also protecting her own destiny.
    ISBN 978-0-06-304819-5 (special edition)
    [I. Fantasy. 2. Slavery—Fiction. 3. Orphans—Fiction.]   I. Title.
PZ7.R1025Sn   2014   2013047971
[Fic]—dc23   CIP
                                                                    AC

Typography by Erin Fitzsimmons
20 21 22 23 24   PC/LSCH   10 9 8 7 6 5 4 3 2 1
❖

I

"BLOCK!"

"Where?"

"I can't tell you where—you're supposed to follow my movements!"

"Well, then, slow down."

Mather rolls his eyes. "You can't tell an enemy soldier to slow down."

I grin at his exasperation, but my smile is short lived as the dull edge of his practice sword swipes under my knees. I slam onto the dusty prairie with a back-popping thud, my blade flying from my hands and vanishing into the thigh-high grass nearby.

Hand-to-hand combat has always been my weakest area. I blame Sir and the fact that he didn't start training me until I was almost eleven; a few additional sessions with a sword might have helped me catch more than three of Mather's blows now. Or maybe no amount of training would change how awkward a sword feels in my hands and how much I love throwing my spinning circular blade of death—my chakram. Predicting an opponent's close-range moves while a sword slashes through my vision has never been a strength of mine.

The rays of the sun prickle my skin as I stare up into the blue sky, wincing at a particularly sharp stone under my back. This is the fourth time in the last twenty minutes that I've ended up on the ground, watching stalks of prairie grass billow around my head. My lungs heave and sweat beads down my face, so I stay on my back, basking in this moment of peace.

Mather bends into my line of sight, upside down over me, and I hope he attributes the sudden heat in my cheeks to exertion. No matter how many times he puts me on the ground, he never looks anything but handsome. He's the kind of good-looking that makes me physically ache, makes me stumble for chairs when I'm caught unawares. A few pieces of his white Winterian hair dangle by his cheek, the rest of the shoulder-length strands held together by twine. The leather breastplate stretched over his chest highlights the fact that he's spent most of his life using those muscles in combat training, and his arms are lean and uncovered but for brassards. Freckles trail all along his pale face, his neck, his arms, a testament to the blinding sun of the Rania Plains.

"Best six out of eleven?" The hopeful note in his voice, as if he honestly believes that I have a chance at beating him, makes me cock an eyebrow.

I groan. "Only if the next six events can be ranged."

Mather chuckles. "I'm under strict orders to get you to win at least one *sword* match by the time William and the rest return."

I narrow my eyes and try to swallow the longing that rushes at me. Sir left with Greer, Henn, and Dendera on a mission to Spring while the rest of us stayed behind: Mather, the future king (who gets to go on the more dangerous missions because he's been trained since birth in the art of fighting); Alysson, Sir's wife (who has never shown the slightest skill in fighting); Finn, one other able-bodied soldier (Sir's rule— Mather always has to have a capable fighter to back him up); and me, the perpetually in-training orphan girl (who, despite six years of sparring practice, still "isn't good enough" to be trusted with the important assignments).

Yes, I've had to use some of my skills on food-scouting assignments, to fight off the occasional soldier or disgruntled citizen of one of the four Rhythm Kingdoms. But when Sir arranges missions to Spring, missions on which we'll be directly benefiting Winter instead of simply bringing back supplies for the refugees, he always has an excuse for why I can't go: the Spring Kingdom is too dangerous; the mission is too important; can't risk it on a teenage girl.

Mather must recognize the way I bite my lip, or the

way my focus drifts, because he exhales in a forceful sigh. "You're improving, Meira, really. William just wants to make sure you can fight at close range as well as long range, like everyone else. It's understandable."

I glare up at him. "I'm not horrible with hand-to-hand combat, I'm just not *you*-levels of good. Lie to Sir; tell him I finally beat you. You're our future king—he trusts you!"

Mather shakes his head. "Sorry, I can only use my powers for good."

His face twitches and it takes me a beat to realize the unexpected lie in what he said. He doesn't have any powers, not really, not like magic, and that shortcoming has been a struggle our entire lives.

I sit up, plucking blades of grass to roll between my fingers, if only so I have something to do in the sudden tension. "What would you use magic for?" I ask, my words so weak they almost float away.

"You mean, besides lying to Sir for you?" Mather's tone is light, but when I swing to my feet and turn to him, my chest aches at the strain on his face.

"No," I start. "If Winter had a whole conduit again, a conduit that wasn't female-blooded, that any monarch, king or queen, could harness, what would you use the power for?"

The question tumbles out of my mouth like a smooth stone in a stream, its edges worn clean by how often I roll it around in my head. We never talk about Winter's conduit, the locket that King Angra Manu of Spring broke when he destroyed our kingdom sixteen years ago, unless it relates to a mission. It's always "We got word that one of the locket halves will be in this place at this time"; never "Even if we manage to get our female-blooded conduit put back together, how will we know if the magic works when our only heir is male?"

Mather shifts, batting at the grass with his sword as if he's waging a personal war against the prairie. "It doesn't matter what I would do with it—it's not like I can use it."

"Of course it matters." I frown. "Having good intentions—"

But he shoots me an exasperated stare before I can even finish. "No, it doesn't," he counters. The more he says, the faster the words come, pouring out of him in a way that makes me think he needs to talk about it too. "No matter what I want to do, no matter how well I lead or how hard I train, I won't be able to force life into frozen fields, or cure plagues, or feed strength into soldiers like I would if I could use the conduit. The Winterians would probably rather have a cruel queen than a king with *good intentions*, because with a queen they at least have a chance that the magic can be used for them. It doesn't matter what I would do with magic, because leaders are valued for the wrong things."

Mather pants, his face tight as he hears everything he said, all his worries and weaknesses laid bare. I bite the inside of my cheek, trying not to stare at the way he winces to himself and smacks the grass again. I shouldn't have pushed it, but something deep in me always throbs with the need to say more, to learn as much as I can about a kingdom I've never even seen.

"Sorry," I breathe, and rub my neck. "Bringing up a sensitive subject while you're armed wasn't smart on my part."

He shrugs, but he doesn't look convinced. "No, we should talk about it."

"Tell that to everyone else," I grunt. "They just run off on missions and come back bleeding and say, 'We'll get it next time, and then we'll get the other half, then we'll raise allies and overthrow Spring and save everyone.' As if it's all so easy. If it's so easy, why don't we talk about it more?"

"It hurts too much," Mather says. Just that simple.

That makes me stop. I meet his eyes, a long, careful gaze. "Someday it won't hurt."

The promise we refugees always make one another—before going on missions, whenever people come back bleeding and hurt, whenever things go badly and we're huddling together in terror. *We'll be better . . . someday.*

Mather sheathes his blade and pauses, his hand on the hilt, before taking two steps toward me and cupping his palm around my shoulder. As I start, my eyes jerking up to his, he realizes what he's doing and pulls his hand back.

"Someday," he agrees, voice clipped. The way he clenches and unclenches the hand that touched me makes my stomach flip over in a spiral of thrill. "For now, all we need to worry about is getting our locket back so we gain standing as a kingdom again and can get allies to fight Spring with us. Oh, and we need to make sure you're able to do more than lie down during a sword fight."

I mock-laugh. "Hilarious, Your Highness."

Mather flinches, and I know it's from the title I used. The title I have to use. Those two words, *Your Highness*, are the wedge that keeps us the proper distance apart—me, an orphaned soldier-in-training, and him, our future king. No matter our dire circumstances, no matter our shared upbringing, no matter the chill his smile sends over my body, he's still *him*, and I'm still *me*, and yes, he needs to have a female heir someday, but with a proper lady, a duchess or a princess—not the girl who spars with him.

Mather draws his sword again as I hunt through the prairie grass for my discarded blade, refocusing on the task at hand rather than on the way his eyes follow me through the tall, yellow stalks. Camp stands a few paces ahead of us, the wide prairie lands camouflaging our pale brown-and-yellow tents. That and the fact that the Rania Plains aren't friendly to travelers has kept us safe for the last five years in this pathetic home—or as close to home as we have right now.

I pause in my search, staring at the camp with a growing weight on my shoulders. Far enough from Spring not to be discovered, close enough to be able to stage quick scouting missions, it's just a smattering of five tents, plus one pen for horses and another for our two cows. Otherwise the Rania Plains are barren, dry, and *hot*, even by the sweltering standards of the Summer Kingdom, and as such they sit empty, a territory none of the eight kingdoms of Primoria wants to claim. It took us three years to get a handful of scrawny vegetables to pop out of our garden, let alone enough crops to make occupying the plains worthwhile for a kingdom. So much conduit magic would have to be used to make the soil yield crops that it'd hardly be worth it, and no one can make a profit from watching the sun set.

But all of this is enough to keep the eight of us alive. Eight, out of the original twenty-five who escaped Winter's fall. Thinking about those numbers makes my stomach seize. Our kingdom used to be home to more than a hundred thousand Winterians, and most of them were massacred in Spring's invasion. The ones who weren't now sit in work camps throughout Spring. However few are left, waiting in slavery, they're worth enduring this nomadic lifestyle we live now. Those people are Winter, pieces of the life we should be leading, and they deserve—we *all* deserve—a real life, a real kingdom.

And no matter how long Sir restricts me to lesser missions, no matter how often I wonder if getting the locket pieces will be enough to win allies and free our kingdom, I'll be ready to help. I know Sir is aware of the dedication pulsing inside me; I know he understands that I share his desire to get Winter back. And someday, he won't be able to ignore me anymore.

On one trip to Yakim, one of the Rhythm Kingdoms, when I was twelve, a group of men cornered Sir and me in an alley, raving about the barbaric, warmongering Seasons.

How they'd rather we kill each other off so their queen could swoop in and pick through the rubble of our kingdom to find what they blame the Seasons for losing: Primoria's source of magic, the chasm atop which our four kingdoms sit.

"They really want us to kill each other?" I asked Sir after we managed to escape. I had fought one of them off myself, but as we scaled an alley wall to get away from them, my pride ebbed into confused shame.

Somewhere beneath the Season Kingdoms lies a giant, pulsing ball of magic; and somewhere in our Klaryn Mountains there was once an entrance to it. Only the four Season Kingdoms' lands are affected by the chasm—in the extremity and consistency of their environments—but every king and queen in Primoria, Rhythm *and* Season, possesses a portion of that magic in their conduits and can use it to help their kingdoms. The four Rhythm Kingdoms hate us for the fact that *this* is all they have, magic in objects like a dagger, a necklace, a ring. They hate us for letting the entrance get lost to age and avalanches and memory, for living directly atop the magic and not tearing our kingdoms apart to dig down and get more of it.

Sir stopped and crouched to my level, then scooped up a handful of melting snow from the side of the road. "The Rhythm Kingdoms envy us," he said to the slush. "Our kingdom stays in winter all year, in glorious snow and ice, while their kingdoms cycle through all four seasons. They have to tolerate melting snow and suffocating heat." He winked at me and pulled up his best smile, a rare treat that made my chest cold with happiness. "We should feel bad for them."

I crinkled my nose at the brown sludge, but I couldn't stop myself from sharing his smile, basking in the camaraderie between us. In that moment, I felt more like a Winterian, more a part of this crusade to save our kingdom, than I ever had before.

"I'd rather have winter all the time," I told him.

His smile faded. "Me too."

That was only the first time I felt—*knew*—that Sir saw the willingness in me. But no matter how often I prove myself, I can never push beyond his restrictions—though that won't stop me from trying. That's what all of us do: keep trying to live, to survive, to get our kingdom back no matter what.

I find my practice sword resting in a patch of trampled grass. Muscles spasming with the effort, I pick it up and frown at Mather, who stares past me into the plains. His face is blank, his expression hidden by the veil that makes him both a perfect monarch and an infuriating friend.

"What is it?" I follow his gaze. Four shapes wobble toward us, heat shaking their silhouettes in illusions of waves. But they're unmistakable even at this distance, and my breath catches in relief.

One, two, three, four.

They're back. All of them. They survived.

MATHER BLOWS PAST me through the grass. "They're here!"

From camp, Sir's wife, Alysson, gathers her skirts into a knot and hurries away from the food she's been fixing, and Finn sprints out of a tent with a medical bag.

I drop the sword and follow Mather, focused on the shapes before us. Is that one Sir? Is he leaning too far forward in his saddle? Did he get hurt? Of course he did. Two of them went to the outskirts of Abril, the capital of Spring, and the other two infiltrated one of Spring's seaside ports, Lynia. Neither is terribly deep inside Spring's borders, but they're still within Angra's domain, and any mission there ends in at least some bloodshed.

Mather and I reach them first. Finn's girth doesn't stop him from beating Alysson, and he stumbles to a halt seconds behind us, tearing bandages and creams out of the bag.

Dendera collapses off her horse, panting on the ground. She's in her late forties, Alysson's age, and her white Winterian hair hangs over a face creased with the slightest wrinkles around her eyes and mouth.

She wraps one arm across her waist and turns to Greer as he climbs off his horse. "His leg," she murmurs, pointing Finn toward the gash in Greer's thigh.

Greer waves him back to Dendera. "She's worse," he says, resting his forehead against his saddle as he takes deep, even breaths. His short, ivory hair clings to his head, matted with sweat and blood. Most days it's easy to forget he's the oldest of our group, hiding his age behind his unwavering determination to take on any task, any mission.

Henn slides off his horse next to Dendera, wrapping one of her arms around his shoulders to keep her up. The way he cradles her makes me want to look away, like I'm watching something intimate. It shouldn't feel any different than the way we all treat each other—a haphazard army with Sir as our commander rather than a family. But I can't help wonder whether, if our situation was better, Dendera and Henn would want to be a true family.

All four of them bleed from various spots on their bodies, torn shirts and makeshift bandages stained brown-red with a mix of dried and fresh blood. Sir is the only one who eases off his horse and stands straight, towering and immovable and watching us detachedly. With all the time

I spend with Mather, I should be better at decoding emotionless looks. But I just hover there, my body frozen with anxiety, unable to move to help Finn and Mather pass out bandages.

My eyes travel up and down each horse, each bag. Did they get the locket half?

"William!" Alysson's shriek precedes her by a few heartbeats as she hurls herself at her husband, injuries be damned. Seeing Sir wrap his arms around her, hold her tiny body off the ground, is like watching a bear clutch a rag doll—power and might alongside fragility and meekness. They fold into each other in a rare moment of vulnerability.

Sir sets down his wife. "It's in Lynia. Got there the day we left."

Finn lowers the handful of bandages he pressed against Greer's leg. Mather looks up from where he holds a small water sack for Dendera as she drinks. I suck in mouthfuls of the hot, heavy air, my mind whirling.

We've been searching for the locket throughout Primoria since Winter fell, but only a handful of times have we gotten leads on where one of the halves would be. Angra keeps half of it moving, bouncing from cities in Spring to remote settlements in the unclaimed areas of Primoria—the foothills of the Paisel Mountains, ports on the sea—to make it harder for us to get both halves back.

Now we're close. My chest swells with the same excitement that I know everyone is feeling, or felt before they ended up here, broken and bleeding. Sir will send someone back for it. Fresh and rested people make for the best soldiers, so he won't send anyone who just returned. Which means—

I rush toward Sir as he looks Mather up and down, then does the same to Finn. "You two, leave now," he says. "They'll move it again soon, since they know we escaped."

I stop. "They'll need everyone. I'll go too."

Sir looks at me like he forgot I'd be here. He frowns, shakes his head. "Not now. Mather, Finn, I want you ready to leave in fifteen minutes. Go."

Finn scurries off, his bulk swaying around him as he hurries back to camp. Obedient without thought, like everyone always is.

I stare up at Sir with my jaw clenched. "I can do this. I'm going."

Sir grabs his horse's reins and starts walking it toward camp. Everyone falls in behind him—except Mather, who hangs back farther, watching us, his eyes calm.

"I don't have time to argue this," Sir snaps. "It's too dangerous."

"Too dangerous for me but not for our future king?"

Sir looks at me as I walk alongside him. "Did you beat Mather in sparring?"

I grimace. Sir reads that as my answer.

"That's why it's too dangerous for you. We're too close to take any chances."

Prairie grass pushes against my hips, my boots tearing into the dirt with every step. "You're wrong," I growl. "I can help. I can be—"

"You do help."

"Oh yes, that bag of rice I bought in Autumn last month saved our kingdom."

"You're most helpful where you are," he amends.

I grab his arm to make him stop. He turns to me, his face streaked with dirt and blood through his white beard, frizzled strands of ivory hair sticking out around his face. He looks tired, hovering between taking one more step and collapsing.

"I can do more than this," I breathe. "I'm ready, William."

I called him Father once. In the wake of his stories about my real parents dying in the streets of Winter's capital, Jannuari, as Spring overtook it, and how he scooped baby-me up and rescued me, it seemed logical to an eight-year-old that the man raising her should be called Father. But he turned such a shade of red that I feared he'd start spitting blood, and he growled at me like he'd never done before. He was *not* my father and I was never, *ever* to call him that again. I was only ever to call him by his name, or a title, or something to show respect. But not Father. Never Father.

So from then on, I called him Sir. *Yes, Sir. No, Sir. You are not my father and I will never be your daughter and I hate that you're all I have, Sir.*

Now he ignores me, pulling his horse onward. His

decisions are final, and no amount of arguing will change his mind.

Like that's ever stopped me. "This isn't enough! And while I can't fault you for caring about the most efficient ways to save our kingdom, I know *I* can do things for Winter too."

A few paces behind me, Dendera moans, still hanging off Henn's neck. "Meira," she says, her voice worn. "Please, dear, you should be grateful you *aren't* needed."

I whip to her. "Just because you'd rather be patching dresses doesn't mean all women should want that."

Her mouth drops open and I pinch my eyes closed. "I didn't mean it like that," I sigh, forcing myself to look at her. She leans more heavily on Henn now, her eyes glistening. "I just meant that you shouldn't be forced to fight when you don't want to, and I shouldn't be forced to *not* fight when I *want* to. If Sir let me go, maybe you wouldn't have to go on missions. Everyone would win."

Dendera doesn't look any less hurt, but she glances at Sir, a quiver of hope hidden behind her pain. She used to be like Alysson, tending to camp, until Sir got desperate—he started needing her for missions just as he started letting me help with food scouting. She's never argued with him, not when he makes her train or when he sends her out on missions like these. But one look in her eyes and I can see how much this life terrifies her, how badly she'd rather be back at camp. She's as uncomfortable with weapons as I'd be in a gown.

Mather strides over to me through the grass, and I think he might try to offer words to break the tension. But after a few paces, he crumples to the ground like the earth sucked him down and refuses to release him. I frown as he grips his ankle.

"Oooww," he howls.

Sir bends down in a quick rush of panic. "What happened?"

Mather rocks back and forth and winces as everyone else moves closer. "Meira beat me in that last fight, didn't she tell you? Knocked me flat out. I don't think I can go to Lynia."

The wrinkles in Sir's face relax. "Didn't I see you run out to meet us?"

Mather doesn't miss a beat, still rocking and wincing. "I ran through the pain."

I suck in a breath until Sir looks up at me, and Mather winks discreetly above a wide grin.

"You beat him?" Sir asks, disbelieving.

I shrug. I'm a horrible liar so I just leave it at that. *Mather is helping me.* A blush warms my cheeks.

Sir has to know we're lying, but he won't risk sending Mather on the chance that he really did sustain an injury. He does trust him, more than anyone here. A moment passes before Sir rubs his temples and shoots a sharp breath out of his nose. "Help Mather into camp, then get your chakram."

I bite back my squeal of triumph but it comes anyway, a

weird blubbery noise that catches in my throat and bursts out of my still-frowning mouth. Sir stands, takes his horse, and marches into camp with renewed determination, like he doesn't want to face me now that he's given in. Everyone trails after him, leaving me to help Mather the invalid.

When the others are out of earshot, I fall to the ground and throw my arms around him. "You're my favorite monarch in the history of monarchs," I babble into his shoulder.

His arms come around me, squeeze once, shooting rays of chill through my body as I realize . . . we're hugging.

I fly to my feet and extend my hand to him, certain my face will be permanently stained red. "We should get back."

Mather takes my hand but pulls down as I pull up, keeping me from leaving. "Wait."

He turns to fish for something in his pocket and I lower to my knees beside him, my eyebrows pinching slightly. When he pivots back, his face is solemn, and the ball of nervousness in my stomach expands. In the center of his palm sits a round piece of lapis lazuli, one of the rarer stones Winter used to mine from the Klaryns long ago.

"I found it when we were staying in Autumn a few years back," Mather starts, his eyes soft. "After the lesson William gave us on Winter's economy. Our mines in the Klaryns, digging up coal and minerals and stones." He pauses, and I can see the child he was then. We moved to Autumn eight years ago, a boy-prince pretending to be a soldier and a girl-orphan who wanted nothing more than to pretend right alongside him.

"I liked to think it was magic," he continues, his face severe. "After our lessons about the Seasons sitting on a chasm of magic, and our lands being directly affected by the power, and Angra breaking Winter's conduit and taking our power in one swift crush of his fist, I wanted—needed—to believe that we could get magic somewhere else. Our world may seem balanced—four kingdoms of eternal seasons, four kingdoms that cycle through all seasons; four kingdoms with female-blooded conduits, four with male-blooded. But it's *not* balanced—it will always be tipped in favor of monarchs who have magic versus people who don't, like their citizens and . . . other monarchs whose conduits break. And I hated being so . . ." His voice trails off. "Help-less," he finishes.

My brow creases. "You're far from helpless, Mather."

His half smile returns and he shrugs. "At the very least, this lapis lazuli was a connection to Winter. And having it helped me feel stronger, I guess."

I bite my lip, not missing how he brushed past what I said.

He takes my hand and rolls the stone into my palm. "I want you to have it."

Giddiness floods my senses when Mather doesn't let go of my hand, doesn't look away from me. And the light flickering in his eyes—this is important to him. He's passing me a part of his childhood.

I pull the lapis lazuli closer to examine it in the dying sunlight. It's impossibly blue, no bigger than a coin, with darker strands of azure running along its surface.

Outside of the lost chasm, magic has only ever existed in the Royal Conduits of the eight kingdoms in Primoria, reserved for rulers to use as needed. Not in objects like this small, blue stone, sitting so inconspicuously in my palm. But I know why Mather wanted to believe the stone has magic: sometimes placing our belief in something bigger than ourselves helps us get to a point where we can be enough on our own, magic or no magic.

"Not that I don't think you'll be fine," he adds. "It just helped me sometimes, having a piece of Winter with me."

I squeeze the stone, coolness gathering in my chest beside the slow, dull thudding of my heart. "Thank you." I nod to his ankle. "For everything. You didn't—"

He shakes his head. "Yes, I did. You deserve to fight for your home as much as the rest of us do."

I swallow. We're still alone outside of camp, with only the faint breeze pushing through the grass and a few scraggy trees nearby. "I should pack."

Mather nods, his face blank again with that maddening, impenetrable nothingness. He fakes a limp into camp, my shoulder under one of his arms to help the charade. I keep a hand around his waist, the other clutching the lapis lazuli. I'm barely able to draw in full breaths, I'm so aware of his body against mine, of how when I look at him, I see the life

Sir says we're fighting for. Something simple and happy, just Mather and me in a cozy cottage in Winter.

But he's not just Mather—he *is* Winter. He will always be Winter first and foremost, and there is a palace in his future, not a cottage.

So I help him over to the fire and hurry to pack what I'll need for the trip, moving and doing in silence because silence is infinitely easier than talking. And now, finally, I'm moving and doing what I've always wanted—helping my kingdom.

WHEN I WAS eight, we moved our camp once again to make it harder for Angra to track us—this time, to Autumn. Until then, my life had been no bigger than the perimeters of our sad little camps in the Eldridge Forest. We passed through Autumn's capital, Oktuber, on our way to their southern forests, filling our carts and loading our horses with supplies.

Autumn was as similar to the foliage-heavy Eldridge as a snowflake is to a flame. The dense humidity of the Eldridge was nonexistent in Autumn's dry coolness, its yellow-and-red forests sleepy and crunchy and colored with warmth. Oktuber was a maze of rickety barns and tents in maroon, azure, and sunshine orange, with the crystalline blue sky gleaming above, a sharp and beautiful contrast to the kingdom's earth tones. But it was the Autumnians themselves who left me gaping—they were beautiful.

Their hair hung in tendrils as dark as the night sky, swaying in the dust kicked up from the roads that wove through Autumn's tent cities. Their skin glistened the same coppery brown as the leaves on some of their trees, only where the leaves were crinkled and dry, the Autumnians' faces were perfectly creamy.

I touched my own skin, as pale as the clouds drifting over us, and ran my fingers across the cap covering my blindingly white hair. My entire life, I had been surrounded only by the other Winterian escapees. It had never occurred to me that anyone might look different, but as I gazed at black eyes set in lush brown skin, I wished for my skin to be that pretty shade, and for my blue eyes to be a dark mystery too.

I told my wish to Alysson, who was tasked with keeping Mather and me out of trouble while everyone else gathered supplies. Her brow pinched in the wake of my admission. "The world is full of lovely people, Meira. I bet somewhere there is an Autumnian girl wanting to have skin the color of snow just as you want skin the color of earth."

My gaze flicked around, but I didn't see anyone watching us, at least not with the same yearning with which I watched them. I tugged at my cap. "Then why do we have to hide our hair?"

Alysson's hand went to her own hair, wrapped up in a blue length of fabric. In retrospect, hiding our white hair didn't do much to keep people from realizing who we were—if

23 ❧

anything, it only made them look at us twice, noting first our hats or fabric-wrapped heads, then our pale skin and blue eyes and how wholly out of place we were. But Sir never backed down in his insistence that we needed to at least try to disguise ourselves, lest Angra get word of our location.

After a deep inhale, Alysson touched my cheek, her fingers cool. "You won't have to hide forever, sweetheart. Someday our features will blend in, not stand out."

I doubt she meant blending into Spring.

I shove my hands into the pockets beneath my heavy black cloak, the dense wool swaying around the weapons strapped to my back and legs. The cloak's hood covers my head, hiding me in shadows as I stroll casually down the dirt road, the darkness of midnight falling on me from the half-moon sky. Every few seconds I peek up through the hood, noting the walls of Lynia just ahead, the gate at the end of this road flanked by flickering torches and a handful of Spring guards.

A shiver runs down my spine, but I keep my posture tall and confident, adding a cocky sway to my step the closer I get to Lynia's north gate. The Feni River gurgles off to my left, marking the northern border of Spring before it flows out to the Destas Sea. A bridge connects to the gate up ahead, linking Lynia to the Rania Plains over the river in a wide swoop of stone and wood. My eyes dart over it, to the darkened field beyond, before swinging back ahead. An escape route to keep in mind.

The Kingdom of Spring stretches to my right, drastically different from the barren, grassy prairie lands of the Rania Plains. In the daytime, rolling hills of lush greenery cascade all around, forests of blossoming cherry trees, fields of wildflowers in a rainbow of colors. In the nighttime, Spring looks far more like what it really is—cloaked in shadows, everything drenched in black.

It didn't take long to travel to Lynia, what with the breakneck pace Finn demanded. A little more than two days after we set out, we reached the port city. We hid our horses in an abandoned barn and waited until night, then split up to approach Lynia from the north and the south. Getting into Lynia is the easy part—getting out will be the fun part.

One other traveler strides down the road in front of me, a man slumped on his horse. He reaches the guards first, mumbles something about finding work at Lynia's docks the next day, and after a few moments of quiet muttering, they let him pass unmolested. I swallow. Based on the recon work Finn and I did, the patrol in Lynia has been increased along the wall and gates, making it impossible to sneak in unnoticed. But it *is* possible to pass as a Spring citizen, and waltz into Lynia with the guards' blessing. I keep my pace steady as I approach.

"Halt," one guard orders, flinging out a hand to block my way.

I step back, careful to keep my face out of the direct light of the sconces on my right and left. "On my way to the Dancing Flower Inn," I recite, the cover Finn and I came up with. My voice rumbles out low and deep to make myself as gender-neutral as possible. "Meeting a man for work."

Which isn't entirely a lie. Well, the Dancing Flower Inn is a lie—Sir told us about it and a handful of other landmarks in Lynia. Our real mark is the Keep, Lynia's seat of government and, according to Sir, the location of the locket half. My eyes flick past the guards—all five of them—to the great circular tower that looms above the other buildings in Lynia. It's in the center of the city, at least a half-hour trip. Finn will have the same from his end of the city.

I swing my gaze back to the guards. Two study me, the rest lean lazily against the wall, their breastplates gleaming in the flickering torchlight—silver armor with a black sun on their chests. Angra's sun. I'm not sure how much tighter I can ball my fists; my nails are already digging into my palms.

"Lots of people coming in for work at this hour. Odd, isn't it?" One of the guards cocks his head, his Spring-blond hair shorn against his scalp, his green eyes translucent in the combination of firelight and darkness. Exactly what I was counting on.

I finally tip my head back, the hood of my cloak sliding just enough for the firelight to touch my face. The flames will wash out my blue eyes just as they do his, making me look, enough for the guards at least, like a green-eyed Spring citizen. Spring citizens have skin a few shades darker than Winterians, but pale nonetheless, and the yellow light should make me look enough like one of them that they'll let me pass. I hope. No amount of tricks of the light could make my hair look anything but white, so it remains tucked safely under a black cap, which will also make me look more like a boy than a girl. I hope. So many *I hope*s. I bite my tongue, keeping my focus on the guard.

His eyes flash over me, one brow lifting in an expression that makes my blood freeze solid in my veins. "And what kind of work are you meeting this man for, girl?" he sneers.

His comrades perk up. The fact that they know I'm a girl isn't ideal, but that's the part of my disguise I'm least worried about—if they know I'm a Winterian, it will be a hundred kinds of bad.

I draw in a calming breath and pull up the coyest smile I can manage, angling my body slightly toward him. "Work you can't afford," I reply, throwing him a wink and strutting past them into the city. I hold my breath, waiting for them to shout at me to stop, waiting for one of them to run after me and try to convince me that actually he *can* afford it. But all I hear is a roar of laughter, and one of the guards applauds.

"Make our king proud!" he shouts, and I hurry into the city, leaving the jeering soldiers far behind before disgust or fear can creep up on me at what I just did.

I yank my focus back to the task at hand. The port on the

northeastern coastal tip of Spring, Lynia is sleepy and calm and lacking any hint of Spring's usual brutality, mainly because the closest Winterian work camp is a day's ride inland. Angra can't have damaged, hollow Winterian slaves sullying Spring's image when trading ships from other kingdoms dock here. Lynia's peace is only a mask painted on so the rest of the world can pretend that cracked and withered Winterian hands didn't make the goods they buy.

The streets around the gate aren't exactly busy, but they aren't empty either. A few taverns stand in halos of firelight, the ruckus of laughter and music emanating in muffled bursts from within. A handful of drunkards stumbles from tavern to tavern, but that's it. As if the rest of Lynia would rather stay tucked in their beds than partake of nighttime frivolities.

I've been in enough of Primoria's cities to know this isn't normal—most cities stay loud and bright even after the sun sets, and sneaking through them is all too easy. But in Spring, everything is quieter and more tense. If I stand still and hold my breath, I can practically *feel* Angra's evil. The way he uses his conduit's magic to pour devotion into his people, so that every Spring citizen responds to every situation like the guard: "Make our king proud!"

Other kingdoms use their conduits as they should be used—to enhance the already existing strengths of their lands and people. To make fields yield a plethora of fruit, to make soldiers strong, to make sick people healthy. But

Angra uses his conduit to enhance the bad—to snuff out anything good unless it benefits him. To make every soul in his kingdom an empty shell of servitude.

I duck down a deserted alley, heart pumping adrenaline in thick rivers through my body, but I don't slow my pace, even as I reach the stack of crates against a wall at the end. In a burst of movement I'm up the crates, scaling the wall, and rolling onto the tiles of the roof next to me, a handful of stories in the air. Spring soldiers may find Lynia's deserted streets easier to patrol, but spotting enemy soldiers on rooftops is a slightly more difficult task.

Chunks of tile crumble under my boots as I push into a sprint, a breath away from the edge of the roof and three stories of night air. I launch into the void, black cloak fluttering behind me through a smokestack's bitter cloud. The next roof slides under me like a field beneath a horse's hooves, nothing but speed and the jolt of running feet meeting solid ground. I drop-roll into the shadow of a chimney and wait a moment, holding my breath. No shouts of alarm. No clanking of armor moving closer.

Towering over the city, I have an unobstructed view of the land beyond Lynia's walls. The silhouette of the Klaryns paints jagged black teeth across the southern horizon, a quiet, sleeping beast that watches over all the Seasons— the Summer Kingdom farthest west, Autumn next, then Winter, and finally the Spring Kingdom on the Destas Sea. I wish we could see each other as the mountains see us—resting side by side in the arms of a watchful giant—instead of as separated, divided, enemies. If we did, maybe together we could find the way back into the chasm of magic.

My fingers run over my pocket, Mather's lapis lazuli ball tucked against my thigh, and I growl at myself. Sir would have slapped me across the back of my head by now to get me to refocus on what I'm doing, instead of what might be done.

I clear the next rooftops without a problem, angling my progress toward the Keep under the blue-black sky. The only thing that concerns me now is the shadow scaling the western wall of the tower. Finn should be a horrible soldier, but for whatever reason his short, stubby blob of Winterian girth has outdone my only slightly taller stick figure of Winterian agility on every mission we've worked together.

Without hesitation I fling myself from the last roof to a horizontal pole protruding from the side of the tower, Spring's flag rippling below me, a black sun against a yellow background. Random things, these flagpoles—almost as though the architects included them in the design should enemy soldiers need a quick way to get inside. When we rebuild Winter, there won't be flagpoles on buildings. Anywhere. Period.

Windowsill, balcony, windowsill, pole—I leap in this pattern until I reach the highest balcony. The warm, orange glow of firelight pours through a gap in the center of thick curtains, and Finn is already there, perched on the balcony ledge, grinning at me.

I swing up across from him and mouth, *I hate you.*

He grins more widely.

We hold for a moment, listening for any signs of life within. According to Sir, this room is the city master's office. No noise echoes back to us except for the steady crackle of a fire and the gentle whooshing of the curtains dusting the stone floor in the breeze. I glance over my shoulder, surveying the night below us. From the balcony, it's a straight drop to the street with a few windowsills along the way. Another escape route to keep in mind—from the Keep, at least.

We ease onto the balcony floor and scoot toward the curtains. Finn peeks through a gap, his eyes flickering in the golden glow, before he nods to me. The room is empty.

Adrenaline makes me twitchy with excitement as I grab one of the curtains, pull it back, and slip inside the office.

The fireplace in the back corner roars, stoked high with logs—the city master must plan on returning soon. High-backed chairs stand in a circle on a lush scarlet rug before the fire, and a desk stands against one wall. Above the desk hangs an old yellowed map that shows the kingdoms of Primoria surrounded by the Destas Sea to the east, the endless Rania Plains sweeping between the kingdoms and out to the west, and impassable mountains to the north and south. A few sconces hang on the walls, but that's it— simple and straightforward. I make for the desk while Finn, still on the balcony, keeps an eye on the closed office door.

Most of the drawers are unlocked, cluttered with quills and ink jars and blank pieces of parchment. My fingers fly through the odds and ends, sorting and searching as noiselessly as I can. The information Sir gave us just before we left flies across my mind and helps calm my racing heart: *We were able to steal a map of the Keep; we think they're hiding it somewhere underneath it, in a cellar, maybe. Wherever it is, it'll be locked, so find the key first, most likely in the city master's office.*

I repeat those words in my head as I fly through drawers, look under papers, shuffle ink jars. Nothing.

Finn hisses as voices waft toward me from beyond the door—someone's coming.

Panic leaps through me, dizzying surges that make it difficult to sort through everything carefully. I slide the last drawer shut, the voices outside close enough that I can make out a few words—"So honored to have you"; "Welcome, Herod."

I stumble into the desk, body convulsing with dread as I meet Finn's eyes across the room. My mouth forms the question: *Herod?*

Finn beckons me to hurry. Nothing about his demeanor changes, his forty-two years making him slightly more adept than I am at controlling emotions. But it isn't just emotions that swell inside me at the name. Memories slam through my head, one after another, gore and horror and fear all stemming from General Herod Montego.

I push away the images of our soldiers stumbling back into camp with bones protruding from their chests, delirious with pain, and I grab onto Sir's advice: *Focus on the goal. Don't get sidetracked. Don't let fear take hold of you—fear is a seed that, once planted, never stops growing.*

No fear—not now, not here. I scan the desktop once more in desperation, the sound of laughter coming from just beyond the door. They're right outside—

A letter, tucked under a heavy iron paperweight in the shape of a wildflower. I grab the letter without pausing to consider what it says and dive for the balcony, boots swishing across the stone floor. One breath after I'm outside, after the curtain flutters back into place, one breath after they would've seen my shadow flicker on the stone floor, the door opens, and voices barrel toward us.

Finn peers through the slit between the curtains, holding up his hand, flashing fingers to tell me how many he sees. Five soldiers. Two servants. Four nobles.

He drops his eyes to the paper in my hand and nods me along, half his focus on the conversation behind the curtain.

I shift in my crouch across from him and take deep, calming breaths before staring at the paper. My hands stop shaking enough that I can hold it in the slit of firelight.

Report: To All Spring Officials
Work Camp Population Statistics

Abril Camp: 469
Bikendi Camp: 141
Zoreon Camp: 564
Edurne Camp: 476

The document goes on to describe how many deaths, how many births, what things were built by what camps. But my hands are shaking again, and I can't focus on the words.

These are the Winterian statistics in Spring's work camps. The numbers are . . . people.

I touch the numbers, my fingers trembling. Such small totals. Did we know it was this bad? I suspected it was—Sir's lessons on the fall of Winter were graphic. The way he described how Angra planned the attack, as if he knew Winter would fall on *that day*, how he stationed every soldier he had throughout Winter, moving them in secret until everything exploded in one unavoidable sweep of destruction. There was nowhere to run—Angra blocked off any retreat into Autumn, or the Klaryns, or the northern Feni River. He barricaded us in our own kingdom, and when he broke the locket, when our soldiers had no magic-given strength to help them stand against him, we fell. Only twenty-five of us managed to escape.

I feel the weight of that now. Seeing the statistics proved what Sir has been saying for years—every day, we're teetering on the edge of Winterians becoming nothing more than memories.

"I trust my king, I do," a voice booms within the room. I snap my head up, all the adrenaline and fear warping into anger. Finn tightens his lips in warning, and I thrust the paper at him in response.

"And I know it was scheduled to be here longer," the voice continues. "But I want it out of my city. *Tonight*. Before any more Winterian scum descends upon us."

The city master. I exhale. The locket half is still here—we haven't lost it yet. My relief is short lived when Finn scans the paper, looks back up at me, and the expression he gives isn't fear or shock—it's just pain. Regret.

My eyes widen. *Did you know how bad it is?* I mouth.

He tucks the paper into his belt and bobs his head once. Yes, he knew. Everyone in camp probably knows. It's just one of the things they don't talk about, one of the too painful parts of our past. And I knew too—I just didn't have exact numbers in my head to fuel my rage.

Herod laughs, and my nerves flare higher. Killing him is going to feel so good.

"Calm yourself. It will be gone within the hour."

"It's safe here." A different voice. Probably one of Lynia's councilmen. "I don't care if the Winterians know it's here. Lynia can keep it protected far better than any other city—"

"Silence!" the city master shouts.

But Herod chuckles. "Ambitious, your man."

"Not ambitious," the councilman corrects. I hear a rustling as someone walks across the room. My heart ricochets around my ribs—they're going to the desk. Will they notice that the paper is gone? "Certain. The safe we built for it—it's perfect. The Keep above—"

Excellent: the location of the locket half. Sir was right—it's under the Keep.

A harsh movement from within is followed by the crack of the councilman's face meeting Herod's fist. Bodies move, chairs fall, and amidst the ruckus Herod's voice rises.

"Do not speak of its location! That was our arrangement—you hide it and never utter a word of the location. It isn't safe so long as that boy breathes."

I bristle. *Mather will keep breathing so long as I am breathing, you murderer.*

But the councilman doesn't react. Something shuffles, and I realize it's papers on the desktop, the *thunk* of a paperweight. I widen my eyes at Finn, who grimaces before the councilman even speaks.

"The—" the councilman starts, clearly confused. "Something's missing."

A pause, then a growl resonates in the stillness. I can taste Herod's fury on the air as his growl morphs into three words that make my heart plummet.

"We aren't alone."

4

BOOTS POUND ACROSS the room. The curtain flashes open as Finn and I leap, dropping face-first off the balcony and into the cool night.

"Winterians!" Herod screams. "Lock it down *now!*"

In the seconds of free falling before I hit the ground, I find myself faced with two options. Continue my fall, drop into a roll on the street, and make all haste out of Lynia in the hope that we can get back in later, or cling to the building and find a way inside. Key or not, we're so close to the locket half that something as small as a jagged piece of metal shouldn't stop us. But the plan was that if either of us ran into trouble, Finn and I were to regroup outside the city. If we leave now, though, getting back in will be impossible. They'll move the locket half without hesitation, and we'll be back where we started.

My body makes the decision before I do. The rock wall shreds my fingers as I scramble against it, and two window-sills fly past before I find purchase on one, body jerking to a halt, wrists screaming at having to support my weight so abruptly. I flail, arrows barely grazing my kicking legs and straining arms as I scramble against the rock, searching for footholds, and use a few chipped pieces of mortar to pull myself up and over the windowsill.

The window pops inward and I tumble inside, blinking in the darkness until my vision adjusts. *Please don't let this room be anything with soldiers inside.* Maybe a kitchen, or a nice cozy bedchamber, or—I look around wildly—a storage room. It's a storage room, empty but for stacks of shadowed crates in the narrow, lightless space. Perfect.

Outside, Herod's voice carries, screaming about Lynia's failures. I peek over the windowsill and spot Finn's plump shadow skirting into an alley. He pauses, face caught in a ray of moonlight as he scans the area. He doesn't see me, and I don't want to draw any Spring attention by waving. He'll go back to camp now, I know—another of our protocols. If one of us goes missing, the other is to leave immediately.

Before I realize the full extent of what I've done, how alone I am now, Finn's gone. He'll tell Sir I vanished in the chaos, and Sir will growl something about how he never should have let me go in the first place.

I have to prove him wrong.

My arms are too rubbery from my windowsill grab to throw my chakram, so I settle for the curved knives hidden in my boots. One in each hand, I creep across the narrow storage room. The door opens easily enough and I fly out, knives ready, heart racing.

But the hall is empty, lit only by a few widely spaced sconces on the walls. The floor slopes up to the right and down to the left. I run left, the sounds of chaotic anger closing in on me from above. No doubt Herod's rushing down the Keep, shouting to the men below that I'm coming. Too bad I'll beat him there.

A few stories later, I stumble out of the hall into the center receiving room, a grand affair draped in gray stone and heavy green curtains. The late night works in my favor— there are no men here. They're all with the city master.

Herod's shouts echo from up the hall, closer and closer. I scan the room, my pounding pulse choking any air from my lungs, leaving me gasping as I survey each corner. A door nearly three stories tall shoots into the air on my left—the exit, most likely. I do a quick count—four other doors lead out of the room, two closed, two open. Through the two open ones I see a long dining room and a small, dark kitchen. That leaves the two closed doors.

I ease one of my knives into my sleeve and attack the first door. It opens without a fight and I stumble into . . . somewhere really, really bad.

To my left and right stretch two long rows of cots, most

filled with the lumpy bulks of sleeping soldiers. A barracks for the Keep's guards. Terror makes sweat slick down my back, candlelight pouring in behind me from the chandelier that hangs over the center receiving room, and I chirp in surprise, then immediately smack my hand over my mouth. No one moves for a moment, and just when I think I might get by, Herod's shout barrels into me, only a story or two above.

"To arms!" he cries, and that's enough to send every sleeping soldier into instant readiness, whipping to their feet and scrambling for weapons.

I grab the door, yank it closed, and sprint for the other closed door. This is close, *too* close, and by the time the soldiers in the barracks open their door, I'm shaking the last closed door—locked—and spitting every curse I've ever heard.

"Snow and ice and frost above." Luckily Sir likes to test Mather and me with inane challenges like *Pick the lock on this chest, your supper's inside.* His tests and the finger-length hook-pick I keep in my hair finally prove useful, though I certainly don't plan on telling him that. I tuck the other knife under my arm and busy myself with the lock.

The soldiers stumble out of their room. Herod draws closer. The lock doesn't budge, whether because I'm too twitchy or my hands are slick with sweat or I just need to practice more lock picking. My chances of making it out of the Keep shrink with each breath I take, each strangled sputter of my heart filling my body.

"Who needs a key?" I growl as a I rear back and hurl all of my weight into kicking through the lock. It breaks open, sending the door thudding against the wall. A set of stairs curls downward with light lifting up from below, a flutter of yellow.

"Stop!"

I whirl. Herod stomps into the hall and his lumbering bulk freezes across the room. Such a perfect chakram shot; damn my shaky arms. But soldiers fill the space between us, most half dressed, clutching weapons and blinking away the blur of sleep. Too many to take all at once.

Herod glares at me and his face reddens. "Winterian!"

I dive into the staircase and slam the door behind me, but my kick broke the lock so the door refuses to close. Though it means I'll lose a knife, I jam one of my blades as hard as I can through the lock and into the wooden frame. It'll hold enough to give me a better lead.

The stairs get slippery the deeper I go, the walls coated in what smells like donkey waste. This isn't just a cellar, and on a deep inhale, I realize exactly where I'm going, where they hid the locket half: the sewers. Oh, fun.

A few stifled breaths later, the sound of gruff voices echoes up at me. I test my arms—not quite as shaky—and draw out my chakram, tightening my hand around the familiar, worn handle.

"Hurry! There's a ruckus above. Best we move quickly."

I stop at the last turn in the staircase, the glow of lantern light strong. They're close. Chakram-range close. My favorite kind.

"I'm not touching that thing. You know what it is! *You* pick it up." From the sounds of their conversation, there appear to be only two of them.

The other man growls. "I'm your superior! I order you to pick up the damn locket piece."

I smile. There's my cue. "Now, boys, no need to argue. *I'll* pick it up."

I emerge from the staircase with my chakram wound back, ready to soar through the air. We are indeed in a sewer—a tunnel opens around me, holding a river of murky waste lined with foot-high walkways on each side. One man and a few horses wait on the farthest walkway, the other man stands ankle deep in Lynia's filth. Very few men, but any more would draw too much attention.

Behind the men, one of the wall's bricks has been removed and in the hole, illuminated by a few lanterns, shines a blue box. Relief fills me up. After years of searching, half of the locket is finally within reach.

I aim my chakram at the captain with his boots mucked up in sewer gunk. His eyes swim over me. "The Winterians are sending girls to do their dirty work now?" he sneers. "Why don't you put that thing down before someone gets hurt?"

I push out my bottom lip and widen my eyes. "This?" I

lower the chakram. It's now aimed at the captain's left thigh. "They gave it to me and said *throw!* I don't even know how it works—"

The soldiers jeer, a deep-throated chuckling that says this is a fight they're sure they'll win. I let the chakram fly as the captain moves forward, my body bending into an arch. The chakram soars through the sewer, slices clean through the captain's leg, and continues its spin back to me in one elegant circle of purpose. He screams and drops into the sewage, grabbing his thigh like, well, like I just sliced through it.

"Oh." I run one hand down the flat side of the blade. "*That's* how it works."

The other soldier eyes me from the opposite walkway, his hands out like he might start dancing. Or running. Probably the more likely option. But then he smiles, and his shift from scared to amused is so abrupt that a flicker of disquiet tightens in my stomach.

Magic.

The word flies through my mind like it was there all along, a quiet pulse of knowledge that told me everything felt off. Wrong. And it *was* wrong, all of it, because the soldier drops his arms and pulls his shoulders up straight, his body morphing before me. Bones cracking and re-forming, muscles stretching with a sickening rip. The soldier isn't a soldier, at least not a nameless, nothing soldier, and the captain I shot laughs from his still-fetal position, his anticipation laced with pain.

That wasn't Herod earlier. Of course it wasn't. Herod wouldn't waste his time mingling with the city master; he would be here, with the locket half, waiting to intercept thieves.

Herod finishes transforming until the only thing light about him is his golden hair, green eyes, and pale skin—the rest of him is shadow, a testament to his master's evil. He's huge too, his head nearly brushing the ceiling, and thick in the shoulders, the body of someone who was born holding a sword. Which does not sound like fun for his mother.

I lean forward to launch my chakram but Herod lunges off the platform, takes one step through the sewer gunk, and throws his body at my knees. I trip off the walkway and go down in the middle of the sewage, my breath knocked out by both Herod's body and the sudden immersion in feces. He grabs the chakram and slides it onto the walkway, out of reach, before pinning my arms above my head in a painful twist, sneering at me as feet thunder down the staircase. The not-Herod and his men have broken through the door.

This could have gone better.

I wiggle in his hands, something in my pocket digging into my hip—a weapon? No, Mather's lapis lazuli ball. The only thing it's good for now is as a painful reminder of Mather, of Winter, of how he'll never forgive himself if anything happens to me.

Herod's fingers tighten around my arms and I flinch.

His grip is just above my one remaining weapon—the knife in my sleeve.

"Sir!" A soldier rushes into the sewer. It's the not-Herod, slowly morphing back into his own form. I've heard stories of the magic Angra uses his conduit for, beyond controlling his people. Tales whispered when people returned from missions in bloody tangles of broken limbs, memories shared in the heat of fever and agony. Angra uses his magic to induce visions so real they drive his people mad, to snap traitors' bones and tear out organs while his people still live, and for transformations like this one.

As Herod drags me up, the only solace I find is that both of us are covered in sewage.

"Bind her. We're taking her to Angra," he orders, and steps way too close to me as a soldier loops rope around my wrists. "Scared, soldier-girl?"

I force myself to look him in the eye. I don't have the luxury of fear. When we're at camp in the safety of our tents and Sir explains all kinds of horrific possible deaths to me, I can't show fear. *Fear is a seed that, once planted, never stops growing.*

But I was there when Gregg, one of our soldiers, stumbled back into camp six years ago. He and his wife, Crystalla, had been captured while on a mission in Abril and thrown into the nearest work camp. Gregg told us about it, babbling in the grip of madness about the grueling work, the decrepit living conditions—and the brutal, inhuman way

Angra made Herod kill Crystalla. Gregg barely escaped with his life, and even that he lost a day later, when the injuries Herod gave him proved too much for his body to handle.

A tremor runs through me, and I know Herod saw it. That seed of fear.

I cannot die like Crystalla.

A soldier lifts me onto a horse and ties my wrists to the saddle. Hope flutters in my chest—they didn't check me for weapons. Whether because of the chaos of my intrusion or the need to get the locket half out of Lynia as fast as possible, I don't know—but I still have my knife. I still have a chance.

Herod eases the locket box from the hole and holds it for a moment, looking up at me. That face, that mocking twitch around his lips—this is the monster in Gregg's story, the one Angra uses to destroy his enemies in the most brutal ways possible. Angra doesn't like getting his hands dirty, not when he can watch as his puppets dance around in such glorious shows as he uses his Royal Conduit to control them. Why be the dog when you can be the master?

Herod tucks the box into the saddlebag nearest me. Before he mounts, he grabs my chakram off the walkway, tossing it between his hands and eyeing me with that taunting sneer. He leaps onto his stallion and slides the chakram into the saddlebag on the other side of his horse.

There's no way I can get it now.

"You try to escape and you'll be dead long before we reach Abril," he warns.

I suck in a breath, twisting my wrists as imperceptibly as I can until my knife drops into my palm. "And I'll kill you before all of this is over."

Herod smiles, the bloodlust on his face glowing more strongly. Nausea twists my stomach in unrelenting knots— he likes when I fight back. Something to keep in mind.

With a shout, Herod tells the men to leave. He grabs my horse's reins and pulls me forward, my leg bumping against his saddlebag. I can feel it, the small square box pressing into my shin. The only thing separating it from me is a layer of leather.

I need to keep him distracted, focusing on body parts other than my hands.

"How are they?" The question is quick and sharp. They, the Winterians in the camps.

I swallow. Two of the ropes are cut. One more . . .

Herod turns to me. He smirks, pulls my horse close so that I'm hip to hip with him. "The backbone of the Spring Kingdom. Though you Winterians die too quickly for my taste."

A few more fibers cut, and the rope falls off my wrists. I fight the urge to stretch my poor, abused arms and concentrate on Herod, on letting him think I'm resigned to my fate.

I turn to him, meet his eyes, and lean a little like I'm

sliding toward him in my saddle. "Well, there's one Winterian I know who isn't dying. At all. And he's going to destroy Angra."

Herod does exactly what I hoped he'd do: he lets go of my horse's reins long enough to slap me. The blow yanks my hand up, the hand that I had managed to slide into his saddlebag and wrap around the small blue box.

I kick my horse, hard, and launch down the sewer's walkway, all so fast that Herod still has his hand in the air before he realizes I'm free—and I've got the locket half.

"*No!*" he screams, gravelly voice reverberating off the stone walls.

I urge my horse on, galloping beside the muck of the sewer until we escape into darkness, out of the lantern light. Arrows fly past but smack off the stone, lost without something to aim at. Hooves pound behind me, shouts and curses follow, and I make a mental note to always, *always* put a knife in my sleeve when I go on missions.

The horse seems to know where he's going, so I just urge him faster. Surely he's as repulsed as I am by the stench and remembers how he got down here—too bad his new rider is covered in sewage. I gag, finally calm enough to feel the stink of feces all over me.

I shift on the reins, keeping my other hand pressed so tightly to my stomach that tomorrow I'll have a box-shaped bruise there. A mark of my heroics—Meira, the first soldier to retrieve half of Winter's locket. A well of pride springs in me, and I hold on to the feeling as tightly as I clutch the box.

The horse curves around one more turn and we fly up to the surface. The cool, fresh night air makes me smile and I kick the horse faster, faster. Not quite free yet.

We're only seconds from the north gate when the guards stationed there realize what's happening. They scramble for the lever that will close the iron bars over me, but it's too late—I push the horse on, throwing a glance at the guard who first stopped me on my way in. His eyes widen with recognition, so I rip off the black cap that covered my hair as I whizz past, galloping across the bridge over the Feni River. White strands stream around me, some matted with sewer muck, but most tossing in the wind. A living snowstorm, a vibrant white reminder that they haven't enslaved every Winterian. Some of us are still alive. Some of us are still free.

And some of us are half a locket closer to taking back our kingdom.

I MAKE IT back to camp in two days, stopping only for a handful of half-hour breaks. I don't see Finn along the way, but I have to believe it's because he sped back to camp with just as much ferocity and beat me there, not because he didn't make it out of Lynia.

I leap off my horse, poor steaming thing, and lead him to a narrow stream where he slurps down water like he's never tasted anything so sweet. As he drinks, I lunge across the stream and stumble up the hill, prairie grass pushing against my thighs. There, under a clear blue sky, sits our camp, like I never left at all.

A horse bearing Lynia's golden *L* on its livery stands in the corral—Finn got back safely. I relax, inhaling the earthy scent of sunbaked grass. No other prisoners of Herod's will come stumbling back into camp bloody and broken. Not today, anyway.

I pull my shoulders back and stride into camp with as much dignity as I can muster, considering I'm still caked with dried sewage. No one's around, though, no one poking at a crackling breakfast fire or scrubbing clothes at the well. Which means almost everyone will be in the meeting tent, the largest of our dull yellow-and-brown structures. I don't bother alerting anyone to my presence—I fling back the flap and stomp in, leaving clumps of gunk on the faded brown carpet.

Our five men cluster around a dented oak table in the center of the room. Their faces are scrunched in varying states of worry, from silent grimacing to outright shouting, so caught up that they don't notice me at first.

"We've got to send someone back for her! Each moment we waste is another moment she could be dead," Greer shouts. His deep voice carries farther than anyone else's, but he rarely, if ever, speaks out in meetings. The skin on my arms prickles. If he's worried enough to talk, they must be pretty concerned.

"I never should have let her go," Sir growls. "How did you lose her, Finn?"

The tent flap rustles into place behind me, and the men turn as one, their words dying in their mouths as five shocked faces stare up at me. Five faces with eyes in a spectrum of blue shades; five faces aged by war and death and sixteen years of nomadic living. A few of them still have bandages from their last mission tied around their limbs.

"Don't work yourselves into a panic, gentlemen—I'm alive," I announce, forcing arrogance to cover just how exhausted I am. I make sure I bump Finn with the most gunk-covered part of my cloak when I squeeze between him and Henn. The locket box tears from my palm like a block of ice that stuck to my skin and clunks against a stack of maps on the table.

Silence. Shocked, stunned, I-have-to-be-dreaming silence. My chest cools and I wait for the softest, most delicate tingle of pride. Placing the locket half on the table completed this mission, and now that it's done, now that I succeeded, I've finally proven what I've wanted for so long. *This.* That I can help Winter. That I can use what I'm good at—thinking on my feet, ranged fighting, stealth—to help my kingdom. But all I feel is . . . tired.

I step back. Staring at me is the usual lineup: Sir, Finn, Henn, Greer—and Mather.

He is the only one whose attention didn't get sucked to the box the moment I placed it on the table. His jewel-blue eyes are unreadable as he stares at me, his face locked in an expression that's either joy or horror. I choose to think it's joy.

"Meira."

I flinch and turn to face Sir, who stands, lifting the box. "Yes?"

He doesn't look at me, just flicks the lock and lifts the lid, his face gray with dreamlike surprise. I can't see the locket half from here, but I know what he's looking at. Sixteen years of fighting, of hoping that once we reunite our conduit's two halves, we'll be closer to getting our kingdom back.

"You . . ." Sir looks up at me. Back at the box's contents. Back at me.

I've rendered Sir speechless. Oddly, that small victory makes me feel lighter than retrieving the locket half and surviving Spring did.

Sir starts to ask something but takes a deep breath, coughing as he inhales the stench emanating from me. "Alysson!" he wheezes. "For the love of all that is cold, will you draw Meira a bath?"

I laugh as Alysson hurries in from an adjoining tent. She reaches for me, twitches when she realizes what she'll be touching, and settles for simply ushering me out with a wave.

"And when you're done, Meira," Sir calls, "you're going to tell me *everything*."

"Yes, Sir," I reply, not bothering to hide my smile.

As I leave, Sir's voice trickles after me. "Snow above. She actually did it."

It's not praise, but it makes me smile just the same. Yes, I *did* do it.

It takes five buckets of water, two bars of soap, and a small fire to get rid of the sewer gunk. Once the last of my ruined outfit is crackling away in the flames, Alysson departs to care for my stolen horse. I pull on a clean, white shirt and black pants—sweet snow above, *clean clothes*—and leave my wet hair to dry in the wind as I trek back to the meeting tent.

I take a deep breath, gathering my remaining strength to face Sir, and plunge inside. The giant oak table has been pushed aside to make room for a cluster of pillows, their threadbare brown fabric stretched taut over stuffings of wool and prairie grass. Two bowls—one holding steaming vegetables, the other cradling a handful of frozen berries—wait inside the pillow ring. The cushions surround something else that makes my breath catch on the velvetiness of the warm air: a circular iron fire pit, far enough back so as not to set the pillows aflame but close enough to let the earthy smell of burning coal absorb into the fabric.

Steam rises off wild turnips and onions, twisting into an aroma of savory sweetness. But it's the berry bowl that makes my stomach do a little dance of excitement as I drop onto a pillow. I haven't had frozen berries since my last birthday, seven months ago, and seeing the bowl of frosted black and red orbs makes more than hunger twirl through me. Alysson makes them for special occasions, or tries to, when enough ice can be found to freeze the berries solid. They're a Winterian delicacy, something all the other refugees eat in revered solemnity.

Speaking of Winterian delicacies . . .

The coals shift, sending up a cloud of warmth. Sweat breaks out across my forehead and my nose tingles with the smell of the heat. It isn't for warmth that we have this fire pit—I think I speak for every Winterian when I say we'd rather be frozen solid than near any kind of spark—it's for memory. It's for the same reason I have a fistful of slowly thawing berries in my palm.

Last year, Finn and I bought food in a small market on the outskirts of the Kingdom of Ventralli, one of the Rhythms. While there, he found this pit buried in a pile of iron knickknacks a blacksmith was melting down. When he spent half of our measly savings on it, I expected Sir to beat him with it and make him try to sell it back. But the look on Sir's face when Finn lugged it into camp launched a pang of helplessness through my body. The gentle, sad pull of wanting.

Winter made this. Or, rather, Winterians mined the coal and the iron that went to other kingdoms like Yakim and Ventralli, which made the fire pit itself. But the coal and iron still came from Winter, a part of our kingdom ripped from the mountains and molded afar.

To improve their kingdoms' economies, rulers use Royal Conduit magic to enhance certain areas of expertise that their kingdoms developed based on geography or the natural talents of their citizens. If a certain kingdom showed an interest in education, the ruler used magic to make their people excel at learning; if another kingdom showed an aptitude for fighting, the ruler used conduit magic to make their soldiers more lethal. Winter sat north of the richest part of the Klaryns, so our queens enhanced our ability to find minerals and granted us endurance and courage in the bottomless, dark places of the earth.

Spring has their own mines in their section of the Klaryns, but theirs produce deadly powders that fuel their cannons, the only mines in the world that harbor it. That's what we thought the war was about—Spring wanted to expand their mine holdings. But when they won, they didn't tear into our mines. They just boarded them all up, like their goal was simply to destroy Winter piece by piece, spirit by spirit, by making us sit back and watch Winter's most valued possession fall into decay.

Once Angra kills us all, he'll probably reopen the mines. But as long as we live, it's more valuable to dangle our useless mines in our faces, taunt us and distract us into making mistakes, getting caught, falling into his open hands. Or at least, that's what we tell each other, to make it feel less like the war was all for nothing.

I pop a berry in my mouth and stare at the orange and dusty black of the burning coals. The berry numbs my tongue, makes ribbons of ice crawl up my teeth, but its chilly sweetness is suddenly not as enticing. I reach one finger out and put it on the edge of the fire pit, farthest from the heat, and hold it there until the burning sensation creeps up my whole hand. The others set up all this because they want me to know that what I did was important—important enough to burn coal.

But it doesn't *feel* important. Not like it should.

I'm reminded now, watching the coals burn, of why I never feel like I truly belong to Winter. I want to understand all this as deeply as Sir and Alysson and everyone else, a reminder of a time when everything was how it should be, but all this is wasted on me, someone whose only connection to Winter lies in stories told by others. I thought that if I had a hand in saving Winter, I'd feel like I deserve it, the kingdom everyone else remembers. I thought I could fill the void left by my lack of memories with purpose. That's what I've always told myself: if I matter to Winter, Winter will matter to me. And today I mattered to my kingdom.

Then why don't I feel anything more for the fire pit than the slight burn on my finger?

Behind me the tent flap stirs, a whisper of noise that could almost be dismissed as the hiss of coals or the wind. My muscles tighten, the hairs on my arms rise. But I don't flinch, don't react, just spear a chunk of turnip with a fork.

A breath later, fingers touch the base of my neck where a blade would go if this attacker were truly an attacker. I shiver, but not from the coolness of my wet hair pressing to my skin.

"You're dead," Mather says, laughter in his voice.

When I first started learning to fight, he would sneak up on me in the weapons tent or the training yard, slinking noiselessly until he touched my neck and whispered that joking threat. And no matter how many times he did it, it still left me screaming like Angra himself had snuck up on me. Sir, of course, did nothing to stop it; he just said I needed to get better at paying attention to my surroundings.

I look up at Mather and pause midchew. He drops onto the pillow across from me, his face stretching in a grin.

"Dead? I let you sneak up on me," I snort. "All this future-king-of-Winter stuff has gone to your head, Your Highness."

Mather's face twitches at his title. "You always say you let me sneak up on you. Too scared to admit you're not as good as everyone thinks you are?"

I swallow. "Aren't we all?"

Mather drops his gaze to the fire pit, the orange glow pulsing in his azure eyes. "William showed me the locket half," he breathes.

My hand tenses around the fork, and I open my mouth to say something, but all I can think of are the same illusion-shattering questions I asked him before I left. Things that make our veil of happiness evaporate like drops of water on a bed of hot coals. So I just stay quiet, and in the silence he looks up at me, one corner of his mouth cocked curiously.

"It's strange to think that the last time any Winterian saw it, it was around my mother's neck." His eyes focus on something beside my head, something hovering in the patched-together memories everyone has told him too. Memories of his mother, Queen Hannah Dynam. Memories of how Angra himself marched into the Jannuari palace, killed her, and broke the conduit in two.

I recognize that look. Mather's face takes on the same aura of disappointment whenever he misses a target in practice, or when Sir beats him at sparring, or when I ask him how he'd use magic if he could. Disappointment in himself, in his inability to do what he set out to do, even when it's far out of his control. He runs a hand over his face to brush it off, and there's that emotionless veil again, hiding his true feelings behind a smile.

I shake my head slowly. "You're insane."

His eyebrows pinch in the suggestion of a smile. "Am I?"

"Yes." I stab another turnip and leave the fork there. "We got the locket half. You shouldn't be feeling anything other than happiness right now—*real* happiness, not your fake smiles—Mr. Heir of Winter."

Mather's face grows solemn. He pauses, his hands open in his lap like he's holding all of his worries. "I didn't feel anything," he murmurs, a slow, absent thought. "When I saw the locket half. It was the only thing I've ever seen of my mother's. I should have *felt* something."

I fight to steady my breathing, and my eyes drop for a beat to the fire pit. Wasn't I just worrying about these same things? I forget sometimes how similar Mather is to me—how we're both young enough to feel separated from Winter in the same ways. Mather's lack of feeling is a bit more pressing, though. After all, he's Winter's king.

But I don't have any way to reassure him, any wise words to soothe his fears—if I did, I'd be able to fix my own problems too. "It's just half of a necklace right now," I try. "Maybe you'll feel something when it's a whole conduit again."

Mather shrugs. "I'm not supposed to have any connection to it, though, remember? I'm just her son." His face flashes with shame and he shakes his head. "I'm sorry. You're right; this is supposed to be a happy day. You got the locket half. Thank you." He leans forward, his eyes intent. "Really, Meira, thank you."

My face spasms with confusion, but I can't do anything to smooth it out. I didn't know he'd put so much weight on the locket half, that he wanted so badly to have a connection to his mother. I don't remember my parents or even know who they were, but it never occurred to me that Mather would hurt so badly for people he'd never met either. Does he miss his father too? Hannah's husband, Duncan, was a Winterian lord before he became king. Does Mather wish he knew him if only to talk to someone in the same situation—king of a female-blooded kingdom?

A heaviness settles in my stomach, filling me with a choking mix of guilt and anxiety—wanting to help Mather, but knowing it's as out of my power as using

Winter's conduit is out of his.

Thankfully at that moment, the tent flap opens to reveal Sir. He takes in the absent food, my wet hair. I hold my breath, remembering why I'm really here—to tell Sir what happened.

Sir sits next to me, silent. He doesn't reprimand me for being so casual with our future king, doesn't berate me up and down for my informality and poo-covered entrance.

Uh-oh.

He withdraws the box from his pocket. "So," he begins. "Would you care to explain?"

Suddenly I feel like the misbehaving child who first begged Sir to let me help out with the resistance. The child who waved swords around like awkward steel wings and showed absolutely no promise in fighting until I tried ranged weapons like my chakram, and it turned out I could be deadly too. The child he always sees when he looks at me.

The chakram. My heart drops. Snow above, I have to tell Sir I lost another throwing disc. With the decline in Primoria's iron production due to the disuse of Winter's mines, weapons have become expensive. And being a Winterian refugee isn't exactly a lucrative career.

I grab a berry, avoiding Sir's eyes. "Isn't anyone else coming? Finn maybe?"

He shakes his head. "Just us. Now talk."

It's an order. He's angry about something, but I have no idea what.

My stomach starts to burn, churning around all the food I've shoved into it. Sir has no right to be angry or disappointed. I retrieved half of the locket. I did what he couldn't do, even after he doubted me. The only thing he should be feeling is awe.

Is that why he's upset? Because I finally proved that he needs me?

I glare up at him. "It was exactly where you said it was. In the Keep. That's all."

"You're telling me," Sir begins, "that you were able to waltz into Lynia's stronghold and retrieve this locket piece with no arrows fired, no men killed, no bloodshed? Because that bruise on your cheek and the lingering stench in here say otherwise. What happened, Meira?"

The wrinkles in Sir's face deepen. He wears his age more heavily all of a sudden, his naturally white hair ivory from his fifty-some years, not his Winterian heritage. He fingers the box before popping it open and showing me the locket half.

It's the first time I've seen it. A silver chain snakes around the back half of a heart-shaped locket, gleaming though it's more than a few centuries old. Half of Winter's conduit. I exhale, my shoulders slouching. I still can't believe it's *here*, a hand's breadth from me.

The moment Sir opens the box, Mather's whole body stiffens. My eyes swing to him, and I want to continue our conversation from moments ago. I want to apologize for earlier, for bringing up the biggest weakness in his life like it was nothing more than a discussion of the weather.

My breath catches against those questions again, the things no one ever dares ask aloud.

Will this be enough? Will reuniting our conduit halves restore our magic, or will Winter forever be the only kingdom in Primoria without magic to make it whole? If so, how will we defeat Spring, a kingdom steeped in magically induced strength, when all we have are eight refugees and a pretty necklace? Will another kingdom even ally with us once we have the locket whole again, if our only heir is unable to use it?

It's possible to live without magic. We've been doing it for sixteen years—barely, but we have. We grew a small garden in the Rania Plains. We train our bodies to be strong. But those things will never be enough when all the other kingdoms in the world have something that transcends human limitations, when Spring is able to wipe through our strongest soldiers, when the Rhythms are able to do the same.

Mather was right: Primoria may seem balanced, but . . . it's not.

Sir closes the box with an abrupt click and I flinch. I was quiet too long. He stands, shaking his head, and a gut-wrenching certainty forces me to stand too.

"It was too dangerous," he says. "When we start looking for the other locket half, you're not to argue your assignments, do you hear me? You're back on food-scouting missions."

"No!" I shout. Sir turns but I grab his arm. I'm starting to feel the effects of traveling—legs wavering, head spinning. But I will not let him take this from me. I earned my keep today, a hundred times over, and I'll be damned if he casts me aside so easily again.

"I brought you half of the locket!" I shout. "What else do I have to do?"

Please, tell me what I have to do to feel like I belong.

Sir looks at me so severely that I drop my eyes from his face and my hands from his arm, blood roaring through my head. I'm so tired, exhausted to the point where I'm not certain this is happening. I can't deal with this right now. I need sleep; I need to collect myself and stop feeling like what I did wasn't significant.

I stomp out of the meeting tent, ignoring whatever Sir or Mather calls after me, and run to my own tent. The size of our camp doesn't allow for dramatic stomping sessions, though, and I fly into it in less than a few seconds. But my tent isn't only *my* tent, so when I shove inside, Finn and Dendera look up at me with wide eyes.

Dendera refocuses on patching a hole in one of her boots. "Just once I'd like to see you leave a meeting with William like a lady instead of a panting bull."

I snarl and flop onto my bedroll. Finn retorts something about me not being a lady, which makes me smile, but it makes Dendera rant about how there's still hope for me. I bury my face in my pillow and tune them out.

Dendera once told me that she had been a member of Queen Hannah's court. She was respected for her opinion and her mind, and no woman under Hannah's rule was allowed to feel small. I've asked her, and everyone, about Winter so often and heard so many tales that their memories are my memories now, and I can trick myself into feeling like I remember. The frozen berries and iron fire pits. The mines in the Klaryn Mountains. The thick, earthy aroma of refining coal hanging over every city.

If I close my eyes and cover my ears and block out everything else, I can see the court Dendera described. I can see the city Sir told me about. Jannuari's great white palace stands above me, its sprawling courtyard filled with ice fountains. It's so cold that foreigners have to wrap in layers of fur to walk from building to building, while our natural Winterian blood keeps us warm even in the worst conditions. And snow is everywhere, always, so much that the grass beneath it is white from lack of sun. An entire kingdom wrapped in an orb of eternal winter.

But here is where my made-up memory always crashes around me. The cold and snow dissolves into explosions. The screaming starts, pushing over the palace complex like a wave, and I'm running through gray streets choked with smoke as hordes of people run too, more explosions corralling us into Angra's grasp. That's what they're doing—corralling the Winterians like sheep so they can lead them to a life of slavery and pain.

Except for us. Originally twenty-five refugees who kept Angra up at night, reduced to the seven who still live with Winter's future king.

But no matter how dire our situation, how desperate Sir gets, he will never see me as an asset. Just the overexcited child he had the misfortune of raising.

THOUGHTS OF OUR kingdom's destruction aren't exactly fodder for restful dreams. Only a little while after falling asleep, I'm shaken awake by nightmares of a shadow engulfing Jannuari's desolate streets, a darkness so complete and absolute that all buildings and people disintegrate into oblivion. I fly up, gasping on my nightmare, thankful that the tent is empty. The only noises come from the fire crackling on the distant edge of camp. It must be suppertime.

I stand, still fully clothed, and pull my white hair into a braid. The sun is just starting to set when I step outside, casting the Rania Plains in the gray-yellow haze of a day about to die.

To my left, the flap of the meeting tent swishes, and my muscles tighten. I have no desire to face Sir yet unless his face is apologetic, which is less likely than the Kingdom of Summer freezing over. So as the tent opens I hurry away from it, running until I reach the southern edge of camp and crest the hill.

The setting sun pulsates directly in front of me, and a hint of relaxation creeps into my muscles. One of the only good things about this place is the sunset. The fiery hues bleed into the landscape until the world around me is nothing but colors—the encroaching black night, the flickering yellow sun, the reaching beams of scarlet, the waving brown prairie grass.

I slide to the ground, elbows resting on my knees as the campfire crackles somewhere behind me and the wind hisses somewhere ahead. In the face of all that has happened, it feels good, really good, to just breathe for a moment. So in my mind, I sketch out the map I saw hanging over the desk in Lynia, my nerves calming as I focus on the withered yellow edges, the faded brown lines, something simple when everything around me is so . . . not.

The Rania Plains—a great swath of empty prairie lands between all the kingdoms. The Seasons—Summer, Autumn, Winter, and Spring to the south, wrapped together in the arms of the jagged Klaryn Mountains. The Rhythms—Yakim, Ventralli, Cordell, and Paisly, spread across the rest of Primoria. Four Season Kingdoms, four Rhythm Kingdoms, eight conduits.

The locket half flies through my mind. I bite my lip,

the thin sheen of calm I constructed shattered by a victory that feels more like failure. Will we always fail, even when we succeed? Getting this half of the locket, getting the next half, forming a whole conduit, gaining allies to free Winter—when will it feel like enough?

"Meira?"

I whip around, heart caught in my throat until I realize it isn't Sir—it's Mather.

He watches me in silence, his eyes flitting across my face. My heart *thwump-thwump*s against my ribs and I don't look away from him, hating how with one glance he can crack me open. Anyone else I'd be able to ignore, to hide my fear from them behind a cocky smile, but Mather sees everything. I know he sees it, because for the briefest moment he drops his expressionless mask and the look in his eyes shows me he feels the same way. A mirror of every part of myself I can't bear to face.

He drops down beside me and asks, his voice quiet, "Was it that bad?"

I frown. "Getting the locket half? What makes you think it was bad?"

"You barely yelled at William earlier. Either you're sick or Lynia was . . . I went on and on about my own problems when you . . ." His eyes linger on the bruise on my cheek as if seeing it for the first time. "You wouldn't have gone if it weren't for me, and I didn't even realize you'd been hurt. I'm an idiot."

"No," I snap. "No. I mean yes, you are an idiot some-times, but don't you dare apologize. You don't need to feel guilty for letting me go to Lynia—I'd do it again, no mat-ter how close I came to being captured."

Mather's face falls and I flinch at what I said. *Captured.* He turns to the sun, unreadable thoughts whirring across his face. I never could tell if his ability to push away his emotions was something Sir drilled into him or whether it was Mather's natural gift. Either way, when we were younger and I'd talk him into stealing weapons or paint-ing the meeting tent with ink, Mather was able to keep a straight face when Sir asked if we were the culprits. I mean, of course we were—we were the only seven-year-olds in camp and were covered in thick black ink. But Mather always held strong in his unwavering lie, repeating with a freakishly believable certainty that he and I were innocent.

Until I burst into tears and admitted the whole thing to Sir. But Mather never got mad at me for pulling him into mischief or for breaking during Sir's interrogations. He'd just smile, throw his arm around me, and say something encouraging.

Mather has always been a king, every moment of his life.

I shake my head. "I wasn't that close to being captured," I amend. "Herod just—I'm fine. Really."

But Mather's eyes dart over every part of my face, and when he finally meets my gaze, he lifts one of his hands, his callused fingers coming to rest on my cheek. A spurt of pain lances across my face when he touches the bruise there, but I don't move, needing to feel his fingers on my skin more than I care about the pain.

"No one who faces Herod is fine," he whispers.

A cooling breeze blows at me as night replaces the roaring heat of the plains. I inhale the mustiness and try not to move as Mather pulls his fingers off my cheek, his eyes shooting once again over my face, as if he's hunting for more injuries. His gaze stops on my lips, hovers there, and I'm torn between needing to know why and forcing myself to pull us apart.

"He stole my chakram, though," I say, grabbing at anything to lighten the mood.

Mather finally smiles. It takes up every part of his face, from his eyes down to his lips, and lights the air around us like a candle in a cave.

But almost immediately it falls, the light snuffing out. "William values you, you know."

I spin away, plucking blades of grass and tossing them into the air. Mather doesn't pick up on my sudden distance—or maybe he does, but knows I need to hear what he's saying.

"William was one of Winter's highest-ranking generals." Mather waves his hand through the air, brushing at a few of the blades I freed. "And he feels like he failed. He sees you as someone who should be dancing at balls, not scaling towers and killing soldiers. Just try to be considerate—"

I turn to him, my face hot. "Considerate to the man who can't even manage a pat on the back when I push us one massive step closer to freeing our kingdom?"

Mather tips his head. "Try to understand that he feels guilty for needing you to help free our kingdom at all. It's not that you didn't do a fantastic job—you did, and everyone's gathered around the fire right now swapping stories about you."

I grin, if only a little. "I am pretty amazing."

Mather smiles back. "I bet you would've survived even without the lapis lazuli."

I laugh and run my fingers over my pocket where the small stone pushes into my hip. I keep forgetting it's there, like I've already accepted it as part of myself. "You're giving credit for my success to a rock?"

He shrugs. "No one has gotten the locket half before. It can't be a coincidence, and I expect you to heap appropriate amounts of praise on me for giving it to you in the first place."

"*You've* had it with you on locket missions before. Why didn't it ever help you?"

Mather exhales and suddenly he's just watching me and I'm watching him and all trace of humor is gone.

"You're right. I guess it wasn't the stone; it was how amazing you are," he says.

Coolness balls in my stomach against the heat that rises to my face. Sitting there, the dying light playing on his strong features, his words lingering between us . . . Mather is the steadiest force I've ever known. Angra has every right to fear him.

With half of the locket in our grasp, we're so much closer to Mather being who he's always been meant to be—and I need to see him as that man. Sir has mentioned a few times that Mather will soon need to wed. And he'll be expected to have a female heir, and I will cheer for him and his beautiful new family, and pretend it doesn't kill me to not be enough for him.

So I stand. I brush the stray pieces of grass off my pants and stare daggers into him on the ground, ignoring the frantic way my hand grips the stone in my pocket. "You are right, as always, Your Highness. I will try to be more understanding with Sir."

Mather looks up at me, his mouth falling open like he wants the right words to tumble out. I've heard Sir tell him too: *You're royalty, she's not, and there's too much riding on your future to squander it on an alliance that won't benefit Winter.*

He stands, his eyes boring into my face. "Remember when I told you the world isn't balanced?"

I hesitate, all the air trapped in a knot in my throat. "What?"

Mather's fingers brush my hand, the one that isn't desperately clutching the stone, gentle pricks of contact that make the knot of air in my throat tighten. He hooks a finger into one of mine, his breathing ragged. "I'll find a way to restore the balance," he promises.

I stare at him, unable to process his words. He doesn't try to explain what he meant or do more than stand there next to me, watching me, waiting.

I know you two grew up together, but he's our future king. He's too important to allow anything more than friendship.

My pulse thunders as Mather's words warp with Sir's, conflicting bits of knowledge that make me dizzy. Mather *is* too important to waste on me. But—

I ease my hand into his, his coarse fingers swallowing mine. Like he'd been waiting for me to reciprocate.

No.

My fingers uncurl, slowly, and I slide my hand out of his. It'll hurt too much when it ends. Not if—*when*. When he marries some foreign dignitary's daughter. When he moves on.

I peel my eyes from him, unable to see whatever emotion flares across his face, if anything, when I pull away. Night throws a number of shadows onto the reaching, clawing fingers of scraggy trees and bushes by the stream, and a gust of wind makes a few of the shadows waver, bulks of darkness that swagger like shuffling boars—

I freeze.

Those aren't shadows.

Everything in my body screams with warning and I curse Herod a million times over for stealing my chakram.

"Mather." The strain in my voice pulls him out of the

tension between us. I can feel when he sees them, his posture sharpening. The bodies in the trees move again, five of them—Spring scouts.

One of the men eases out from behind a tree, standing in full view. He knows we see him. He tips his head, body masked in the darkness of early evening, and I can imagine the smile tugging at his mouth. *My master will be thrilled I found you.*

The other scouts follow his lead, materializing from the grass and bushes until they stand before us, shoulder to shoulder, hands twitching at their waists. Waiting for us to move. One snaps his head toward the horse pen and back again so quickly I wouldn't have caught it if I'd blinked. They're going to steal our horses to get back to Spring; they probably abandoned their own a few hours back to avoid being spotted. They'll try to kill some of us before they leave, to whittle our numbers even lower before they tell Angra where we are so he can stage the final strike. So he can be the one to kill Mather himself.

We can't let them return to Spring.

We need weapons. We need to alert the others. We need to—

Mather makes a decision before I do, grabbing my hand and dragging me into camp. I flip one last look behind me. The five soldiers move, tearing over the grass toward the horse pen.

This is my fault. They tracked me. I led them here from

Lynia, straight here, because Sir is right—I *am* just a child who shouldn't be fighting in a war.

Mather pulls me faster and something bounces out of the collar of his leather breastplate. The locket half. It gleams in the setting sun's light, faint and flickering in the shadows, yet embedded with powerful and fiery potential. It's Winter's essence.

I rip my hand out of his. "Warn Sir!"

Mather skids to a stop but I'm already gone, surging into my tent. His voice fades behind me as he starts running again, drawing closer to the others and farther from me.

"Scouts!" he shouts. "Scouts, five of them—"

Finn has a chakram too. I find it along with a holster as Sir bellows from the other end of camp.

"All right, new chakram," I mutter. "It's time to let Herod know we don't appreciate being followed."

7

MY WHOLE BODY coils like a tightly wound spring as I rush back toward the horse pen. In the dark I can barely make out the five shapes moving around our horses, throwing saddles and bridles and cursing at each other to hurry.

"Meira!"

Sir's voice slams into me, warped with panic, and a small part of me leaps with desperation, wanting to hide until whatever is scaring the adults goes away. He tears past me, and to keep up I have to pump every bit of energy into my legs as I sprint over the grass. Everyone else is close behind— Dendera, Finn, Greer, Mather, and Henn. Alysson is the only one not among us, the only nonfighter in our group.

The scouts don't pause as we draw near, don't whip out weapons or try to slow us down; they just hurl themselves with renewed vigor into freeing the horses. The Spring soldier nearest to me uses a knife to saw at the rope tying a mount to the fence. I lurch to a stop and my new chakram flies from my palm, slicing through the soldier's neck in a quick, smooth hiss of motion before rebounding into my hand. The soldier jerks back like he smacked into a wall, the knife slipping from his fingers as he falls, knees clunking into the grass, mouth agape at the starry sky above him.

I leap over the fence and into the horse pen alongside everyone else, a wave of Winterian death. The soldier I killed lies in a heap next to where I land, and I can't stop myself from looking at his face. He's young. Of course he'd be young. Not all soldiers are withered in years, covered in the blood of all the people they've killed, ready to die themselves.

I swallow. There's no room for emotion in war—another saying of Sir's.

Two of the men turn to form a makeshift barrier between one of their comrades, almost mounted on a horse, and us. Expressions murderous, they take in the soldier I killed and reach for the swords at their waists. But Sir is running, gaining on them, and they don't know it, but they're already dead.

Sir kicks off the fence and hurls himself into the air, curved knives in each hand. His blades flash in the night, graceful and deadly, and he arches like a snake preparing to strike. The armed soldiers haven't even fully swung to face him when Sir lands on the first, sliding the knives through the soldier's neck and into his torso. The force of the landing throws that soldier into the next one, and when Sir rips the knives free from the body, he uses the motion to slice the other soldier's throat. The two men fall, gurgling as blood pulses out of the wounds in their necks, while Sir pivots to the soldier they tried to protect, the one still fumbling to free the horse.

The man scrambles to face Sir, his eyes dropping to the bodies at his feet. "Please," he whimpers and grabs at the horse, misses, falls to the ground between the two men Sir killed. "Please—I beg you—"

Sir towers over him. "Where is your weapon?" His voice sends tremors of warning across my skin, the first sensation I've felt since I killed the soldier.

The soldier cowers. "I don't—"

Sir grabs a sword from the hand of a nearby dead man and thrusts it hilt first at the blubbering soldier, who hesitates. "Take it," Sir growls.

The soldier takes the sword. The moment the blade is fully in his grip, Sir lunges, slamming his knives into the soldier's chest. Cloudy eyes stare at me as the man's mouth bobs up and down, begging for one last breath, just one—

One final dying moan, and he drops weightless alongside the other Spring soldiers.

Night makes the dead men look like nothing more than glistening bodies curled in sleep. When the sun comes, it will reveal the blood, the gore, streaks of red covering the grass inside the horse pen. A tangy iron stench hovers over the area, making my lungs burn. It should rain, a thundering, screaming storm, to wash all this away. The remnants of five lives—

I stop.

One, two, three, four.

Four. Not five. There were five soldiers, weren't there?

I scan the area. Dendera and Mather straighten the saddles and other supplies the Spring soldiers tore through. Greer, Henn, and Finn poke through the corpses, taking weapons. Sir crouches over his kills, wiping the blood off his knives with one of the men's shirts.

And just behind Sir, behind the horse that the last man had been trying to mount, a piece of rope dangles from the fence next to the open gate. Cut.

My arms tremble with dread before I even get his name out of my mouth. "Sir."

He looks at me, sheathing his knives.

I point to the dangling rope and open gate. "There were five scouts."

Sir turns and stares at the rope. His eyes flick beyond it and there, already a small speck on the horizon, is the last soldier barreling in a cloud of dust on one of our horses. The man is far enough out of range to be uncatchable. He'll tell Angra where we are.

Anxiety pours into my stomach, filling me with the knowledge of what's going to happen next. Sir pivots to face me, his eyes leaping from me to Dendera to Finn to everyone. *No, don't say it, don't—*

"We're leaving. Now. Pack only what's necessary," Sir announces, already untying horses from the fence. "Convene north of the camp in five minutes."

His words smack into me. "We're running?" I squeak, holstering the chakram. "Can't we just—"

Sir steps toward me, and even in the dark I can see his eyes are bloodshot. That's the only way he ever shows emotion, in his eyes. "I will not take chances, not when we're finally so close. Start packing or mount a horse."

He spins away, taking a few steps through the grass until he reaches Mather, grabs his arm, and hisses something that makes the expression on Mather's face mimic the shocked, angry one on my own. Sir hurries to the rest, spitting the same orders at them—pack what you can, no time to waste. They separate, scurrying into camp to obey him.

Sir doesn't see them as he talks. His eyes dart across the horizon, stoic, calm. A boulder in the ocean, standing strong against crashing waves. Herod may be big and dark, but Sir is big and light—just as towering, just as threatening, with strength built on the pure pull of revenge.

With him leading us, how did we ever lose to Angra?

"Meira."

I flinch. My focus was so fixed on Sir that I didn't hear Mather approach. He smiles, but it's marred by the sweat streaked across his cheek, by the panic around us.

"You let me sneak up on you?" he guesses, trying for lightness.

I shrug. "I have to let you think you're good at something."

He nods, lips relaxing as he watches me with a calm, solemn stare. Like we've never had to abandon camp or run off separately into the night until we all reconvened somewhere safe. We've done this at least a dozen times since we were small enough to remember, but he's looking at me now like he's never had to leave me before.

"Mather?" It comes out as a question.

He swings toward me, stops, pulls back, dancing around like he can't gather up the courage to do something. My throat closes, shock choking me, not letting me dare hope that he's going to do what I think—

Finally he sweeps in and lifts me against him. A tight, whole-body hug as his arms come around my back, holding me to his chest with my feet dangling in the air, his face in my neck.

"I'll find a way to fix this," he tells me, his words vibrating across my skin, tremors that shake my very foundation.

Slowly, carefully, I relax into him, my arms going around his neck. "I know," I whisper. When he starts to put me down I cling more tightly, keeping my mouth to his ear. I have to say these words, but I can't bring myself to look at him as they spill from my lips. "We all know, Mather. You'll do everything you can for Winter. No one has ever thought less of you, and I think—I know—that Hannah would be proud that you're her son."

He doesn't respond, just holds me there, panting into the space between us. I want to push my face down to his; I want to stay like this, lingering just short of kissing, forever. The conflicting desires make my pulse accelerate until I'm sure he can feel its rhythm beating on his chest. I can feel his, the fast thump of his heart galloping against my stomach.

In a quick burst of motion he sets me down, slides one hand around the back of my neck, and plants a kiss on my jaw, his lips lingering on my skin, leaving permanent trails of lightning in my veins. His chest deflates, the tension on his face unwinding as he pulls back from me. I catch a glimmer in his eyes, the finest sheen of tears. He doesn't say anything or agree with me or do more than give my fingers one final squeeze.

Then he's gone. Hurrying into camp to pack or saddle his horse or whatever Sir ordered him to do.

I stand in the middle of the horse pen, one hand on my jaw. My eyes flick up, searching for Mather amidst the chaos.

What was *that*?

But I know what it was. Or at least, I know what I want it to be—what I've always wanted it to be. What I constantly have to tell myself can never, ever be. But why now, in the midst of leaving, when I can't corner him and make him explain or figure out some way to ignore that it even happened? Because it did happen. My jaw feels like it's been branded by his mouth, and no matter how many times I repeat, "He's our future king" to myself, I can't get the impression of Mather's lips out of my skin.

I don't *want* to get their impression out of my skin.

Sir slides in front of me, dragging two horses already saddled. "Pack your things."

I yank my hand down. Mather's words and his lips and his arms around me fade to the back of my mind, and I hold them there, anchors in the face of all this uncertainty.

"No," I growl at Sir. *No, we can't just leave. We have to stay; we have to plan something better than running.* "I can't let them—"

In one swift motion, Sir grabs my arm and flings me onto the nearest saddled horse. He leaps onto his own and takes both my reins and his, shooting me a glare that tells me not to argue.

His glares have never stopped me before. "We can't let them destroy this home too!"

Alysson and Dendera swing onto their own mounts as we trot out of the horse pen. We ease to a brief stop in front of the meeting tent, long enough for Finn, Greer, and Henn to throw passing nods at Sir that yes, everything will be destroyed before we leave. Sir flicks the reins and as we continue I catch the faintest crackle of fire from inside the tent, the pop of flames devouring anything of importance, maps and documents. They probably used the fire pit. We won't be able to bring it with us. Angra will find it, the only part of our past we possess, filled to the brim with ashes.

As I fumble with the pommel for something to hold on to other than a weapon, Sir's fist around my reins falls, his hand unfolding just enough to cup mine. It's so subtle I can't tell if he's trying to comfort me or making sure I don't rip control of the horse away.

"It's not your fault," he grunts. "It's no one's fault."

My throat closes and I just sit there, numb and small. It is my fault; I led the scouts here. And I know that staying is pointless—Angra will send far more than five men now, and with only eight of us, the odds are laughable. A death sentence. But I can't just do nothing—doing nothing will kill me faster than facing Angra's whole army on my own.

Sir pulls our horses to a stop when we reach the plains on the north side of camp. A heartbeat later we're joined by every horse, every person, everything they were able to grab in the time Sir allowed. As for our livestock, I hope Angra will treat them better than he treats our people.

"Split up, two riders each. Once it's safe, we convene in Cordell," Sir announces. He points at Dendera, who sits on a horse beside Mather on his own mount. "Keep. Him. Alive."

Dendera bows her head and stays that way until Sir jerks on his horse's reins. It rears with a mighty whinny, filling all the horses with adrenaline. Over the roll of noise Sir eyes me and nods, beckoning me to follow. When he heaves northwest into the now-dark plains like one of Angra's cannonballs, I trail a breath behind.

Everyone else follows, a brief stampede before we split off. I look back as Alysson gallops north with Finn, Greer and Henn head east, and Dendera and Mather go northeast.

Mather looks at me, his eyes grabbing mine with the same intensity as before. He urges his horse on beside Dendera's, then they're gone, barreling into the night.

Sir pulls his horse back alongside mine. The wind whips against my cheeks, drying the tears as they fall.

Not my fault. Sir said so, and Sir only tells the truth.

After an hour of all-out galloping, we slow. Sporadic groups of trees and shrubs are all we see, their dried, dead silhouettes splayed against the night. We keep going, riding until the sun rises. Until it sets again. Until the horses simply can't go on any longer. Then we dismount, make sure they have a little water nearby, and leave them. Sir takes all their gear off first—the saddle, the reins, the blankets and small plated armor. He hides the useless parts in dried-up bushes, keeps what remains in his sack; and with a final pat on their flanks, we continue northwest for two days on foot, stopping only to sleep and scan the horizon for Angra's men.

Sir keeps his supply of food rationed just enough to drive me mad with hunger. Small streams of muddy water run every so often, edible plants are even scarcer, and shade is nonexistent. There's just sun, sky, yellowed grass, and dead, scraggy shrubs for hours.

I hate heat. I hate the sweat that drips between my shoulder blades, the way the sun's rays bake every bare area of skin raw. But I hate silence more, and Sir won't talk. Not just his usual quiet—he's downright mute. He doesn't look at me, doesn't acknowledge me, for hours upon hours of endless walking.

Just when I think I'll have to tackle him, he drops to his knees next to something in the grass. A stream, little more than an arm's length wide. It's the clearest water we've seen since we started, and the fog of heat lifts in a burst of relief when I sigh at the small spattering of half-alive green plants clustered around the banks. Tough vegetation that gets roasted in the sun, but it's more edible than most of the Rania Plains' delicacies, like crow.

Sir glances at me as he takes the pack from his shoulders. "We camp here tonight and head for Cordell tomorrow. No one's following us. The sooner we get to safety, the better."

Though the temptation of clean water sits a few paces away, I stay frozen. He's talking to me. "Why are we going to a Rhythm Kingdom? I thought you hated King Noam?"

Sir turns to the water, his shoulders slumping a little, but he doesn't respond.

"I can't help until I know the plan. And like it or not, my help is all you have now."

The bite in my voice startles me and I drop my arms. I move forward, hesitate, unsure what reaction will come. But when I step up next to him, all I see are the trails of dried blood that swirl off his hands and into the water. He's had Spring blood on him for days. Of course he has—when would he have been able to wash it off?

The face of the soldier I killed flashes through my mind. *My fault. All the men who died at camp were my fault too.*

Sir nods to his left. "Upstream," he says, ignoring my snap.

I shrug out of my chakram's holster and drop it in the grass before marching to the left, kicking my way through bits of undergrowth. Every part of me feels bloodied, dirty, like I'm coated head to toe in the guts of Angra's soldiers. I drop to my knees and dunk my head into the water up to my shoulders. The coolness washes away a bit of the heat, flowing over me and chasing off my panic. My regrets.

I've killed before. I've seen Sir kill before. I've seen everyone at camp, even Mather, speckled with blood and limping from battle. I shouldn't care that a few Spring soldiers have died; they've killed thousands of our people.

My lungs start to burn but I stay down, keeping my breath trapped inside until the painful need for air is the only thing I feel. Nothing else. I don't have room for anything else.

Fingers wrap around my arm. Before I can shake myself awake enough to realize who it is, I inhale. Water flows into my lungs, icy hot panic rushing into my chest along with the unwanted water, and I yank free of the stream, sputtering and heaving. Sir drags me into the grass, slamming his fist into my back to get the rest of the water to pour out of my nose in a rush of earthy grime.

As soon as my lungs clear I launch to my feet, shaking dirt and water out of my eyes. "I'm—I'm fine. You startled me. I'm fine."

But Sir doesn't look convinced.

"None of this is your fault. And you've killed before," he says. His creepily perceptive general senses finally work in my favor for once. "You'll kill again. The trick is not to let it incapacitate you."

"I don't." I curl my hand into a fist, dirt gritting between my fingers. The rest of me is calm, careful, forcing every bit of anger out in my clenched hand. "I don't want it to get easy. Not even if it's Angra himself. I want to feel it, always, so I'm never as awful as him."

Or you. I don't want to end up as hard as you.

I twitch at the thought, more guilt heaping atop the rest. He wasn't always this way, I remind myself. Alysson told Mather and me about the night Jannuari fell to Angra's men. The night twenty-five of us escaped, cloaked in a snowstorm created by Hannah's last pull of magic before Angra broke her locket in half and killed her.

"William was the only reason we made it," Alysson told us as we huddled near the fire one night, waiting for Sir to get back from a mission. "We could see the flashes of cannon fire and clouds of smoke over the city, and we wanted to race back to save our countrymen, but William kept us moving until we crossed the border, until we got away." She paused then, stroking one hand down Mather's cheek. "He was the one who carried you on his chest the whole ride out of Winter once we broke free of Jannuari. Every time one of us begged him to go back and help save our kingdom, he'd put his hand on your little head and say, 'Hannah entrusted us with the continuation of her line. This is how we will save Winter now.' Even though a war raged behind us, even though we were caught in a chaotic blizzard to hide our escape, even though we wouldn't reach safety for days, William was so gentle with you. A warrior with a tender heart."

Sir had never told us that story himself, and after Alysson told it to us once, we never heard it again. But I'd watch Sir after that, looking for the tenderness that Alysson mentioned. Occasionally I could catch a flicker—a twinge around his eyes when Mather faltered in sparring, a twitch of his lips when I begged to learn how to fight. But that was all I ever saw of the general who once carried a baby for days to safety. Like all of his actual tenderness was gone, but every so often his muscles convulsed from the memory of it.

That's how we all are, too hard for what we should be. We should be a family, not soldiers. But all that really connects us is stories, and memories, of what should be.

Sir nods. He's clean now, every speck of blood gone except the stains on his clothes. Like it never happened. "Not wanting to forget how horrible it is to kill someone is part of what makes you a good soldier."

"Did you just—" My fist relaxes. "You just called me a soldier. A *good* soldier."

Sir's lips shudder in his version of a smile. "Don't let that incapacitate you either."

The sun dries the water on my cheeks and starts to singe my skin again. This is a weirdly peaceful moment for Sir and me. I fight down the giddiness that threatens to ruin it.

"Should we hug or something?"

Sir rolls his eyes. "Get your weapon. We head for Cordell."

WHY SIR PICKED Cordell as our meet-up spot is still a mystery. Granted, it is the closest able-bodied kingdom to our former camp. But I remember the rants Sir's gone on about Cordell. King Noam's a coward, hiding behind his wealth, hoarding his conduit's power like all the other Rhythms, and on and on.

So when we aim our course northeast the next day, I have to ask. Even though I've already done so half a dozen times and gotten no response. But Sir and I did have a rather anger-free interlude, *and* he called me a soldier, so that has to be worth something.

"Why are we going to a Rhythm for help?"

Sir glances at me, his face half amused, half annoyed.

"Persistence can get you killed."

"When sparked by torture, it can also get answers."

Sir snorts. "Rhythm or not, Cordell is closest. And we're in a hurry now."

And also desperate, if Sir expects us to get help in Cordell. Nothing is ever that simple, and if I can guess the reason for Sir's decision, something is definitely wrong.

"What's our next move?"

Sir focuses on the horizon, the endless cream-colored waves of prairie grass and the beating sun. "Rally support," he whispers. "Get an army. Free Winter."

He says it like it should be easy. Just what we've been working toward for sixteen years.

And now, because we have half of Hannah's conduit, it's finally within reach. My whole life has been focused on getting the first locket half—I never really saw or questioned beyond that.

"Wait—we don't have a whole conduit yet. Why would Noam agree to help us? And where is the other locket half, anyway?"

Sir glances at me but keeps his lips in a thin line. "It's a risk we have to take, because of the location of the other half." His voice is flat, and I can tell there's something he's not saying, but he presses on to my other question. "If you wanted to make a thing hidden, safe from the world, so you always knew where it was, where would you keep it?"

"With me, I suppose—" I flash to him. "No."

He shrugs.

"Angra has the other half with himself? On his person?"

Sir doesn't respond, letting me piece it together. His puzzles are a little annoying.

"So Angra kept one half constantly moving around the world so we'd have a horrific time getting it back while he had the other half around his neck all along?" I shake my head. "And here I thought getting the first half was an accomplishment."

"It is," Sir corrects.

One corner of my mouth quirks up and I revel in those words. *It is.*

"Why didn't you go with Mather?"

The question pops out before I realize I've been thinking it. Not that Dendera isn't capable of fighting alongside Mather too; despite the fact that she'd rather not be a soldier, she's our second-best close-range fighter. But Sir is still the best, and the best should be with Mather.

"We can't be caught together." Sir swings his pack around and tugs it open. "Both of us are too valuable to the cause."

He hands me a strip of jerky. I look at him, waiting for more explanation, but he sticks a square of cheese in his mouth and settles back into silence just as easily as he left it.

That's it. Not because he cares about me, not because he wants to protect me. It has nothing to do with me. It never has.

I force down the dried beef, my hand flipping the little blue stone in my pocket. The carved surface is gritty against my fingers, and I imagine rivers of strength and fearlessness flowing from it, up my arm, and into my heart. I imagine it really is a conduit, my own source of inhuman strength tucked into my palm—both a symbol of power and a reminder of Winter.

I yank my hand out of my pocket. I don't need made-up strength. I'm strong enough on my own—*me*, Meira, no magic or conduit or anything.

But . . . it would be nice. For once, to not be so weak. To not look at all we've done and know we still have so very far to go before we can be safe.

To be powerful.

We stop to make camp when the sun sets. By that point, the heat together with my lingering self-doubts about Sir loving me have turned me into a twitchy ball of anxiety. So when he takes the first watch, I force sleep to cleanse my thoughts. Shockingly it comes easier and more quickly than any sleep I've had in a long time, as if the way Sir talked to me today caused some small amount of stress to lift.

I hate how important his opinion is to me.

I close my eyes, curl into a ball in the golden waves of grass, and slide into dreams like the stars slide across the black night sky.

Cottages encircle me on a cobblestone road, fences dusted with snow and ice, windows warped with frost. A thick cloud of smoke blankets the sky, chugging from the chimneys of the industrial buildings on the edge of the city.

I'm in Jannuari.

I know these streets like I know the beat of my own heart. Scenes I built out of stories and other people's memories, stolen images and emotions. But fear paralyzes me where I stand on the cold stone road, snaking around my limbs in violent clamps and urging my pulse faster, faster, faster. I've seen Jannuari in my dreams for years, listened with rapt attention to stories about it. So why am I terrified?

A wave of bodies rushes into me, surging down Jannuari's twisting streets. We're running, desperately running, as explosions ricochet around us.

This is the night of Winter's fall.

"No," I breathe. We can't run. Angra's herding us. He'll take us all away, imprison us—

"NO!" I scream it over and over, clawing at the people around me. But they don't budge, don't hear me, terror locking them behind impenetrable walls of need.

Then I'm safe.

It happens so fast—the change—that I fall back and smack into the wall of the room I'm in now. A small, cozy study, lit by a warm fire pit on the left. The earthy musk of burning coal instantly relaxes me, the smell of memories that aren't mine. The window across from me is open to the night, letting in the occasional snowflake.

The people in the room don't notice me. They're too focused on a woman standing by the door, a woman who can't be older than thirty, with flowing waves of white hair and the softest, calmest face I've ever seen. Like nothing, not even Angra's cannons, can shake her.

There's a locket around her neck. The conduit.

Hannah.

"*I'm sorry,*" *she whispers, tears spilling over her cheeks.* "*I can't tell you—*"

"*No!*" *Sir flies up. Sir. And Alysson's next to him, and Dendera behind him, and Gregg and Crystalla. Alive. They're all here, alive—*

A scream starts to rip from my throat before a hand clasps firmly over my mouth. In the dimness Sir glares at me, his own mouth pressed into a grimace behind his white stubble. The dream leaves fogginess in its wake, and I blink in confusion, my pulse settling back to a normal beat. I've dreamed about Jannuari before. I've even dreamed about Hannah before. Everyone has, I'm sure—Winter dominates every moment of our waking lives, so why not our dreams too? This is nothing to be concerned about.

But I can't get the uneasy feeling to leave me, especially when Sir nods to my right, drawing my attention to hoofbeats.

Horses thunder across the plains, sending vibrations running up my palms as I lie flat on the ground. Sir lowers his hand from my mouth when realization shudders through me.

Spring? I mouth.

He shakes his head. "Coming from the southwest," he whispers. "Going northeast."

I squint. Clearly Sir expects me to know who the galloping army is, but I'm at a loss. The kingdoms southwest of us are Summer and Autumn. Summerians only leave their kingdom to send collectors to fill their brothels, but rarely do they travel so far beyond their corner of the world, especially when Yakim and Ventralli are much closer and just as full of potential slaves. Autumn has its own collapsing-kingdom problems; they had been without a female heir for two generations before their current king bore a daughter, but she's only one. Due to the nature of conduit magic, bearers aren't able to fully use it until they are at least teen-agers. They need to be able to consciously push magic here and there, and children aren't able to harness the amount of magic within a Royal Conduit, or control what they're able to summon.

But Autumn does have one powerful ally—Cordell. King Noam's sister married the king of Autumn two years ago. It was her marriage to the Autumn king that bore his female-blooded kingdom a daughter in the face of Angra's attacks—once Winter was assimilated into Spring, Spring turned its greed to the weakened, heirless Autumn. Their attacks increased after the birth of Autumn's princess in an effort to conquer them before she grows into her power. And with Noam linked through blood and marriage to Autumn, one of the most powerful Rhythms was forced to care about a Season for reasons other than its proximity to the Klaryns.

That's why Sir wants us to go to Cordell. Noam *has* to help stop Spring now—either has to help or let his sister and niece get slaughtered by Angra. If those hoofbeats are any indication, he's already helping.

I pound the ground in excitement. "Cordell!" I squeak. "They're Cordellan? Riding back from Autumn?"

Sir touches his nose in a sly, I-taught-you-well way before he leaps up from the grass and blows out one long, ear-piercing whistle. The sound echoes in the dark and the hoofbeats, dozens of them, stop.

My chest thuds. I really hope they are Cordellan. And that at least a few of them have sympathy for travelers, Season or not. Because if they cling to the Rhythm-Season prejudice or if they're Spring—

But Sir doesn't make mistakes like that. I hope.

I stand too. The shadowy mass of the army looms a few paces ahead of us. One shadow, the darkened figure of a mounted rider, pulls out of the mass and canters forward. As he gets closer, his Cordellan gold-and-hunter-green uniform—and the medals that dangle from it, marking him as an officer—become visible. He's got a sword in one hand, reins in the other, so he can keep riding *and* impale us if needed.

The officer halts far enough back for us to see his face. "Identify yourselves or—" He stops and his eyes open so wide their whites gleam in the darkness. "Golden leaves," he swears, and I start at the words. It must be a Cordellan reference. "Winterians?"

I run a hand through my white hair, pulling it over one shoulder, and swallow the lump of anticipation that wedges in my throat. This is the moment when either he'll spit on us and say something derogatory about the barbaric Seasons or he'll help us.

Sir steps forward. "William Loren, general of Winter. And this is Meira"—he waves at me—"also of Winter. Our camp was attacked by Angra and we are on our way to Cordell."

The officer lowers his blade and my body relaxes slightly. "Anyone seeking refuge from Angra is most welcome in Cordell. I am Captain Dominick Roe of Cordell's Fifth Battalion."

Apparently Dominick lowering his blade signaled an all-is-well to his men, for they instantly put away their own weapons. They're not going to spit on us—they're going to help us. I smile.

"You are offering a warm welcome for us in Cordell?" Sir presses.

Dominick points at two of his men and they obediently push through the crowd, both pulling riderless horses beside them. His face flashes with a grimace—though, in the darkness, it might have been just a trick of moonlight. "All I can truly offer is an escort to Bithai."

Bithai, Cordell's capital. We can't ask for better; an entire regiment of soldiers led by a captain who clearly dislikes Angra and doesn't hold to the Season-Rhythm prejudice. Sir must've spent his watch making wishes.

"We accept," Sir says. "Your generosity will be repaid."

The two men Dominick pointed to offer us the horses. I settle onto one and catch Sir's eye as he adjusts himself on his mount. His shoulders unwind and he slumps a little in his saddle, looking relaxed for the first time since I got back from my mission to Lynia. Because since then—

My chest aches and I close my eyes. I can't afford to think about what has happened. Can't afford to wonder or worry about who got away, who made it to Cordell. Not until we get somewhere safe—or at least as safe as we'll ever be.

The waves of creamy prairie grass vanish around midmorning the next day. I pull up straighter in my saddle, eyes wide as I take in the vibrant change of scenery. I've never been to Cordell. We've had no reason to go to a kingdom Sir hates when there are others who will sell us food and supplies. But now I wish we had come before. It's beautiful.

The grass beneath the horses' hooves is such a vibrant green that my eyes hurt. Hills roll around us, gentle and sloping, with perfectly placed maple trees just starting to turn orange and gold. We pass a farm and are engulfed by a flowery, airy scent—lavender, one of Cordell's most popular and pricey exports. Some soldiers wave to a farmer and his workers, who drop their tools and buckets to wave back.

We continue on, leaving the workers to their effervescent purple fields. The soldiers, drawn by the green and the sun and the aroma of lavender, whoop and holler with the joy that comes from being home.

Sir doesn't seem invigorated by the men's excitement. He surveys each farm we pass, each speck of a village, more than likely taking count of how many lavish buildings there are, how many fields seem a tad too plentiful. His face doesn't change and in that not-changing I see the same anger he gets whenever he rants about Noam.

Just as Winter focused its magic on mining, Cordell focuses its conduit on opportunity—on helping its citizens work a situation in their favor so they get the most out of it. Opportunistic, resourceful, swindlers: whatever they're called, they can even "make leaves turn to gold"— a Cordellan phrase Sir explained in our many lessons, referring to the fact that they're so good at turning a profit it's as if they make leaves on a tree turn into gold coins. That explains Captain Dominick's curse earlier— *Golden leaves.*

But while Cordell has endless resources, Noam is not known for making political alliances with anyone other than just-as-wealthy Rhythms. His sister's marriage to the Autumn King was a scandal he eventually condoned when he found ways to make it beneficial to Cordell, but lowering himself to assist Winterian refugees?

After three hours of winding through fields of green and lavender, we see an even more magnificent sight rise before us: Bithai. The city sweeps over a wide plateau surrounded by about twenty different minifarms, all abuzz with midmorning activity. The closer we get, the denser the houses, the people, until the regiment clomps onto a cobblestone road that connects to a drawbridge and the gated city.

As soon as we pass under the gate, the city explodes around us in a ruckus of merchants shouting, carriage wheels clanking down roads, and donkeys braying into the morning wind. Buildings line up in perfect symmetry along gray cobblestone streets, the avenues folding and bending in precise angles through the city. Each structure, whether house or store or inn, is a mix of gray stones stacked beneath curved, brown-tiled roofs. Flags snap in the breeze above us, banners with a lavender stalk in front of a golden maple leaf on a green background. Everything is clean, deliberate—fountains and vines decorating random corners like the entire city is supposed to be part of the palace grounds. Which makes sense—Bithai is Cordell's entryway, Noam's best display of power. Of course he'd keep it as perfect as he could.

Citizens wave as we ride through, cheering the soldiers, shouting encouragement to their long-gone men. A few women drop baskets of produce and practically knock horses over in their attempts to kiss their husbands. More often than not, civilians pull back from Sir and me, their mouths twisting in confusion at the sight of two Winterians in Bithai. But the soldiers are too distracted to care about political prejudices, and they fall into the waving and the cheering with enthusiasm, their faces lighting with relief at being home. The sentiment makes me smile.

Loyalty. Pride. I can feel it in the air, in the way the men shout greetings to passersby and ask for news of Cordell. These men love their kingdom. These men have what I see missing every day from Sir's eyes, from Finn's set grimace, and Dendera's distant gaze—a home.

The regiment slows to a gentle trot and turns onto one last wide road, maple branches arching over us. Light filters through the canopy, a few leaves drifting down and dancing around the wrought-iron fence that follows both sides of the gold-brick road.

Sir pulls up alongside me. I try to catch his eye to get some clue about what we're planning to do next, but he just stares ahead. So I do the same.

Oh, sweet snow. Seriously?

The regiment pulls to a stop, and I have to bite my tongue to keep from asking if Noam is trying to compensate for something. Because I can understand wanting to have a lush kingdom, and wanting to have an impeccably pristine capital . . . but this?

A gate cuts off the main palace grounds from the entry road. This gate is gold, towering at least three times taller than me, and covered in climbing, green metal vines. Scarlet metal roses bloom along the vines, azure birds perch on metal limbs. But, worst of all, a pair of looming maple trees sits, one on each side of the gate. Entirely golden, their leaves clink in the wind with a pretty—and completely excessive—melody.

"Their kingdom's heart," Sir whispers. It's his sudden quietness that makes me realize the men's enthusiasm has been replaced by a deeper air of solemnity.

"It isn't"—I catch myself and drop to a whisper—"real gold, is it?"

Sir gives a curt nod. My mouth dangles open. No wonder Sir hates Noam; he used enough gold to run a kingdom to make two *trees*.

The regiment dismounts, leaving Sir and me to follow. When we all stand in front of the gate, the Cordellan men drop into waist-bows and linger for a moment, hair swaying in the breeze, before a gentle murmuring rises from their bent forms.

I ease closer to Sir. "Are they chanting?"

Sir nods. He doesn't look happy. But it's not an I'm-going-to-punch-Noam-in-the-throat unhappy—it's wistful and slightly envious. "It's the Poem of Bithai."

The soldiers finish their not-at-all-creepy murmuring to the two gold trees and gather their horses. Captain Dominick moves among his men, all now busy leading their mounts to the right, down a separate road that wraps around the back of the palace grounds.

Dominick motions to the gate. "General William, Lady Meira—"

Lady. My nose curls, the title rubbing up my spine. That

had better not stick—I'm not sure I *want* to be a lady.

"—if you will please follow me, I will take you to our king."

Sir's neck is red. This trip is going to destroy him from the inside out. Not that I feel any better about being here—most of the experiences I've had with Rhythms left me feeling worthless in a less-than-human way. Jeers as we walked down streets; rotten vegetables hurled at us as we rode out of town. Why should Cordell be any different? But no one has been cruel so far, so I trail behind Sir as Dominick leads us through the gate into a lavish garden.

A fountain spits water into the air in the center of a small stone walkway, the whole thing lined with bright-red azalea shrubs and shoulder-high lavender bushes. Bits of pollen float through the air, darting around like bugs chasing each other through sunbeams. To the right, a stone walkway meanders into a forest of maple trees, a hidden path for midnight trysts or assassination attempts.

In front of us stands a palace of the same gray stone as the rest of Bithai. This building dwarfs all the others, though, gleaming with four stories of glittering windows, ivory balconies, and thick velvet curtains.

Just as Dominick waves us into the palace, a shout makes me whirl around. Sir stops too and eases long enough to smile, a soft, truly relieved pull that fills me with comfort.

"Meira!"

I turn toward the forest as a blur of white hair and blue

silk swoops out of the green darkness—Mather.

A smile bursts across my face, erasing all the lingering remnants of exhaustion from the trip. He rushes forward and swoops me into a back-cracking, body-pinning hug.

I don't even care that my ribs just popped.

9

MATHER BEAMS UP at me with that blinding smile and doesn't put me down. I try in vain to fight the blush that I'm sure is turning my pale face red. He's definitely been in Bithai a bit longer than us—his hair is pulled back with a ribbon, he's wearing a sky-blue shirt over clean ivory pants, and Hannah's locket half gleams from his neck. Noam has one point in my I Won't Kill You book: he took care of Mather.

Mather chuckles low in his throat. "Took you long enough to get here."

His words vibrate through his neck and make me painfully aware of the fact that I'm holding on to his neck at all. My fingers tremble but I can't pull away, and I just laugh down at him, feeling his muscles tighten.

"I didn't realize it was a race," I manage, the memory of

our last hug flashing across my mind. His face reddens, a light tinge of pink. *Is he thinking about it too?*

"It was, and you lost," is all he says, his laughter washing over me.

Sir clears his throat. Mather squeezes me one more time and sets me back on the stones where I find it difficult to balance. Who shook up the world?

"Who else is here?" Sir asks. Straight to the point.

Mather doesn't seem as peeved by Sir's abruptness as I always am. "Everyone."

I exhale. We're all here. We all survived. A bit of my guilt unwinds—we lost our camp, but none of our party. I wouldn't have been able to recover if one of us had died because of me.

Sir exhales too. "Excellent. Have you met with Noam?"

Mather nods. "Yesterday. Dendera and I have been here for two days—" He glances at me, then back at Sir, and doesn't continue whatever thought he had. But he suddenly looks like someone punched him in the gut, and all my senses jump to alert.

Something's wrong.

Sir nods once again and turns to Dominick. "Show us to your king."

Dominick pivots on his heels and leaps up the stairs to the palace. Two guards stationed there swing the doors open, eyeing our vibrant Winterian hair. Well, Sir's and mine aren't vibrant at the moment; our heads—like the rest of us—are caked in travel dirt and sweat. But I'm guessing by Sir's determined march behind Dominick that we aren't going to get a bath before meeting Noam.

A bath. I fight down a squeak of longing as we stop in the palace's foyer.

The only source of light is the chandelier above us, which lets off a gentle white glow. The rest of the décor is dark—polished wood walls, black marble floor. Comfortable yet expensive through and through. Rectangular panels line the walls; I can't tell if they're doors or just decoration.

One, on our right, swings open.

Dominick rushes forward and pulls back in a sharp salute to a man within the room, out of sight. "My king, I have—"

"More Winterians. Yes, I assumed as much."

The deep voice matches the warm darkness of the surroundings. Homey almost, a voice I'd expect from a grandfather, not a king.

Sir surges forward, nearly shoving Dominick away. "Noam."

Once, when I talked Mather into stealing a bottle of Finn's Summerian wine and we got a bit tipsy, Sir sentenced me to two weeks of scrubbing dinner dishes for being "disrespectful of our future king's position." But Sir has no problem snapping the Cordellan king's first name like he's a misbehaving toddler.

Noam steps into the foyer, arms crossed. He's big—not

quite as big as Sir, but still commanding. His golden-brown hair hangs loose to his shoulders, edged with gray around his face and even more gray in his beard. He's got deep and mysterious eyes that make me feel both naked and invisible all at once, like he can read all of my secrets with just a glance. And his conduit, Cordell's dagger, sits in his belt, the purple jewel on the hilt glowing ever so faintly in the dimness.

Noam, face impassive, turns his dark eyes to Sir. His gaze travels over Mather before stopping on me, and he grins.

That can't be good.

"That is all, Dominick. Thank you."

Dominick pulls back like he expected more. But then he bows, mumbles something about coming back to report on Autumn later, and marches out the front door.

"William," Noam says though he's still staring at me. "So glad you made it. Nasty business, dealing with the Shadow of the Seasons. The Seasons can be quite"—he pauses—"volatile."

I hold back a snort. Volatile. And he hasn't even met me yet.

But my snort gets caught on what he called Angra—the Shadow of the Seasons. I'd forgotten that's what the Rhythms call him. Like he's nothing more than a gray haze cast by the rest of us, and maybe if we move the right way, he'll disappear.

Sir steps into Noam's line of sight and I blow a sigh of relief.

"I'd hoped we could discuss it in a more private setting." Sir looks at Mather. "My king said you had already spoken with him, but I have some matters I would like to discuss as well."

Sir's never called Mather "king" before. Future king, yes. Royalty, yes. But never king. King Mather Dynam. A flutter of unease rushes through me. I know he's our king, and I knew this would happen. I just thought I'd have more time, until we found the other locket half, at least. Not . . . now.

Noam waves over two servants. "Get Lady Meira settled. We need her looking her best for tonight."

Both Sir and I blanch. Sir, blanching. I don't think I like Bithai anymore.

"Excuse me?" Sir grunts.

Noam smirks. "The ball. My court has been waiting in Bithai for two days, expecting a celebration. Now it can begin. Surely your *king* has told you."

The way he says the word *king* makes my skin crawl. I look to Mather, whose face is as red as the azaleas outside, and his jaw set so hard his teeth have to be completely flattened.

The servants move toward me. "Come this way, please," one says.

Sir nods at me. But there's something behind his eyes, something he's barely holding on to, that makes me want to set my chakram to work ruining Noam's pretty foyer.

The servants start off and, after another pause, I follow. This must be what sheep feel like before we cut their heads off and roast them over open fires.

Noam's voice carries as we leave the foyer. Like everything else in Bithai, it's intentional. "Yes," he says. "We may yet come to an arrangement."

I whip around but Sir, Mather, and Noam have already gone into what I can only assume is Noam's study. The door shuts, cutting off anything else I might hear.

"Lady Meira, this way, please."

Lady. Really?

I surrender to following the servants. The foyer ends in a ballroom—*the* ballroom, I'm sure, where whatever party Noam's planned will happen tonight. It's big, opulent, with marble and chandeliers and lush green plants and lots of gold. I'm a little sick of Cordell's wealth.

Two staircases wrap around the room, one on each side. The servants take me up the left one, circling around so I have a 180-degree view of the ballroom. I make a point not to look at it, focusing instead on the mud caked on my boots.

We get to the second floor and commence to weave through so many identical halls that I begin to think Noam's plan was to get me lost in a maze of annoyingly expensive finery. Wood paneling so polished I can see my filthy reflection as we pass, crystal chandeliers that throw shifting dots of light across my body, maroon carpet so plush and velvety that my boots leave indentations. The same dark accents and expensive yet comfortable feel as the foyer.

Finally the servants stop in front of a door. Its polished surface lets me watch my scared expression swing inward as it opens, and behind the door is, I hate to say it, exactly the bedchamber I'd design if I had endless resources and nothing more to worry about than room furnishings.

It's simple and pretty. Where I had expected it to be as over-the-top as Noam's gate, it's nothing but a canopy bed (a really nice canopy bed), an armoire (a really nice armoire), and an intricate lavender rug stretched over a wood floor. Balcony doors stand open opposite me, heavy white curtains rippling in the wind as I walk into the center of the room.

Both servants are only a few years older than me, dressed in plain but simple dresses made of cloth in Cordell's hunter green. Brown-blond hair hangs in smooth strands down their backs and one of them, her wide brown eyes giving the illusion that she sees everything, steps up to me. "Is this to your liking, Lady Meira?"

"Meira."

"Yes, that's what I said. Lady Meira."

I frown. "No, just Meira. No lady."

"I'm afraid I can't do that, Lady Meira."

I grind my teeth and turn back to the servants. "Fine. What are your names?"

"Mona."

"Rose."

"Well, Mona and Rose, what can you tell me about what Noam's planning?"

Mona keeps her head bowed meekly and Rose simply shrugs.

"We know nothing except that we are to have you dressed and ready by eight."

I squint at them. "And if I refuse?"

Mona's eyes widen. Rose, clearly the one in charge, puts a hand on Mona's. "I hope you don't. King Noam made it clear that our future in his service depends on you being at the ball."

One of my eyebrows shoots up. "And you always do exactly what your king demands?"

Rose bobs her head slowly like she isn't sure why I'd even ask such a question. I expect the same from Mona, but when I notice her hesitating, wringing her hands, I can't stop a curious grin. Rose sees my sudden change in expression and faces Mona, who throws up her hands and nods so violently that I fear her hair will shake right off her head.

"Of course I obey him!" Mona declares. "I just—it would be nice, wouldn't it? If we, I don't know, had our own magic?"

115

Rose's face turns as red as her namesake flower. "No Cordellan wants for anything, and you stand here, *in front of a guest*, and say such things?" She whips to me. "I apologize, Lady Meira—Mona is new to her position."

Mona relents, dropping her hands and bowing her chin against her chest. But she doesn't respond to Rose—she turns to me, her eyes on the floor. "Forgive me, Lady Meira."

I almost forget to bristle at being called "Lady" when I see her small flicker of fire snuffed out. I can't get the surprise off my face—the only time she spoke up was at the thought of having her own magic? Of not being indebted and linked to Noam?

I hold on to the thought, trying to figure out how to place it in my mind. I'm reminded of the lapis lazuli ball in my pocket, the small circular stone pressing into my thigh. Mather wanted to believe that it was magic, that anyone could just pick it up off the ground. It would make the world much simpler—no one would have to depend on their king or queen to help them. No one would have to stay within the boundaries of their kingdoms to partake in their bloodline's magic. We'd be much less . . . trapped? That doesn't feel like the right word, at least as someone who's been fighting her entire life to get this kind of magic. But maybe in other kingdoms, kingdoms that have had magic for centuries, they ask these questions. They wonder what it would be like to be free of our world's strict lines.

I shake my head at Mona. "Don't apologize. It's fine to ask questions." Even if I'm not sure what my answers to those questions are. All I know is Winter needs magic to be free. That's all I can see right now.

Rose snaps to me. "It most certainly is *not* fine when such questions contradict our king's clear orders." She lifts an eyebrow and a finger simultaneously, ready to turn her threats to me.

I back up to the canopy bed and flop out onto it, arms splayed. "No need to get riled up. I'll go to the ball."

When Rose starts talking again, I can hear the smile in her voice. "Excellent. There's a bath prepared for you through there, Lady Meira."

My head pops up in time to see Mona point to a door on my left.

"We'll be back after you've rested," Rose says, and ushers Mona out.

As they close the door, I sit up. The lapis lazuli ball pushes against my hip, making me think of Mather, of Sir, not of magic and who should or shouldn't have it. I wiggle the stone out of my pocket and roll the small blue ball around on my palm, the repetition soothing my nerves.

Noam wants me for some reason. Stranger still is the fact that a Rhythm king sees something in a Season refugee worth using at all. And Mather and Sir both know what it is, but they're in a meeting right now with Noam, so my current options are to either sneak around the palace in hope of finding answers in one of these many rooms or take a bath and a nap.

As if my body has already made its decision, I let loose a yawn, my eyes blurring as tears rush in.

I rip off my travel clothes and pile the whole mess of things in the corner with my chakram guarding it on top. The lapis lazuli ball rolls off the pile, thumping against the wood floor and coming to rest on the thick carpet. I pick it up and set it on the bedside table, staring at its blue surface. I know it's ridiculous, but a small part of me relaxes, knowing a piece of Winter is there if I need it.

Scented soaps and bubbly water quickly erase any lingering worries, filling my senses with lavender and steam. Oh my. I could get used to this.

After spending much too long turning wrinkly, I emerge from the bathroom and frown as the fog of relaxation lifts. Something is wrong. I scan the room twice, mind fuzzy, before my eyes drop to the floor and see—

Nothing.

My things are gone. My chakram, my boots, everything. Only the lapiz lazuli ball is still on the table. A nightgown is now spread out on the bed, a gleaming ivory garment that was probably meant to be a fair trade for my clothes. I should be perturbed, except the nightgown is softer than rabbit fur. I ease it over my head and the fog of relaxation drops back on me. And when I slide between the silky sheets and the warm feather quilt, I forget why I should have been perturbed. Or why I should have gone back to Noam's study and demanded answers. Or where Noam's study even was because all these halls look the same, and his trees are ridiculous, and, sweet snow, this bed is comfortable . . .

"*I'M SORRY. I don't know what else to do. He'll be here in a matter of hours.*"

I'm in the study from my earlier dream. The warm fire pit, the musk of burning coals, the open window letting in flakes of snow. The twenty-three who escaped that night and would come to live in the Rania Plains with two infants, all huddled together in preparation for leaving. And Hannah, her silent strength wavering as she kneels beside . . . Alysson?

Why am I dreaming about this again?

Alysson sits on a chair in front of Sir, who leans over the back of it with his head to his chest. They're both somber, half crying and half not, trying to stay strong before their queen. Alysson has her arms cupped around a tiny wad of blankets.

"*I don't know what else to do,*" Hannah whispers, stretching long, pale fingers to touch the bundle in Alysson's hands. One tiny hand shoots up and Hannah takes it, wraps both of her hands around it.

Mather.

"You don't have to go," Hannah says. "You don't have to obey me."

The queen of Winter, groveling before her general and his wife.

Alysson looks up at her queen, one hand still around Mather and the other moving to grasp Hannah's. "We'll do it," she whispers. "Of course we'll do it. For Winter."

"We'll all do it." Sir now. He looks up, alert and focused. "You can trust us, my queen."

Hannah stands, her fingers absently stretching down to her son. She nods, or bows her head, staying quiet so long that when a distant explosion crashes, everyone jumps.

"I'm so sorry that I did this to you all," Hannah whispers. "So sorry . . ."

"Lady Meira?"

I fly awake expecting explosions, ready to grab that tiny baby and run. It takes a couple of deep breaths and a few moments of focusing on the canopy before I believe that I'm not in that study—I'm in Cordell. I'm in Noam's palace with Rose bending over me, excitement stretching across her face.

It was just a dream. *Another* dream about Hannah. But why did it feel so real?

"Are you ready to be made beautiful, Lady Meira?" Rose asks, overlooking my steady blinking at the canopy.

I cock an eyebrow. "Are you saying I'm not already beautiful?"

Rose's face collapses. "No! Of course not—I mean—"

"It's fine, Rose. I'm joking." I swing my legs over the bed and assess the situation before me. Three additional servants have tagged along with Mona and Rose, each holding either a bag or a piece of clothing. This is part of whatever Sir is planning, I guess—prettying me up, like trussing a chicken before cooking it. Can't go to a ball in my travel garb, and I wince that I didn't realize this sooner. I've never worn anything fancier than the same threadbare clothes I've always had. I'm not sure whether or not I *want* to be fancier—every time Dendera described ball gowns to me, my only thoughts were *Sweet snow, that sounds like a lot of unnecessary fabric,* and *Skirts were probably invented as a device to keep women from running away.*

"Of course, Lady Meira," Rose says, and turns to the servants. "Girls! Let's get to it!"

I fling my hands up. "*Whoa*—now? Wait! I want my clothes and chakram— Ow!"

All five girls descend on me at once. They yank me out of bed and shove me onto a dressing pedestal that makes me feel like one of Noam's silly golden trees with people twittering below me.

"Mona, legs and feet. Cecily, bodice and sleeves. Rachel and Freya, hair and face." Rose falls into step as a general would over a gaggle of confused captains, ordering and scolding. The girls tug me this way and that, shoving me into layers of fabric and dousing me in weird powders and oils. One grabs my hair and jerks it up into a curly design— one paints something glossy on my lips and cheeks—one shoves stiff-heeled shoes onto each foot—one tugs the strings on a corset so tight I can taste the inside of my stomach.

"Are you—sure—all this—is—necessary?" I sputter between tugs on the corset. I understand wanting to be more put together for a ball, but surely all this discomfort isn't really needed? Can't I just slip on a simple dress? Or, better yet, not go at all? But Sir and Mather will be at this ball, and I don't want to wait until it's over to figure out what they're planning. If I have to suffer through a few too-tight corset strings, then fine.

Rose, finger on her bottom lip, lifts an eyebrow at me. She turns to the armoire without a word and pulls it open. On the inside of each door is a mirror, and even though the racks within are stuffed with dresses and nightgowns, I'm too focused on the reflection staring back at me to notice much about the clothes.

Noam's servants are talented. Or I'm prettier than I thought.

The dress they stuck me in—or are still sticking me in—is a deep ruby red, billowy, swishy, with an intricate gold design threaded into the bodice. The gold loops up into two sheer straps that slide just under my collarbone, showing off the necklace of braided gold one of the girls has fastened around my throat. My hair, a giant array of pinned-back curls, hangs messy yet deliberate with a few white strands dangling free around my face.

"Well?" Rose crosses her arms. She seems way too satisfied with herself.

I click my mouth shut. Maybe being a little fancier isn't a horrible thing. "You're . . . good at what you do."

Rose sighs as the girls back up, finished with their assault. A few of them coo at me, "Aren't you so beautiful! He'll fall for you for sure—"

I throw a finger up and look around. "Wait. He who?"

Mona closes her bag of supplies. "Prince Theron, Lady Meira. He'll be smitten!"

Noam's son. I frown, absently clutching the fabric of the skirt. I knew I was forgetting something.

The girls start to leave, Rose herding them out with sharp orders to see if other guests need any last-minute assistance. I leap down from the dressing pedestal and grab Rose's arm.

"General William and King Mather." Saying his title flows out surprisingly easily, and I start in discomfort. "Where are they?"

"Getting ready themselves, Lady Meira. They did say that if you were to ask for them, they would meet you in the library before the ball."

"And when is the ball?"

"In ten minutes."

I smack my fist to my forehead to fight down a sudden migraine. "Lady Rose, if you wish me to attend this ball, you will tell me exactly where the library is. Now."

Rose points down the hall and to the left. "Two lefts, one right. First door on your right."

I start to say thank you, but realize—I'm wearing a ball gown. How many times will I have this opportunity? I drop into a sweeping curtsy, skirt fluffing out in my descent, fabric swallowing me up. Rose applauds as I leap up and start to run out the door. Then I pause, grab the lapis lazuli, and stuff the small blue stone into one of the gown's pockets. Just something to hold on to.

Two lefts. One right. First door on the right.

I repeat the instructions as I run, trotting past scurrying servants and fancy-looking people I don't know. Cordellan royals, probably. Running in a dress is hard enough, but running in a ball gown is like trying to run while wrapped in a tent, so eventually I concede defeat and heft the whole mess of silk into the air. A few passing courtiers raise their eyebrows, but I hurry past them, too glad to move my legs freely to really care about their shocked looks. I was right— skirts *are* inventions meant to make running harder.

The library door is already open when I dash in, but the room is empty. Books line shelves three floors high, and windows just as tall let in rays of dying sunlight. Three balconies wrap above me and a grand piano stands in the center of the bottom level, but there are no people, not even a servant dusting old books in a corner.

I scurry into the room and scan each level for any sign of Sir or Mather or Dendera, anyone. The more empty corners I see, the harder my heart hammers.

They're not here.

Their absence shakes me out of the lightness of preparing for the ball, of getting to take a bath, of the luxury and finery of Bithai. Here I am, standing in Cordell's library, playacting like some foreign damsel, all ball gown and lavender-vanilla perfume. I should embrace this. I shouldn't care that I won't find out anything before the ball, because this type of normalcy is what Sir wanted for me, isn't it? To dance and laugh and wear frilly dresses. To lead an easier life.

But however nice it is to have a tub full of steaming water, however pretty my gown is, *I've* never wanted this kind of life. Dendera would talk about the days when Winter was whole and its court was intact, when Queen Hannah would throw lavish balls like all the other kingdoms of the world. The ladies would dress in fine ivory gowns and the men in deep blue suits, and everything glittered silver and white. I would listen to Dendera's stories and smile at the images, but it was the tales of Winter's battles that filled my dreams. Tales of protecting our kingdom. Fighting for our land. Defending our people.

Not that the courtiers were any less worthy of Winter than the soldiers who fought for it, but I never wanted the life Dendera said she'd had. I wanted a life of my own, a life where I could feel myself *being* a part of Winter. And that, to me, came through fighting for it.

A piece of parchment on the music stand catches me, and I pick it up. Something about the way the script bends in a frantic, scratched hand, like whoever wrote it was in a hurry to get the poem down, draws me to it.

> *Words made me.*
> *They shifted over me from the moment I took breath;*
> *Little black lines etched into my body as I wriggled and screamed*
> *And learned their meanings.*
> *Duty. Honor. Fate.*
> *They were beautiful heart tattoos.*
> *So I took them and kept them and made them my own,*
> *Locked them away inside me and only took them out*
> *When other people got their meanings wrong.*
> *Duty. Honor. Fate.*
> *I believed in everything.*
> *I believed in him when he said I was his greatest duty.*
> *When he said I would be his greatest honor.*
> *I believed no one but him and his three words.*
> *Duty. Honor. Fate.*
> *I believed too much.*

There's a pain in it, the same I-want-more-than-this pain that makes my dress a little less pretty. It sucks my breath away. I'd expect something like this just lying around if we were in Ventralli, which is known for its artists, but not in Cordell. Cordell is all money and power and fertile farmlands. Who wrote this?

"Lady Meira?"

I fly around, parchment fluttering to the ground, gown whooshing in a great funnel of red. At first I think it's Noam. Same tall build, same golden hair, same dark-brown eyes. But this man isn't old enough to have gray in his hair; he's only a few years older than me, and his skin is smooth, sporting just a patch of stubble on his chin. He's much more handsome than Noam too, not quite as harsh, like he's more apt to sing a ballad than lead a kingdom.

I smooth my dress. "Prince Theron," I guess.

An intrigued light brightens his face. Then his eyes drop to the parchment resting between us on the carpet, words up, and the light falls. He dives, grabs the paper, crumples it in his fist like he can disintegrate it through sheer will.

"Golden leaves," Theron curses, catches himself, and grimaces, the paper in his hands cracking through his careful foundation of manners. "I'm sorry. This isn't—it's nothing."

I frown. "You wrote that?"

His mouth tightens. Fighting with admitting to it or getting this conversation back on course.

I motion to the paper he gently sets on a table. "It's good," I say. "You're talented."

A little of Theron's panic ebbs away. "Thank you," he says cautiously as the corners of his lips lift. It's not Mather's full-face smile, but it still disarms me, making my legs weak under the layers of skirts and petticoats.

I clear my throat, pulling my focus off Noam's shockingly attractive son and back onto why I'm here. Even if Sir or Mather shows up now, we would have to talk in front of Theron. So I lift my skirt in a slightly more ladylike way and walk toward him.

"Apparently I'm wanted at a ball," I say. "I don't want to risk incurring the wrath of Rose. Are you on your way there as well?"

Theron nods and puts a hand on my arm as I pass him, gently enough for me to feel an indescribable tingle rush up and down my body. A single spark of lightning created by his fingers on that one small spot of my arm.

"I am. Would you mind an escort? I thought it might be a good time to get to know each other." His eyes flick back to the parchment. "Well, properly."

How far away could the ballroom be? "Yes, thank you."

Theron offers me his arm. I pause, eyebrow cocked, before slipping my hand through it and resting my fingers on the green velvet of his sleeve.

"So," I start as we pull to the left in the hall, "you're the king of Cordell's son. How's that?"

Theron chuckles. "Beneficial sometimes, horrible others. You're beautiful—how's that?"

The heel of my shoe catches at a weird angle and I stumble forward. No one has called me that before. Dendera said I was a "pretty thing" once, and Mather . . . I exhale, running through every interaction I've ever had with him, and deflating a little as I do. He's never said anything like that to me, and until now, I never realized he hadn't—or how much I wanted him to. It makes me agonizingly aware of the fact that Theron's looking at me, and I just stare at him, not sure what to do.

"Forgive me," Theron says, his face pale. "I shouldn't have been so forward. We're still getting to know each other. I promise, over time you'll see I'm much more charming than I first appear."

"Well, I hope we get plenty of time alone together so you can convince me of your charm." My eyes flash wide when I hear what I said. "Oh. No. I mean—well, I mean that, but not as presumptuously as it sounded."

Theron bobs his head. "We have all the time you desire, Lady Meira. I will not rush you."

We make another turn and one of the two grand staircases sweeps down in front of us. The giggly chatter of party guests mingles with the music lifting from the ballroom below, something light and string-based. Food smells drift up—honey ham, lavender tarts, the sharper tang of liquor, the nutty aroma of coffee. For a second I just breathe it all in, my stomach grumbling under the lush scents, then—

"Wait," I say, my mind working over his words. "Won't rush me to what?"

Theron's face flashes with confusion, putting pieces together I can't see, and he pulls back, taking his arm away from me. "No one's told you," he breathes.

At the same time, the pieces click in my head. "You know! You know what Noam and Sir and Mather—"

Theron nods. He's got a serenity to him that Noam doesn't have, something graceful and calm that makes every move look deliberate. "Yes," he whispers. He looks to the railing, the ballroom below, and back at me. "I . . . I'm sorry. I assumed someone told you. My father and King Mather have come to an arrangement. We aid Winter—"

I clap with delight. Sir did it! Winter has an ally.

But Theron isn't done. "—so long as we are linked with Winter."

My hands freeze mid-clap. "Linked?"

He exhales. I feel him take my hand before I see it, his skin warming my fingers in a grip that's tight, intimate.

I jerk back, slamming into a small decorative table behind me. The vase on it falls over and clatters on the floor, water and flowers sullying the thick carpet.

But I just stare at Theron. King Mather made a deal with Noam.

He linked Cordell with Winter. Through me.

I'M A PAWN they used to create an alliance with Cordell.

My tongue sticks in my throat, choking me as I stand there, staring at Theron. This has to be a figment of my overly active imagination, because the king of Cordell would never agree to wed his son—the heir of one of the richest Rhythms—to a mere peasant from a Season. I'm wrong. I have to be.

"Tell me Mather linked us to Cordell through a treaty, or something. A meaningless piece of paper," I beseech him. "Tell me this isn't . . . what I think it is."

But Theron doesn't say anything, which only feeds my panic more. His mouth opens absently, but he just sighs, his eyes flitting over me in silence.

I grip my stomach, the fabric of the gown smooth against my fingers, and swallow the tight knot in my throat. Mather did this. My chest swells with a new emotion—betrayal. How could he—why did he—no. *No.* I will not lose my mind over this, because it still doesn't make any sense. Why would Cordell agree to take *me*? There has to be something Mather and Sir didn't tell me.

Well, obviously there's a lot they didn't tell me, but they're down at the ball right now. And I will *make* them talk.

"Are you all right?" Theron finally speaks, but he doesn't try to touch me again. This would be easier if he was horrible, if he didn't care if I was all right. But he looks hurt. Is he just a pawn too?

Remembering the poem he swiped off the floor—probably.

"I'm sorry," Theron says. He looks at the railing, motions toward the ball. "I know this is sudden, but this ball is for you. Me. Us."

Us. It sounds like a foreign word.

I pry myself away from the wall, my roaring determination to march down to that ball and face Mather and Sir and demand answers now replaced with dread. Because when I see Mather and Sir, they'll see me with Theron. Mather will smile and congratulate me and try to explain why this is the best thing for Winter. That the only good we can do for our kingdom is marry to create an alliance because we're useless children. That the kiss before we left camp was a good-bye, nothing more. That even though I've never seen Winter or its enslaved people or set foot on its soil, I'm expected to sacrifice everything, because until Winter is free I don't matter.

I instantly hate myself for thinking that. Other Winterians suffer enslavement while I'm engaged to the crown prince of Cordell—someone bring out the sympathy parade, poor Meira is engaged to a handsome prince.

My life could be worse. A lot worse.

Then why does the thought of taking Theron's outstretched hand make me feel empty?

My fingers are stuffed into my pocket, grasped tightly around the piece of lapis lazuli. I yank my hand free, fighting the urge to hurl that stupid rock as far away from me as possible. I don't want any of it. I don't need Mather or Sir. I never did.

I place my hand in Theron's, and his warm fingers tighten around mine as we move toward the staircase. Having him hold on to me gives me strength I didn't expect. Something infinitely more powerful than the fake strength of the blue stone, still weighing heavy in my pocket.

We're there. Staring over the railing at all the many Cordellans who wait below. Dignitaries mostly, the men wearing hunter green and gold-trimmed uniforms like Theron's, the women wearing gowns in reds and blues and purple jewel tones like mine. And in the far back corner, the Winterian delegates, dressed in what I assume are borrowed outfits too—sharp green suits for the men, billowy gowns for the women. Sir and Dendera and Alysson and Finn and Greer and Henn and Mather.

Mather stares up at me, and even from all the way across the ballroom, his face ripples like he's grinding his teeth. When I meet his gaze, hold it, he looks away.

The music glides to a halt, violins fading in gentle whines. Below us and to the left a platform has been erected for the orchestra, but Noam now stands on it too, one hand upraised triumphantly toward his son and me.

"Ladies and gentlemen, honored guests," he begins. He's so happy. Exuberantly happy. "May I present Prince Theron Haskar and his bride-to-be, Lady Meira of Winter!"

Bride-to-be.

I gasp, drawing in breath after breath, unable to get any air into my lungs. It's real. This. Theron.

The crowd pulls back as if Noam announced that he was stripping them of their titles, their delight at the ball turning to shock. Clearly Noam's arrangement isn't something all of his courtiers welcome with open arms. Somehow, knowing that makes me feel a little better. Not much, but enough that when the crowd breaks into halfhearted applause, I'm able to wave slightly at them all.

Mather sees my reaction and turns to Sir, who snaps something to him before they both move toward the great glass doors on the right side of the ballroom. Doors that open to manicured green hedges, cobblestone walkways, bubbling fountains under a nighttime sky.

So that's how they want to play it.

As Theron and I reach the ballroom floor, a herd of nobles attacks us, blabbering questions that sound innocent but are at the core insulting. Questions such as "I thought you and my daughter had gotten along so well, Your Highness" and "Won't you dance with my niece? She so enjoyed your company last winter. I mean, not *Winter*. Our season. Our *normal* season."

Theron's mouth hangs open, unable to get in a word. The fat duke whose niece had such a nice time last winter grabs his arm, persistence making his blubbery face pink.

"I insist, my prince!" he says, and drags Theron into the crowd. Theron looks at me, eyes darting to the duke and back. Should he fight it? Should he stay with me?

I shake my head and wave my hand in front of my face to mimic being hot in here. Theron returns my wave with a single head bob. He understands.

Once he's gone, the rest of the courtiers eye me, their narrow gazes examining me like I'm some mythical being come to life. I drop a curtsy and turn away from their assessments, making for the terrace doors. Let them think whatever they like. Let them conspire and say horrible things about me. This isn't my kingdom. At least, it shouldn't be.

I throw open a door. Stars glitter in the black sky above me, small twinkling eyes that watch as I slam the door shut and dive into the fantastic nighttime chill of Cordell's autumn. The pureness of the cold hits me, threatening to pull out the scream I've been holding in for the past ten minutes.

"Meira."

I pivot toward Mather and Sir, standing in the entrance to a hedge maze. Half of me wants to run to them and cry and beg to leave, half wants to start throwing rocks at their heads.

But I'm a soldier. A Winterian soldier. And apparently a future queen of Cordell.

So I pick up a handful of rocks from beside the path and hurl the small stones at them as I step forward.

"You—giant—awful—traitors!" I stumble to a halt a breath from Mather. The last rock hits him in the shoulder and he flinches back, rubbing the bruise.

"Meira, calm yourself," Sir says, putting his hand on my arm.

I grab his wrist and slam him back into the hedge, my other hand going to his throat before I know what I'm doing. I'm pinning Sir to a wall of shrubbery. I never thought I'd be in this situation.

"Why?" I growl at him. "Why would you do this to me?"

Sir doesn't fight; if he did, I'd be on the ground with a few broken fingers. "We had no choice."

"No," I spit. "*I* have no choice. You forced this decision on me. *Why?*"

"I did it," Mather answers.

My whole body convulses. No, he didn't. He couldn't.

Because Mather of all people knows what it's like to have Sir say he'll be married off to some random royal he's never met because that's all he's useful for. Didn't Mather tell me he knew how horrible it felt to be valued for the wrong things?

Didn't I mean anything to him?

I release Sir and turn, my body numb from head to heels.

"When Dendera and I got to Bithai, I met with Noam," Mather starts. "I explained what happened. We have half the locket; we're that much closer to getting our conduit back. And now, with Noam already helping Autumn, I told him Winter's interests and Cordell's are nearly identical. If he overthrows Spring, Autumn will be saved. But—"

"Autumn does not need Spring overthrown."

The voice booms out of the darkness and we all turn, focusing on the looming shape at the entrance of the hedge maze.

Noam. I'm going to yank his eyes out through his nostrils.

I'm not sure whether Sir reads my thoughts or my sudden strike-to-kill expression, but he grabs my wrist to hold me back.

"Autumn needs time. They need a few years to keep the Shadow of the Seasons at bay while Princess Shazi grows. Once she's old enough to use her conduit, Autumn will be able to handle Spring on its own." Noam steps to the side, leans casually on a statue at the hedge maze entrance. "It is not in my best interest to stage all-out war with a Season."

Mather lurches toward him. "What makes you think Shazi will be able to hold off Spring once she's older? Regardless of Autumn's strength, Spring will not be satisfied staying within its own borders. You've seen Angra's evil! He will spread anywhere he can—"

Noam holds his hand up. "We have been down this road, King Mather. And you know my stance."

Mather growls. "My mother did not surrender her power to Angra. She did not give up."

But Noam ignores him. "Angra is not so ambitious that he will attempt to expand to a Rhythm. The Seasons' problems will remain among the Seasons, and my niece will not be as weak as Hannah." Noam turns his smile to me. "And I believe Winter has potential. I believe you will be able to reopen your mines and rebuild your kingdom. So yes, Cordell will aid Winter. We will give you support and safety, as long as our support and safety do not extend to a Cordell–Spring war."

I shake my head, unable to piece his words together. It doesn't make sense. He'll help us—but he won't help us? He thinks Winter will be restored, but he won't do anything to get us there. What does he think will happen?

Something he said stands out, and I gasp.

"You'll take our mines because you're linked to Winter now. You'll try to find the chasm." I pull out of Sir's grip to surge toward Noam, my fingers wanting to reach back and grab my chakram and slice through his skull. "You'll tear our kingdom apart to find it!"

Noam steps toward me. "Politics do not leave much room for free gifts, Lady Meira. I cannot afford to give another kingdom something for nothing. Yes, I expect payment."

Fury rises up my body and I start panting. "You have everything," I spit. "*Cordell* has everything. You even have Autumn now—and still you want another Season's resources? You might not find it, you know that, right? What makes you think you'll have any more luck than the people who have lived there for thousands of years?"

Noam puts a hand on his conduit, the purple jewel on the hilt glowing against his hip. "It's time a Rhythm tried where the Seasons have failed. Yes, Cordell is linked to Autumn, and yes, I will scour that kingdom for the chasm entrance—but if it isn't in Autumn's section of the Klaryns, what then? You are young. You have been removed from politics. But you will soon learn that this is how things work—this is your new world."

I fall back to Sir. "No. Tell him we don't do this, not in Winter. We don't let—"

But Sir's eyes drop. His entire body looks like it might dissolve and I've never, in all my life, seen him show so much emotion at once.

We're entirely at Noam's mercy until he decides either to help us or fling us back out into the dark where no one else will come to our rescue. I had always assumed

Sir had a plan for who our allies would be after we got our locket back. If this is the best option—a trap—then would anyone else even bother helping us? Or would the other Rhythms rather wait for us to disintegrate under the Shadow of the Seasons and then swoop in to claim our kingdom and, by extension, access to the chasm of magic? With their own internal struggles, none of the other Seasons are strong enough to overthrow Angra.

We're stuck.

I back up a step. Mather puts his hand on my spine, leaves it there, his thumb moving slowly over the fabric of my dress.

No, no, *no*.

"Lady Meira." Noam sweeps his arm back toward the ballroom. "This ball is in your honor. It will raise suspicion if you are gone too long."

I shake my head but start to walk forward, my feet taking me toward the light of the ball. When I'm parallel to Noam, I stop. "Why me?"

Noam's smile falters for half a heartbeat and he casts an amused glance at Sir. "That is part of the arrangement, that you will be given a proper title in Winter. By Cordell's golden leaves, have you been led to believe that you would fade into history once Winter has been reborn? That you wouldn't matter to your reestablished kingdom?"

I look over my shoulder at Mather, Sir. Next to Noam, who stands cool and relaxed, they both look defeated in the flickering light of the ballroom. Noam has said more things that make sense in the past few minutes than Sir ever has. That sad realization makes something click, something that shuts off the ache deep in my stomach.

I never wanted to fade into nothing, but Sir never told me I wouldn't. He never let me believe I mattered to Winter beyond my responsibility to lead a normal, safe life once our kingdom was free from Angra, regardless of how fervently I tried to prove to him that I was more. He just let me think I would be lost in all this, that I wasn't important enough to matter further.

And now this is it. This is how I will matter to Winter. As a marriage pawn.

"Yes," I whisper. "I did believe that."

Walking away from Mather and Sir feels like a nightmare. A nightmare in which I want Mather to run after me and fight off Noam and admit he could never do that to me, marry me off to someone else, because he's been in love with me all along.

Noam opens the door to the ballroom for me, smiling as the music and laughter of his court rushes out. "You are part of this family now," he says when the door shuts behind us. "And it would benefit you greatly to remember that my son has options. Many more *beneficial* options that do not involve us in a war. My kingdom progresses, adapts, and changes, while your people fester in stagnation like stones eroded in a stream, sitting atop power but not caring in the least that it's there. This is a favor, granted only out of my generosity."

I hold back a growl. Noam slips his hand around my arm, pulling me to a halt, and as his thick fingers tighten against my skin, a memory sweeps into my mind, one of Sir's lectures on court lineages. Noam had a wife. Theron's mother, Melinda DeFiore, a princess of Ventralli. In my mind's eye, I see Noam kneeling at her bedside, her frail body sinking slowly into the tight grasp of death. She was sick, very sick, but there's something wrong with Noam—did he let her die?

I shake my head. When did Sir tell me how she died? He must have. I remember it so vividly that sometime in all his lectures, he must have mentioned Queen Melinda of Cordell's death.

Noam shakes me out of the flash of memory by tightening his grip on my arm, holding me the same way Theron did. No, not the same way. Theron was gentle, made sure I knew I could pull away at any time. Noam clutches me like he owns me. He owns everything in Cordell and is used to every person, animal, and plant bowing under the power of his conduit. And even though I'm not Cordellan and his conduit can't actually affect me, I still feel the power he wields when he curls his hand around mine and squeezes. He *does* own me now.

Couples spin past us to fast-paced orchestral music.

Their laughter falls into the background of Noam's sudden glare, still disguised by his pleasantly calm aura.

"You need me," he hisses. "*Winter* needs me. You will begin proper training to instruct you in the ways of etiquette and Cordellan history. I advise you to *not* refuse this training and to obey me in all things."

A tremor runs up my arm. In that moment as he feeds on my fear and revels in power, I see Herod, hissing threats like he was a cat and I was a bird with my wings trapped in his claws.

I yank my arm out of Noam's grip. "Is that what your wife did? She disobeyed you?" I spit, throwing the accusation out like a chakram into a dark room.

As his face collapses, some of my dislike of him unravels. It's the last thing he ever expected to hear from me, from anyone, and it shakes him off whatever pedestal he keeps himself on.

"What—" Noam's mouth falls open. Closes. Opens again, and when it does, his shock shifts away in favor of anger and he grabs my wrist in a threat.

I dig my nails into his skin. "You may have me trapped in this." I tug him off me. "But you aren't the first man to underestimate me, so may I advise you to start treating me with a little more respect, *King* Noam."

Before he can respond, I spin around and dive into the rows of dancers, darting back and forth between them until I reach the center of the moving bodies and swooshing fabric.

Colors swirl around me—glistening gold, dark green, blue taken straight from the deepest part of the Destas Sea. The colors and music combine to create a strange lull in the chaos, a weirdly peaceful hub in the center of the ballroom, surrounded by music and the rotating circles of people. It almost relaxes me.

Almost.

I cup my hands over my face and exhale, inhale, exhale again. *Just keep breathing.* No matter what happens, no matter who turns on me, no matter what pompous swine thinks he has power over me, I am still me. I will always be *me*.

Who is that, though? Apparently it's this girl in the ruby gown and smudged face powder, getting examined by Cordell's upper class. Someone who can treat the king of Cordell with as much revulsion as he treats me. A lady. That can't be right.

It's definitely not someone important to Mather or Sir. Definitely not someone who will have any standing in the new Winter, no matter what Noam thinks. Just someone who gets bounced around in whatever position needs to be filled, used and used like a candle on a moonless night until I burn away into a puddle of compliance and obedience.

I wanted to be a soldier. Someone who would *earn* standing in Winter. Someone Sir would look at with pride. Someone Mather would look at and—

No.

This is who Sir wants me to be. He's made it startlingly

clear that if he had his way—and look, he's finally having his way—I'd never be a soldier. And Mather can just leap off Bithai's four-story palace and land on a golden tree.

A hand cups my elbow and I jump back when I look into Mather's eyes. He scoops me into his arms, arranging us into a proper dancing pose as if he can sense how dangerously close I am to hitting him. "I just want to talk," he pleads as we move through the sea of bodies to the music.

"Well, I don't," I retort, and pull out of his arms. People eye us as they swirl past, but I refuse to start dancing with Mather again despite the way he holds his arms out, his face pinched and his eyes glassy.

He brushes the emotion off his face, one solid sweep of nothing. Hiding it, pushing it away, pretending it doesn't mean anything to him when it should mean *everything*.

I shake my head. I will *not* cry. I will not show emotion either. "I thought you said you knew," I start, the words grating against my throat. "That you knew how it felt, to be deemed worthless for reasons beyond your control. Yet here I am, a pawn in a marriage arrangement, because you and Sir deemed me worthless for anything else. Thank you, Mather. Thank you for finally showing me my place."

Mather gasps, running a hand through the strands of hair that have fallen free of the ribbon holding the rest back. He shakes his head but doesn't say anything. Either he can't or he *doesn't*, and the tears threatening to spill out of my eyes finally do. I wipe at them furiously, and just as

I start to slide into the crowd, Theron appears.

He looks as bedraggled as I feel, only he's spent the last few minutes dancing as well as being his father's plaything. His eyes shoot to Mather before he looks back at me and lifts an eyebrow.

I stop myself from looking at Mather. This is my place now. This is where I belong.

"I'm sorry," I tell Theron. The loud music drowns out my voice, making it look like I'm just mouthing the words into the air.

Theron's lips tilt in a smile that doesn't reach his eyes. "So am I," he says, and holds out his hand.

I feel when Mather leaves, taking the heavy air of tension with him. My eyes latch onto him when he joins Sir outside the crowd of dancers, and a lump rolls around in my throat and beats down on my heart when he looks back at me. His eyes flick to Theron, back to me, and he pushes Sir out of the way to head for the staircase. Sir grabs his arm and barks something at him, and Mather responds by barking right back.

Then he leaves, vanishing up the stairs and down the hall.

Sir turns away, finds Alysson, and leaves too.

"Lady Meira?" Theron forces a smile, his hand still extended. Something about it feels permanent, like taking it means everyone else I care about will disappear.

They already have. And all I have now, all I'll ever have,

is standing in front of me with a lopsided half smile and narrow eyes from his own stress.

I shake my head. "Just Meira," I say as I take Theron's hand and let him pull me into him. My cheek barely reaches his face, my temple stopping just beside the stubble on his chin. A delicate scent of lavender and something like worn book pages emanates from him. We sway back and forth, gentle and steady though the music that pulses from the orchestra is still fast and strong. As if we're saying, *We make the music here. Not you.*

"Just Meira," Theron echoes. He adjusts his arms around my back and looks across the distance between us, then nods decisively. "We'll be all right. Together."

I can't say anything. I turn my face to the side and close my eyes, fighting against the coolness that swarms me with his words. *Together.* The two of us, just us, while everything around us is swept away.

"Don't you want more than this?" I breathe, finally looking up at him.

His eyes are soft, relaxed, but my question makes his softness tense. His lips pull apart and the answer that comes sounds so much like the thoughts whirring through my head that, for a moment, I think maybe I said it.

"Every day of my life."

IT TAKES BOTH Rose and Mona to get me out of the
dress. And when they finally do, instead of meekly accepting another nightgown and crawling into bed, I demand they
return my stolen clothes and kidnapped chakram. After a
few good minutes of them telling me that's not what ladies
wear and me telling them I'm their future queen so they'd
better obey me—it took me several tries before I could say
it without crying—they relent and retrieve my things.

"We cleaned them, at least," Rose says, and hands me my
shirt. It does look white now, not brown and crunchy.

"And I had one of the guards tend to this." Mona lifts my
chakram. "It's sharpened."

Mona is my favorite.

They leave and I tug on my much more comfortable
clothes. That stupid blue stone is in my pocket before I can

analyze why I still want it after everything Mather did, why I feel better with it in my possession than leaving it behind. I loop my chakram into its usual place of honor between my shoulder blades and race from the hallway door to the balcony. Moments before my feet leave the bedroom floor, I grab one of the white curtains and propel myself out onto the balcony railing. The speed I picked up from the sprint shoots me out into the air and I bet my life quite literally on the chance that the curtain won't rip in two.

Somewhere between my being fully airborne and breaking my leg on the ground below, the curtain catches and holds, swinging me back in toward the palace. The familiar surge of adrenaline rushes into me, the same freeing burst I felt on the mission in Lynia. A pure rush that makes me see more clearly, makes my head lighter. I release the curtain and grab for a ledge just above my balcony. It would have been possible to climb out of my room without the curtain theatrics, but not nearly as fun.

Once I'm there, a few easy jumps and pulls get me to the roof. It's made of the same curved tiles as the rest of Bithai's roofs, but instead of a steep slope to the ground, it's flat and walkable. Good for lookouts in times of war—and for a restless future queen who feels like exploring her new home.

My nose curls involuntarily at the word. This isn't my home. I've never even been to my real home, and now here I am with a replacement I never asked for. I should feel grateful, lucky even—most Winterians call a Spring work camp their replacement home. But I can't feel anything more than frustration.

I start running on the shingles. The palace is huge, wings shooting off at every crossing, occasional domes of glass hinting at skylights. But it's the tower jutting out of the northernmost wing of the palace that calls my name.

It's empty and a little dusty, its disuse proof that Bithai hasn't seen a war in years. I pull myself over the railing and kick aside an overturned table. Finally one place Noam doesn't keep pristine.

I can see why they built the tower here. It's open on every side, giving a complete view of the city and the kingdom beyond. To the east, most of Bithai sleeps under a clear sky and a half-moon. To the west, farmlands roll off into the horizon, green and dark in the absence of city light. To the south . . .

I dig my fingers into the railing. To the south are the Seasons. Spring, with its brutality and blood, and Winter, with its snow and ice and coldness that never ends, with its queen who haunts my dreams through images of the refugees and baby Mather.

Mather.

I feel liable to explode, everything in me hot and heavy and choking off air. I hate him for caring, for making me think he liked me too, for giving me a flash of hope as small as a stone and a kiss on my jaw when both of us knew we could never, ever be more than what we are.

"You shouldn't blame him."

On a sharp breath, I yank my chakram into my hand and aim it at the shadow behind me.

Sir.

I tense my hand against my weapon. "You've got nerve."

Sir steps away from the corner of the tower he just climbed up. "I couldn't let the day end without you knowing the truth."

I laugh. It's hollow and makes a shiver dance down my back. "Well, it's already tomorrow, so you're a tad late."

Sir surges forward, tears the chakram out of my hand, and tosses it to the floor. Before I can fight back, he rotates me to face the south and keeps a hand firmly on the back of my neck.

"Snow above," he hisses. "You've never seen what's down there. The closest you've come to Winter is the outermost towns in Spring, the aftermath of Winter's fall. But you've never seen the Winterians in the camps. You didn't see Angra lead them away; you didn't look into their eyes as they realized what was happening, that Angra was going to use them until they died. Don't snap at me like you know what's at stake. You don't know anything, Meira, and I'm sorry if this marriage is hard for you to accept, but it will happen. You wanted to matter to Winter? *This* is how Winter needs you."

I jam my elbow into Sir's stomach and rip his hand off my neck. He stumbles back, coughing, a look of shock falling over him.

"*No.*" I point a finger at him because I'm not sure what else I can do. My arm shakes, an outward sign of my inward roiling, rocking anger. "You do not get to lecture me like this is some lesson you're trying to drill into my head. This isn't our training tent. This is my *life*. You know this is horrible, Sir! You know everything, so if I don't know anything, why don't you tell me? Why doesn't Mather tell me himself instead of sending you to do it for him?"

Sir stares at me for a moment, quiet, the rush of fight gone. His eyes are wet, hair frayed, body slowly caving in like he's been beaten against the rocks one too many times. He *was* our rock, though.

I pull my hands through my hair, a moan escaping my lips. Something deep and hidden, urged on by the child in me who cries whenever Sir's upset. "What happened, William?"

He hugged me, once. When I was six, still small enough to sleep in the tent he shared with Alysson, I woke up one night screaming. Drenched in sweat, crying so hard and loud my body ached for days. Sir was instantly at my side, alert and looking for an enemy.

"I saw them," I whimpered.

"Who?" He was so concerned, his brow pinched, his eyes wide. Like he expected a Spring soldier to leap out of the shadows.

"My—" I couldn't say it. *Mother. Father.* I didn't even see them in my dream—I saw who I thought they were, who my mind created. Two loving people who were slaughtered in the street, their baby tumbling from their arms before Sir scooped me up.

In my dream, though, they were burning. Screaming at me from a building engulfed in flames while Angra stood outside, a monster of a man holding a staff. His conduit. Orange-and-red fire danced up and down the ebony surface of the staff and across the ground, feeding the inferno of the building. I stood behind him, screaming for him to stop.

Angra turned to me. "Not until you're all dead."

When I told Sir my dream, he stayed quiet for a long while, his face a war of emotions. Fear and regret and something deep—guilt, maybe. Or blame? But it flickered off his face and he wrapped his arms around me, nestled me against his chest, and let me lean into him.

"It's not your fault," he whispered. "Meira, it's not your fault."

Sixteen years, and that's all I've gotten from him—one hug in a moment of weakness. When I lower my arms, Sir's staring southward, like if he focuses hard enough, he can actually see Winter.

"I came here. Fourteen years ago," he whispers.

I don't move.

"Two years after the attack. Took me that long to beat down my pride. Cordell had been one of the kingdoms we called for aid when Spring finally got too strong, but they didn't come. No one did, Rhythm or Season."

Sir straightens and presses his hands to his eyes, shakes away some emotion. "When I got here, I pleaded with Noam from every possible angle. We needed anything he could give, and he had *everything*. But . . ." Sir pauses, chin falling to his chest as he goes deeper and deeper into memory. "Noam hasn't changed in fourteen years, and he wanted the same thing then that he does now. The same thing all the Rhythms want—access to our kingdom, to our mountains. A legal and binding connection to the possibility of more magic."

I nod. I didn't know that Sir had been here before. It makes sense—his hatred of Noam, his passionate anger toward Cordell. I keep my lips pinched together. He's never talked to me so openly before.

"There was nothing left, though. No Winterian royal court to barter with, beyond Mather, and Noam didn't have any daughters, not even a niece. So he proposed an alliance between you and Theron, under the condition that once our kingdom was restored, you would be given a title and standing in the new Winter, something worthy of a future Cordellan queen." Sir sighs. "But you were so young. So small. And I couldn't—I had no right to promise you off like that. You weren't even mine. Who was I to make a marriage arrangement for you?"

A lump forms in my throat. I swallow but it doesn't budge.

"But that was fourteen years ago. Fourteen years and we're still no closer to anything. Yes, we have half of the locket, but we can't get the other half without killing Angra himself, and we'll never get close enough to do that without support. We need help. Until its heir comes of age, Autumn is too weak and Summer would rather watch us die than make the effort. No other Rhythm has deigned to negotiate with us. So even though Noam's a Rhythm, even though I know he's using us—" Sir pauses, voice catching. "We have no options other than to trust that he will actually help. When Angra's scout escaped our camp, I took Mather aside and told him what would happen. That Dendera would take him to Bithai, and he would meet with Noam, and he would tell him we accept."

I drop onto the railing, the tower spinning.

"Don't blame Mather; he was following my orders. And now you are going to follow them too." Sir's voice rises from the peaceful lull of storytelling to his abrupt bark. "You are going to do this, Meira. You are going to do what we need you to do."

I shake my head, but Sir just repeats it: *You are going to do what we need you to do.* Not what I want to do, not what I *can* do. What they need me to do. For Winter.

I almost laugh at the irony. After all, I wanted to be needed, didn't I? But my laugh dies. No—I wanted to matter because of who I am and what I can do, not just because I'm a Winterian female, and our new ally had a suitable Cordellan male to pair with me. I wanted to *belong* to Winter, to earn my belonging.

My eyes gradually drift from the floor of the tower to Sir's face. He's regained some of his in-control attitude and doesn't look quite so broken now.

"Was Hannah sorry?" I whisper. "Before Angra attacked, was she upset about something she did?"

Sir's entire face freezes as if Angra stabbed Mather in front of him. But he shakes his head, his face setting in a blank stare, and his refusal to answer slams against my question.

I grab my chakram from the floor, holster it, and swing a leg over the tower railing, straddling the stone wall. "I know there are things you aren't telling me. Big things. Reasons why all this is happening, and someday, Sir, I will find out. I only hope your reasoning is good enough for me to forgive you."

I drop down the tower and roll on the roof, breaking into a run, the cold night air blowing me faster, the darkness and gleaming stars taking me somewhere I don't have to feel.

157

I crawl back into my room through the open balcony doors. Another nightgown waits on the bed for me, but I'm too shaken to bother putting it on. I just lay the chakram and the lapis lazuli on the bedside table and sprawl out on the quilt, fully clothed, keeping my eyes pressed shut.

Breathe, breathe. That's all I focus on, air moving in and out of my lungs, until I drift away from reality and into sleep.

At first I think I'm in Noam's palace, but the ballroom is set up all wrong. A great white marble staircase rises in front of me, the room folding out in a square. The same white marble floor makes the entire room glow in the calm, quiet darkness of night. This is Jannuari's palace. Winter.

I exhale, blowing a cloud of white into the air as peace descends deep into every limb. I'm in Winter. And she's here again. Hannah. I can feel her presence, a gentle aura waiting nearby.

In a distant hall, a baby cries.

I run up the staircase, weaving down hallways paned with ivory marble. White candles flicker on tables as I fly past, adding eerie shadows to every twist and turn.

Finally a room appears on my right, the door thrown open, light streaming out. I hurry in to see a bassinet in the center, soft white light rippling out of it. Hannah stands next to it and baby Mather screams again, wailing like he's being attacked.

I step forward as Hannah's ice-blue eyes flick up to me.

"I can't talk to him," she says. She moves around the bassinet, close enough that I catch a whiff of her perfume. "But Angra isn't watching you."

"Angra?"

Hannah shakes her head and looks around the room, her face pan-icked, anxious, like something might jump out and get us. "He's coming. But you can hear me, can't you?"

I nod. "Yes, I can hear you." I pause. "My queen."

Where there had only been light in this room, there is now a shadow in the corner. Black and thick, impenetrable. Hannah reaches for me but curls her fingers into her palm.

"Hurry," she says. "Do what you must."

"What?" I step toward her and she twitches back to Mather.

"Do what you must," Hannah whispers to the bassinet. The shadow in the corner grows and grows. It sweeps between us and as I scream out to Hannah, the entire world goes black.

Magic.

It's the first thing that flies into my mind after I wake up, the blackness and lingering scream from my dream van-ishing in the morning light. I roll onto my side and my eyes fall on Mather's lapis lazuli ball on the bedside table. That stupid blue rock.

While this isn't the first time I've dreamed of her, Han-nah has never spoken to me before. *To me.* Like I was there, back when Jannuari fell. A wave of trepidation makes me shiver. Is that what Mather gave me? Some weird rock that induces nightmares and visions? I don't need any other rea-sons to hate him right now. It can't be magic. I'm having these dreams because I'm fatigued to the point of night-mares. That's it.

All this on top of the late-night ball means I'm frazzled, I'm exhausted, and I just want to hurl my chakram at something.

Rose and Mona have other ideas about how I should spend my day, though. After a quick breakfast in my room over which we have an argument about the importance of attending etiquette classes, I climb off the balcony. Rose throws quite the fit when she sees me leap out into the air, but I swear Mona hides the smallest smile behind her hand. Mona is still my favorite, and despite Noam's threat last night about obeying him, I refuse to buckle this easily. I may be trapped in this arrangement, but that does not mean I've become Noam's future queen-shaped slave.

So I take it upon myself to explore the palace grounds. I'm just doing what I must, as Hannah told me to. Whatever she meant by that cryptic warning. But it wasn't really a warning; it was my riled mind's interpretation of events—I hope.

I jog off down a cobblestone path, skirting groups of royals who either perk up at the sight of me or start whispering to each other, eyes narrowed and noses crinkled disapprovingly. Probably because I'm wearing my travel clothes and have a chakram strapped to my back. The nose-crinkling royals grow in number and I realize I'm jogging through a garden area, a place where proper future queens would flit around in fancy gowns and coy giggles. Where they would let the world move on around them while men make decisions.

I will *not* be that kind of queen, no matter that Cordell isn't actually my kingdom. But what kind of queen will I be? I know only what kind of soldier I've always tried to be—active, alert, eager, desperate to be a part of Winter. Is that the kind of queen I'll be too? Or will Noam see to it that I remain a helpless figurehead, some pretty ivory statuette to position just so in one of his alcoves?

All of my thoughts echo back to me in a wave of shock. How I thought about being queen definitively—what kind of queen *will* I be. Not maybe, not might. Like I've accepted the life that Sir and Mather thrust on me. I know I have no choice—I know this is my role now. But I still don't want this life, and a part of me sneers at the part that knows I need to find a way to not hate it.

I can't keep thinking these things, can't keep strolling aimlessly through pretty gardens and pretending I belong here. So I leap over a few hedges, wiggle between a row of tightly placed evergreens—and pop out in a wonderful, wonderful place.

The noises of battle surround me, soldiers grunting and swords clashing and arrows twanging through the wind. Men in various states of undress leap around each other, sparring with weapons or fists in roped-off rings. Behind them all, a barn stretches in both directions, doors thrown open, horses whinnying from within and more men carrying stacks of armor in and out.

Cordell's training grounds.

Which means . . . *I can shoot things.*

A range sits on the far left, at least two dozen targets set up alongside a few tall wooden poles for ax and javelin throwing. Some soldiers hurl daggers, knives, others fire good old-fashioned bows, and still more fire crossbows, gleaming metal things that make me giggle just as excitedly as Rose and Mona did over my ball gown.

I can feel my chakram pressing into my shoulder blades, begging to join the fun. So I step up to the range, pull the chakram out, wind back, and let it sing through the wind. The blade spins down the line, nicks the top part of a wooden pole, and whips back up the row until it thwacks to a stop in my palm. A rush of relief descends over me.

"Meira?"

I turn and my chakram tips to the side, itching in my hand, ready to throw and throw until I hurl away every bit of the past few days. But I just stand there, eyes narrowing to hide the fact that my initial reaction is to gape at Theron's bare expanse of glistening skin. He's shirtless—and it's clear that Cordell subjects its men to rigorous chest exercises.

He leaves a group of soldiers by the barn, their bodies angled slightly toward us and their mouths open mid-conversation. Each of them stands sweaty and armed, swords and knives dangling absently from their hands and belts.

And Theron is no different. He slides a sword into a sheath at his waist, an amused smile making my already warm face heat up even more. All the soldiers around us have stopped shooting, their heads tilted in such a way I can tell they aren't exactly used to women showing up on their field. Or hitting their targets.

Theron nods at the chakram. "A fine Autumnian creation. My aunt sent us a shipment of them shortly after her wedding. Your weapon of choice?"

Yes, throwing. Something safe to focus on. Safer than, say, the way the Crown Prince of Cordell's arm flexes as he hefts an ax out of the ground beside me.

In response, I reposition myself in front of the pole and let the chakram loose. It whirls through the air in a beautiful arc and brushes across the target, a hair off from my last hit, before flying back to me. *Sweet snow, that feels good.*

I look up at Theron. "And yours?"

Theron sizes up the ax in his hand. He looks around us, taking in all the still-gaping men and the fact that many of them are now pointing at my pole and shaking their heads in wonder.

"Why should I give away my greatest strength so soon?" Theron looks back at me with a teasing grin, and my grip on the chakram's handle tightens involuntarily, as if that's the only thing keeping me up under his smile.

"First day as Cordellan royalty, and you're already terrifying the soldiers."

Mather's voice knocks into me from behind. The sudden combination of Theron in front of me with Mather closing in makes me feel like I'm caught weaponless on a battlefield.

Mather. *King* Mather. King Mather who negotiated the deal that makes me look at Theron and feel terrified and nervous and lit up all at once.

I turn on him, mouth full of all kinds of nasty, steaming curses, curses befitting a rugged soldier, not a lady. But everything I want to say dies the instant I see him. Because—*mother of all that is cold*—he's shirtless too, with only the locket half dangling around his throat and his freckled skin reflecting the sheen of a good workout. Not that I haven't seen him shirtless before, but it isn't a sight I'll ever get used to. He was obviously sparring with some of the men—I must've glided right by him, grouping his half-naked body in with all the other half-naked bodies. In my defense, there are a lot of good examples of Cordell's training rituals here. Mather's abs and arms, which look like they could snap a cow's neck, aren't *that* impressive next to Theron and three dozen soldier bodies.

I force myself to meet Mather's eyes. And immediately find myself staring at his chest. I swallow and grind my teeth together. All right, clearly the training yard is kept behind a wall of evergreens to keep out gawking girls—like me.

"Did they outlaw shirts in Cordell?" I mumble, and face the target, tipping my head down to my chakram to hide the blush creeping bit by bit up my neck.

Theron chuckles but bites it away when neither Mather nor I say anything else, and he shifts uncomfortably beside me, twirling the ax in his palm. I can feel him eyeing Mather, both of them caught in an awkward web surrounding me. I'm at the center of a weird possessive feud between the Winter king and the Cordellan prince. How in the name of all that is cold did that happen?

But I feel no sympathy for Mather. Not as he steps closer to me, his boots swishing over the grass, his breath exhaling slowly, painfully. I'm all too aware of how much attention is on us when he stops beside me, close enough that I can feel him if I shut my eyes.

"Can we talk?" he murmurs.

The hair on the back of my neck stands up straight. *No. Why should I talk to you ever again?*

But I'm not supposed to be mad at him. It's all Sir's fault.

I look back at Theron, who isn't looking at me anymore. His body has pivoted to face the target beside my pole and he pulls his arm behind him, every muscle in his back tensing as he winds the ax around. Winding and winding, tighter and tighter, until all of it breaks in a single thrust that sends the ax flipping end over end through the air. It whacks into the center of the target, the handle wobbling from the force.

Theron turns to me, half his face alight with the beginnings of a smile. "My weapon of choice doesn't matter," he says, continuing our conversation like nothing happened. His eyes flash to Mather over my shoulder. "No matter what I use, I always hit my mark."

My eyebrows launch skyward. Mather sucks in a breath behind me. Every single body in the entire training yard holds still in curiosity, and alongside that curiosity is a tension of warning, the gentle nudge of a fight about to start.

Mather steps closer to my back, his voice low and controlled in my ear. "Meira, please."

Theron glances to the side, his eyes locking onto mine as he beams, full and bright, and turns to walk down the long line to retrieve his ax. He'll hit his mark no matter what he uses. No matter what situation he's thrust into. No matter how little control he has over his life.

I can't fight my laugh as I turn to Mather and holster my chakram. "What can I do for you, my king?"

Mather blanches. Running a hand over his face, he regroups quickly enough, and a determined stiffness washes over him. He nods to the barn. "Come with me."

13

HALF OF THE barn is made up of stables with horses poking their curious heads out of enclosures, while the other half is a wide room filled with oak tables and cabinets and rusted iron weapon racks. The open barn doors make the place airy and cool, while the light dusting of straw on the stone floor gives it a distinctly masculine feel.

Mather struts determinedly into the room but stops when he comes to the right wall. He stares up at it, arms crossed, and juts his chin out. "I thought maybe when Winter has such a place . . ." His voice fades, his eyes losing a bit of their annoyance from moments ago.

I stop beside him and mimic his arms-crossed stance. A map covers the wall. Detailed and practically life-sized, it shows every part of Primoria from the northernmost Paisel Mountains all the way down to the southernmost Klaryns.

The Eldridge Forest and Rania Plains sit in the center, a splotch of green and yellow with the Langstone and Feni Rivers nearly cutting the entire map in half.

What makes this map unique, though, is the way the kingdoms are portrayed: a small illustration of each Royal Conduit shines in the center of its respective kingdom's territory lines.

I groan. "This is what you want to talk about? Geography?"

Mather shakes his head, his brow pinching. "No, I—" He stops and runs a hand down his face, grappling for the right words. When he starts talking again, he's angry, his words clipped and tight. "I wanted you to see this. To see everything. I wanted to explain to you—snow above, would you just listen to me?"

I snarl at him. "Because you deserve to have me hear you out?"

"No," he admits, and I start. "Because you deserve to hear what I have to say. *You* deserve it, Meira. This doesn't have anything to do with me."

I roll my eyes but make no move to leave or to speak again, which Mather takes as permission to talk. He looks back up at the map, his eyes lingering on Cordell. In the center of Cordell's territory lines, a dagger gleams beneath a scripted *M* for male-blooded.

"Paisly's female-blooded shield," Mather says, almost to himself, a soft hum of noise as his eyes travel the map. "Ventralli's male-blooded crown. Yakim's female-blooded ax, Summer's male-blooded cuff, Autumn's female-blooded ring, Spring's male-blooded staff, and—"

He steps forward and stretches his palm out to rest on Winter. Flanked by Spring to the east, mountains to the south, Autumn to the west, and the Feni River to the north, Winter's locket dangles over the expansive mass of land, the heart-shaped pendant etched with a single white snowflake in the center. The *F* just above it is mocking. A visual representation of one of our lifelong struggles.

"Between meetings, I've hardly had time to breathe," Mather says. "But a few days ago, I came out here to get some air, and I saw this. Captain Dominick said they put this map here to remind the men of Cordell's place in the world. So they can look up and always know who they are. A piece in the bigger puzzle of Primoria."

I frown. "That doesn't sound like something Noam would encourage."

Mather's shoulders tighten. "Noam didn't commission it." He glances back, his hand on the picture of the locket. "Theron did."

The way he says Theron's name puts a nick in Mather's otherwise reverent tone. Like that one detail is a black smudge in a beautiful tapestry.

Mather curls his fingers on the map, tugging against the drawing of the locket. The back half of the real one sits around his neck. Next to the palm-sized picture, it looks sad. Empty.

"Noam may like to pretend Cordell is the only kingdom in the world," he continues, his voice getting progressively harder, "but part of what makes his men so passionately Cordellan is this map. This reminder that they could be Rhythm or Season, Yakimian, Ventrallan, Summerian—but they're not. They're Cordellan. And that fact is what pushes them to fight for their land." Mather smiles in a sad way that isn't really a smile. "I want Winter to have that."

He pulls back from the map and steps toward me, close, closer still, until he's barely a hand's width away. We're alone, all the other soldiers out in the training yard.

"I didn't want this," he whispers, the words cutting between us. "I want Winter free, but I don't want—I don't want him. For you. I don't want you to think that you're worthless, that this is the only place for you, because it's not, Meira—it never could be, not with everything you are."

My pulse thuds against my ribs, anxiety and anger rolling through me, and I can't bring myself to look into his eyes. *Just stop talking. Just please stop talking, you giant, stupid—*

"I don't know what else to do." Mather's breath blows across my face. "Before we left camp, Sir took me aside and told me what I was going to do. It hollowed me out in a way I'd never felt. It was the first time I truly understood how much we have to sacrifice to overthrow Angra, how much our lives don't matter in the bigger task at hand. I always thought we would find a way to . . . to overcome this. To be together, and I swear to you"—Mather takes my chin in his thumb and finger and pulls me to look at him—"I swear to you, I will find a way to fix this. I told you I'd restore balance, and I will."

"No."

The word hangs in the air. I blink, confused, but I know I'd say it again. Why? I've wanted him to say this forever, haven't I? Why would I feel anything but *Yes!* in the wake of his words?

Mather squints at me. "I will. I *can*. I won't let Angra destroy even more of our lives. No matter what William says, there has to be another way—"

"No!"

I shove back from him, a part of me tearing off and staying in his hands. Each word hurts. It piles on top of Sir's words last night, churning together in some great wave of confusion. And all I know is that Mather's hope for another solution is a taunting, all-consuming temptation that I can't afford to feel; already I can taste the first waves of relief cresting over his words. But there is no other way. No other hope. Sir spent fourteen years trying to find another path to take. Letting myself believe that Mather might be able to save me, only for me to end up still in this marriage game . . .

I don't think I'd survive it.

"I'm doing this, Mather," I say, my voice thin and weary. "For our kingdom, for our people. For *you*. We need Cordell. We need this."

Mather pulls back like I slapped him. Redness creeps up his neck, sweat glistening on his forehead. "You want to marry Theron?"

My eyes narrow. "What?"

"You want to marry Theron," he says again, and everything in his body sags. "You don't—"

Want me.

His unspoken words drape over me, weighing me down and down until I think I might crumple onto the straw-covered floor.

"You're an idiot," I spit, though I hear how loudly I didn't refute his accusation. "This doesn't have anything to do with that. It's about allies and saving *our* kingdom. You have to stop—nothing's changed; nothing's different between us. It's just as impossible as it always was, and this is how it has to be."

"I'll find a way around it," Mather returns. He steps toward me, I step back, a weird dance through the barn. "I was always going to find a way. I told you before we left—I told you I would fix this!"

"How was I supposed to know that's what you meant? All I ever got was Sir's voice hammering into my head that you were too important to waste on me!"

"I never felt that! You've always been *everything* to me. I didn't know how to handle how much I needed you growing up—snow, I still don't, all right? I'm trying, though. Do you think I'm that arrogant? That I let William make me believe I was too good for you?"

"What else was I supposed to think?" I'm shouting now, my voice tearing at the barn's rafters. I step back once, twice, knowing I'll never be able to get far enough away from him. "You may be able to look beyond the reality of our situation and imagine some other outcome, but all I ever saw, all I ever *see*, is a reminder that our lives aren't our own."

"You think I don't know that our lives aren't our own?" Mather grabs the locket half in a fist. "I'm the *king*, Meira!"

I cup my hands over my ears and shake my head, blocking out anything else he might say, anything that might make me stop talking. "None of it matters. It doesn't matter what I want or need or love, because Sir will always be there to remind me that Winter has to come first."

Mather stops. His face relaxes, one small muscle, and around my hands cupped over my ears, I hear him echo one of the words I said.

"Love?"

No, I didn't say that. I'm not that stupid.

A footstep makes me fly around. Behind all the other sounds, men grunting in the yard and swords clanging and arrows firing, it shouldn't have mattered, shouldn't have stuck out.

Theron stands in the doorway, body hardened like he caught us rolling around on the floor. "Is everything all right?"

I throw a hand up, mouth hanging open. Yes. No. It never was, it never will be.

Theron doesn't wait for an answer. He turns to Mather, the gleam of sweat on his skin glinting in the sunlight behind him. "King Mather." Theron steps forward. Steps back. Looks like he wants to run out to the training yard and start hacking at someone. "I heard you have skill with a blade?"

I frown. This can't be good.

It isn't. Mather pauses, maybe considering how furious Sir will be, but a moment later he flashes a tight grimace that makes me fear for Theron's life.

"Don't worry, Prince Theron. I'll go easy on you."

I pull at Mather's arm but he shrugs out of reach and marches at Theron, ducking out of the way at the last second to move around him and into the training yard. Theron follows with his own hard stomping.

The yard again falls into a shocked silence when the three of us parade toward the sword rings. Mather ducks under the rope of one ring and rips a training sword out of a case, huffing around the perimeter like a penned bull.

"You can't do this!" I grab Theron only because Mather's already in the ring. Theron is my betrothed, after all. I should be worried for him. *More* worried for him. Right? "Don't do this. You're both—um—important."

Theron's mouth relaxes and I think he might back down. But a voice rings out, and I have to bite my tongue to keep from grabbing my chakram and slicing off one of the soldiers' heads.

"Show him, my prince!" the soldier calls from the opposite side of the sword ring. "Show him how we fight in Cordell!"

Theron closes his eyes in a quick, almost pained grimace. When he opens them again he puts a hand over mine where I cup his arm. "If you want us to stop, we will."

More men are cheering him on now. Shouting his name—"Theron!"—so loud and so confidently that I can see Mather deflating before me.

This is what Mather meant. What he wants for our people. Not just a poem murmured to two ridiculous trees or a map reminding them of their place in this world. Pride. Tradition. Something like the happiness on the soldiers' faces when they returned to Bithai from Autumn, like the pride when they cheer now for their prince.

Mather paces back and forth, tearing up dirt under his boots. The louder they cheer the angrier he gets. "Come on, Cordell!" he shouts. His voice pounds through the hollering men, drawing their cries to chaotic levels. "Show me what you can do!"

I glare at him and his chin tips down, his intensity waning ever so slightly. But not enough. Not completely. He's doing this.

And Theron is too. His men are begging him to. Crying out for him, for Cordell. "Prove our strength, my prince!

Prove our power and might!"

No man can refuse to answer that call. And watching Mather across the ring, feeling just how alone and weak and small we are surrounded by people who have a kingdom and an identity—

I'd answer that call. However stupid or selfish or wrong, I'd answer it. I wheeze in that realization, one hand going to my chest as I suck down gulps of sweat-heavy air. I'd answer the call of my kingdom, of the Winterians, crying out for me to prove myself to them.

To prove that they really *do* come first, always, no matter what.

When Theron releases my hand and pulls out of my grip, I don't say anything. I should. I should beg him to turn away from this and walk back inside the barn and ignore the cries of his people, but my own voice screams in my head, warping the Cordellans' words back at me.

Prove yourself, Meira! Prove yourself to Winter. You want to matter to your kingdom, and you want your kingdom to matter to you?

Then prove it.

Do what you must. Not what you WANT. What you must.

Prove it!

One of Theron's men hands him a practice sword. My eyes latch onto the movement as Theron hesitates, fingers twitching, and takes it.

The moment Theron touches the hilt, Mather dives. Silent and deadly, he flings his body in a graceful albeit slightly too aggressive flourish, swinging the sword wide at Theron's head. Theron ducks, rolls to the opposite side of the ring, dust swirling as he rights himself and uses the momentum to swipe at Mather's legs. Mather's left knee buckles just long enough for Theron to get traction to stand—and then it's madness.

It's the kind of sword fight Sir has told stories about, with two opponents bent on chopping each other to pieces but both so equal that neither can get an upper hand. Theron beats Mather to one side of the ring—Mather kicks out Theron's legs and drops him to the ground—Theron flips backward and slaps Mather's blow aside—Mather uses that blow to catch Theron's knee—

The soldiers' cheers grow with each strike. I don't even know who they're cheering for anymore, just that they're thrown into a frenzy by two royals beating the pulp out of each other. The higher their screams rise, the more my heart throbs, caught up in the fever of the sword fight and how I'm teetering on the edge of those two words still jabbing into me.

Prove it.

Mather wraps his sword around Theron's and yanks it free, hurling it over the crowd. Panic flows into me, panic at it going too far, at the blinding insanity of the crowd, at the way the soldiers scream with anticipation and Mather slams his foot into Theron's chest. Theron drops to the ground, the wind knocked out of him, and Mather closes in, his sword in both hands over his head, moments away from cracking down on Theron's skull.

I'm under the rope and in the ring before I can breathe. "Surrender!" I scream as I tear toward them. "Theron, surrender!"

Neither of them hears me. Neither of them flinches or breathes or sees anything beyond this fight.

I stumble between them, my arms flailing out toward Mather as my legs brace over Theron. Mather's sword shoots up through the air, rising and rising, cutting the breeze ahead of his final screaming threat as I reach for his arms, his sword, something to prevent this.

It stops. The entire area freezes as if Noam stiffened every Cordellan with his conduit.

I exhale, body still thrown out in one last feeble attempt to keep Mather from making a really, really big mistake, and the noise that silenced everyone comes again.

"MATHER!"

Sir. His white head bobs in and out of the tightly packed Cordellan soldiers, weaving his way to us through the throng.

"Golden leaves," Theron hisses from the ground.

I don't see Mather's face. I don't see much of anything when I turn and Theron looks up at me, blood speckling his chest, a few red-black splotches in the shape of Mather's spiked boot.

"Medic!"

It's Dominick. He drags a tiny man with an overflowing pouch of bandages, and they duck under the rope, instantly yanking Theron's hand off his chest.

Dominick turns to the men still gaping at their prince and the foreign Season king. "Fun's over. Back to training now!"

The men hurry away. It's such a violent switch in priorities that my brain can't catch up, stuck on Theron's blood and Mather's anger and the echo of the Cordellans' shouts, of my own voice in my head, screaming at me to choose.

To choose Winter. To always choose Winter. Over Mather, over Theron, over . . . me.

A sword drops behind me, the metal clanking in a hollow ring on the dirt. I turn, the world spiraling even more.

"Meira." Mather holds his hands out, staring at them like he's covered in blood. "I didn't mean to—I don't know what—"

The whole training yard shakes when Sir leaps into the sword ring. He stomps forward, ready to rip into us with his own threats. But his eyes fall to Theron on the ground, Mather standing over his sword, and me in the middle of it all.

A wave of fury sweeps over Sir's face when he returns his gaze to Mather. He doesn't say anything, just takes two quick steps forward and grabs Mather's arm, dragging him out of the sword ring as neither looks back. When they get a good distance away, far enough that I can't hear what they say, Sir growls something that makes Mather shake his head once, twice, and shout something in return.

Fingers brush the back of my hand. Theron stands beside me, and he doesn't smile or nod or do anything I expect him to do; he just stays there next to me, blood tingeing the bandage on his chest. A calm and steady reminder that I'm not alone.

"Are you all right?" I ask, nodding to the bandage.

Theron drops his gaze to the wound and shoots me a roguish grin. "It takes more than a boot to stop me." He touches the fabric and purses his lips. "But I should probably cover it up. Just in case my father—"

His eyes go to Mather and Sir, still in a heated argument a few dozen paces away. When Theron looks back at me, he inhales and stands up straighter.

"No need to cause more trouble," he says, and points toward the palace. "Care to come with me? I'll wash up and show you around, if you like. Far less"—he pauses—"dangerous activities."

My gaze darts from him to Sir and Mather and back again. Should I stay and talk with Sir? Should I go over and try to defend Mather?

I pull my shoulders back. "I'd love to."

14

THERON LEADS ME up the servants' passage to his chambers, winding through the bowels of the palace to avoid any run-ins with Noam. We walk up three flights of stairs and down unendingly long halls, all far less luxurious than the main walks of the palace—just simple green carpets and unpainted wood walls and milky white candles on brown tables.

Maids with baskets of linens and errand boys with messages tucked under their arms scurry past, performing the daily tasks that keep a palace functioning. Everyone we pass stops to drop a bow to Theron, their faces easing from the focus of work to the pleasure of seeing someone they know.

Theron nods to each of them. "Is your mother feeling better?" he asks a passing maid, who dips a curtsy as she says yes, quite, the doctor worked a miracle. "I hope your brother is enjoying his new post," Theron says to an errand boy, who beams at the mention and says he is, my lord, he was made lieutenant.

I trail behind, eyebrows rising higher with each brief conversation. He knows all of them. Every single one. And not only that, but he seems genuinely interested in them, remembering not only dozens of faces but also the smallest details about how that back acre of farmland is doing, did the trade with Yakim go well last week, is your daughter settled with her new husband yet?

We stop in front of a door in the third-floor hall. Theron turns the knob, moving on like none of the interactions were anything out of the ordinary, and I cast a glance behind us. None of the servants seem to think anything is unusual either. Is he that familiar with them? I can't imagine Noam allows his son to mingle with those "beneath" him.

"Are all royals in Cordell so"—I pause, searching for the right word—"attentive?"

Theron looks over my shoulder at a chatting group of maids. His eyes drift, just enough that I can tell his thoughts are on a not exactly pleasant memory, and he forces a smile to cover his tracks. "No one else sneaks around the back to get to their rooms as often as I do," he jokes, and before I can ask more, he dives into the room, leaving me to follow.

Tucked beside a bureau, the door opens onto a sitting room just large enough to be spacious but not so large as to be extravagant. A dining table lies on the left while an array of chairs and couches cluster together around a fireplace on the right. The furniture sits atop a thickly woven green-and-gold rug, the colors mimicking the dark shades of the rest of the sitting room. A chandelier hangs over the dining table and paintings of Cordell's lavender fields or vibrant green forests or rivers trickling through yellow prairies line the walls. It's fine yet functional, a place I could picture both a strategic meeting taking place as well as a vicious card game.

"I'll be just a moment," Theron says as he shuts the door behind us and disappears into the bedroom on the right.

After a moment, the sounds of water splashing into a bowl drift out. I wander around the sitting room to distract myself from the fact that Theron's bedroom door is open and he's probably a bit more than shirtless now.

Sweet snow, I've never thought about a man being undressed so much in my life. Even at camp with Mather, I never thought about the fact that he'd be in the bathing tent after me, and he'd be, um . . . I mean, maybe I thought about it, but I never got quite so flustered. I press my hands to my cheeks and exhale.

I stop in the middle of the room, hands still on my face, and narrow my eyes. There's a lot of stuff in here. A *lot* of stuff. More than furniture and decorations. I turn in a circle, surveying the tightly packed space. I was so distracted by thoughts of boy matters that I overlooked the slightly messy, slightly unkempt quality of Theron's sitting room—all right, the *very* messy, *very* unkempt quality.

Framed paintings of every size and shape sit in haphazard stacks around the room, leaning against the bureau and the wall and the chairs, with smaller paintings spread across the tabletop on a thin cotton sheet. Elaborate masks covered in jewels and gold accents dangle from ribbons on the corners of paintings. Books in towering stacks lean against the fireplace and on small end tables, and crowd the bookshelves so tightly I fear the entire structure will burst in an explosion of paper and dust. They're large books too, great archaic things that look so old, so fragile, that I worry I might disintegrate them just by breathing too hard.

I lean over the dining table, my eyes flitting across palm-sized paintings of oak trees and books with yellowed pages poking out of the covers. One rectangular tome with a gold-embossed title reads *History of Trade on the Feni River*. Another book next to it reads *Stories of Mountain Dwellers* in thick leather thread. Beside it sits a stack of fresh parchment, a few illegible lines scratched in the same frantic hand as the poem in the library. Theron's work. I squint but can only make out a few words this time—*true* and *could* and some others—and turn to a collection of oval portraits in a small box, each painting encased in a thin silver frame. I run my hand over one of a woman with her hair done up in a taut bun, staring grimly at the painter as though he and he alone was responsible for pulling her hair so tight.

A cupboard door slams behind me and I flinch away

from the table to peer into the other room. All I can see is a canopy bed drenched in pale white light from an open window. The cupboard slams again from within and I step toward the door just as Theron steps out, pulling his now-wet hair back into a ponytail. He's changed out of his training clothes and into something more princely—black pants with thin gold stripes running down the sides. A close-fitting white shirt buttons up to his neck under a black vest, hiding his bandaged chest.

He tightens his hair. "What would you like to see first? We have quite the menagerie in the forest, an art gallery in the north wing—"

I cock an eyebrow. "An art gallery? Are you sure there are any paintings left in it?" I wave my hand at the room. "From the looks of things, this prince business is just a front for your life of art thievery."

Theron glances around the room and absently moves to the nearest stack of books, lifting one and running his fingers down the spine. He looks up at me, an expression of mock hurt on his face. "I rob libraries too, I'll have you know. And I have two good reasons for this"—his eyes narrow as he considers—"collection."

"You want to have a standby profession in case being king doesn't work out?" I guess, smiling, even as I realize how truthful it might be.

Theron shrugs, setting the book back on the stack. "Partly that. But mostly it's because my father thinks this obsession is wholly unbefitting of a future king, and as long as I keep my chambers clogged with relics, he refuses to come here." He beams at me. "But also because many of these belonged to my mother."

"Your mother?" I run my eyes over the bookshelf, remembering Sir's lectures. Theron, half Cordellan, half Ventrallan, is probably expected to take after his father's side more than his mother's.

I reach out and touch the spines of the books on the shelf. They remind me of the fire pit Finn brought back. Holding on to some part of your past even if it means also holding on to the pain of never again having it. That pain is less horrible than the pain of forgetting.

"I'm sorry," I say, though I'm not sure what I'm apologizing for. *I'm sorry your mother isn't here anymore. I'm sorry your father uses you.*

Theron shrugs it off and steps closer, standing at the other end of the bookshelf. "Do you read much?"

I trace the lettering on the spine of one particularly fat book. "Only as much as Sir made me. I prefer to slice my time away." I smile but Theron just watches me, his lips cocked thoughtfully.

He pushes away from the bookcase and toward a stack of paintings in the corner. "I have a landscape I think you might like," he throws over his shoulder, sorting through great square frames. "An older one, but it's in good condition—"

He keeps talking but his voice fades to a murmur, a

distant lull at the back of my consciousness. I stare at the fat book I've been running my fingers over, the letters spelling out a title that makes my mind squeeze with sudden curiosity. It's old, very old, one of the brittle tomes that looks liable to disintegrate into a cloud of dust at any moment. I read the title again.

Magic of Primoria.

Magic like . . . my dreams of Hannah?

I know nothing about magic beyond what Sir told me through lessons, but there has to be a reason for my dreams—if they aren't caused by stress, that is, which is still a possibility. But if that's not it, they have to be coming from somewhere else—the stone? Another source of magic? And if there's magic coming from somewhere else, then there has to be a source of magic other than the Royal Conduits. I mean, there's the chasm, but the magic there only affects the Seasons, just as all the Royal Conduits affect only their citizens within a certain radius. Maybe, if I was in a Season Kingdom, I could attribute my Hannah dreams to remnants of magic emanating from the chasm— not that I've ever heard of that happening—but here, in Cordell, what could be causing them? If it even was magic. If I'm not just losing my mind.

As I sift through my thoughts, a weight of doubt drops in my chest. *Thousands of years.* That's how long it's been since there's been anything but the eight Royal Conduits, since the chasm of magic had an accessible portal through the Klaryns before it was lost to avalanches or sabotage. If there was another magic source, if there was more power, *if there was anything else*, someone would have found it by now. Wouldn't they?

None of this stops me from pulling the ancient book off the shelf and holding it in both hands. A seal sits in the bottom right corner, deep red wax rubbed almost smooth by the years. An indecipherable phrase curves around a picture of a beam of light hitting a mountaintop. I can make out a few of the words—OF THE LUSTR—before it fades into age-warped gibberish. A maker's seal? Whatever it is, I run my fingers over it, biting my lip in thought.

Doing some research can't hurt, right? And it's a far better alternative to sitting in Bithai's palace getting primped as a future Cordellan queen while Sir and Mather and Noam go on making decisions without me. This way I'm *doing* something. Something small, but still something.

It's a start.

"—yet interesting, I think," Theron is saying.

I turn to him, hugging the giant book to my chest. He holds a painting by the top corners near his waist, the base of it barely brushing his boots.

All breath flows out of me, sucked away like the painting is a vortex of wind and I'm caught up in the storm.

It's Winter. Or, well, it could be a Rhythm Kingdom in its own winter season, but when I see that painting, it's Winter. A forest there, the trees bowing and bending under the weight of ice, their brown branches frozen into glittering columns. Drifts of snow flow around the base of the trees, broken only by boulders or small snow-covered bushes. Everything sits in the peaceful stillness of morning, the sun's rays just barely cresting the trees and turning everything the hazy blue-yellow of dawn.

Prove it.

Those two words again. My fingers tighten on the book the longer I stare at the painting, something like determination coursing through me. Sir was right. I don't know anything. I don't know what Winter feels like, what forest this painting depicts. I don't know anything, I've never seen it, because it's gone. Just like that, one horrible war, one vicious takeover, and thousands of people were slaughtered, imprisoned, destroyed. Just like that, an entire kingdom was shattered, and the most I've ever been able to do is hope that someday I have my own Winter memories.

I've been so selfish, haven't I? Selfish and narrow-minded and *wrong*, because I wanted to matter to Winter, but *in my own way*. Within my own set parameters that would also fit who I wanted to be. I choke on a laugh, hating that it's taken me this long to realize that Sir was right. Damn him—I long for the day when he's wrong for once.

I don't even realize I've moved until Theron clears his throat. I'm kneeling on the floor before the painting, staring, the book still clutched to my chest in one hand while my other goes out toward the trees like if I reach hard enough, I can grab some snow off the branches.

Theron shifts his hold on the painting and looks down at it. "I can have it hung in your room if you wish."

I nod and jerk my hand back around the book. "Thank you," I breathe, and look up at him. He smiles, soft and careful, his eyes shining as they dart across my face.

Muscle by muscle, his smile fades. "We'll get it back."

I hug the book tighter and swallow, forcing a sudden rush of tears to the back of my throat. "We?" I shake my head. "*They* will. My part is—" I stop, breath pinching, and wince. It shouldn't hurt. This is right, isn't it? This is what I *need* to do—marry into Cordell. For Winter.

Theron leans the painting against the back of a couch, one of his hands absently hovering over it. His eyes drift out like he's remembering some long-ago tale, and when he focuses on me, I stand, quiet, holding the book like a shield between us.

"I almost joined Ventralli's Writers Guild when I was eleven," he says.

My eyebrows rise. "Really? What happened?"

"Nothing good," he laughs. "I wrote to the Ventrallan king at the time—my mother's brother-in-law—and got his special approval to join. I arranged for a place to stay and travel to get there and how many men would escort me. I was so proud of myself, and I wanted it so badly." Theron's gaze drops to a space over my shoulder, staring into the past. "Five days before I was to leave, my father sent his steward to my rooms to tell me a carriage was waiting to take me to a military base on Cordell's coast. That I would live there for the next three years and study under one of my father's colonels.

"My father knew my plans to go to Ventralli. I told him as I was making them, but I didn't know until that day that he never intended to let me go. That his heir would be brought up in military methods and resource management, not art and poetry." He frowns and looks back at me as if he'd forgotten I was here. "But that didn't stop me from having all this"—he waves around the room—"and from inviting the best Ventrallan writers and poets and artists to visit Cordell. There will always be a *they* in your new life, Meira. *They* make decisions; *they* mold your future. The trick is to find a way to still be *you* through it all."

"Are we really allowed that luxury?" I ask. I don't even think about how forward it might be or how little I know him—all I can think is how much I *do* know him. He wanted something more out of his life. He wanted to be an artist, though his father wanted him to be a king. And here he is, the heir of Cordell, standing amidst piles of books and paintings. He's both. He adapted to everything his life thrust at him.

Theron exhales, his shoulders bending ever so slightly. "I need to believe so."

I frown. Is it possible? To be both what Winter needs and what I want? Instead of fighting for *only* what I want, or surrendering to *only* what Winter needs, to find a balance between the two?

I hold up the book. "Can I borrow this?"

Theron nods before he even sees what it is. "Of course. Take anything you want." He nudges the painting. "And I *will* have someone put this up for you. Now"—he tries again, a bright smile washing over his face—"the menagerie?"

THE NEXT MORNING, when Rose and Mona come again with pleas for me to attend etiquette class, I shock them and myself by agreeing.

Rose, holding a sky-blue gown and a navy ribbon, stops beside the wardrobe. Her eyes narrow, and after a pause she scurries over to stand between my bed and the balcony. "Is this a trick?" she asks, and I don't miss how she tries to hold her arms out, as if to block me from sprinting around her and leaping off the balcony.

I slide off the bed, on the side opposite the balcony doors, and calmly meet her eyes. "No. I'll go."

Rose puckers. "Wearing a proper outfit?"

I frown. "Yes."

"Without your weapon?"

A groan bubbles in my throat. "*Going* isn't compromise enough?"

Rose's pucker sharpens and she clucks her tongue. "Weapons have no business inside the palace."

She takes a few quick steps across the room and lays the gown and ribbon on the bed. No sooner does the fabric relax against the mussed sheets than her hands move to my nightgown, undoing the buttons down the back like she's afraid I'll change my mind if she doesn't move fast enough. I start to flinch, start to fight her off on instinct, when my muscles still. I can do this. All of this—the marriage, whatever classes Noam ordered, *and* help my kingdom in ways that I never even dreamed of but that will still make me feel like I belong to Winter.

If Theron can do it, I can too. I can weave threads of myself into a tapestry already designed by others. It's possible. And this could be good—I'm in a position of power, aren't I? Far more power than being an ordinary soldier. This *will* be good.

So as Rose tugs the gown over my head, and Mona runs a brush through my hair, I pull my shoulders straight. I'm a future ruler of Cordell. How would a future ruler act? Mather bursts into my mind, his steadiness, his calm demeanor in the face of . . . everything. Act like Mather. I can do this.

"I'm bringing my chakram," I say. When Rose whips her head up, I level my eyes in a stare. Calm, in control, steady.

"I don't intend on using it, but I will have it with me."

Rose's lips twitch. Her eyes narrow, a tight sweep of a glare, before she drops back to work tying the dark-blue ribbon around my waist.

I can't hide my smile. One small victory.

The next week flies past in a whirl of Cordellan history and curtsying properly and learning which fork to use while eating salad. I clearly surprise Rose and Mona by paying attention, and every time an instructor compliments me on answering a question correctly, they twitter excitedly from the back of the room. But I've always been a good student—in camp, it was only when I saw Mather sparring without me that I started to get twitchy and disruptive, and Sir would throw his hands in the air and shout at me until I broke down in tears. Now, though, I really am trying to be good at this whole future-queen thing.

If only because, every morning, I find a way to be *me*.

In the earliest cracks of dawn, when the sun is still fighting a black–blue war with the night sky, I slip on my clothes—my *real* clothes, a shirt and pants and boots—and scurry through the still-sleeping palace to the library, where I stashed *Magic of Primoria*. This coupled with my chaotic schedule of classes and meals in my room means I haven't seen any of the other refugees since Mather and Theron's disastrous sparring session. Certainly not for lack of trying on their part—I dart down side halls when I see Dendera coming, scale walls when I hear Finn's voice around the corner. I have no desire to face anyone until I can present a revelation. Until I can prove that I can still be useful in this position as *me*.

Part of me wants to sneak out to the shooting range each morning instead of creeping to the library. I haven't used my chakram since I started queen training, and even though I take it with me to every lesson, it's starting to feel too much like a prop. But the other part of me, the part that's resigned to this arrangement, knows how important it is that I try to read *Magic of Primoria*.

Emphasis on the word *try*.

Every line on every page of the almost-disintegrating-in-my-hands book is filled with the tiniest of tiny words written in cramped, illegible script. The letters bleed into one another from age and from the fact that the writer pushed the lines so close together that the text looks like one big blob of ink. As if that wasn't enough, the lines I actually can decipher are beyond unhelpful, either filled with archaic language or riddles, but mostly just history I already know. How the chasm of magic has rested beneath all the Season Kingdoms for as long as anyone can remember, a source of mystery and magic that has existed as long as our world itself. The chasm sits deep, deep beneath our land, so even if a Rhythm did conquer a Season Kingdom and chose to dig through it in an attempt to get the magic, they'd be digging for decades.

There used to be an entrance to the chasm through the Klaryns, a shaft that was opened one day when miners stumbled into it. No one knows where the mine actually was—shortly after it was discovered, it was lost to landslides or deadly weather. But I like to think it was in Winter's part of the Klaryns—after all, what other Season Kingdom is as good at mining as we are? Then again, we haven't been able to find another entrance to the magic chasm since the first one vanished, so maybe we *aren't* that good.

When the entrance was open, thousands of years ago, an expedition was sent to retrieve magic. According to legends and a few of the more legible lines in the book, the magic sat in the center of an endless cavern, a great ball of energy snapping and crackling as it hung in the negative space of the cave.

To be removed from the cave, the magic needed a host, an object imbued with its powers. The great ball of energy pulsed around the cavern, striking rocks here and there like uncontrollable, chaotic fingers of lightning. And the rocks it struck became infused with magic. So monarchs started leaving other objects close to the source, waiting for the bolts of magic to strike swords or shields or jewelry and fill them with power. They also tried more dangerous ways of creating conduits, of letting the magic strike their servants. This led to the discovery that only objects could be hosts for the magic—people didn't turn into conduits so much as they turned into overcooked meat.

That was how the Royal Conduits were created. The monarchs of the world ordered their conduits made first, connecting them to their bloodlines through even more magic. But those ended up being the only conduits ever made, because just after the eight Royal Conduits were created, the entrance to the chasm disappeared and our world changed forever. Not only did we have magic now, but we had prejudice too—the Rhythms hated us for losing something so vital. They might have hated the Seasons before anyway, for any number of reasons, but it's the loss of the magic source that hangs with them to this day, even when no one can remember our lives being any different than they are now. There have always been the eight Royal Conduits, nothing more, nothing less.

That's all I can decipher. And the more I stare at *Magic of Primoria*, the more my flicker of doubt grows into a full-on flame. What am I even looking for? I've had the same Hannah dream every night this week, the one where I see her surrounded by the refugees in the study. But I can't figure out any connection between the dream and the things I do or don't do—I even tried hiding the lapis lazuli ball and not touching it for a few days, but I still had the dream. So it isn't magic? But what did I even want to find, anyway? Some long-lost source of magic that I could present to Sir, proving that I can matter to Winter in my own way in addition to linking us to Cordell?

I slam the book closed and press my back into the balcony

railing behind me. The early morning light casts yellow rays through the towering windows on my left. It's almost time for more queen lessons, but days of being awake so early are catching up to me, and I just want to crawl back into bed and forget about trying to be a proper Cordellan lady. My fingers tighten on the book's cover and I regret leaving the chakram in my room this morning. A few easy slices and this uncooperative tome would be nothing but confetti.

"Sustenance?"

I look to my right to see Theron peeking over the top of the staircase that leads to the third-floor balcony where I set up camp. A tray of steaming dishes sits in his hands, and my stomach answers with an unladylike gurgle. Theron is the only person who knows about my early-morning sessions—he comes here each morning himself to return books or get new ones, and running into him is an inevitability I don't mind.

He continues up the stairs, dropping to sit beside me but facing the library below. "I figured you'd be hungry, since you didn't come to breakfast again," he says, and sets the tray between us. "My father is appeased that you're attending those lessons, but your friends are—"

"Deserving of every speck of worry and stress I give them?" I fill in, reaching for a crusty slice of bread from a basket.

Theron laughs. "I was going to say that they're scaring my court with how often they have whispered disputes behind potted trees, but 'deserving of stress' works too."

"Someone should tell them potted plants don't keep sound from carrying." I stuff small bits of bread into my mouth but keep talking, reveling in this small act of impropriety. It's all too easy to forget that Theron's a prince, that his station is so far above mine I couldn't reach it if I was standing on top of the Klaryns, that I should be proper and ladylike and curtsy when he approaches, all things I learned in yesterday's etiquette lesson. It's too easy to do a lot of things around him, and I'm still trying to figure out why that is.

Theron nods toward the book still pressed between my legs and chest. "Dare I ask how it's going, or will you threaten to cut it apart again?"

I groan. "I don't want to talk about it. This porridge is good. What's in it, strawberries?"

"You're still not going to tell me what you're doing?"

"No," I say to the food tray. There's no scenario in which telling someone you've been having dreams about a dead queen ends with them not believing you've fallen into the dark abyss of insanity.

"I can be helpful," Theron offers, his voice light. "I am, in fact, trained to help an entire kingdom, so I think I can channel some of that training into helping one beautiful woman."

I look up at him, my eyes narrow despite the smile that crawls across my face. "That's not fair, throwing out compliments like that. Do you know how dangerous those things can be?"

Theron shrugs, grinning, his cheeks tinged just the slightest bit pink. *He's* embarrassed?

He drops his grin into a pout, puckering his lips and pulling his eyebrows tight over his nose.

I glare.

He pouts harder.

"You're impossible," I growl, and rip open the book.

Theron laughs and scoots a little closer to me. "Impossible, endearing. Synonyms, really."

I mock-laugh and scan the indecipherable pages again, pain instantly pulsing through my head at the sight of all that black, swirling ink. "I'm trying to learn more about magic," I start.

Theron gasps. "While reading a book called *Magic in Primoria*? No!"

"Impossible, endearing, hilarious. Also synonyms."

"So you agree I'm endearing?"

I glare at him and open my mouth, only to find I have absolutely nothing to say. He smiles, waiting, and my gape becomes an incredulous snort.

"As I was saying," I start again, and Theron waves a hand in surrender to tell me he won't interrupt. "I'm trying to learn more about magic. The Royal Conduits and where they came from and"—I run my fingers down the swirls of black ink—"and everything. Anything I can learn. Maybe there's some loophole, something that means we could defeat Angra without needing our locket."

As I talk, the amusement on Theron's face fades, and he eyes the pages under my hands. "What have you learned so far?"

"Nothing I didn't already know. This book is unreadable." I flip to one of the passages I can actually make out—but just because I can read the words doesn't mean they make any sense. "Like this, for instance. 'From the lights, there came a great Decay; and woe was it unto those who had no light. They did beg, thus the lights were formed. The four did create the lights; and the four did create the lights.'" I slam my head back against the railing. *"What?"*

Theron's face stays serious. I recognize the expression as his "art" face, the same look he got when we were in his room and he was looking at the painting of Winter. Curious, focused, like the whole case of books behind him could fall over and he wouldn't even flinch.

His lips move soundlessly, repeating the passage to himself. "Four? It said four twice?"

"Yeah." I look back at the book. "The same thing twice too. 'The four did create the lights; and the four did create the lights.'"

Theron nods. "The kingdoms of Primoria. Four and four. The Rhythms and the Seasons. They created something . . . resources? No, something magic-related. A metaphorical light? Perhaps the conduits? So light could be a conduit."

He leans over the book and points at the passage, inserting his words as he goes. "From the conduits, there came a great Decay; and woe was it unto those who had no conduit. They did beg, thus the conduits were formed. The Rhythms did create the conduits; and the Seasons did create the conduits."

He beams up at me but it flies away when he sees my glare. "What?"

"*What?*" I stab a finger at the passage. "I've been staring at that for three days and you come in here and figure it out in three *seconds*."

Theron's smile returns. "Told you I'm helpful."

I will not give him the satisfaction of me smiling back. "What does it mean, though, O Wise, Learned Prince? It still doesn't make sense. A great Decay came from the conduits? But the Rhythms and Seasons created more conduits? But they only created the eight before the entrance vanished. So what, exactly, is the Decay, and why is it capitalized? A metaphorical decay, a literal decay . . ."

Theron leans back, arms resting on his knees, and stares at the library below. "That's why literature is so fascinating. It's always up for interpretation, and could be a hundred different things to a hundred different people. It's never the same thing twice."

I close the book with a groan. "I don't need a hundred different interpretations. I need to read a book that says, 'Here's how to defeat Spring and restore power to your king, and while you're at it, here's how to prove you matter when no one else thinks you do—'"

I stop. I'm staring at the bookshelves and not at Theron, and I don't think I'll ever be able to look at him again without shriveling up from embarrassment. Which might make the whole marriage thing a bit awkward. I can still hear what I said hanging around me, my weak, weak admission, and I can't bring myself to breathe, let alone face him.

Theron doesn't give me a choice. He crawls up onto his knees and moves into my line of sight, his forehead wrinkled and his eyes darting over mine like he's trying to figure me out the same way he figured out that passage. After a moment of silence, he grimaces.

"You matter" is all he says.

I flinch, cold tingles bouncing all around as he stares at me with that certainty in his eyes. It's similar to all those tense, lingering stares Mather would give me, yet at the same time *not*. When Mather looked at me, I never knew what emotions he was hiding behind his seriousness, if he liked me or if he was trying to figure out if he did. But with Theron—it feels more purposeful. Like he's staring at me because he wants to, not because he's questioning himself.

Neither of us says anything else, exhaling slowly into the space between us, too afraid to move away, too afraid to move closer.

A door slams below us, echoing up the three floors of the library. I jump, shaken out of my trance. It's probably

Rose—I'm late for today's lessons. But the voice that fills up the library makes me groan with a different weight.

"Meira," Sir says determinedly enough to practically pull me over the third-floor balcony.

Theron sighs. "There's only one door out of the library," he says as if reading my thoughts.

I groan again. There's no escaping Sir now. Unless I barrel past him and run as hard as I can into the twisting halls of Bithai's palace. The mature reaction.

Theron stands and reaches out a hand to help me up. "He won't yell at you when I'm present."

I slide the book onto the floor, slip my hand into his, and want to smile. I want to do a lot of things when he pulls me to my feet and we're so close, so very close, for one short second, and I wonder if marrying him would be such a horrible thing.

Theron leads me down the stairs, still holding my hand. I'm all right with that, in a way that makes me think my answer to the do-I-want-to-marry-him question might surprise me.

We reach the bottom floor of the library and there is—everyone. Sir, Alysson, Dendera, Finn, Greer, Henn, and Mather. All standing in a tight group in the middle of the room, faces in various states of anger or frustration.

Sir steps forward to meet us halfway, his arms crossed tight over his chest. His eyes fall to Theron's and my hands, intertwined, but he doesn't say anything, and shivers run up and down my arms, spreading through my body the longer we stand there not speaking.

"Prince Theron," Sir starts, keeping his voice strangely calm. "We need a word with Lady Meira. Alone."

I stifle the urge to whimper. Not because Sir wants to talk to me—because of how he said it. Lady Meira. It feels so formal. Too formal. I don't want Sir to be formal with me.

Theron pivots to face him. "I must respectfully decline, General Loren."

Mather makes a huffing sound from behind Sir. My eyes dart to him, and we're stuck now staring at each other while I do absolutely nothing to distance myself from Theron. Mather looks at our hands and back up at me, his face constricting into anger, regret, anger, anger, anger—

"Is something wrong, King Mather?" Theron asks around Sir.

Mather starts forward but Sir snaps out an arm and slams it into his chest. Mather stops, panting like he did in the sword ring. I expect some kind of guilt to sweep over me, or at the very least a rising wave of discomfort, at seeing Mather. But all I feel is tired—tired of getting nothing but unreadable emotions from him. Tired of waiting on him. Tired of *him*.

We don't need another encounter like the one in the sword ring, though. I can handle this on my own. I always have.

I pull Theron's hand until he looks down at me. "I'll

be fine," I promise, though it sounds strange to my own ears. I've never had someone worry about me during Sir's interrogations. It makes me feel both strong and weak at the same time, like I could lean too much on him, on the support he's offering, and lose myself behind him.

After a moment of considering, Theron nods. He squeezes my hand once and backs away, making for the door while politely acknowledging everyone he passes.

The door closes behind him and I have barely two seconds to inhale before someone rushes up on me. I blink, trying to focus on Sir's face, but it isn't Sir.

"It's one thing to be alone with the prince in the library," Dendera spits. "I can almost overlook that. But his *bedroom*? Do you have any idea the kinds of rumors that have been circulating about you? Then you avoid us for a *week* after—thank the snow above that you've been attending those lessons, but that isn't enough!"

Dendera's face is flushed, her hair sticking out in frazzled pieces like she hasn't slept in days. Has she been worrying for this long? Both times I evaded her, she *did* look flustered, but I assumed it was from my avoidance of her, not from my being in Theron's bedroom. I can see why it would be improper for normal courtly ladies, but for me it seems a tad silly. I'm still in training anyway, aren't I? A short while ago I was covered in Lynia's sewer gunk as I barely evaded capture—I'm lucky I'm alive to even *be* improper.

"You're joking, right?" I ask, though I have a feeling it'll just anger her more.

It does. She scoffs, spit flying from her mouth. "You think I'm joking?"

Sir steps in, putting a hand on her arm to pull her attention elsewhere. "Dendera—"

"Talk to her, William! She can't keep doing these things! She has responsibilities now. I never see her long enough to talk to her about colors or food or decorations—"

I shoot a glance at Sir. "What is she talking about?"

Dendera quiets when Sir looks at me. Everyone seems to take one giant step back, like they know that whatever Sir is about to tell me isn't going to be received well.

Sir's face is impassive. "That's what we came to talk to you about, Meira," he starts. A part of me relaxes when he doesn't use my title, just my name. Just Meira. "The wedding is scheduled for the end of the month, and Dendera is on the committee in charge of the celebration, so she needs your cooperation—"

"The *what*?" I screech. "Wait, wait, *stop*. The wedding? At the end of—that's in two weeks! I'm doing the training, these stupid lessons—"

Sir keeps going, ignoring my outburst. "She needs you to cooperate. There's still a lot to be done if we're to cement this alliance."

I stare at him. At all of them. Everyone watching me and backing him up and—

Mather won't look at me now. His back is to me as he clutches the piano, head down, the muscles in his shoulders moving under his shirt as his grip tightens on the polished black lid.

"So that's it?" I whisper. It catches on tears in my throat, tears that come when I realize this *is* how my life will be now, and I should have expected the wedding to happen quickly, what with how close we are to getting our conduit back. But I can't even present some great revelation about magic and how it works and what they need to do with the conduit and how Hannah's been talking to me because Hannah *hasn't* been talking to me, not really, and I can't even read a stupid book and I've been spending all my time learning how to use fancy forks.

There's nothing else. This is really all I can do. I can't think of anything else.

Sir's face finally breaks a little. His lips twitch, his eyes redden.

But I shake my head before he can say anything. "Fine. That's fine. I assume plans are all set? Noam's ready to send men down with you to Spring to get the other locket half?"

No one says anything, and their not saying anything pushes me to talk faster, harder, grabbing onto the hole in their otherwise solid wall of superiority.

"That has to be it, right? Because I can't imagine you'd be in such a rush to get me into this if Noam wasn't also keeping up his end of the deal. If preparations weren't being made on both ends."

Dendera flinches. Her eyes dart to Sir, and Finn looks at Sir, and everyone looks at Sir because he's the one who's supposed to lead us through this.

His jaw tightens. "Noam will uphold his end of the bargain when we have fulfilled ours."

I run Sir's words through my head. Noam isn't doing anything to help us. He's just letting us pretend that he's going to fulfill his end while Dendera and Alysson and Finn and everyone stares at me like I'm some doll they're playing with.

I snarl at Sir. *"No."*

Sir reaches for me but I shove through his grip, pushing by everyone—Dendera, who shouts something about floral arrangements, and Alysson, who says something about calming down, and Mather, who says nothing because that's what he does, he just stands there while I'm supposed to close my eyes and obey.

If I have to close my eyes and obey, Noam does too.

16

AS I FLY out of the library and down the hall, Theron unfolds himself from the wall beside the door and falls into step beside me.

"You didn't tell me they were already planning our wedding," I snarl as I march, working my way to the ballroom and from there to Noam's study. "I guess I should have realized we wouldn't have a lot of time to get to know each other."

Theron keeps pace with me. He throws a glance behind us and I follow his gaze, my eyes locking on the herd of Winterian refugees behind us. Sir is at the lead, and when I look back at him his face darkens.

"Meira, stop!" Sir shouts. Mather grabs his arm and says something that keeps the procession from following me any farther. A wave of gratitude flies through me for half a breath before I shoot around a corner and lose them.

"I'm sorry," Theron says when it's just us hurrying down the hall. "I didn't want to tell you until I had a chance to talk my father into delaying it." He spins around a corner after me and nearly smashes into a servant carrying a tray of vases. The servant cries out, both of them fly in opposite directions, and miraculously nothing falls as Theron continues down the hall beside me.

"Why does he think he can pull strings and make us dance around like this?" I growl.

Theron doesn't say anything.

When we get to the ballroom I charge down the stairs. Halfway across the floor Theron realizes where I'm going and flings himself in front of me, walking backward because I don't stop.

"Meira, this isn't going to fix anything—"

"Don't care."

"I've talked to him every day since he announced the engagement; if I can't change his mind—"

I grit my teeth. "I. Don't. Care."

Theron stops walking and I dart around him. I don't think; I don't do anything as Noam's study looms in front of me. All I know when I pound my fist on the closed door is that I am so, so tired of this. So tired of Noam and Herod and Sir and Angra and all these arrogant, puppet-master *men* who hold all the strings and refuse to give them up. Life could be so easy if they would just let it go, if they would just let *me* go, because I am so tired of this. . . .

I slam my fist on the door again. "Noam!" I shout.

No answer.

I try the handle. Unlocked. Stupid king.

"Meira, wait—"

Sir has finally caught up to me, as has everyone behind him, all staring like I'm an escaped animal from Bithai's menagerie. Sir takes a step forward and I snarl. Maybe I *am* an escaped animal, and maybe they *should* look at me with that little flicker of fear. This is who I am, isn't it? The untamed, unpredictable, useless orphan girl. I don't want to hate them this much. I don't want to blame them for this. But I do, and that hating and blaming makes my chest burn until I think I might incinerate from the inside out.

"Congratulations, everyone," I announce as I open the door to Noam's study. "You've finally broken Meira, the crazy, orphaned soldier-girl. She's snapped, all thanks to the mention of floral arrangements."

Dendera whimpers but I put her behind me as I step into the study. Noam isn't in here. No one is. A desk sits directly in front of the door with tall auburn bookcases all around, mimicking the dark and cozy aura of the entryway just behind me. Papers and quills and ink jars clutter the top of the desk, books sit on stacks of other books and a ledger leans open on a stand.

"He's not here, Meira," Sir says behind me. "Leave this—"

He puts a hand on my arm, reaching over the threshold to me.

Don't you dare touch me.

I snarl at him. "You can't order me around. You aren't my father, *Sir.*"

I slam the door on him before he responds. Before anyone responds. Before they realize I've locked the door and barricaded myself in Noam's study and my little tantrum just went from little to really, really big.

"Meira!" Sir shouts from the other side of the door. He slams his fist against it and jiggles the knob and slams again. "Open this door right now! Do you have any idea of the consequences of breaking into the Cordellan king's study—"

Alysson and Dendera start shouting too. I swear I hear Finn, Henn, and Greer chuckle, but I could just be imagining it in my delirious tantrum state.

I drop into Noam's chair. What *am* I doing? I do know the consequences of breaking into the Cordellan king's study and locking myself in here, because if he finds out—when he finds out—I'm pretty sure my time in Cordell will be spent in prison, if anything. Not that Noam's helping us now.

Or is he?

I grab the ledger off the stand and flip through it,

looking for some clue that he might actually be helping us, but the only entries are calculations for crops and trade amounts. I drop it back on the stand and look over the nearest stack of papers. Correspondences with a duke in Ventralli, complaints from a farm on the outskirts of Bithai that got flooded. I shove it all aside and start pulling open drawers. Extra quills and blank papers and—

The top left drawer is locked.

I pull again. It holds tight. I grab a letter opener off the table and break the lock just as a new voice joins the fray outside.

Noam.

"She *what?*" he bellows. "She's your charge, William; your responsibility. I give you shelter and aid and allow you free rein of my palace, and this is how Winter repays me? By Cordell's golden leaves, I swear I will—"

I rip open the drawer to papers, lots of papers, and grab the first one. Calculations for iron? The next looks similar but shows estimates for precious gems. Another is a map of . . . mines? Winter's mines, dozens of lines swirling through the Klaryns. And then . . .

A letter.

Every bit of frustration, the tantrum I just had, floats up out of me. All that's left is the steady pulse of realization, the dull, empty thud that echoes through my chest with each word on each page of this letter.

To the King of the Spring Kingdom,

Cordell is now joined with Winter on the promise of engagement. My son and heir, Prince Theron Haskar, will take as his wife a surviving female refugee of Winter. I hereby enforce Cordell's ownership of Winter and all its holdings as now owned by Spring through a binding and unbreakable contract of proprietorship through marriage.

Due to Cordell's newfound authority in Winter, I am also prepared to offer Spring the trade of the heir of Winter, Mather Dynam, as a show of good faith that Winter is entirely under Cordellan influence.

I'm shaking so hard I can't see the words on the letter anymore.

Noam betrayed us. He's going to sell us—no, not us. Mather. He's going to sell Mather *to Angra* so that Angra will let Noam take control of our . . . *holdings.* So Noam can take the riches out of our mines and gut our kingdom until all the magic comes pouring out. So Noam can get what he wants because he always gets what he wants—he isn't helping us, he's just using our connection to start ripping through the Klaryns.

I knew he was using us . . . but not this ruthlessly.

The door to the study whooshes open, slamming into the wall and knocking books off shelves. Noam glares at me, his face so red it's purple, one hand on the door and the other on the frame.

"This is beyond unacceptable—" he starts, then his eyes drop to the open drawer, the letter in my hand, the others in my lap. His face gets even darker and he clears the space between the door and the desk in one giant step.

I can't form words through my shock as Noam's hand winds back. His fingers curl into a fist, everything in his body morphing into muscle and strength and the dagger at his belt pulsing purple, glowing as Noam's fist barrels through the air toward me—

"Stop!" Theron shouts.

Color whirls, limbs flail. Noam's pressed against a bookcase, Mather holding him there by his collar, Theron standing just behind Mather. Both of them glare up at the Cordellan king like neither would have any objections to the other maiming him.

"To arms!" a soldier outside the study shouts and the ring of metal fills the air, swords drawn and knives unsheathed. The rest of the Winterians and five Cordellan soldiers press into the room with drawn blades.

Theron spins on his men. "Stand down!"

Noam grunts against Mather's fists pressing into his neck. "Ungrateful boy! I'm your father!"

"You're a coward," Theron hisses, so low and so soft I barely hear him above the ringing in my ears. He turns to me, his eyebrows tight above his face. "Meira, why—" but he doesn't finish, just stares at me, calm and scared and waiting.

Noam betrayed us.

"Meira," Sir growls. He pushes around the Cordellan soldiers to stand before me, his arms trembling, his eyes straining to keep his anger tucked carefully inside.

"What have you done?" he whispers.

I wheeze, hearing his words. "What have I done?" I pant. "What I did was ignore your obnoxious, arrogant, controlling actions for one blissful moment, and uncovered Noam's plot against us."

My body goes cold as I grab onto the realization that if Sir had his way, I'd be looking at dress patterns or sitting in another etiquette lesson, not holding an incriminating letter. Not putting an end to this charade.

I'd be who he wants me to be, and that weak, innocent girl would never have found *this*.

I shove up from Noam's chair and thrust the letter at Sir. "I'm not sorry."

Mather looks back at me, then at the letter. His anger fades to confusion and he loosens his hold on Noam's collar. Noam eases away, smoothing out his shirt, but doesn't fight back, a satisfied smirk falling over his face as Mather joins Sir in reading the letter. Everyone else holds, the Cordellan soldiers still armed and ready to kill us should Noam give the word.

I watch Sir realize it. I watch his frustration at me

disappear beneath the sharp stab of knowing he failed, we failed, Noam failed us. Cordell was our only hope, and here is proof that we are, always will be, slaves upon whom other kingdoms prey.

Sir hands the letter to Mather and turns to Noam. He doesn't say anything, just stares at this great king who was supposed to help us. The silence in the room is oppressive as Mather hands the letter off to Finn, and soon the others are huddled over it, reading and gasping, muscles tightening in rage.

Noam pulls his shoulders back. "A year after Winter fell, Yakim sent a regiment of men to your kingdom. Tried to take it from the Shadow of the Seasons by force, and Ventralli tried the same thing. Did you know that? Neither let it go public. They were embarrassed, because they had identical failures—Angra slaughtered them. Every single man. The Winterian climate was too harsh, and because Ventralli and Yakim had their conduits so far away, in their respective countries, Angra had the advantage, what with his kingdom adjacent to Winter and his conduit so close. After watching my Rhythm brethren die so spectacularly, I decided on a less aggressive approach."

Mather's shoulders rise and fall with each breath, his hands in fists. But his eyes are defeated, vacant, as are Sir's and Alysson's and the other refugees', broken and lost and unable to speak around the distress of it all.

And Theron stands before his father. The letter is in his

hands now, his face gray as his gaze swings from the words to Noam. Like he can't decipher the meaning, or doesn't want to.

"I would forge an undeniable connection to Winter," Noam continues. "One Spring could not ignore. One the other kingdoms of Primoria would not be able to argue. I've waited fourteen years for you to come crawling back to Bithai and accept my offer, William. The moment that boy-king of yours appeared on my doorstep, I sent the letter to Angra to smooth over any bumps Cordell might face on our way to owning Winter—and to begin building a bridge between Spring and Cordell, so that if it turns out that neither Autumn nor Winter yields an entrance into the magic chasm, Spring will let us into their kingdom too." Noam smiles, so completely powerful. "You'd think slaughtering Hannah would have satisfied Angra's bloodlust, but the Seasons have never been anything but barbaric. And barbarism is far too easy to predict."

As Mather twitches to move I swing my body around in front of him and hold him there, one hand on each of his wrists, my head bent into his chest. Low growls bubble in his throat, but he doesn't try to fight.

"Now that this whole nasty business is out in the open"— Noam claps his hands behind me—"don't we have a wedding to plan?"

A roar launches up out of me and I turn on him, keeping my body between Mather and Noam. "Why would we agree to this now?" I shout. "We have nothing left to lose!"

Noam's smile doesn't waver, but his eyes flick from pleased to threatening as a few muscles around his brow twitch. "There are only eight of you, Lady Meira. And you are in *my* domain. You can either marry my son willingly or by force. I have not waited this long and worked this hard to *not* control Winter, and it only needs to look official— whether you choose to become Bithai's prisoners afterward is entirely up to you."

I can't tell whether I'm holding Mather back or he's holding me back. I can't feel anything else in the room, don't know what Sir is doing or if that's Alysson who is crying or anything outside of Noam's awful sneer, and I regret for the umpteenth time this morning leaving my chakram in my room.

"But I digress." Noam waves his hand like he's shooing a bug out of a window. "I'll give you a moment to collect yourselves, but then, Lady Meira, I do believe you have classes to attend, and King Mather and General William have meetings, do they not? The dukes from Cordell's coastal provinces are so looking forward to meeting our new ally."

Noam keeps babbling about what we *need* to be doing, about meetings staged to make everything look the part. Like he knows we'll accept this fate, and the horrible thing is . . . we will. As Sir corrals us out the door, I see it in his eyes. The same defeat I saw when I first confronted him about the marriage arrangement. All these years of fighting, all these years of barely surviving under Angra's attacks, and he's giving up because one arrogant king made a mess of our lives?

The door to the study slams shut on us, separating the Winterian refugees from Noam's men. Theron stayed within the study, and I realize maybe I should worry for him, but all I feel is a thudding emptiness when I face everyone else and see the same shock rendering them immobile.

I shake my head incredulously. "Angra's coming for us, isn't he?"

My question makes the veil of shock hang heavier, and no one so much as breathes in agreement. No one except Mather, who pulls his shoulders straighter, and when I slide my gaze up to him, the look he throws me is the single most terrifying emotion he's ever shown. A violent mix of fear and brokenness and a slow smile that gets negated by the tears in his eyes.

"Not for us," he amends. "For me."

Sir snarls. "Mather . . ."

But Mather takes one step backward, and my hands go out to him like I already know what he's going to say, like his words are an earthquake and my body shakes with the tremors.

"If this is where it's going," he starts, "if this is the fate Noam chose for us, I won't let every last one of you die in the fray. I'm done putting all of you in danger for a cause we can only guess at. I'm done being a pawn."

222

Mather's eyes meet mine and my heart drops.

"I'll fulfill Noam's agreement," he says. "I'll make it so Angra couldn't care less about the rest of you, and you'll finally be able to free the Winterians. We don't need magic, not if you can get Noam to fight off Angra. Not if—"

"Mather!" His name pops out of my throat, a scratching, clawing croak. "Noam won't help us no matter what deal we fulfill—"

"So I shouldn't at least *try*? With Angra no longer searching for you, imagine the good you could do! All this trouble, all this pain, for . . . what? Magic that may or may not come back? Magic we can't even use, even if we *got* it back? No, I'm done. I'm—"

Sir's fist comes out of nowhere, a solid white rock that slams into Mather's cheek. Mather crumples onto the floor, body caved over on his hands and knees, while the rest of us gape and stare and gasp ragged breaths. Sir *punched* Mather. I can't feel anything beyond shock, disbelief, my eyes having trouble telling my mind what they saw.

Vicious red blotches paint Sir's face as he crouches down and rips Mather's head back so he can hiss into his face. "You are the king of Winter—you are not a coward," he growls, and the anguish that leeches out of Sir's voice shakes the same emotion into my body. "The only time you will *ever* face Angra is to run a sword through his chest, and if I hear you speak like this again, I will teach you the true meaning of the word *sacrifice*. We will figure this out—and it will not involve you handing yourself over to Angra."

Mather gawks up at him, just as aghast as the rest of us. Most of what Sir said was right, except for one thing. Mather didn't suggest fulfilling Noam's agreement because he's a coward—he suggested it because he's our king, because he's tired of our lives being like this, because he saw a way to end it all.

Sir grabs Mather's arm and yanks him to his feet. Mather puts a hand to his face, covering the already purple bruise there, and eyes Sir with the wary look of someone who regrets what they just did.

I open my mouth to intercede when a Cordellan soldier bursts through the doors at the end of the entryway, the ones leading outside the palace. He barely gives us a passing glance as he flings himself at the door to Noam's study, yanks it open, and topples to his knees inside. Noam, Theron, and the soldiers within whirl toward the open door, Noam's face tight with rage.

"My king," the soldier sputters, gasping for breath. "I bring grim news. It's Spring. They're—"

Noam stomps forward. "What is it, man? A messenger? Damn king hasn't—"

"No, my king," the soldier interrupts. "A Spring battalion crossed our southern border an hour ago—they've burned three farms and refuse to negotiate. They're marching on us, my king. Angra's men are marching on Bithai."

17

SPRING IS HERE. In Cordell.

Noam flies out of the room, shoving past us, vanishing before anyone can say a word. Because if we were able to get a word in, we would have pointed out that all his machinations were for nothing. Spring is attacking him, which means there is no deal. Angra not only won't agree to give him Winter, he won't agree to anything.

All Noam's playing with us, all his lying, was futile, because now Angra has betrayed him. Mather was wrong too—handing himself over to Angra wouldn't have stopped anything. Angra won't rest until all of Winter is his, completely, every last piece of it.

I inhale, breathing down a sudden surge of anxiety as the soldiers file out of the room after Noam. We're alone, the Winterians standing in the hall and the Prince Heir of

Cordell still hovering by his father's desk.

Theron didn't know about his father's plan. He couldn't have, not the way he looks at me now as he crumples the letter in his slowly tightening fist, his face a mix of regret, anger, and sympathy. I jump when Mather's fingers move against mine and I realize I'm holding on to him like he's the only thing in this palace keeping me from falling into a hundred different pieces. When did I take his hand? After Sir punched him? I still can't believe that really happened. That Mather suggested, for the briefest of moments, dying for us.

My hand tightens on his, my chest pulsing with a medley of emotions. Fear for what he wanted to do; sorrow that, for a moment, I could have lost one of my friends; relief that Sir didn't agree to his insane suggestion. But of all the emotions I feel, I'm most shocked for the ones I *don't* feel. There's no giddiness at holding his hand, none of the things I used to harbor for him. Mather is my king, my friend—my best friend—and I am his soldier. I'd hold Dendera's or Finn's hand the same way, if they needed it, if they threatened to let themselves die for us.

The reasons why I'm holding Mather's hand changed so fast. But this isn't about him, or anything that's happened between us. This is about a soldier protecting her king. This is about Winter. And Mather *is* Winter.

Sir is the first to wake out of his shock. Of course he is. He starts spitting orders at everyone. "Finn, Greer, Henn,

Dendera, Mather—to the armory. If any of the Cordellans give you trouble about getting gear, come find me. Alysson, stay with Meira. Neither of you are to leave this palace. Prince Theron—" Sir starts, then realizes he has no responsibility to order Theron about.

Theron looks at him, teeth grinding together. "Armory too."

Sir turns to Mather. "I want you battle ready in fifteen minutes."

Mather nods, his face set in a mask that could hide a plethora of emotions. Fear. Anger. Regret. Everything. He drops my hand and jogs down the hall after Finn, Greer, Dendera, and Henn, not looking back at me or letting me know at all what he's thinking. Maybe he's not thinking, can't think, after all this.

Sir points at me. "Meira—"

I grimace. "Stay in the palace—I know."

His jaw clenches. "I was going to say be careful too."

My mouth falls open. But Sir has already hurried down the hall, toward the front doors that Noam just exited.

Theron sets the letter on his father's desk. "I didn't know," he promises when it's just us and Alysson and a few soldiers down the hall.

I inhale, amazed at how hollow I feel. Like the chaos of the past few seconds has drained everything out of me. "It doesn't much matter now, does it?"

Theron looks up at me, something working behind his

eyes. A few quick steps through the study and he bursts into the hall, grabbing my hand. "Lady Alysson, would you please accompany us? I will place you under watch of my personal guards."

Alysson gapes at him. "Your Highness—" she starts but Theron is already walking, dragging me down the hall. She follows, but soldiers come from around the corner to fall in behind Theron and me, cutting us off from Sir's wife as they stand guard over their heir.

Theron pulls me closer to him and we stop at the entrance of the ballroom. "Shall we head to the armory?" he asks. His voice is low enough to be blocked from Alysson by his wall of soldiers.

I look up at him. He keeps his eyes on me, a strange light glowing behind them.

"But Sir—" My voice falls out from under me as the gleam in Theron's eyes intensifies. In the aftermath of all that happened, in the midst of all that is happening, it's such a warm relief that I smile back.

Theron shakes his head. "Wants you to stay in the palace? You and I both know that's not where you'll do the most good."

I stare at him, letting his words roll over me. "You'll let me fight?"

"Once we get to the gate, whether you fight or return to the palace is up to you. But I'm not going to hold you back, if that's what you mean."

"Why?"

Theron's mouth twitches. "Because I've been at my father's disposal my entire life," he whispers. "And I will not stand for this game monarchs play. These are *our* lives. I will not let my father or General Loren or even Angra continue to tell us that they aren't."

His poem rushes back to me, his jerky handwriting on the parchment in the library. Theron cocks up a corner of his mouth, studying me in a way that doesn't feel possessive or condescending. It feels equal.

Warmth gathers in my stomach when I smile back. It's hardly the time for smiles and lingering gazes, but I can't help it. It kicks away a small bit of the anxiety of facing Spring, as if having Theron beside me will keep me safe through this. Not as a protector—as an equal. I'm not the only one caught in this. I'm not alone.

My mind flashes to the last time someone helped me like this, when Mather faked an injury so I could be the one to go to Lynia and get the locket half. Mather did it because he knew I wanted it, but Theron is doing this because he knows *he* would want it.

I look up at Theron. They're so similar. And yet so not.

Theron nods at the soldiers behind him. "Escort Lady Alysson to safety."

"Yes, my lord," one of them says and turns. Alysson starts to walk away with them, assuming we're somewhere in the hodgepodge of men. The moment her back is turned,

Theron and I slip in the opposite direction, diving through a door and into the servants' hall.

I know what I have to do to prove that I can be useful as both a future Cordellan queen *and* myself—fight in this battle. Protect this city and the Winterians. Sir will hate it.

At this point, I couldn't care less.

We wait for Mather, Greer, Henn, Finn, and Dendera to get their gear and leave before we enter the armory. But it turns out Cordell doesn't have armor suited to my small stature, so an extra layer of padding later, I'm marching beside Theron out of the armory with one of the beautiful metal crossbows strapped to my back. Too few of Cordell's soldiers use the Autumnian weapon, and I'd stand out in the ranks of the army. The longer I go without Sir noticing me, the better.

"Don't you look battle ready."

I don't turn as Mather jogs up beside us. He's outfitted in armor that matches Theron's—everything from a breastplate down to greaves, chain mail clinking under it all. He's got just as many weapons too, a sword and knives and even an ax strapped to his back, and the bruise on his cheek is a flaming purple-red now.

Mather eyes me but I refuse to look at him. "You've never listened to William, have you? Not when we were children and not now."

I don't respond, even as I realize that Theron is on my

left, Mather my right. Both of them are wound as tight as I get before I launch my chakram through the air, and shooting looks as sharp as knives at each other.

We'll deal with that later. I just hope later isn't after Bithai's been ransacked by Spring and we're scrounging through debris.

The closer we get to the main entrance to Bithai, the more hectic things are. Soldiers run toward the gate while citizens run away from it, dragging carts or livestock laden with whatever valuables they can hold. Residents of Bithai's outer villages, come to take shelter within the city's stone walls.

"There's a tower by the gate. My father will be there along with your general," Theron says. He looks at Mather like he's trying to decide what else to add.

Mather nods. "How many men do you have in the city?"

"Five thousand. Not nearly the bulk of our army, but enough."

"Conduit?"

Theron beams, letting slip the smallest bit of pride. "My father may be known for pouring his conduit magic into opportunity, but he also gives much of his power to defense when needed. I think you'll be pleased, King Mather."

Theron's smile does nothing to ease one out of Mather. He stares at Theron, through him, and nods. "I hope for Bithai's sake that you're right."

The streets leading up to the front gate may be busy, but

the gate itself is chaotic. Citizens pour in from the land beyond, cattle bleat, babies wail. A few soldiers try to instill some sort of order, but the overall feel of the area is to get in as fast as possible, in any way possible.

The tower Theron mentioned looms on our left, spiraling high above the wall to give those within a view of the south. A few captains linger around the door and as we draw closer, the muffled shouting of their fearless leader makes even the air feel nervous.

Captain Dominick is one of the few by the door. His dark hair hangs in sweaty strands and when he turns to us, his tense face relaxes almost imperceptibly.

"My prince, a messenger reported that Spring's current speed puts them at our gate by late afternoon."

"Thank you, Captain," Theron says. He shoots a look at Mather, hard and daring. "Shall we?"

Finally, *finally*, Mather lets his mouth twitch in a small grin. "Your kingdom, you first."

Theron tips his head and darts into the tower, his armor clanking as he twists up the spiral staircase. Mather starts to follow so I trot behind him, nearly smacking into him when he slams to a halt.

"You can't come like that," he snaps down at me.

My lip twitches in a snarl. I was prepared to hide somewhere in the tower to avoid Sir, and Mather owes me at least his silence, doesn't he?

"If you send me to the palace I'll just sneak out and you

won't know where I am or be able to keep track of me. Trust me, this option's better for everyone."

Mather cocks an eyebrow. "I know."

"What?"

He sighs and waves over a running soldier. "Your helmet, please."

The man pulls off his helmet. Mather takes it in one hand and wraps my braid in a knot at my neck in order to slide the helmet over my head. The visor is still up and I feel like I'm looking at him, hazy and distant, through a tunnel, memories overlapping this moment with all those times I sparred with him. All those practice fights when it was just us, two children pretending to be soldiers. Or two soldiers pretending to be children.

"Don't speak," Mather says. "Don't draw any attention to yourself. If William realizes it's you, you're on your own."

"Nothing I haven't dealt with before."

That makes him pause, one hand on each side of the helmet. I think maybe he wants to say something else, but he just drops the visor down with his thumbs.

"When it starts, stay near me or, so help me, Meira, I will march you back into Bithai myself."

I nod, the hollow core of the helmet clanking back and forth. It smells like sweat and old iron in here. Iron that was probably mined out of the Klaryns, which makes me feel ever so slightly more at home.

Mather vanishes into the tower without another word. I

hope my disguise is convincing enough, Spring's approaching threat distracting enough, that Sir doesn't notice the slightly skinny soldier-boy in the room. I'm not sure what I fear more: Sir's wrath or Angra's.

I squint through the narrow eye slits and trail Mather up the stairs.

Seven stories later, Noam's screaming flies at us through an open door. The great circular room is the highest in the tower, allowing views in all directions of the lands beyond Bithai. High-ranking generals scatter throughout, leaning over maps or trying unsuccessfully to avert their eyes from their wailing king.

Spit flies from Noam's mouth, his arms wave, his armored body paces nervously. His conduit sits in a metal belt at his hip, its usual place of honor.

"Damn you, William! Damn you and every single one of your white-haired nuisances. I knew I should never have let you cross my borders, let alone sacrificed my son in all of this. Damned Seasons. Good-for-nothing barbarians who refuse to surrender to stronger forces—"

I file along the wall next to two other guards. They nod at me like I'm supposed to be there. So far, so good.

"Your kind is too beyond reason to negotiate," Noam continues. "I should have seen it before. But no, I tried to give you mercy, debased my kingdom by joining with a Season, and *this* is how I am repaid? Now Angra marches on me! Give me one good reason why I shouldn't hand all of you over to Spring right now."

The tantrum I threw hours ago seems like nothing compared to the way he stumbles around, back talking and fumbling his reasoning. Noam truly believes he was doing us a favor? He thinks we should be grateful to him. That nothing he did brought this upon us, as though he wasn't the one who tried to negotiate with the Shadow of the Seasons.

Sir doesn't react to any of this, leaning against the far wall and massaging the skin just above his nose. He's never lowered himself to respond to screaming or threats—not that I have firsthand experience with that or anything.

Theron trudges into the middle of it, already tired though the true battle is hours away. "Father, stop—"

Noam whips toward him like he forgot his son would be here. "Yes! Of course, son. Break it off. Break it off now. We're done with Winter. The engagement is dissolved."

"No," Theron growls, a low noise that shakes awareness into everyone in the room.

Noam frowns at him. "What?"

"No," Theron repeats. "I meant stop making yourself look like an ass, *Father.*"

Sir flips his head up, hand still held absently before him, eyes wide in a shocked amusement.

Noam rears back. "Don't tell me you—*Spring* is coming— they did this, they brought them here—"

"No, *you* brought them here. When you wrote that letter,

you told Angra exactly where they were. What did you think would happen?" As Theron shouts, madness flickers in his eyes, something waking up after years of watching his father in silence. The men around him stare in wonder, clearly shocked at seeing their prince yell at their king. "That Angra would bow down to you? That he would negotiate and trade and act fairly? Angra wants to *kill them*. He will stop at nothing to get what he wants, and negotiating has never worked with him. You think Winter didn't try to negotiate before it fell? You think Autumn hasn't tried to strike a deal with him since Spring turned on them? You'd know how truly vengeful he is if you ever bothered to go to Autumn."

I frown. Noam has never even *been* to Autumn, the home of his sister and niece, the place where he sends thousands of his men to fight?

"You cannot speak to me like that." Noam throws a hand up to silence him, but Theron shoves it away.

"I can. You've wasted too much time already. Our men need a leader right now, someone to tell them how to survive the approaching army, not a blabbering idiot. Your great plan failed, Father. Own up to it."

Noam's mouth drops open. As does mine. As does every single mouth in the room.

From the trembling light in Theron's eyes to the way his hands quake ever so slightly at his sides, he seems to be realizing how far over the edge he's gone. "You have to do this." His voice drops to a hiss. "I'd take that dagger from you right now if I could, but you're still the oldest living male heir of Cordell. So act like it."

Noam looks every bit the cornered dog, stray and wild, desperate for an escape. After a few long minutes, he relaxes, pulls his shoulders back, and looks his son in the eye.

"You'll make a fine king. Someday." He adds the last word like a threat.

Theron bows his head.

Noam turns to the nearest general and puts a hand on his dagger. "Your regiment will be our left flank. Have them ready. And you—right flank."

He spouts commands like nothing happened. Like he purposefully staged his little outburst as some odd pre-battle ritual.

Theron's shoulders slump when his father turns away, but Sir steps up beside him and murmurs something that makes Theron straighten.

Mather steps up too. "That was brave."

Theron wipes a hand down his face. He looks drained, as if he might fall over and sleep for a week. But there's something else in his eyes now, something roaring beneath the surface.

"And should have been unnecessary." Theron turns to Sir. "I'm sorry. For everything. Cordell is far better than—" His eyes flick to Noam. "I apologize, King Mather. General Loren."

Sir waves him off. Behind them, Noam points at the field beyond and shouts an order at one of his generals.

"I agree with one thing he said," Sir offers. "You will make a fine king, Prince Theron."

Compliments from Sir *and* Mather in the span of five minutes. If it were me, I'd pass out with gratitude, but Theron just stares at the stone floor.

Sir plows right on past it too. I'll never understand men. "For now, Mather and I are needed with our people."

Theron nods. "Of course."

Sir jogs down the staircase, Mather a beat behind him. As Mather passes me, he meets my eyes, and mouths, *Try to stay here.*

It is one of the safest places to be. Unless Angra's cannons rip through the tower, in which case it's a long, slow tumble to the ground.

I swallow and stand a little straighter. Noam is busy channeling power into various regiments by willing the conduit's magic to pour into men here, officers there. The hum of the tower has switched drastically, no longer buzzing with concern or anxiety. Amazing what a calm leader can do to a group of men.

But it isn't only Noam's magic that's calming them. Theron moves around the room, talking with each general, sending some off to prepare their soldiers. His serenity eases them into submission whereas his father uses brute force. Theron's steadiness, his certainty, remind me of someone.

He reminds me of Sir. They have the same solemn surety when faced with life-or-death situations. The same boulder-in-the-ocean stance.

Halfway across the room, Theron glances at me. Does he recognize the overstuffed armor he helped force me into?

A moment passes and a small smile uncurls his lips— not gleaming enough to arouse suspicion, just a small token that says, *I'm watching out for you too.*

I smile back even though he can't see.

18

AS THE SUN hovers a few hours past noon, I find myself with my back to Bithai's most outlying buildings. The ones the citizens were all frantically running away from, seeking shelter within the city's high stone walls while soldiers took up their stations on the sweeping fields of green.

Noam, Theron, and a few high-ranking generals stayed in the tower by the gate while the rest of the men, myself included, were pulled down to add numbers to the field. The sea of soldiers stretches so far around me that I can't see the green of Bithai's grass, just silver armor and dark weapons and ready, waiting bodies. Cavalry take up the outer flanks, rows and rows of infantry fill the center, and two long lines of archers stand at the back on the sloping edge of Bithai's plateau. Which is where I am, the metal crossbow loaded in my grip.

The past few hours have been filled with preparations, getting lined up and making sure everyone had proper gear. Now that everything is set, it all has time to catch up to me. I inhale, exhale, my breath heating up the helmet, my pulse hammering in my ears and echoing around the metal that encases my head. The waiting is the worst part—with food-scouting missions, I never had a chance to get nervous. They were so fleeting that by the time they were over, I hadn't even realized I was supposed to feel more than a rush of adrenaline. But now, listening to my heartbeat and watching the horizon and waiting, waiting, waiting for battle—it's horrible.

The rest of the Winterians stand behind the archers in their own group. Noam can't help us with his conduit, can't pour strength or will into us because we aren't Cordellan and, therefore, remain unaffected by his magic—the same way we couldn't affect any of his people if our conduit was whole. And we're the reason why Spring is attacking—if we all die, it becomes a bit of a lost cause, regardless of Noam's empty threat to hand us over to Angra.

Mather made sure to position himself a few paces behind and to my right, mounted on a horse should he need to swoop in. He hasn't moved to make good on his own threat either, and I breathe a little easier every time I see that he hasn't vanished to surrender to Angra. I look back at him, desperately wanting to rip off my accursed helmet. Iron smell or no iron smell, this thing's nothing but an airless metal oven, and no Winterian likes heat.

Mather shifts on his horse, eyebrows coming together in a question. *You all right?*

I nod. He shifts again, says something to Sir, who shakes his head fiercely.

My body thuds with longing. I should be there, back with them, not hiding among Noam's archers. Come battle time, when Noam wills his regiments to move one way or another, I'll be at a loss as to which way to go. If Noam wills his archers to shoot left and I let one fly right, it'll give me away.

I shake off my worries, refocusing on the weight of the metal crossbow in my hands and the energy surging around me. Captain Dominick sits three rows ahead in the infantry, overseeing his men on horseback. No one says a word, no one shouts orders, no one even breathes too loudly. We're all just waiting in the heart-shattering anticipation of death marching toward us.

The sun drops lower. Lower still. It's at this moment, when the late afternoon's heat is barely playing with us, that a ripple runs through the men. They stand straighter, all eyes sweeping south. Spring's army has been spotted.

I've never seen a Royal Conduit–led battle before. Sir told me about them, of course, reiterated Spring-versus-Winter battles in such epic detail that I could almost smell the cannon fire on the air. Through the conduit, rulers can will entire regiments to move as one, shift people around like they're arranging items on a tabletop. It's not a forceful push; more like a subconscious suggestion—soldiers can choose not to follow their leader's conduit-channeled instructions. But it's usually in the soldiers' best interest to follow their leader's will.

Sir's history lessons roll through my head alongside what I read in the magic book. Each Royal Conduit is like a horse; use it too much or too quickly and it tires out, and leaders have to wait for it to rest before they can use it again. Use it too often, too aggressively and, well, we don't know what could happen—no one has ever been stupid enough to let it dry up completely, if it even could. The monarchs can feel when the magic gets low, a tug at their instincts like that uncomfortable feeling of something wrong. And it's a passive magic—only when the bearer consciously chooses to draw it out does it work.

If Noam uses his conduit steadily, it could give Cordell a huge advantage. Angra never leaves his palace in Spring, and Herod, who is most likely leading this charge, won't have the same control over his men. Angra's magic may make their minds numb with a devotion to Spring that lasts beyond Spring's borders, but he won't be able to tell them how to move, where to attack, when to pull back. For all our sakes, I hope that advantage is enough.

When the Cordellan soldiers perk up, we do too. I risk one more glance behind me, noting who's here and who's not. Alysson's the only one missing. Which leaves seven of us.

The archers raise their crossbows and I fumble to match their rhythm. The crossbow is so much heavier than my chakram, bulky and dense, but I can do this. I've done this before. I've just never done this as part of an army, wearing a constricting helmet.

I keep my finger on the trigger, my breaths coming slower and slower. No one fires yet, we just keep our crossbows aimed at the sky.

"Come *on*," the man next to me hisses.

His anxiety pushes at me, a flame that catches and spreads like wildfire through the group. Soon everyone is twitching for the battle to start.

Then the sound everyone was waiting for, the vibration that sends everyone's anxiety rearing higher.

Cannon fire.

A single shot comes from somewhere distant, too far away to hit anyone. A warning meant to announce Spring's arrival. The shot fades to an echo and Spring's army rises up over the horizon in the fading sun of the late afternoon, their soldiers nothing but a black mass that sweeps down over Cordell's distant hills like a plague. Another cannon fires, then two more, closer and closer—

Thwack.

The archers let loose the first round. I snap to fire with them, launching my arrow in an arc over the infantry. *Are they within range already? Are they close enough to—*

Yes, they are. Spring's so close, in fact, that before our

arrows even complete their arcs, three cannonballs rip holes in the first lines of Noam's infantry. The black mass of Spring soldiers is close enough now that I can see them running toward us, weapons raised, shrill war cries tearing out of their throats.

Five seconds. Four seconds. Three.

Two.

One.

The force of the two armies colliding sends a shock-wave through the men. They return Spring's war cries with screams of their own, howling into the air as the familiar numbing focus of the fight sweeps over me. I fire three more rounds along with the archers before I realize the group has split in two, half running one way and half running the other, fanning to spread out Cordell's force.

I step to my right, second-guess, then step to my left as a line of infantrymen heaves backward, slamming into me and throwing me to the ground. I roll to the side, flip around, narrowly avoiding stomping boots and clomping horse hooves as Dominick's men move in one giant mass to the back left. Noam's pulling them around—why?

A hand grabs my arm and before I can process who it is, I'm clinging to a saddle and hefting my leg up to straddle the horse.

"I trained you to blend in better than that," the rider throws back at me.

I freeze, arms around Sir's waist, cheeks warm in shame

and frustration at being caught. On the bright side, I can take off the helmet now.

As I yank the metal oven off my head and toss it to the ground, Sir urges his horse to a trot behind Dominick's regiment. They continue to pull behind the rest of the infantry, moving to the left and back. The rest of the infantry closes in to fill their gap.

"Are you going to take me back to the palace?"

Dominick's men swing to the right, aligning themselves behind the leftmost cavalry.

"You're going to stay with me," Sir hisses. He motions to my crossbow. "Cut down the closest ones first. Whatever you do, whatever happens, *do not stop firing.*"

I yank an arrow into my crossbow as Sir kicks his horse into a gallop. We shoot past Dominick's soldiers, bearing wide around the cavalrymen until we line up with the first row of riders.

"Three counts," the cavalry captain tells Sir.

"Your mark."

The captain raises his sword into the air. I lean around Sir, scanning the horizon for what we're going to be fighting. And there, from Bithai's lush green hills, a wave of nightmares rises.

Angra's cavalry crests a hill in front of us, horses coated in armor, soldiers raising crossbows or swords or axes. More infantrymen in black sun armor run between the pounding hooves.

That's why Noam pulled Dominick's regiment here. On the far left, if that cavalry breaks through, they'll be able to work their way between the rest of Noam's army and Bithai's gate.

Another rider gallops up beside us. Mather. He meets my eyes, steady and sure, as Spring's riders draw nearer. Just one more hill, and they'll be within arrow range.

"One," the captain shouts, breaking me away from Mather's eyes. "Two."

I lift my crossbow into the air. This is it. I've been in hand-to-hand combat with small groups of Spring soldiers, but never a battle. A strange calm settles over everyone, something not urged from Noam's conduit. A deeper instinct that blocks everything else.

"Three!"

Sir and I heave forward with Noam's cavalry. The world slows until there's nothing more than the pounding of our horses' hooves, the screaming of the soldiers, the wave of arrows that rises up from Spring's archers and paints the sky with violent streaks of black.

I fire my crossbow, fire again, slowly lowering my arc as we draw closer and closer to Spring's riders. In those final seconds before we collide, Sir reaches down and touches my leg. Mather turns to look at me, his eyes wide in the calm before the storm. I feel everything happening around me as if watching from a dream.

Years of training take over. Our horses merge seamlessly

into Spring's cavalry and arrows fly, swords slice through the air and into throats, knives lodge in chests. My crossbow sings out the hum of arrows flying, a symphony that ends in satisfying *thwack*s into shoulders and knees and other weak points in Spring's armor. My crossbow isn't a weapon I'm holding—it is me, and I am it, and the two of us bring down soldier after soldier like we were made to do nothing else.

Sir rears his horse around and I break out of my stupor long enough to note that we've crossed through all of Angra's cavalry. At first I'm flooded with the sweet, pure burst of relief—there are so few of them! But then I see what waits for us behind the cavalry.

"MATHER!"

Sir's scream rips holes in my body. I whirl around to see Mather nearing us. He's almost here too. He's almost—

I don't have time to finish the thought.

Cannons wait for us. Dozens of them, pulled by oxen over the hills. Soldiers stand next to the iron monstrosities, and even from so far away, I can see, feel, taste their glee as they light the explosives that will send death barreling toward us. That's all I have time to absorb, the horrific weight of the soldiers' impending joy at our demise, and just as my eyes register that the black balls slamming into the earth around us are cannonballs, an invisible force shocks me off the horse and cracks me like a rag doll against the ground.

Fire-red pain lances across my vision, radiating out from

a solid break in my chest. Sounds deaden against the roar of agony that fills my head, and something beneath me reeks of iron, wet and warm. But it's not the comforting smell of iron mined from the Klaryns.

It's blood.

The muted noises rise to a horrible ringing. I push up, one of my ribs screaming out in anger, but I don't care as more cannons fire, more of Noam's cavalry gets launched into the air.

It was a trap, and now there are more Spring men running at us around the cannons, and the remaining Spring soldiers we didn't kill from the initial charge fly back to surround us. Here and there a few clumps of Cordellan riders stay up, hacking at enemies, firing blindly. But it's no use. We're too cut off from the bulk of our army, helplessly lost in our stupid rush to destroy Angra's cavalry.

I scramble up. The armor and extra padding lock my broken rib in a pathetic makeshift cast and I'm able to stumble forward, debris clouding the air, bodies littering the way. The stench of blood and sweat clogs my lungs, growing with each explosion, each scream.

Mather. I think I shout it but I can't hear myself. Maybe I only mouth it, a feeble cry in the dark. *William!*

A cannonball hits the ground nearby, knocking me down with its invisible force. I collapse on a body that reaches up, a bloodied hand gripping my shoulder. Panic numbs everything in me for one beautiful, horrifying second when

I see who is grabbing me, how bloody he is, how mangled in the filth of battle.

Sir.

Whenever he described situations like this before, the scenario seemed like a distant, foreign thing I would never have to face. Injuries on a battlefield. Excessive blood loss, broken bones, ripped flesh—

This isn't real. This can't be real. Not now, not him.

A Spring soldier wails in front of me, a Cordellan sword through his chest. The sound of his dying scream warps in my ringing ears as Sir's lips move. I lunge to him, shouting, willing the ringing to lessen enough so that I can hear him through the screams and explosions.

His lips move again. "Meira."

Blood and dirt and sweat make his fingers slick as I grip his hand. "What do I do?" I shout. "Tell me what to do!"

Sir smiles through the bloodstains on his cheeks. The blood trails down to show its source—a gaping wound in his belly, ripping open half his chest. Dark blood pulses out, brittle white bone protruding from the cavity.

"Meira," he says again. His hand comes up to cup my cheek, his thumb rubbing at my temple.

"What do I do?" I scream again. Another cannonball strikes somewhere close by; they're coming closer and closer. They'll hit us soon. We're still in range. I have to move him, get a medic—

"I'm sorry," he wheezes.

Sir's eyes drift out and he stares vacantly at a space beside my head. When he looks back, his gaze is distant and hazy as if he's seeing through me.

"No," I growl. I shake his shoulders, trying to pull his focus back to me. "No! You listen to me, William Loren. You do not deserve this!"

Sir nods. "I served Winter."

Another cannon. A Spring soldier howls above me, sword raised, and I reach for my crossbow. It isn't there—it got torn away with the cannon blast. Before I can scramble for another weapon, a Cordellan arrow comes whirring out of the ashes, and the soldier crumples beside Sir's legs.

So many bodies, Spring and Cordellan alike. So much death and blood piling up so quickly—

Sir's thumb moves on my temple again. I bend over him, shielding him from debris, from blood, from all of this. "No," I mumble. It's all I can do, all I can say, eyes blurring with dust and hot, pulsing tears. "No, no, William, don't—"

Sir wheezes. He looks at me again, and one last ray of clarity brings recognition to his eyes. "Meira," he whispers. "You have to save them."

"Of course," I croak. "I'll do it. I promise I'll do it. But you have to help me. I can't do it without you!"

Sir shakes his head. "Did you hear Bithai's poem when we first arrived?"

I nod, and Sir presses on.

"No," he says. "The words. Did you hear the words?"

When I shake my head this time, Sir inhales, closes his eyes, and lets memory say it. The gentle poem rolls out, past Sir's wheezing breath, past his pain.

> *"Cordell, Cordell, today we come*
> *To kneel before your blessed throne.*
> *Let all who find refuge be glad*
> *They hide behind your walls of stone.*
> *Cordell, Cordell, if we must leave*
> *To battle, travel, or to die,*
> *Let those who do not come again*
> *Forever in your presence lie."*

His eyes open again. "Winter needs that," he rasps. "Winter must have that."

I shake my head again, tears pouring down my cheeks. "No, William—Winter needs *you!*"

Sir smiles. The smile catches as his thumb stops moving, everything in his body hardening like a pond freezing in winter. The sudden, scary pause echoes through me. He's not moving. He's not breathing. He's not—

Alive. He's not alive anymore.

Slowly, so slowly, his hand drops and collapses against his chest.

"Meira!"

Someone calls my name, voice ragged with fear. I grab

Sir's face, my dirty fingers digging into his hair. He stares into the sky, his eyes absent and empty, an expression that branded its horrible meaning into my mind long, long ago. A candle without a spark, a sky without a sun, the look people get when they cease to be people, start being bodies. But he is too strong for this expression, his face too hard, too wise, to support the sheer nothingness cascading over him. I refuse to let him go, not like this, not while I will always, always need him.

"William," I sob, and shake him, his blood squishing between my fingers. "Look at me! Please, I'm begging you, look at me. . ."

All I ever wanted was for you to look at me.

"Meira!" Mather slides to the ground beside me, throws his arms around my shoulders.

"No!" I claw at him, pushing him away, but he fights me to my feet. *"No!"*

We stumble back, trip on another dead body. Like Sir, staring up at pockets of blue sky through holes in the wafting debris, just another casualty in Angra's war.

I shove Mather away, rage coursing fresh at Angra's name. This is his fault. All of this, his greed and his conduit and Winter being weak, so weak . . .

Mather's arms leave me long enough that I turn back to Sir and reach out in one final grasp for him.

Please, you can't die too.

Coldness streams down my arm, flies from my fingertips.

I can feel it crawling across the battlefield and over Sir's body, spreading like frost over the ground. It touches every blood vessel, every nerve, turning everything around me into a field of ice. Is this what shock feels like? Is this how it feels to have a piece of who you are ripped from your life—cold and desolate?

Mather pulls me away like nothing happened. "Meira, we have to run! It's not safe!"

I stare at him. Doesn't he feel cold too? How can he not feel it? But his panic, the way he drags me through the battle, tells me he didn't feel anything.

Cannon fire pierces the air, spinning and whistling in the dust, and I react without thought—I shove my shoulder into Mather, throwing him sprawling to the ground as the earth next to me explodes. The weightlessness returns, heaving me up and up, slamming me back into the blood-soaked ground. Something else pops in my chest, and pain flares.

I try to pull myself up, to see where I landed, but only manage to get to my elbows before blackness swarms over me in the form of twisting agony. As it descends I see Mather too far away, screaming, getting dragged toward Bithai by a few of Noam's men.

"Meira."

A shadow drops over me. At first it looks like Sir, but it can't be Sir, it can never again be Sir, and I whimper in the terrible truth of it all.

The shadow crouches down. He sneers at me, a sickening movement that clashes with the men wailing for their lives behind him, against Mather getting sucked away to safety. Against my great rush of terror when I recognize that face.

Herod.

"You stole something from me," he hisses. "It's about time I take it back."

As he bends down, pain, and fear, and exhaustion sweep over me, throwing everything into darkness.

SNOWFLAKES DRIFT AROUND me, turning the air over the ivory field white and cold.

I'm in Winter.

"I thought I'd have more time." Hannah stands beside me in a white silk gown, the locket gleaming from her neck. Her eyes are glazed, whether from tears or the cold I can't tell.

"What?" I feel a flicker of alarm. I shouldn't be in Winter. Last I remember, I was . . . somewhere else. Where?

"I thought I'd have more time," Hannah repeats. "The connection to conduit magic never breaks, but it was too soon earlier. I've been trying to give you time, but time has run out." She faces me, and I know now that those are tears in her eyes, tears that crest over her lids and tumble down her cheeks. She steps forward, reaching one hand out to me.

"Wait." I pull away. I can't remember . . . anything. Why I'm here, in a dream again, why my stomach hangs with a painful weight. Why . . .

Sir's dead. And I've been captured by Herod.

I fall to my knees, gasping on snowflakes. "No . . ."

Hannah steps closer. "Once you arrive in Spring, Angra will use his dark magic to watch you like he's been watching Mather since Winter fell." Her face softens. "I'm sorry I can't explain what I'm about to show you, but I don't have time for more than this now."

She puts her hand on my forehead. I moan in protest, but the moment her skin touches mine, scenes fill my head, images and pictures of . . . the past. Hannah is showing me the past. I don't know how I know that, but the truth zings through me as certainly as the images, and I draw in ragged breaths to keep myself from descending into panic.

Dozens of people stand on a dark lane, holding stones and pendants and sticks in unrelenting fists. The objects glow faintly, gentle pulses of light under the deep black sky. The people turn as a different group approaches, also holding glowing objects. The two groups don't hesitate—with a scream and a bellow they attack. Fists split bones as if they're no more than brittle pieces of wood; bodies fly through the air, thrown like fistfuls of straw.

Normal people shouldn't be able to fight like this. But these aren't just normal people—those objects are conduits. People once had their own conduits? But only the Royal Conduits were created before the chasm disappeared. . . .

Or was that wrong?

A shadow rises from the fight, drifting out of each thrown punch, each snarl of hatred. The larger it grows, the angrier the crowd gets, like each feeds the other. Anger for more anger, evil for stronger evil—

From the light, there came a great Decay.

More black clouds of Decay appear, rising out of towns, villages, all from people who use conduits to do terrible things. A murder, a theft, a woman cowering as her husband beats her. Each time someone uses a conduit for corrupt ends, the Decay grows; and each time the Decay grows, it finds people, seeps inside them, and makes them do even more corrupt things.

And woe was it unto those who had no light.

Eight people stand before me on the edge of a cliff in a great underground cavern. A brilliant ball of light from the endless depth beyond all but blinds me, and as I realize what this is, everything I've ever felt evaporates, leaving only gentle awe.

The lost chasm of magic.

They did beg, thus the lights were formed.

The eight people stack stones and pendants and sticks on the edge of the chasm. Conduits, still glowing softly in eight separate piles. On the very top of his or her pile, each person places an object that does not glow. A locket, a dagger, a crown, a staff, an ax, a shield, a ring, a cuff. I run my eyes over the eight people again. Four male, four female.

The four did create the lights; and the four did create the lights.

Snapping fingers of energy strike the eight piles one at a time, unstoppable waves of power drawn to the new conduits like lightning to metal. Magic fills up the Royal Conduits, connecting with their rulers, their bloodlines, their genders.

The scene changes again, flashing by me. The clouds of Decay dissipate now, waning under the power of the Royal Conduits as the rulers chase the Decay from their lands. People rejoice as the Decay's fog leaves them.

Then I see something I recognize all too well—Spring. Cherry trees stretch in a sea of pink and white around a man with curly blond hair, nearly translucent green eyes, and pale skin. He stands at the entrance to his city, holding a staff. And around him hovers the last black cloud in Primoria, pulsing weakly.

"You are true strength," the man tells the cloud, and opens his arms to it.

I scream, needing someone to hear me, needing someone else to see that they didn't destroy all of it. The Decay still exists—and it's in the ruler of Spring.

"Tell me how to save them."

The scene changes. Centuries pass. I'm in a bedroom in Hannah's palace, Jannuari visible beyond open balcony doors. The Decay has faded to a distant, forgotten legend, and the only thing anyone in Winter fears now is Spring. Hannah crouches at the foot of a canopy bed, tears streaking down her face.

"Tell me how to save my people from him," she begs. Who is she talking to?

Then I see it. The small white glow in her hand where her fist sits against her chest. She's holding the locket, begging it to tell her what to do. Has any other monarch done that before? Used their conduit as more than just a source of power, but as a source of authority?

Hannah's locket responds to her pleading, a radiant white chill that ripples out of her hand. The magic pours into her, and through that pouring comes . . . this. All of this knowledge. The past, why the Royal Conduits were really created, what Winter is truly facing in Spring.

I fight the urge to curl in a ball and never leave this place. It's safe here, there's no Decay, no evil, and my chest aches with everything that awaits me outside of my dream.

"You will understand how to use all this when you are ready," Hannah says, and I jump. *I thought this was a memory of her, not actually her, but she swings her tear-rimmed eyes to me as I release a sob that burns my throat.* "It's you now, Meira. Wake up."

Warm, flickering gold throbs beyond my eyelids, and I squint in the rays of sun passing above me, columns of dancing light under a clear blue sky. The wind churns the scent of dead grass and dried earth, so pungent that I instantly know where I am—the Rania Plains.

It's you now.

I close my eyes, biting back the sobs that come as Hannah's dream plays through my head. Why did she show me all of that? Why *me*?

Because Sir is dead and Mather is gone. I'm the only one left, the one about to face an evil created thousands of years ago, so long ago that not even myths remain from that time.

I bite back another sob, drawing in deep, slow breaths. I can't worry about that now; I have to focus on figuring out where I am. Step by step, breath by breath, I open my eyes and survey the world around me.

I'm in a cage. Wooden bars keep me trapped as a great, lumbering ox pulls me on. Men trail alongside, their breastplates showing Spring's black sun. I'm Herod's prisoner. Gregg's story comes hurtling back to me, every detail crisp and clear from when he returned to camp so many years ago, a battered soldier who had just watched his wife die. The way the words tumbled out of his mouth like he didn't even know he was saying them, just kept coming and coming, telling us every detail about how Herod killed Crystalla. . . .

Nausea roils and I turn over, barely making it to the edge of the cage before my stomach pushes out what few pieces of food I haven't digested yet. I cling to the bars, heaving and fighting down tears as an all-too-familiar shadow crosses over me.

"Good morning, Meira. It's *Lady* Meira now, though, isn't it? I haven't gotten a chance to congratulate you on your engagement. A Season managing to snag the wealthy Cordellan prince. I didn't know Rhythms were stooping to charity now."

I focus on the grass rolling beneath the cage's wooden wheels, on the smells of earthy dead plants and sour vomit. Not on Herod's booted feet, keeping pace beside me, his fingers curled around one of the bars.

"I'm moving up in the world." I heave again, coughing out air. At least there's nothing left for me to vomit. My ribs, silent during my need to puke, scream at me now until I roll onto my back. Even that doesn't entirely appease them. I need medicine, a splint better than my padding and armor. I doubt I'll get any of that here.

Herod laughs. "How quickly the mighty fall."

I close my eyes, the sunlight casting red and gold on the insides of my lids. I will not give Herod the satisfaction of seeing me break. I will be strong.

People had conduits once to make them strong. I saw them, conduits like stones and pendants and sticks. I shove the dream away, refusing to let it poison me with more worry, but something catches me and won't let go.

People had conduits *like stones*.

The stone in my pocket, the one that Mather gave me, that he wanted to believe was magic when he was a child. A piece of lapis lazuli that Winter mined. It could be . . .

This is insane.

But I have nothing left to lose for trying, do I?

I shut my eyes tighter, focusing on the lapis lazuli ball, on whatever might be inside it. I imagine the stone's strength flowing into my body, twirling through the cavity of my chest, and filling my ribs with vitality and health.

Nothing happens.

I do it again, gritting my teeth, begging the blue thing to do something, please, to help me in some way—heal just one rib, just one—

Something jabs my side. Hard. I gasp in the sudden shock of pain and swallow down a wave of nausea, my focus shattered by the hilt of Herod's sword.

"You've slept enough," he says. "Angra will want you conscious when we arrive."

I shut my mouth tightly once my stomach calms, body

curled away from Herod and ribs well beyond the point of screaming pain. Stars poke my vision, threatening me with a long, slow sleep, and I try to hold my chest in a way that would make the pain stop. There's no relief. No help from magic. The snuffing out of that one flicker of hope makes me feel even more hollow, but I can't think about that. I have to stay awake. I have to know what dangers lie ahead.

Like magic more powerful and potent than we ever knew, a great, destructive force contained in one man. If it went into Angra's ancestor . . . has it been passed down, generation to generation, like the Royal Conduits themselves? Why hasn't it spread throughout the world again?

There is only a handful of magic sources now, though, and the Decay grew when people used magic for evil. Maybe there isn't enough for it to spread beyond the Spring monarch, so it stays in him, leeching power from him and him alone.

I shudder. No, it's just Angra. It's just the man we've been fighting for years, an evil, sadistic monster who uses his Royal Conduit for evil. Just his Royal Conduit. Nothing more.

Angra is never *just* anything, though.

The wheeled cage clunks down, the steady swishing of the wheels through grass giving way to the *clomp-clomp* of wheels on stone. We've passed onto a bridge, one of the many that link the Rania Plains with Spring over the Feni River. The narrowness of this bridge tells me we're no longer with the bulk of Spring's army. We must have broken off to reach Abril, Spring's capital, more quickly.

As the cage thumps into the grass on the Spring side of the river, the empty expanse of the Rania Plains changes to blossoming trees, the kind with white-and-pink buds that cast floating petals into the air. Spring's forest is pretty, honestly. But a marred pretty, a mask.

Herod jabs me in the back with his sword hilt again. "Sit up. We're nearly there."

"Sitting is easier said than done right now," I croak, but one more jab from his sword hilt and I wiggle into a semi-erect position, black dots swirling through my vision.

Abril sits in the northwestern tip of Spring, close to Winter. There are no outlying villages nearby, no signs of life outside its massive stone walls other than the occasional field of crops cutting through the forest of eternally blossoming trees. Laughably peaceful representations of a kingdom that has been anything but.

The small army of men around my cage descends from a side path onto a wide main road that cuts through the trees. Abril's walls rise before us, casting the surrounding land in shadow, looming rows of black behind the pink-and-white trees. After a few moments of shuffling, we pass through a gate and into the city itself. I cling to the details around us, forcing my mind to stay active instead of losing myself in the dread pulsing in the pit of my stomach.

Angra's banner, the black sun on a yellow background,

dangles from four- and five-story buildings, the tall structures encasing us in an eerie shadow. As we roll by, heads
pop out of smudged windows, eyes peek through cracked
doors, but I see no people in the streets and hear no chatter
of city life. Like they've been choked so long under Angra's
suffocating use of his magic that they've forgotten how to
be alive.

We cross a bridge and the buildings get a little nicer,
windows cleaner, walls painted and whole. People stand
around now too, smirking over another Winterian prisoner,
another show of their king's dominance.

Fear is a seed that, once planted, never stops growing.

Sir's voice whispers that phrase in my memory, keeping
the fear at bay.

A black iron gate sits at the end of one last road. Soldiers march on the wall above it and eye us from towers, a
reminder that Spring is a kingdom crafted by war. When
we pass through the gate, a grand green yard rolls around
us, leading up to a palace of black obsidian. Even from as
far back as we are I can see colored etchings in the rock,
green ivy vines, butter-yellow and sunset-pink flowers—
Spring in darkness. It's both poetic and sad how well it
embodies this land.

The gate shuts behind us, and Herod nods to the men,
who near the cage. I stifle a cry as they drag me out, my
bones grating, shocking bursts of pain as I collapse, helpless, hanging off two men. Dried sweat and bits of vomit

cling to my skin, crunching as I move, and a few cuts along my leg burn. But I'm just here, draped between Angra's soldiers, wholly at their disposal. Helpless and useless and alone—

The piece of lapis lazuli is still in my pocket. A piece of Winter. I straighten a little, wincing. I may be alone, the stone may not be magic, but I am *not* weak.

We start to move forward and something clinks to my right, a shovel banging on stone. It makes Herod flinch enough that I jerk my head toward it.

I wish I hadn't. I wish I'd kept looking forward, let my worries about Angra suck me into a numb thoughtlessness.

Off to the right, in a garden, a group of Spring guards stand watch over a pile of gray bricks, a deepening hole, and . . . Winterians.

Everything about me drops away, flimsy and weightless. Three Winterians, their white hair matted with sweat and mud, their pale faces gaunt, stand waist-deep in the dirt. It's a wonder their bony arms can even hold a shovel, let alone dig with one—they're so frail, so thin, they could be mistaken for ghosts.

Tension cuts off the air to my lungs. I want to cry out to them, run to them, fight off the guards, whisk them to safety. But I can't do more than croak feebly in their direction.

One of the Winterians stops digging. She lifts her head, face caked with mud, and when her gaze meets mine across the lawn, light dawns on her face. A ray in the shadows of Spring that makes me heavy with guilt—she can't be any older than me.

"Get back to work!" one of the guards yells, and readies a whip. It curls around the girl's forearm and yanks her forward, but she keeps her eyes on me, her face alight with wonder.

"No," I whisper as the guard raises the whip again. "Stop!"

Herod steps between the Winterians and me. The whip cracks, and Herod leans in so all I can see is his face. "Keep moving," he growls, and pushes the soldiers holding me. We plunge up a set of gleaming black steps as the whip cracks harder and faster.

"Stop!" I scream as we enter the shadow of Angra's palace. "Stop it!"

I reach back for her, for all of them. As I do, a deadly will rises in me to help them. As hard and fast as the whip, as brilliant as the girl's hope. But the soldiers pull me inside the palace, yanking me away from doing anything more than hurting.

ONCE THE DOORS shut, all links to the surrounding
city vanish, sealing the palace around me like a tomb.

The entry hall is a cave of gleaming obsidian with
sconces throwing yellow light onto the reflective surface,
a never-ending echo bouncing off walls that toy with it
just for entertainment's sake. The only breaks in the light
are portraits of Spring's past rulers that hang at perfectly
spaced intervals on the walls. A woman, her long blond
hair pulled over one shoulder in a tangle of curls, beams
at the painter. A little boy with pale green eyes stares into
the distance, his blond curls exploding out of his head in
disorderly rebellion. The same two people are in at least a
dozen portraits, posing in front of Spring's cherry trees or
rivers or plain blue backdrops. The riots of color in these
paintings don't belong here; this place should be nothing

but darkness. *Who are these people?*

When I see the signature of the artist in the bottom corner of one painting, my body falls slack. *Angra Manu.* If Angra really painted these, then the outside of his palace makes more sense. He embraces art in a way that would make Ventralli proud.

I turn my gaze downward, staring at the black floor instead of at the bombardment of life and color and happiness painted by the king who has brought nothing but death to Winter.

The doors at the end of the hall groan as a soldier pulls them open. I'm not allowed even a moment to gather my wits before we enter the throne room, wide and dark and filled with the poetic collision of sunshine and shadow. A series of windows has been cut into the high ceiling, circles of sunlight that create a path to the dais at the other end of the room. On that dais, the largest beam pours directly onto a towering obsidian throne, the rock absorbing the light in a subtle yet daunting show of power.

But it isn't the throne that sucks away the most light—it's the figure slouched on it. The figure who shields his eyes as if the sun pains him, gripping a staff as tall as I am.

All these years of fearing him, and I've never seen Angra. He rarely, if ever, leaves his palace, never bothers with leading his army or getting his hands dirty. From this distance, I can see the blond curls cascading over his head, so very similar to the man who joined with the Decay in Hannah's vision. They're undeniably related, and it makes me wince. I still don't want to believe that the vision was real.

We get to the middle of the room and stop. I'm sure Angra can hear my heart humming in my throat, could smell my fear as soon as we set foot in his palace. It's so quiet here—there's no distant shuffling of courtiers, no gentle hum of voices in the next room. This fake calm is more frightening than if Angra was raging in anger. He's the eye of a storm, everything around him waiting with growing anticipation for his madness to break.

Herod steps forward. "My king," he says, voice echoing through the empty hall.

Angra stays silent. Herod nods at the guards and I grunt as they chuck me forward, my armor clanking on the floor. I can't suppress my cry, the feeble sound bouncing off the walls.

Herod laughs as I writhe on the obsidian. "I have brought you a token of Winter's weakness."

"The boy?"

Angra's voice stabs at Herod's mistake—I am not Mather, and no matter how much Herod might enjoy toying with me, he failed.

A low growl resonates in Herod's throat. "No. The thief who stole half of the locket."

Boots descend the dais and glide across the floor. I don't move, hands around my torso, eyes closed, neck bent. Sir trained me for this. For Angra, for Spring.

They make decisions; they mold your future. The trick is to find a way to still be you through it all.

Theron's words run through my head, his smile, his gentle surety. I cling to that image, to anything that will help me remember that I am Meira, and they cannot take that away from me.

Angra stops beside me. I can feel him there, a warm presence just beside my huddled body. He bends down, his staff making a heavy clunk as he adjusts it on the floor.

"She's hurt," he says. The booming echo is gone from his voice, reduced to a whisper that rolls over me.

I open my eyes and a desperate wail bubbles in my throat. This man doesn't just look like the king who bonded with the Decay in Hannah's vision—this man *is* that king. The same translucent green eyes, the same pale skin, the same gleam on his face when he tips his head and adjusts his grip on his staff, black through and through, with a hollow ebony orb on its tip. This is the same king.

How is that possible? Could Hannah's visions have been more recent than I thought? No, I *felt* how long ago it was. But Angra doesn't look any older than the man in his twenties he was in Hannah's vision.

I know Angra was the one who led the charge against Winter when it fell sixteen years ago, but this man couldn't have been old enough to ransack our kingdom. Now that I think about it . . . *I don't know who was king before Angra.* Sir's lessons never touched on Spring's history beyond our war with them. Is this mystery that cloaks him part of the Decay? He never leaves Spring. He never shows himself in public. It would be all too easy to hide this power, this immortality, from the world.

I pinch my mouth shut to hold in the wail, my need to scream fighting me like a wild horse pinned inside a gate. If this is all true, what else is he capable of?

Angra stares at me, unconcerned. His pale green irises flicker and his yellow curls bounce when he moves—the same wild, untamed locks of the boy in the paintings. Was that him too? He painted portraits of himself—and a woman?

He tips his head, his mouth lifting as he surveys me. He looks young, calm, filled with something that terrifies me more than Herod's malice—an ancient determination and patience. And around his neck, dangling above a black tunic, hangs the front half of Hannah's locket.

I gasp. It's so close. The silver heart etched with a snow-flake, its shine muted and dull on Angra's skin.

"Would you like to be healed?" he whispers suddenly.

I frown, tearing my eyes away from the locket. He wanted me to see it. He wanted me to know he has it just like he has me, dangling and useless. But I hear his question, and my ribs scream out *Yes!* while the rest of me quivers in the dark, waiting for this all to shatter around me.

Angra leans closer. Madness dances behind his eyes now as he revels in the sight of me writhing at his feet. "You are in pain. Don't you want me to heal you?"

"Go heal the Winterian girl," I manage. "The one your soldier whipped."

Angra smiles. He takes pleasure in me fighting back too.

I don't have a chance to add anything else. Angra's fingers curl around his staff and I'm thrown into a world of searing red, everything collapsing behind a single shriek that echoes off the walls. It's me. I'm screaming, arching on the ground in breathless pain. My chest caves in, every rib cracking and bending under an invisible force that crushes me, presses me into dust. I scream again and all the bones pop back out, realigning and knitting back together. I can feel them healing, the bones itching and tingling, telling me exactly where they run through my torso.

It stops and I roll to the side, mouth open, unable to say anything, do anything. On top of the pain, more certainty makes me hum with fear. If Angra was just a monarch like all the others, and his staff was nothing more than a Royal Conduit, he wouldn't be able to affect me, someone not of his kingdom's bloodline. But he can use his magic to break me, to heal me—so he must have something helping him. Something more powerful.

Something like the Decay.

That thought is like the final blow of a fight, the one that makes me waver toward unconsciousness. Everything Hannah showed me—Angra's true power—his agelessness—

It's real.

"You still wish me to heal the girl?" Angra asks.

I shake my head, a spiraling migraine making the world shift.

Angra leans the staff down so I can peer into its black orb. "You are one of the few who escaped me," he says. "You couldn't have been more than an infant."

He twists his hand and the pressure returns, collapsing on me like a boot pressing on a bug. I draw in a few quick breaths and focus on the light filtering through the ceiling. *Focus, Meira. Don't—*

I'm able to bite back a scream as the first few ribs crack, but it falls out of my mouth as Angra snaps the rest. The scream turns into a pathetic whine as the pressure rises, ribs reshaping and knitting back together with agonizing slowness.

"How, exactly, did a child manage to evade me?"

My ribs heal again. Sweat trickles down my face, and words come in broken gasps. "Two . . . children . . . escaped . . . actually."

He twists his hand again. Quick this time, every bone snapping at once and knitting together in less than a few seconds. Stars flash over my vision, darkness and swirling light.

Angra glares up at Herod. "Where is the boy?"

I choke on Herod's pause. "My men are pursuing him."

The hope in those words makes it impossible to breathe. As long as Mather lives, there's still hope for Winter.

Angra grabs my hair, forcing me to stare up at him. "Your resistance is crumbling. It's only a matter of time before I kill Hannah's son myself."

The hope in my chest flares against his threats. *You're wrong, Angra, because Mather is alive. There is still hope.*

But it snuffs out as quickly as it came, as thoughts collide in my mind—*Sir is dead, and this war is worse than we thought.*

Angra beams. "I thought so."

His hand trails down my horrible, traitorous face, giving away my emotions. As his fingers touch my skin, his image swirls. His face contorts, darkness pulls in, and the blackness of his throne room fades to a milky white. As it did when Hannah touched me, my mind's eye pulls me into a memory not my own.

A field of snow stretches into the distance, frozen white perfection beneath a clear night sky. The moon, a sliver against the speckled black night, sheds light on a small gathering of men and horses. One holds a lantern that casts light onto the black sun breastplates of Angra's guards. And Angra himself, his appearance unchanged from how it is now, sits on a thick warhorse in front of his men. He wears a heavy, black cloak, and his staff sits in a holster on his saddle. . . .

Angra tears his hand off my face. "What did you—"

I stare at him, mouth half open. A voice in the back of my mind urges me to reach out, and I grab Angra's hand with a strength I didn't think I still had. The image returns, stronger now, as though I'm standing next to Angra on one of Winter's fields.

Hooves beat in the distance as three riders come toward us. They stop, the field around us empty but for snow and this clandestine meeting of Spring and Winter.

Hannah pulls her horse forward and dismounts. She wears nothing over her gown but a bloodred cloak, the flow of scarlet on snow a shocking contrast. "Thank you for meeting me."

Angra's horse dances under the unspoken tension in the air. The guards behind Hannah hold weapons, ready to leap to their queen's defense, while Angra's men look furtively at their king for any sign to attack. But Angra just swings one leg over his saddle and dismounts.

"How could I resist, Highness? Especially after your enticing message." Angra steps forward, black cloak swishing through the snow. "You said you had a deal I couldn't refuse."

Hannah folds her hands beneath her cloak and looks up, blue eyes shining in the weak moonlight. "I will lay down my life for my people."

Angra's face flashes with shock. "No riddles. What do you propose?"

The locket pulses white from Hannah's neck before she speaks, her voice steady and sure. "I will let you destroy Winter's conduit and kill me. I will let you end Winter's line."

"If?" Angra's tone is mocking.

"If Spring's army never sets foot in Winter again."

Angra sneers, making my skin crawl. "This doesn't have to do with how few men you have left? I know that our last battle left Winter weakened, but I never thought it would drive you to such desperation. Do you plan to make good on your end now?"

Angra pulls a dagger out of his belt and shoves it against Hannah's throat so quickly I barely see it happen. Her guards fly forward, swords out, and Angra's men ready their weapons. But neither monarch moves, frozen knife to neck with each other.

Hannah waves a hand at the men behind her and they back up. "Yes," she whispers, and a gasp ricochets through them. Yes? She's going to let him kill her now? But Hannah's face doesn't betray any fear, even with Angra's knife moments away from slashing through her throat. "Does this mean we are in agreement?"

"We are. But I wonder, Highness, how far your deal extends." Curling the knife into his palm, he backs up. His eyes slide down Hannah's body and linger on her stomach, his face radiating amusement. "You don't know yet, do you?"

Hannah's hands move beneath her cloak, clutching her stomach as her lips part in confusion. "We have an agreement, Angra. We can end this!"

Angra pulls himself back onto his horse. "We do have a deal."

"Then kill me. Break my locket and kill me. End this!" Hannah is pleading now, her red cloak rippling around her as she steps toward Angra across the snow.

"Don't worry, Your Highness." Angra glares down at her, his green eyes flashing. "I agree to this deal. But I will destroy you when I see fit, when it causes you the most pain."

Hannah's face collapses. "What do you mean?"

Angra smirks. "You aren't the last of your line." And he's gone, plunging his horse across the snow with his soldiers riding hard behind him.

21

HANNAH SURRENDERED.

The truth makes it painful to breathe. Hannah handed herself over to Angra. In Bithai's garden the night of the ball, Noam had been so certain that Hannah had yielded, and Mather had been just as certain that she had fought against Angra until the end. Noam was right, though. She did surrender—but not in the way he meant. It was a sacrifice, not helpless submission. A sacrifice like the one Mather tried to make for us.

Tell me how to save them. . . .

In my dream, Hannah asked her conduit to show her how to save her people. Is that what it told her? That the only way to protect them would be to die? But she didn't know she was pregnant, and that the end to Winter's royal line meant murdering her son too.

Angra's staff barrels through the air and slams into my cheek, making my head smack into the floor and roar with electric fingers of pain.

"You brought magic into my palace, general." His voice cracks through the air like his soldier's whip.

Magic? Terror lances through me—terror that Angra will take away whatever magic source I have, terror that I could actually *have* a magic source at all. *The stone? Hannah? Whatever it is, how am I using it? Hannah said she couldn't speak to me once I got into Spring, that Angra would watch me with his dark magic. Was it really the lapis lazuli then?*

Herod coughs a laugh. "Magic? She's harmless."

Angra swings his staff at Herod and knocks him to the ground before whirling on me. "Whatever remnant of magic you have, you're out of luck, girl." Angra stomps forward and pulls me roughly to my feet. He makes sure to only touch my armor, not allowing skin-to-skin contact again. "Your weakened magic cannot win here."

Angra would never have been satisfied with ending Winter's line, with breaking the locket, killing Hannah and Mather and letting us go about our lives. He wouldn't have been satisfied until we are where we are now, his slaves, Spring standing on the fading carcass of Winter. Even Hannah's sacrifice, something so much larger than anything I could ever do, wouldn't have changed anything. But *why*? What was all of this for?

"What do you want from us?" The question spills out of

my mouth, shaking and feeble.

Angra releases me, takes a step back. "Power," he says like that explains everything.

I shake my head, fighting the urge to collapse in gasping sobs. "Winter isn't powerful! We're nothing now."

Angra purses his lips like I'm a toddler throwing a tantrum. "Winter will not stand in my way," he whispers half to himself. He nods at Herod before I can decode his senseless explanation. How are we standing in the way of anything?

He's insane. There is no reason for what he's done, nothing we can do to satisfy him. And knowing that makes everything so much more terrifying, because it means there is no end to his horror. There is no box it can be contained in, no way to predict what he'll do.

He just wants to watch us bleed.

"Strip her armor," Angra tells Herod. "Rid her of anything she has."

I lurch back as Herod stands, grabs my arm, his face reddening, spit flying from his mouth. A rabid dog leashed to Angra's wrist. He shoves his face into my hair, his breath warm and heavy from the battle and the long march to Spring.

"I'll teach you your place," Herod growls as he undoes the straps on my armor, the mess of padding and dented metal clattering to Angra's floor. I'm left in a stained cotton undershirt, tattered pants held up by a fraying leather belt, and my worn boots. I hadn't realized how much of my strength lay in having a layer of metal between Herod and me. My knees buckle, my insides rolling over like a whirlpool.

He'll find the stone. He'll take it away. Then he'll destroy me.

Herod's fingers grope across my neck, my arms, trailing down my body as he searches for objects. His fingers leave numbness in their wake—until he brushes over the lapis lazuli.

"Don't—" I start, my body twitching involuntarily.

Herod smirks up at me as he eases out the stone. I fling myself forward, my fist sliding through air, but he easily ducks my exhausted attempt at fighting and jams his arm back into me. I crash onto the obsidian floor with a dull thud, pain cutting through my elbow and hip.

But none of that holds my attention more than the thoughtless way Herod chucks the lapis lazuli ball to the dais, where it clatters at the feet of his master. All I can do is stare at the stone, that brilliant blue piece of rock, and see the day Mather gave it to me. How certain he was that I should have it, a remnant of our lost kingdom. I never thanked him. Not enough.

My insides crumble as Angra curls his fingers around the stone, closing his eyes for a moment as if trying to absorb its magic himself. He looks at me, a grin tearing across his face. "Was this the magic, girl?" he asks. "If so, it's empty now. And if it wasn't what you're using, believe me, I will find the source and rip it out of you."

His words break my panic. It's not magic? It was all just Hannah? One last vision before she has to leave me alone in Spring? Loneliness swells inside me, cutting through every nerve, leaving me holding back sobs in the horrible nothingness around me.

History, the past, whatever Decay Hannah fears—it doesn't matter anymore. Because it's gone, every bit of it wrapped up in Angra as he grips the stone in a powerful fist. There's nothing left to help me now.

Herod grabs me off the floor, the look on his face telling me he isn't done yet, not this easily.

Breathe, Meira. Don't think, don't analyze, don't even react.

Angra relaxes into his throne. "Not now, general," he orders, and I freeze as if I know what he's going to say. I do, don't I? I've known since we first entered Abril.

"Take her to them," Angra growls. "I want them to break her before you do."

Herod pauses next to me, his disappointment silencing him as he flings me around and the two guards march me back down the dark hall.

The dusk sky seems bright compared to Angra's palace, even with the light streaming into his throne room and the encroaching darkness out here. I blink it away and notice, heart dropping, that the Winterian slaves are gone. Only their shovels remain, sticking out of the dirt. I have a feeling I'm about to find out where they were taken.

"Put her with the rest. Oh, and Meira?"

I keep marching down the stone path, my body jolting with each step. I'm healed, but Angra's magic made me unsteady, wobbling with each footfall like a leaf on the wind.

"I will see you again," Herod calls after me. "Very soon."

He laughs, voice fading as he returns to the palace. The doors slam and the smallest bit of tension unwinds from my muscles. He's gone, for now.

The guards take me through Abril's slums, the buildings getting worse and worse the deeper we go. Rotted wood collapsing into rooms, piles of rancid garbage littering street corners. Spring citizens watch us as we pass, smirking at the newest Winterian prisoner. But the lives around them—their collapsing houses, the dirt smudged on their children's faces. How can they be proud of destroying one kingdom when their king doesn't even care for his own?

The soldiers and I reach a barrier of spiked wire that vanishes into the city. Its high walls cut off the slum from what I can only assume is a—

"Winterian work camp. Welcome home," one guard grunts, and unlocks the gate.

It takes all of my remaining strength to keep walking, one foot in front of the other, as they close the gate behind us. These aren't even buildings; they're cells. Just like Herod said. Cages with three solid sides, a roof, and one gated door, small and cramped and stacked on top of each other like blocks. Some are empty but most hold hollow, vacant Winterian prisoners watching with soulless eyes. They don't care. How could they? Angra's beaten any care out of them, left them to rot in these hovels until he needs them for work.

The soldiers shuffle me down the long row of cages. Dust coats my boots, the wind sings in my ears like a desperate wail. Cages stretch for rows and rows, so many that my stomach aches with nausea again.

Three other camps like this sit throughout Spring. Angra really did imprison an entire kingdom, enacted the worst dominance over his victims by turning them into slaves. As a child it was always impossible to imagine—so many hundreds of people locked away? But now . . .

How did we let this happen?

The guards shove me into an empty cage on the bottom row. There's nothing in here, no cot or food or furniture. Just a dirt-covered space with a view of more cages across from me.

"Don't get comfortable," one guard spits. "We'll be back for you."

I glare at them through the bars, fingers tight on the iron. "Go ahead and try," I murmur, but they're gone, the newest Winterian slave already forgotten.

I'm alone now. And I don't have to bite my tongue or stay strong or not let them see me break. That sad freedom rushes at me, and everything that's happened, everything I've seen and felt, bubbles up in my throat. I back to the wall and slide to the ground, pulling my knees up and burying my face against them. The Winterians across from me are watching. They're gaping and wondering and whispering, *That is one who lived out there while we were in here. Why hasn't anyone saved us?*

Because we failed. Because I let Sir die. Because our only ally is rolling in the desecration of their own kingdom. Because we only have half of Hannah's locket, and it took us this long to even get that. Because Angra is so much more powerful than we ever knew.

My shoulders tremble and I pull myself tighter, fighting sobs. Sir trained me better than this, but I don't have any strength left to keep myself stoic and calm. Mather was always the one who was able to hide his feelings no matter the situation. And if Mather is on the run, and Theron, and Bithai fallen, and Angra as ancient and evil as Hannah said—I'll probably die in here.

I force a soundless scream into the cave of my legs, gripping my hair and squeezing into myself. No. This isn't how it was supposed to end—

The lock on the door clicks, but I can't find it in me to care. Let Angra come for me, or Herod even. There's nothing else they can take from me.

Feet shuffle in and the door locks again. Someone's in here with me.

A second passes. Two. Whoever it is kneels beside me. I keep my eyes shut, sniffing in the darkness of my knees, and stiffen when a hand unfolds on my shoulder.

I look up. It's the Winterians from the palace, the two men and the girl who got whipped in the dirt. She has the marks on her arms to prove it, jagged cuts caked in dried blood. But she's smiling, a comforting smile, and light shines deep behind the bruises around her eyes.

She drops a half-empty bowl of stew on the ground, forgotten in the way she stares at me. "You're here," she breathes like she's just as shocked as I am. Like this is some dream come to life, and she's afraid if she doesn't say it, I'll vanish.

The two men sit behind her, their eyes on me, a dull flicker of interest hiding behind their wounds as they sip at their own bowls of stew. They're more wary of me than the girl is, but the weight of their lives sits even heavier on them.

I exhale, inhale, still unable to believe the girl touching me is real. They're all real, and here, and alive. Seeing them from a distance was hard to accept, but this is impossible.

The girl says nothing else. She sits next to me, our hips touching, and curls her arm around my shoulders. She's so thin that I'm afraid I'll break her if I touch her at all. But we just sit in silence, the men staring through the bars, the girl holding me or me holding her.

As sunlight fades over the work camp, a small voice

resonates from the back of my mind, something that makes the horrors not quite so overwhelming:

You will understand how to use all this when you are ready.

It really was Hannah, talking to me. And if she thought it was important to tell me about the past, to try to help me figure out something, then maybe there's still a way to win this.

The girl shifts. She's asleep now, her head on my shoulder and her breathing slow. I lean my head onto hers and close my eyes.

Sir and Mather and Theron might be lost, but the Winterians aren't. And as long as they live, I'm not entirely alone.

THAT NIGHT, SLIPPERY, fleeting dreams suck me down like a hungry wave. Dizzy and disorienting, soulless eyes and faces from my past, and darkness, always darkness. From that blackness come monsters, clawing fingers and bloody teeth lunging for my throat—

I fly awake, every nerve tight. But there are no monsters here. At least, not in this cage.

My panic fades a little at the sight of the three people staring at me. The two men, both at least ten years older than me, and the girl. Her blue eyes gleam, set in a sunken, pale face, and she studies me like she can see my whole life story written across my forehead.

"I'm Nessa," she says, and points over her shoulder. "Conall and Garrigan, my brothers."

Garrigan nods but Conall keeps his eyes level with mine.

His expression is a vibrant contrast to Nessa's—she is open and willing, he is closed and decided. Decided, from the look of it, that I am just as much a danger as the Spring soldiers moving around our cage.

It's morning.

I jump up, back scraping along the rough wall. Will Angra send for me? Will he let Herod torture me into submission, until everything about the past sixteen years comes tumbling out of my mouth? My chest fills with lead-hot pressure, pinching off air.

"I'm Meira," I manage around a tongue that feels more sand than anything, my eyes darting between Nessa and the door, waiting for soldiers to burst inside and drag me out.

"If they were going to take you so soon, they never would have brought you here to begin with," Garrigan offers. He holds some of Conall's distrust, but his face softens, offering me the smallest bit of kindness.

"How can you know that?" Conall snaps, watching the door.

"The same way I do," Nessa declares proudly, taking my hand. "She's here for a reason."

Conall turns a glare to me, like I'm the one who made her say that. I don't have the strength to pull away from her hand, though, needing her small bit of comfort, and I just stare at him until he swings his gaze back to the door.

"Where did you come from?" Nessa asks, the question

popping out of her mouth like she's been holding it in since I got here. "Winter? No, of course not—they say no one lives there anymore. One of the other Seasons?"

"I was in Cordell before I came here," I say. Conall's glare makes me feel guilty for talking to her, like any word I say will only strengthen her slowly growing hope. Nessa still looks at me with a hint of caution, but the brightness in her eyes is . . . beautiful. It's hard not to want to make her happy, and just that word lights up her whole face.

"Cordell," she echoes, and releases my hand to face Garrigan. "That's a Rhythm, right?"

Garrigan's mouth twitches in a smile, cracking his face like he doesn't do it often. "Our Nessa's going to be a world traveler one day," he says, and I can't miss the pride that swells in him. Pride in his little sister, in her ability to still dream beyond these bars.

"Or a seamstress," she amends, her face flushing red. Whatever blip of happiness she managed to hold on to vanishes, and she looks at me with a sad shrug. "Like our mother."

"Quiet," Conall growls, a bite of warning as keys rattle in our door.

I pin my body to the back wall. No matter how Nessa and Garrigan tried to reassure me, or how uncaring I was last night at the thought of Angra coming for me, dread still churns in my stomach, a flicker of survival that's impossible to snuff out entirely. They can't take me. Not until I figure out . . . something. Some way to escape a long, slow death at Angra's hands, a way to help the others around me escape the same fate.

The door swings open. Conall and Garrigan march into the sun and Nessa grabs my arm. "Don't worry," she whispers, and guides me forward. "It'll be all right. It'll be—"

"You." A soldier turns from shouting at Conall and Garrigan to watch me emerge from the cage, his eyes a dark sort of greedy, and my stomach turns.

But the soldier nods toward the end of the road where the uncaged Winterians have gathered. "With the rest for now."

Relief surges through me. Angra hasn't called for me today.

Nessa pulls me forward and shock fills me up like it'd been waiting outside the cage for me all night.

This is the first time I've seen the Winterians of the Abril work camp. Of *any* work camp.

More Winterians join us from the second layer of cages, gathering into a haphazard cluster to march down the road, dust swirling around our shuffling feet. Dozens of people crowd around, frail bodies in tattered rags, clothing brown from years of sweat and dirt. Children too. If Angra had wanted to simply slaughter all Winterians, he would have done so long ago—it would have been a kinder fate. But instead he keeps them locked up, letting families grow and generations spawn in captivity. It's a cruel victory to show dominance over another by destroying them—but it's crueler still to do so by destroying their families.

Winterian children watch me as they stand stoically beside their parents. Their faces say they've learned not to show weakness. Weaknesses get used until all you can do is scream at the unfairness of a life like this, a life of living in cages stacked atop one another, of growing up in a place where you aren't even seen as a person. A life of waiting in torment for the twenty-five mythical survivors to set everyone free.

I meet a woman's eyes. She's Dendera's age, her top lip curling at me, and I flinch back. A man beside her echoes her grimace, and another beside them, so many looks of derision that I feel no safer here than in Angra's palace.

Misery wraps around me, hot waves of disgust at myself, at their lives, at everything that happened to our kingdom. *How long did it take them to stop hoping we'd free them? How quickly did Angra beat the hope of escape from their minds?*

How quickly will he beat the same hope from me?

Looking at the faces around me, at their sixteen-year-long suffering . . . what could I possibly do to stop any of this? What could *any* of us have done—Sir or Alysson or Mather or anyone? It's too big, the wounds too deep.

A soldier cracks his whip into the crowd, throwing a few slower Winterians to their knees. One elderly woman, two old men. Red welts line their arms but we hurry on, pulled by the current of fear. We should fight against the soldiers who whipped them to the ground, stand up for our countrymen and the injustice Spring did to them.

We should have done a lot of things.

Nessa squeezes my hand between both of hers. She hasn't stopped hoping, and any wariness she feels pales next to her faith. I almost prefer the glares, the lingering snarls of the others. Their anger is understandable, something I can accept. But Nessa—

Did I look at Sir like that?

The question flies through my mind, a string of words that wraps around my throat and squeezes off air. All the refugees looked at Sir like that, didn't we? He was our source of hope. He was the beacon that would lead us to freeing our people, to getting our kingdom back.

And he died. Just like that. Our hope snuffed out in one swift and careless moment.

I tremble under thoughts of him, his shadows in my mind making every part of me ache and writhe. I can't be Nessa's hope. I can't let her think I'm any more capable than anyone else, because I can die just as easily. I can't do to her what Sir did to me.

We stop when we reach a crowded gate. Soldiers sort through us at the front, marching groups off to various areas of the city for work.

"My brothers and I will be back in the palace grounds," Nessa whispers, her hand tightening on mine. "I don't know where you'll be. I don't know if—"

I force a smile. "It's all right."

Nessa's lips twitch and she nods.

Minutes later we're at the front of the line. Conall and Garrigan grunt numbers to a soldier by the entrance. 1-3219 and 1-3218. No names here. Angra stripped them of everything—country, home, life. Why not their names too?

The soldier orders them to the group bound for the palace. Nessa, unwilling to let go of my hand, approaches the same soldier.

"1-2072," she says, and the soldier consults a list.

"Palace grounds." He glances at me and squints, sizing up my appearance next to Nessa. I'm too healthy, too well fed. He checks the list and cocks one eyebrow.

"Angra has something special for you," he says. "To the wall, R-19."

R-19. R—Refugee? Refugee 19. Because I'm the nineteenth Winterian refugee who Angra will kill. Herod probably saw Sir die in Bithai, so he was the eighteenth. Gregg and Crystalla, seventeen and sixteen.

Nessa leads me past the soldier into the groups of sectioned-off Winterians. When a few people stand between the soldiers and us, she pulls my ear to her mouth. "The wall is where they send those they wish to push beyond their limit," she whispers, her fingers digging into my hand. "Work but don't strain yourself—just make it look like you're working hard. Maybe you can get through without—"

"Nessa." I shush her. Her concern hurts, a heavy expectation I don't know if I can fulfill.

"You didn't come here just to die," she exhales, half a question, half a promise.

I close my eyes. *Why did I come here?*

Conall puts a hand on Nessa's shoulder. "We're leaving."

Nessa pulls away and marches to join Garrigan. I suck in a breath when Conall's shadow shifts, his tall frame looming over me.

He narrows his eyes when Nessa gets out of earshot. "We've tried escaping," he growls. "Climbing the fences, fighting off guards, digging under the walls. All it results in is more death. The last ones who came promised rescue but vanished before they could do anything; they acted like we hadn't already tried *everything*. Nessa wept for weeks when our hope left with them. I won't see her go through that again."

Gregg and Crystalla. My jaw tightens. "I don't want her to go through that either."

"What you want doesn't matter here. The sooner you realize that, the better."

"I know."

Conall's eyebrow lifts sardonically. "Good luck, R-19."

He turns and joins his brother and sister in the group meant for the palace. He doesn't look back, doesn't care that I'm left standing alone in the sun. Why should he? I'm just one sixteen-year-old girl. I wouldn't believe in me either. I *don't* believe in me. But as Nessa starts up the road with her group, she looks back, her eyes flashing with hope.

Maybe this is what Angra wanted. For me to instill false hope in them, to raise them up and shatter them even further. To taunt them with escape, then kill me in front of them.

But it doesn't matter what Angra wants. Conall was right—it doesn't even matter what I want anymore. All that matters now is surviving.

Soldiers lead us to the southern edge of Abril and out of the city via a small gate. As it groans over us, we're shoved into such a harshly different world that I pause for a breath.

The wall is a jagged protrusion of black rock that shoots away from Abril into fields of slaughtered forest. Stumps of cherry trees litter the landscape, making way for the newest addition to Angra's city. This field of stumps, dirt, and piles of black rock is even more barren and hopeless than Abril itself. A testament to what it takes to spread Angra's kingdom—nothing must remain, no plants, no sign of life. Everything must be dead to make way for Spring.

I approach one of the black rock piles, leather straps sitting in a mound next to it. They're holsters that a few Winterians latch around their shoulders, and then others load chunks of rock into the cradles against their spines.

"Get to work!" a soldier shouts, and cracks a whip above our heads. I grab a holster and slide it on. As soon as I do, a heavy chunk of black rock is nestled against my back.

"Up the ramps," the rock-giver whispers. His aged eyes have the same flicker of curious hope as Nessa's, but he bends to lift another rock from the pile and load up the next in line.

I shift the rock against my back and march for the ramps. Eight stories of platforms stretch into the air, linked by zigzagging ramps that take lines of Winterians up and down the wall-in-progress. The platforms are all made of the same questionable wood as the slums, the kind that could snap in a strong breeze. But if they do break, a few Spring soldiers will be dragged down with us. Some small justice.

I almost laugh at the thought. Justice would be the Winterians hurling these lumps of black rock at the Spring soldiers. Justice would be us sprinting for the field up ahead, the section of Spring that isn't yet closed off from Abril.

The rock grates against my shoulder blades when I pause on a ramp, hovering far above the ground. That field *is* close. Vibrant green crops billow in the wind, nearly ready for harvest. Proof that Angra uses his conduit for something other than evil, however small that is. The wall's purpose is to stretch around this barren section of earth and widen Abril to that field's edge. Soldiers stand between us and it, but for now, for this moment—there is one way out of Abril.

Conall's words bounce through my mind. *We've tried escaping. Climbing the fences, fighting off guards, digging under walls. All it results in is more death.*

I hesitate. If they've tried . . . then I shouldn't? No. I have to, if not for them, then for me. I'm trapped here as much as they are.

If I can get out beyond the soldiers, I can sneak out of Spring and talk to Hannah again. Or I can go back to Cordell and find Mather and Dendera and the others.

The man in front of me shifts the rock against his back as he takes one more step up. But something in his step, or his weight, or the way he jostles the rock makes him teeter forward, his thin boot snagging on a jagged plank of wood. The wood tears through fabric and flesh, cutting apart a section of his foot and spilling blood in a dark pool on the platform.

The man pauses. Half a heartbeat, half a breath. Barely long enough to even absorb what happened, but in that moment his face spasms in a wince of pain. In its wake, he flicks his eyes to the nearest soldier up on the platform, and just when I realize I'm holding my breath . . .

The soldier whips his head to the man. His eyes drop to the blood trail, to the man's still-twisted face of pain. "The work too much for you?" the soldier asks, a dare in his voice.

I open my mouth to speak, to do something that might let the man fade into the background. As he turns and heads up the next ramp, the soldier yanks the man around, spinning him on the dry wood. The man swings out, caught off balance by the black stone, arms flailing to regain his balance. But it's too late, the movement too sporadic, the rock too large.

The man wavers on the edge of the platform, five stories in the air. His hands claw in empty desperation, looking for purchase as the black rock in his holster shifts, moves, drags him back. The closest thing to him, the only thing he can grab, is the soldier.

I fly forward, air stuck in my dry throat, one hand leaving my holster to reach out like I might be able to stop this. But as gravity takes hold, the soldier smiles, lifts one foot, and plants a firm kick in the center of the man's chest.

A soundless scream boils in my mouth as the man topples from the platform. His body plummets through the air, the black rock dragging him down and down, soaring past the bottom five platforms in painfully slow motion. He smacks into the dry earth below, a puff of dust and debris obscuring his crippled corpse from view.

I'm frozen there, trapped against the platform. But no one else flinches. No one cries out that their husband or brother or son just fell to his death. They just keep moving around me, trudging up the platforms and ramps, walking like they can erase the man's memory with each footfall.

Someone bumps into me as they pass and I'm dragged back into the current of mindless work, pulling me past the soldier, his eyes flashing at the body so far below.

The field in the distance thrashes in a breeze I can't feel from here. No one would follow if I tried to escape. They'd just fall through the air, resigned to the fact that they never had a chance of winning. Or they'd be slaughtered in the wake of my feeble escape.

My vision blurs, but I keep walking. I keep the image of the man's face in my mind, hold it against my impulse to run as fast as I can, to kill as many of the soldiers as possible.

I glance at the ground below, at the dust clearing to reveal the man's body morphed into a disturbing, haphazard splotch on the dirt. Something wells up in me. Something dangerous and crippling and deadly, something rising from the part of me that flinches whenever Winter's conduit is mentioned and no one asks the questions I'm always thinking:

What if it isn't enough? What if nothing we do is enough?

But there is no other option—either we keep trying or our kingdom ceases to exist.

As the day drags on, the temperature rises to the point where my eyes start to swim around in my head, sweat making everything slick. Stretches of time flash past in which I swear I'm back in the Rania Plains, traipsing behind Sir as we make our way toward Cordell.

Damn my intolerance to heat. I will not give Angra the satisfaction of fainting. He will not get to see me die so soon.

The work too much for you today?

I bite away the memory. Everyone around me seems to react to the heat the same way I do, stumbling, gasping in the stuffy air. They don't do more than that, though; there's no complaining or collapsing. No matter how it goes against our Winterian blood, they've almost gotten used to the heat of Spring.

By noon, I'm relieved to see that we get a break.

Almost relieved.

The gate leading into Abril creaks open. The Winterians standing in the rock line around me drop their holsters; the rest file off the ramps to stand around us. I follow suit, eyes darting toward whatever is coming at us from Abril.

Winterian children. Some barely old enough to speak let alone work, all hobbling into the work site with jugs of sloshing water. They spread out among the workers and offer up their burdens, wide blue eyes gleaming from hollow faces, thin arms trembling under the thick clay jugs.

A boy not much older than four or five approaches my line of workers and sets his jug on the ground. He dips a ladle in and lifts it to the person closest to him, a man Sir's age who slurps down mouthfuls of water. The boy repeats the process for each person in line until he gets to me.

"No water for her—Angra's orders!" a soldier behind us shouts, cracking his whip beside the boy's feet. The boy jumps, water splattering over his hands and splashing onto the dirt. His blue eyes dart up to mine as he braces for the impact of the soldier's next blow.

I fly back, more from instinct than rational thought. Rational thought vanished the moment I saw water, and desperate thirst reared up instead. All I can see is that jug, but I take another step back. I don't need water. I don't need to draw attention to anyone else.

"No," I croak. "He's right. None for me."

The soldier, whip held at the ready, frowns at my retreat. But I turn, grab my holster, and close my eyes when another chunk of black rock is loaded against my spine. The boy moves back to work, water spilling over the brim of his jug. No pain, no repercussions. No water either. As long as I bow my head and take it, there won't be trouble.

That's all I can do. Stay out of the way, make sure I don't bring trouble to people who have already suffered so much until I can do—*what?*

Soldiers tossed the dead man's body away hours ago, leaving a bloody splotch of dirt next to the platform entrance. I walk through it, staring at the dried blood, feeling the boy's eyes on me, just another body in Spring's arsenal of workers—like the man who fell to his death, a vessel the soldiers destroy for sport.

Dizzy thirst makes me trip, but I keep walking. *Just one more step, Meira. Just one more.*

23

WE WORK UNTIL nightfall.

As the sun drops over Abril's walls, a bell sounds, pulling the Winterians down the ramps. We drop our holsters
in a pile and leave the unused rocks for tomorrow's work.
The wall is a bit taller now, but feeling accomplished for
building this city is as likely as feeling indebted for the
measly stew we're given upon our return to camp.

I slurp mine down along with a mug of water and scurry
away before someone can punish me for getting nourish-
ment now too. When was my last meal? Breakfast in Bithai
before the battle? Whenever it was, it was too long ago, and
my stomach isn't pleased with the surge of nutrients.

"You're still here!" Nessa cries when a soldier pushes me
inside our cage. She leans forward from her seat between
Conall and Garrigan, her brothers too busy over their own

bowls to care that I survived the day. "Did you get food? Do you need more?" She lifts her bowl of half-eaten stew up to me.

A spurt of laughter catches in my throat. She's sacrificing her food for me, when I probably ate more in Bithai than she's eaten in her entire life.

I slide to the ground, back scraping along the wall. "Keep it. I'm fine."

Conall's face flashes with the briefest show of surprise. He expected me to take food from her, someone much worse off than I've ever been? I stare back at him. Did I come off as selfish, or did he just assume that's how I'd be?

I shift in the dirt, my stomach clenching even more uncomfortably around the stew. I probably did come off as selfish. That's what I've been all along, isn't it? Not wanting to be a marriage pawn, even if Winter needed the ally. Wanting to go on missions, even if someone stronger and faster and more skilled than me could have done the job better.

Before I can answer whatever question Nessa just asked, my eyelids sink down, pulled by the weight of all those rocks I lugged up the ramps today. Somewhere distant, Nessa whispers to her brothers and other Winterians murmur cautious conversations masked by night.

She's here, another refugee. And she survived the first day.

I survived today. Others did not.

Days pass. Days of up and down the ramps, of hastily eaten stew, of falling asleep as Nessa and her brothers watch me warily from the other side of the cage. Some nights Nessa talks to me, asks questions about my life. I tell her what I can until Conall's glare becomes physically painful; then I stop, curl into a ball in the corner, and try to sleep. Try, because their voices always keep me awake.

"You shouldn't get attached," Conall chastises so often his words are branded on my mind.

"I don't care. *You* should see if you're still capable of getting attached to anyone," Nessa shoots back.

I'm not sure who I agree with. Conall, that no one should get too attached to me, because who knows how long I'll live, or Nessa, that it doesn't matter. The repetition of work and misery makes it impossible to do more than poke at these ideas feebly.

Until my ninth night here.

A knot of terror locks itself in my throat, tasting like blood. I burst awake, a nightmare black as death chasing every bit of sleep from my body. There's something here, with us, in this room. Something dark and horrible and—

Nessa starts from where she crouches in front of me, dust puffing around her boots. "You're dreaming!"

I fly back, body slamming into the cage's wall. Nessa swings around on her knees while her brothers stand back, eyeing me as if I chanted in my sleep.

"We are Winter," Conall states.

I frown. "What?"

He smiles. It's faint, beaten down by a lifetime of torture.

Nessa stands, offering me her hand. I take it, afraid to put too much weight on her frail bones.

Conall and Garrigan move to the back corner of our cage, the part blanketed in the darkest shadows of late night. The camp is quiet in the exhaustion of a day's work, the closest soldier the one who walks along the barbed fence.

I move to the cage's door, my fingers wrapping around the iron bars. The lock that holds us in is as big as my palm, thick and old, and I touch the back of my braid absently. I don't have any lock picks there. Would I pick it, though, if I could? I haven't done anything to escape in the days I've been here. I can't decide if it's worth the risk—to myself and to everyone around me.

It's so quiet now, so still I can almost forget everything else. No whips or shouts of pain or hollow faces scrunched with impending death. Just black sky and stars and—

Something creaks behind me and I spin around.

A door.

Garrigan pulls it up out of the ground, dust and rocks tumbling off the old planks of wood. Below it, dropping into the earth, a hollow tunnel falls into darkness.

"What is that?" I breathe.

Nessa looks at me over her shoulder. "They want to meet you."

Conall steps up to the hole first and plummets into the

blackness. A thump tells me he didn't fall far, and sure enough, two hands shoot back up for Nessa. She drops forward and vanishes into the dark, and only Garrigan remains with me.

"Where does it lead?"

He motions to the hole and offers a weak shrug. "You'll be fine," he promises. In his eyes is a perfect blend of Nessa's hope and Conall's sternness. Garrigan is the glue that keeps them from tearing each other apart.

I slide across the ground. My boots nudge dirt into the tunnel, a blackness so complete I can only feel Conall staring up at me, can't find his eyes or his outline.

Two hands reach for me. "Come."

I exhale and fall forward, letting his thick hands catch me and set me on a dirt floor. The door thuds shut above us and I hear Garrigan smooth dirt back over it, the quiet swishing of pebbles on wood the only noise.

Fingers find mine, but they're not Conall's. This hand is delicate, cold, like a porcelain doll come to life. Nessa leads me to the side of the tunnel and presses my hand flat on the rock, jagged edges of dirt and thick boulders protruding in awkward bumps. Should I—

I stop. There's something on the wall, uneven ruts filling almost every smooth space.

"What is it?" I put both hands to the rock and follow the carvings. They're everywhere, twisting down and up, shooting over the low ceiling and darting across the floor.

Nessa fumbles with something beside me and a quick scraping noise brings a flicker of fire to life. She lifts the candle, her pale face glowing yellow in the light.

Conall watches us from the perimeter of the candle's light, his disapproving glower a heavy weight. "We don't have time."

"Hush," Nessa tells him. "She needs to see it. And it's good for us to see it too."

That makes him quiet, and his eyes dart to the walls around us, his expression relaxing ever so slightly. I exhale, my own tense muscles unwinding.

"They're memories," Nessa continues, her eyes on the ceiling. "Memories of Winter."

Thousands of words curl around this narrow hall, filling the rocks with jagged sentences, stretching all the way down to a door at the end.

One paragraph has been etched in black stone, the words worn with age.

My daughter's name was Jemmia. She wanted to go to Yakim to attend Lord Aldred University. She was nineteen.

Another is carved into the rock itself.

On the first day of proper winter, every Winterian would gather for a festival in their town's market. We would eat frozen strawberries and ground ice flavored with wine to celebrate winter's birth the world over.

More and more:

Havena Green worked at the Tadil Mine in the Klaryn Mountains.

My father died a soldier, fighting on the front lines when Spring attacked. His name was Trevor Longsfield and his wife was Georgia Longsfield.

All Winterians are cradled in bowls of snow on the fifth day after their birth. I've never seen a Winterian baby cry during this ritual—in fact, they seem to enjoy it.

Winterian wedding ceremonies are held during the first morning snow. The bride and groom drink from a cup of water, and the water that remains is frozen in a perfect circle to represent unity. The circle is buried underneath the ceremony site.

A duchess of Ventralli visited once and complained that Jannuari's frigid air made our kingdom unbearable. Her butler promptly responded, "My lady, Spring has been trying to change Winter's chill for centuries. I doubt you can do it faster than them."

My eyes swim with words carved into the wall, words curved around impenetrable boulders and faded with age. All of them soaking into me, spiraling around in the flickering candlelight. I've heard some of these traditions before in Sir's lectures—frozen berries and celebrating the first day of proper winter. But the rest, babies in bowls of snow, each individual history . . .

I wish I had known this. I wish I had had these words with me every moment of my life.

"When Angra attacked, he burned everything, archives and histories and books. So we decided to record our history in the tunnels." Nessa cradles the candle in her palm, the light casting an ethereal glow around her body.

"Tunnels?" I look at her, my forehead pinching.

"When they made the Abril work camp," she says, "they did so on an existing slum in the center of the city. Winterians built it, though—Spring soldiers just supervised. Lots of the original buildings had basements, cellars that we left intact. They became tunnels for us, a secret world the Spring soldiers didn't know about. All the tunnels lead—"

"Out?"

As soon as I ask it, I hear my own mistake. If the tunnels lead out, no one would be here at all. I look away from Nessa and Conall before either can respond.

Nessa steps up beside me, her fingers going to an etching where she traces the first letter. "These tunnels offer their own type of escape. Conall and Garrigan taught me to read by these carvings. It's important to remember them," she tells me, and Conall, who looks a little less annoyed. "Just in case."

"Just in case of what?" I ask, but I already know.

When Nessa speaks again, her voice is sad. "Just in case no one who remembers survives."

I turn away so she can't see the tears brimming my eyes. Because when a sixteen-year-old boy becomes Winter's king, and there are no records to show him Winter's history, we will have to rely on our people's fading memories to show us what to do.

Those seem like trivial problems, though. Problems we would be grateful to have, normal issues about the competency of rulers and the succession of traditions. Not like whether our people will even survive to have traditions.

I run my hand along one line, wishing I knew which person had written what, and that I could memorize these words so I could tell Mather. Were he and I placed in bowls of snow when we were five days old?

One last etching catches me, the letters coated in dust.

Someday we will be more than words in the dark.

It's hard to walk under all of this, but Nessa takes my hand and pulls me forward. Clearly this isn't our destination. How can something be more important than this? I want to stay down here, memorize every single word until I can't think or feel or breathe anything else—

But we reach the door, a few sad pieces of old wood nailed together, and Conall swings it open, showing me something that is infinitely more important than words in the dark.

People in the light.

Nessa blows out her candle and I squint in the sudden brightness, one hand up to shield my eyes. She pulls me through and Conall throws the door against the tunnel, closing us inside a great circular room carved into the earth, rocks poking out of the walls and floor and ceiling, too big or cumbersome to move during construction. Candles stand in clumps of long-melted wax, mountains of creamy white that flicker with orange peaks. They're everywhere, filling every crevice, giving the room a delicate glow. More doors lead out all around the walls, like the room is the center of a wheel and the tunnels are spokes. From those doors, spilling into and filling up the cavernous room, come more Winterians.

"Ow." Nessa pulls at my hand. My fingers have dug into her fragile arm for support.

"Sorry." I jerk away. "What is this place?"

"We carved this room to connect to all the remaining basements and cellars." Conall answers instead of Nessa, his deep voice stoic. "We're in the middle of Abril, too far to tunnel out under the city itself, so this seemed like the best alternative. Had to keep busy during sixteen years of imprisonment somehow."

I swallow. "Why are we here?"

He flashes a tight glare at me. "You survived the first few days; they want to meet you. However stupid it is to have so many people down here at once." He pauses as he reevaluates my question. "But the better question is, why are *you* here?"

I stare at him, eyes hard, and say the only thing I can. "I should have been here all along."

Conall pulls back, his brows lifting.

"Is this her?"

The voice echoes through the room, silencing the murmurings around us. All eyes are on me, and I wonder how long they've been staring. Probably from the moment they got here. With no soldiers to cower from, no punishment to fear, they're free to gape and wonder and hope, so long as they're in the confines of this haven they've built.

The owner of the voice pushes through the crowd. It belongs to a woman, her old frame hunched under sixteen years of hard labor. But the moment her clear blue eyes lock on mine, she straightens, throwing off any exhaustion.

"You," she whispers. Her withered fingers extend when she reaches me, and she puts one hand on either side of my face. She stares at me, through me, seeing something deep behind my eyes that relaxes her face in satisfaction. "Yes," she says. "You are Meira."

I pull out of her hands. "How do you know that?"

The woman smiles. "I know everyone who escaped Angra that night. The last ones who came here told us about all of you."

Crystalla and Gregg. I back up as if I can get away from the pang of memory. The woman's face is serene, calm. She still hopes for rescue too.

The Winterians around her are not so certain. Most look like Conall, dark and angry, curious about this new visitor but not wasting energy on any hope of escape.

The woman pushes forward. "There were originally twenty-five of you, yes? Last we heard, the number was ten."

She waits, and I know she wants news of the outside world, of the survivors and how many are left to lead the charge against Spring. *Eight,* I almost say. But no, it's seven now. And who knows how many others died in the battle for Bithai? Dendera, maybe. Finn. Greer or Henn. Maybe Spring reached the city and even Alysson is—

My chin falls. "Seven. Maybe fewer."

Quiet muttering ripples through the crowd. The number makes their frowns deepen, and I can feel their blame flare higher. How we let them down.

The woman lifts my chin, smiling like nothing's changed. "The king?"

A bolt of agony hits me. Mather. I've managed not to think about him too much since I got here. His final, parting scream echoes through my mind, desperate and petrified, as he was dragged back into Bithai while Herod stood over me. . . .

"Alive," I whisper. "Running for his life, but alive."

The woman nods. She hooks her arm through mine and turns me toward the crowd, my back to Nessa and a grumbling Conall.

"I'm Deborah," she says, leading me to the center of the room. We're surrounded by Winterians on all sides, a sea of white hair, blue eyes, and wariness mixed with some small spurts of hope. "I was the city master of Jannuari. Of the Abril Winterians left, I'm the highest ranking." Deborah pauses like she's waiting for me to respond.

I adjust my arm still hooked in hers, fingers stretching through the air. It's warm down here, too warm, and I can feel all those eyes watching me. So I ask the only question I can. "What do you expect me to do?"

Tell me how to save you. I don't know what to do.

Deborah is quiet for a moment, her face distant like she's working through a plan in her head. She looks away from me, toward the crowd, and squeezes my hand.

"This is Meira," she announces. "She is one of the twenty-five who escaped Angra the night Winter fell. Living proof that his evil is not as absolute as he would have us believe."

I stifle a moan. It's exactly what Sir told us. That our lives matter simply because we exist—living, breathing evidence that Winter survived. Sir would love to see this cave

315

they built and know they created some small freedom in Angra's prison. He'd find a way to turn their hatred into adoration and, better still, find a way to get them out of here.

He should be with them. Him or Mather. Not me.

"She has come to us as a beacon, like the others who passed through Abril—"

Gregg and Crystalla probably stood in this exact spot, probably toiled at the wall. And they died. No one here knows more than that they left—that Angra took them from the camp and they never came back.

"—a light to shine hope into our misery," Deborah continues. "Her presence signifies an awakening, a reminder we so desperately need that we are more than Angra's slaves!"

The crowd murmurs to themselves. Those who look at me with hope start to smile, start to nod, but the rest simply shrug off Deborah's speech like they've heard it all before. Like her words are this room, a hollow and forgotten thing. Just another trembling sword raised against the greater might of Spring.

Deborah lifts my hand into the air, her old face ten years younger in her joy. I can feel her words coming, bubbling up with her hope, Nessa's hope, all those fragile faces waiting for her outburst.

"We are Winter!" Deborah shouts.

The same phrase Conall said moments ago. Its meaning stokes the hopeful ones into cheers, a handful of voices against the doubtful scorn of the others. Deborah has to see them, the ones who glower and whisper while their countrymen cheer. She has to know the danger of false hope by now. It's cruel of her to give them this; it's cruel of her to tell me I will meet any other fate than death here.

I yank my hand down and Deborah faces me. "No." My response is instant, thoughtless, urged by something cowering in a corner of my soul. "No. I'm just—I'm only one girl. What do you even think I can *do*? It isn't fair of you to let them—"

Deborah cocks an eyebrow. "*Fair* would be none of this ever happening to begin with. *Fair* would be you living out a carefree existence in Jannuari, with a warm bed and a loving family. Nothing is fair, Meira."

I step back. All of this reminds me so much of Sir that my chest aches. I don't want that life as much as I should. I want . . .

But nothing comes. None of my usual certainty about what I want, who I want to be, and the only thing I think, feel, know at all is: *It doesn't matter what I want.* My desires don't matter here. They never did. While I took merciless advantage of the fact that I never had to deal with growing up in slavery, they were here. *Here.*

It's just me now, like Hannah said. Sir should be here, it's true. Mather should be here. But they *aren't*. And since it is just me, I owe it to them to do everything I can to free our people. Even if I die here, I will die mattering, and that's what I've wanted all along, isn't it? And I will, just not within my own set parameters—I will matter in ways beyond my comprehension of the word, because I will matter in whatever way my kingdom needs me most. That, I think, is a truer mark of belonging somewhere—being willing to do anything, *everything*, that needs to be done, regardless of what I want.

As soon as those thoughts fill my mind, a dam breaks and need floods me, cooling my cheeks, tingling my limbs. I fought so long and so hard to be *me*, to be Meira in all of this, to help Winter in my own unique way. But this isn't about what *I* want, it's about what Winter needs. It's always been about what Winter needs.

As Deborah stares down at me, as the Winterians cheer in soft, quiet groups again, I realize that they make me more *me*, more present than I have ever felt in my life. Like I've been waiting all along to understand how much bigger, better, more invigorating this is than anything I could be on my own.

Deborah puts her hand on my arm, one gentle squeeze. "Your presence is proof that there is life outside of Angra's walls." She smiles at the crowd. "Even the strongest blizzard starts with a single snowflake."

Eventually the excited chatter dissipates into expectant silence. We can't stay down here too long—this cavern was made so a few people could have a reprieve every so often, not so everyone could be here at once. The only reason they risked it today is because of me. The thought makes panic flare through me, and I hurry after Nessa without prodding.

She and Conall lead me back through the tunnel. Two knocks on a wooden door above us and Garrigan pulls it open, reaching down to help out first Nessa, then me. Conall pulls himself up and closes the door, shuffling dirt and rocks back over it before arranging himself by the barred opening, Garrigan on the other side. One look in their eyes, at the way they survey the road beyond our prison, tells me they're keeping watch over us. Not that they could do much to protect us from soldiers, but it's a small comfort knowing they're here.

Nessa sits next to me and wraps her arms around her knees. It's only slightly lighter here than in the tunnel, the sky still caught in those last fleeting moments where the sun hovers behind the horizon, just waiting for its moment to break through the shadows and flood the world with radiance.

Nessa looks at me, her eyes flashing. "Conall will come around. Everyone else too. They just don't trust themselves to hope."

I keep my eyes fixed on her in the dimness. "Why do you?"

She looks away, picking at a spot on her dress. It's a two-sizes-too-big declaration of her time here, stained and worn through. "When I saw you in the palace grounds," she starts, her words a hum against the silence of the camp. Every other cage is quiet, forced into a terrified muteness by the threat of monsters in the dark. "I *felt* you when the soldier whipped me to the ground. I've never been able to get through that without screaming, but when I saw you watching us . . . I don't know. I had the strength not to scream."

I pull my arms around myself and stare at my boots. "You're so much braver than I could ever be, living here all these years. I don't believe that I did anything to help you."

Nessa settles in closer to me, her head dropping onto my shoulder with a yawn. "I do. And soon everyone else will believe too."

"Gregg and Crystalla," I whisper, "did you believe the same of them?" *Because they failed.* But something keeps me from adding that, something that doesn't want to remind Nessa of how hopeless we are.

She shrugs. "I wanted to."

I wait for her to explain, but her gentle snores are all that come. It is nearly morning. Who knows what horrors today will bring? I need every bit of strength I can get.

As I slump into the wall, careful not to disturb Nessa, my eyes travel to Conall. From his crouch next to the bars he watches me, dark-blue eyes flickering in the night. He looks to Nessa and back again, something in his expression unwinding.

Mather has the same eyes. The same unreadable, endless sapphire eyes. My heart spasms, but before I can drown in memories of us or the past, I slam the door on thoughts of him.

I nod at Conall and hold my breath. After one heartbeat, two, he nods back.

WEEKS PASS. EVERY morning I spend a few horrific minutes wondering if today is the day Angra will send for me, but he doesn't, and the soldiers lump me with the workers bound for the wall. I work without water until sundown, gulp down cold stew, and collapse in the cage. And every day, through the working, through the waiting, I ask myself the same question, over and over.

What can I do to help us?

I keep this question to myself, tucked carefully in the back of my mind so no one else can get punished for plotting an escape. But every answer I come up with is flimsy and weak. Take down one of the guards—to what end? Shove a few of the soldiers on the ramps to their deaths—and get pulled down myself? There has to be *something*.

My muscles never get used to the up and down of the

ramps, and my legs convulse each night until I pass into restless fits of dreams, dark and scattered flashes that make no sense. Sir and Noam arguing in the Rania Plains, golden prairie grass lashing around them as storm clouds roil above. Mather standing over a dead Spring soldier, eyes on the locket as he holds it out like he wants to drop it into the earth. And Theron caught in a place as black as night, tearing with bloody fingers at shadowy beasts.

Will I ever know what happened to them? Will I ever get to pay my respects to Sir, to stand over his grave and say a final good-bye?

My other dreams, the ones Hannah showed me, are the ones I cling to. The history of magic, the true reason for making the Royal Conduits. Even the flash I saw when I touched Angra, of him meeting Hannah in Winter's fields, whispering of a deal being struck. There's something in all this, some solution Hannah was trying to get me to piece together, but all I can come up with are more unanswerable questions.

She said the Decay used people as its conduit. Dark magic *chose* its host. If dark magic could choose its host—then what about our magic? Where did Winter's magic go when Angra broke our locket? Did it choose to go somewhere else? Those are questions no one dared asked for sixteen years, because it hurt to consider any alternative—or to think that the magic was gone. So we just plastered on fake smiles and assured each other that it was waiting for us to reunite our conduit's halves, waiting for us to reconstruct its host.

But what if it went somewhere else? Found another host?

Or what if it's really gone?

Those questions are too long-term for me, though. I need something to help me *now*—so I carry the dreams around with me, poking at them from every angle as I traipse up and down the ramps. It all has to fit together.

But I have no idea how.

At night, Nessa tells me about her life. She's my age, sixteen. Her father was a cobbler who made the best shoes in Jannuari, and her mother was one of Hannah's seamstresses. So fierce was her parents' dedication to Winter that when Angra attacked, they ordered Conall, seventeen at the time, to protect Garrigan, twelve, and newborn Nessa while they went to help the fight. They died that night, and both Conall and Garrigan have spent the past sixteen years fighting to stay alive for her.

Nessa talks about these memories as if they're hers, the same way I would repeat stories to myself until I was positive I had been in Hannah's court too, and could remember a kingdom locked in snow.

"How do you know all this?" I ask Nessa one night when I can't take it anymore. When staring at her becomes too unbearable, like looking in a mirror of what my life should have been. Raised in a work camp, forced to build Abril as soon as she was old enough to stand. Surrounded by the remains of a family and the even more scattered pieces of a kingdom, every shattered soul clinging to memories that aren't Nessa's or mine.

"My brothers, and the memory cave," she tells me simply. Like it's enough to hear passed-down stories and read about our history from hastily scribbled lines on walls of rock. Like those minuscule bits of information are enough for her, just to have something.

Nessa dives back into her story, about a gown her mother made. It had been intended to be a simple state gown, but the stitching was so intricate that Hannah had opted to wear it for her wedding to Duncan, Mather's father. Nessa lays the words out before me in a carefully woven tapestry of a past that doesn't belong to either of us. That will someday.

I lean against the wall, knees to my chest. I can't help but think she's right—any small bit of information is enough. But we deserve more than that.

And I'm tired of waiting for *someday*.

Someday we will be more than words in the dark.

That night stays with me through the next few days as I trek up and down the ramps. The memory cave, the words etched in stone, and Nessa's hopeful sigh.

"These tunnels offer their own type of escape."

And I realize through all these flickers of desire, these pulses of what could be, that what the Winterians need above all is just what that cave offers, but on a grander scale: hope. Hope to make their lives brighter; hope to help them endure. I have to believe that Mather is still out there, rallying support and preparing an army to march on Spring, and that someday, he'll tear down Abril's walls. But whether or not I live to see that day, I will go down in a vicious swirl that will make Angra rue the moment he ordered Herod to put me in here—and that will prove to the Winterians that hope still exists.

Excitement fills me up, makes me jittery and ready to put a plan, any plan, into action. I regret that I let myself wallow so long before I actually *tried* to do anything.

And, one day, a plan forms in my mind. A plan to bring down more than just one or two soldiers—a plan to bring down enough of them that the Winterians have to take notice, have to feel the weight lift. Not freedom, but the first step in a longer journey. A boost in morale.

The city runs with the efficiency and order of a carefully controlled machine—every soldier in his place, every door tightly bolted. This means that schedules are the norm, and weeks of the repetition embed the soldiers' routines into my mind as well. When they get us every morning; when they dismiss us every night; when they change shifts. The repetition makes them efficient, yes, but it also gives them a huge weakness: it makes them predictable.

I know, for instance, that the soldiers stationed on the ramps will change shift every day at noon and that the ramps will clear of Winterians, who gather around the children and their jars of water. For the briefest moment, not only are the ramps clear of Winterians, they're also packed with double the number of Spring soldiers—those leaving and those taking up their new posts.

And though Herod stripped me of weapons long before we reached Abril, I still have the smallest piece of metal on me—the buckle holding my belt around my pants. So after another endless day working at the wall, I crawl into the cage with Nessa, Conall, and Garrigan, wait for the soldiers to lock us up, and carefully work the buckle out of the leather strap.

Nessa and her brothers eye me as I hunch in the corner, wiggling apart the buckle and using one piece to whittle the other. Scraping metal on metal, so focused I don't know if Nessa tries to say anything to me before she falls asleep, and by morning, I have a beautiful little knife in my palm. As long as my index finger, one edge worn into a blade. I squeeze it so tightly that the edge bites into my skin as I join the rest bound for the wall.

The routine at the wall is unchanged. Holsters, rocks on our backs, trekking up and down, up and down the creaking wood. Before I head up the ramps, I eye the structure, a quick glance that goes unnoticed. The first plank of wood slopes up from the right side of the structure, connected to the ramps above with wooden posts at every corner. But if the other posts were weakened and the bottom one were to snap as the Spring soldiers changed their shift midday . . .

If it brings even the smallest blip of hope to the Winterians, it will be worth it.

I twist the makeshift blade in my hand, keeping it poised between my fingers, and with every back and forth, back and forth repetition up the wood planks, I reach out and slide the blade against the posts that hold us in the air. The posts are as thin as my wrist, the wood already warped and brittle under the sun, and it doesn't take much effort to make small nicks. But only on all the right-side posts, and only enough to slowly, imperceptibly, break them down over the next few days.

Back and forth. *Chip.*

Back and forth. *Chip.*

Three days of this, and I'm making progress. I can see thin lines developing on the posts, inconspicuous enough that everyone else brushes right by, mistaking them for the wood's natural wear. And as the sun stretches higher in the sky that third day, scooting closer to noon, my heart thumps harder and harder in my chest. It's nearly ready, nearly brittle enough. But what if I miscalculated, and the whole thing comes down too soon? What if I send dozens of Winterians tumbling to their deaths? I don't have time to answer my own worries. I didn't miscalculate. I won't kill anyone but Spring soldiers, and the Winterians will see that fighting back is still possible.

This will work.

Noon comes with the creaking of the gate. It echoes over the yard, a screeching wail that makes adrenaline burst within me. I take a deep breath and slow my pace on the ramps, falling to the back of the line of Winterians heading down for their noon water break.

I exhale, dragging my feet, watching the last Winterian trudge into the dirt.

Now.

Spring soldiers file past me, stomping up the ramp to their posts. I count them, adding their numbers to the ones already above me. Twenty-four.

Now.

I swipe the knife through the final post one last time, deepening the gouge I've been making for the past three days.

NOW.

With a sharp bump, my shoulder connects to the post, snapping the weak thing in half. I keep walking, focusing on the people ahead of me, the Winterians sipping water out of clay ladles. Not on the ramps, the other right-side posts breaking, one after another, all the way up.

Pop. Pop. Pop. Pop.

Everything holds for one moment, the intake of breath before the agonizing wail of terror. Then, as if they all realized what was happening at the same time, every Spring soldier shouts, the planks disintegrating under their feet in one great crack of splintering wood.

The Winterians gape at the collapsing structure. Other Spring soldiers dash forward like they might be able to help, like they might be able to stop it. And I swing around on my heels to watch it fall, to watch it all crumble, unable to get rid of the wicked grin on my face.

I hope you feel them die, Angra, I think, my nose flaring in a growl. *I hope you feel their bodies break.*

"You!"

In the chaos of the structure falling, in the cloud of dust that explodes up around the shattered wood, a soldier looks at me. His face scrunches in a livid rage, one hand pointing toward me.

"You did this!" he snarls.

I don't know how he knows. Maybe he saw me bump the post; maybe he saw my smile. However he knows, I confirm it by grinning and holding up the wonderful little knife. I don't care anymore. I showed the Winterians that fighting back is still possible. I don't need to look behind me to see what emotion cloaks them—wonder or relief or fear. Whatever it is, it'll eventually turn to hope. It will eventually start their blizzard.

And I would have been able to go numb in that thought, to let whatever fate descend upon me like a deluge of rain, if not for the sudden cry that pierces the air.

"Don't hurt her!"

The little boy. The one who got scolded for offering me water that first day, the one who has watched me every day since, his round blue eyes apologetic and curious and determined all at once. Every day he looks at me, his fingers tight on his ladle of water. And every day he twitches toward me half a step, like he wants to break the rules, wants to help me, but he always gives in to his fear before he gets farther.

But today he casts off his fear, slamming his ladle on the ground in a shatter of clay. He races across the yard toward me, flying around the dozens of slack-jawed Winterians who stare at the still-settling mess of wood and dust and rocks, the debris interspersed with the bodies of Spring soldiers.

All attention sucks to the boy, his little legs pumping over the ground, shouting as he goes, "Don't hurt her! I want her to live—don't hurt her! STOP HURTING US!"

His voice rips into me, sharper than the knife in my hand, deadlier than the structure that just collapsed. I grip my chest, my fingers digging into the space over my heart.

He's going to get himself killed. Because of me.

The soldier whirls as the boy stumbles to a halt in front of him. The boy's round face is red in his anger, his hands in tight little fists, his eyes alive with fury. He snarls up at the soldier like that's all it takes to stop an attack, and stands there, holding his ground.

The soldier blinks in surprise before he reacts. I see it all happen in a flash of terror and I scream, a single word bursting through my confidence, through my satisfaction at killing so many of Angra's men all at once, through any excitement I had in coming up with this plan.

"STOP!"

Nothing stops, though. Not the soldier, not the men beyond him, scrambling to pick through the rubble, dragging out a few still-alive comrades. Not comprehension creeping over me, showing me what I just did, what's happening around me.

I could have killed my own people. And now the boy will suffer for it.

"Winterian scum," the soldier hisses, yanks a whip off a hook on his belt, and unwinds it in a single crack that sends the boy crumpling to his knees, ripping flesh from his brittle bones.

"Stop!" I cry again, and lunge forward, but cold hands pull me back and the small knife flies from my grip, scattering into the dust. I yank on two Winterian men who hold me but they don't relent, their faces set in determined glares.

"You're making it worse," one grunts, and shakes me back. Even farther from the boy, who screams again, the whip's cracking the only other sound to break his pain.

"I can't just stand here," I bite back. "I can't do nothing anymore."

I don't regret bringing the ramps down. I don't regret taking action. But I will always regret letting any Winterian hurt when I could have helped them, when I could have saved them.

Tears spring to my eyes, blurring everything. The men

release me when I shove them off and fling myself toward the boy. His back is a bloody mess now, thick lines of maroon running through a smear of scarlet red. I slide to my knees in front of him, cradling his white head as he holds himself in a ball on the dirt. Grabbing onto him like I should have grabbed the man, his heavy black rock pulling him off the platform, rolling through the air like a magnet getting dragged to its mate. Helpless and alone, falling and falling, left to die while a battle rages on around him, while I get thrown through the air by a cannon and Mather gets dragged to Bithai . . .

The whip pops but I catch it this time, the leather licking around my arm and holding tight. I grab the thicker end and yank, pulling it out of the soldier's hand in one flesh-biting jerk. The soldier's eyes flash wide before he barks for help from nearby men, from other soldiers struggling between saving their comrades and the growing panic around the boy and me.

I pivot to the boy, the whip still around my forearm. "You'll be all right—" I start, but see his back. Blood pours down his sides from the ripped flesh, his ribs sticking out as white islands in a bloodred sea. He doesn't move, doesn't cry, doesn't do anything but stay curled on the dirt.

My hands go back to his head. "I'm so sorry," I whisper, my forehead pressed to his matted hair. He squirms, a flicker of life in my palms. "I'll make this better, somehow, I'll save you."

This is so wrong. And I can't change it, couldn't stop it, made it worse—*I did this to him.*

A chill turns my limbs to ice, makes my lungs freeze so much I'm sure frost puffs out with my breath. Everything about me turns to snowy chill, my hands hardening in a cage around the boy's head. So wondrously cold, every fiber in me twisting like ice-covered branches in a forest. Am I slipping away now? Is the horror of this pushing me to death?

This was how I felt when Sir died. This uncontainable chill, everything in me going numb.

Soldiers break through the snowy vortex of my panic, their rough fingers grabbing me and hauling me up, yanking the whip off my arm and tearing me away from the boy. I pull against their grip, kicking out at them, fighting to get back to the child.

The boy peeks at me from between his fingers, his blue eyes rimmed with tears and . . .

Relief.

He's relieved. I gawk, not sure if what I'm seeing is real or some distorted image I want to be real with all my heart. My eyes travel past his face to his back, his back that should be bloody and gruesome, but . . . isn't now. His torn shirt shows clean white skin gleaming in the hot sun, not a scar or a scrape or a single lingering cut. Like he was never whipped at all.

The soldiers holding me notice it too. Everyone feels it,

this moment, echoing through the Winterians as they're filled with the same relief. He's healed.

A wave of cold slides through me, and I want to bask in it forever, let icy flakes coat my body, whisk me away to somewhere peaceful and safe. No one else around me seems aware of the sudden cold I feel, and I wonder if I'm hallucinating.

The soldiers wake from their stupors before I do. Their hands tighten on my arms, fingers slipping in the blood that cakes my skin from where the whip bit into my fore-arm. They drag me away, through the crowd of Winterians who gape as I pass.

She brought the ramps down. She healed the boy.

A Winterian man steps forward. One of the many who looked at me with suspicion and hatred, who echoed Conall's distrust of me. His face relaxes in a smile so genuine and pure I expect the entire foundation of Abril to shatter in two, and he lifts his arms into the air, tips his head back, and screams. His cry of joy is the shock wave that sets off the rest, the screams and cries rippling through the Winter-ians like their excitement had been building since the first post snapped. Spring soldiers look up from the bodies of their dead comrades, their fallen ramps. Their prisoners have never had such joy before. How do they stop it?

I'm so lost in the euphoria around me that I don't notice the guards dragging me back into Abril until the gate closes behind me. But even as the heavy iron bars drop into place, the cold in my body doesn't dissipate. The Winterians' cheers don't fade.

Angra can hear them, I'm sure. He can feel the shift in the air, the joy spreading like wafting flurries of snow through the Abril work camp. My grin returns, bursting across my face.

Soon he'll know the blizzard started with me.

THE CLOSER WE get to Angra's palace, the more my relief and amazement fade.

This is the moment I've feared since I arrived, when Angra will torture me into submission. He'll make me beg for death until I tell him how I brought down the ramps, how I healed that boy, and when I don't explain it—*can't* explain it, at least not the boy—he'll make Herod break me.

A shiver eats up my insides. No, I'm not afraid of Herod. I'm not afraid of Angra. *I'm not afraid.*

But Angra will kill me before I talk to Nessa again. Before I can do anything else to help them, maybe even save them. And after seeing what happened to the boy . . .

I want to dissolve in a fit of incredulous laughter as the soldiers pull me through Abril. The boy is all right. Even as I think it, shock chases away my need to laugh, snuffing it out like a candle getting sucked up into wind.

How did *I do that?*

Nessa, Conall, and Garrigan look up from their work in Angra's garden as we pass. Nessa's expression flashes from numb to panicked in two blinks, her body coiling with helpless realization. She surges toward me but Garrigan stops her, wraps his arms around her as he whispers something quick and low in her ear.

Conall sees me too, his glare dangerously dark. I tear my eyes away from him before I can see his disappointment, before his eyes tell me, *I knew you would die too.*

I won't die. Not today. Not after what happened, what I did, what I can do for them. But what *can* I do for them? I don't even know how I did it, where it came from—I healed the boy.

I healed him.

"Leave us."

Angra's voice ricochets around the throne room. A group of high-ranking advisers stands huddled around his dais, the black suns and gold trim on their uniforms gleaming in the filtered light from the holes above. They turn away at his command, all eyes falling on the battered Winterian girl two of his soldiers drag down the long walk to the throne.

One of the advisers is Herod. He smirks and eyes his king like he's asking for permission, but Angra's voice booms out again.

"I said *leave us*."

The advisers gather the papers they had scattered on tables around Angra's dais and file out through various doors. I'm left draped between the two soldiers at the base of the dais. Angra leans back in his throne, one hand as usual clutching his staff. His green eyes are sharp and deadly, and he stares at me as if I'm a prized dog he's considering buying.

"Report," he growls.

The soldier on my right snaps to attention. "She brought down the work ramp at the wall and killed and injured many of our men. She also—" He stops, his eyes darting to my face and pulling away like I might strike him dead with just a stare. "She healed a slave."

My lungs refuse to let in more air, tightening like they know how hopeless it is to continue breathing. I don't know what I am, what I can do, but Angra will torture me until he either finds out or I die.

Angra stands. "Dismissed," he says. Both soldiers spin away, the sound of their boots on the obsidian floor fading into silence. The doors shut behind them.

It's just Angra and me now. Angra and me and the dull, empty thudding of my pulse echoing off the heavy black rock of the throne room. I tighten every muscle against the fear in the back of my mind.

No matter what happens, no matter what he does, I am part of the bigger current of Winter, and that is something he can never take from me.

Angra's fingers play idly on his staff. "Brought down a ramp, did you? *And* healed a slave?" His face is impassive, and that lack of emotion is somehow more terrifying than anything else. I surprised him. And he doesn't like being surprised.

Angra steps forward. He smiles, composed, in control, analyzing me with taunting words until he can figure out what I did, how to stop me from surprising him again. "Clearly you have not learned a Winterian's place if you think you can do such things without repercussions. But fear not—Herod will be more than happy to show you how a slave should act. Maybe I should have had him tutor you in etiquette from the start."

The mention of Herod is like a bolt of lightning on a clear day, sharp and jolting. I stumble backward, eyes popping open, and draw in a quick inhale of breath. Angra's smile widens. He can tell he found a weakness.

"Killed my men," he muses, half to himself. "And healed a slave. It won't take long to figure out how you did one, but the other? You came here with nothing but that stone, so what, exactly, gave you the power to heal someone?" Angra takes one step down the dais. "Has a little dead queen been helping you? Is she feeding you information in the hope that you will succeed where even her son has failed?"

I gape at him. Hannah. How did he know—

But Angra steps the rest of the way down, stopping

close enough that I can see the anger lingering behind his expression, the threat of explosion should I press the wrong button or refuse to play along. "I see everything," he hisses. "I control everything. I know she's still connected to Winter's magic, but I didn't think she'd be stupid enough to use her power in my kingdom, especially through a worthless girl. You're going to tell me what Hannah has said to you, how she is feeding you magic, then I'm going to squeeze every bit of that magic out of your body."

I swallow, my throat tight. The little boy's eyes appear in my mind, so wide and awed and relieved, his small back healed.

"I don't know," I whisper. My own words shock me. I didn't mean to speak. I just—I did something. I'm powerful.

"I think you do," Angra disagrees. He lifts an eyebrow and looks at the orb on his staff. Darkness leaches out of it, one long string of shadow that swerves through the air, wrapping around his hand like a vine hugging a tree branch. The line of shadow uncurls from his hand and makes one great swoop arcing in a wide circle around my head. Toying with me, taunting me with how close the magic lingers to my face. Its darkness plays off the beams of sun that fall down through the holes in the ceiling.

I gape at it. I've never *seen* magic before. This—this isn't magic.

This is the Decay.

"And I'm sure Hannah's put some rather interesting bits

of information in your head," he continues. "I'd like to see what she's been doing to you."

I'm panting now, the shadow hovering in front of my nose. "All your power, and you don't already know?"

Angra's face twitches, revealing his true boiling anger beneath his smug facade. "You were put in a cage with— who was it? I-3219, I-3218, and I-2072. What I do know, R-19, is that my need to know what is in your head is greater than my need to keep them alive. Should I bring them here? Because I'm guessing you care whether or not they live."

I bite my tongue to keep from reacting. Angra's forehead relaxes in a pleased realization. The shadow line pulses before my face, the manifestation of his threat.

"Ah, you do care. I thought so." He steps closer, too close, less than an arm's length away with only the shadow line hovering between us. "You probably would also care," he continues, voice a low purr, "if I ordered my soldiers not to bother bringing them here. If I had them killed where they stand. Or even better, if I let Herod torture them. Maybe I should—"

"I'll kill you," I spit, and lunge forward a beat before flailing back from the swirling line of dark magic, my hands clenching into fists. I can't stop my frantic desire to tear Angra's heart out, but I know it's useless; I can't stop him from making Nessa or Conall or Garrigan Herod's next toy, can't evade that pulsing rope of darkness that creeps closer and closer to me, until I'm afraid to breathe too deeply lest I suck it inside me.

"Will you? Because I think you don't have a choice. No one does."

Blood pools in my mouth. I've bitten clean through my tongue now, the sharp lucidity that comes from that pain the only thing keeping me from leaping at Angra through the aura of dark magic. I focus on the pain, not on the cloudy line of darkness, not on Angra's lulling words. His gentle, pulsing voice that sounds so calm, so sweet, until the meaning of his words shines through. Beyond us, the black obsidian of the empty throne room reflects the sunlight, watching us like a bodiless audience.

"It is freeing, not having a choice. And after a while, people no longer need to be forced to do certain things. Like Herod, for instance—he has taken quite fervently to the choices I make for him. He'll enjoy destroying you."

Cold. Everything is cold. The world is ice, coated in thick, solid wonder, nothing but gleaming surfaces and clouds of frozen breath. I'm locked in it, a part of it, my limbs hardening into the jagged branches of an ice-covered tree, stuck in a suspended state of hibernation while the world freezes around me. My bones shift with a grinding sensation, moving against the ice, shattering it as my body heaves forward, fingers curled in claws, mouth opening in a bloody screech as I dive through the shadow at Angra's face.

The moment the black cloud touches my skin, I realize my great mistake. Desperation opened my mind to him, and my defenses crumble as the shadow dissipates into my head, diving back into my skull and filling every crevice with a dusty and ancient evil. I pull to a stop, sucked out of the cold, cold, cold of the world and into my own heat-drenched torture. The shadow wiggles through my thoughts, dives into my memories, kicking around in my brain as I'm flung backward and forward uncontrollably.

A flicker of Angra's smugness returns. His power is in me now, pushing around my mind, nestling inside me like ink in books.

You will tell me everything, I feel him say. The words are my own thoughts, greedy and deep, and I grab my ears as if I could pull him out of my head. *Or I will let Herod have you first, then those slaves you were with, then every Winterian I own. I will make him kill them all.*

No, he won't. I'll stop Herod; I'll kill Angra before he ever does that to anyone else.

Faces and images from my past swirl as Angra sorts through my head—Mather and Sir, the Rania Plains, Theron holding me as we danced in Cordell. Snow falling, gentle white flakes dusting Jannuari's cobblestone streets . . .

Cold sweeps over me, wondrous cold. I'm standing in Jannuari, bare toes digging into the mortar between the cobblestones as flakes stick to my eyelashes, making the world glitter. Why am I here? It's so cold, every nerve in my body tingling with the wondrous iciness.

I know how to break you, comes Angra's voice. *I know how to break all of you who long so badly for what you cannot have. You show your weakness in your desperation.*

No, I'm in Abril, not in Jannuari. I'm in Angra's palace and the Winterians need me and Nessa will die if I don't stay conscious. I'm not magic; I'm not anything special. I'm just Meira.

No, not *just* Meira. I'm—I'm something—

It's so cold. I love the cold.

Tell me what you want most in life, Meira. I will use your weaknesses. I will warp your mind until you shatter in my hands. I control you, Winter, everything.

Angra reaches one hand up with agonizing slowness and rests it against my forehead. More snow, falling and falling, peaceful flakes lulling me into Jannuari where it's quiet and calm and I've never felt so safe in my life.

The locket. Angra still wears half of the locket around his throat, the white snowflake on the silver heart. We've been looking for the conduit for so long.

I will break you now with what you want most. Your perfect world.

26

ANGRA'S THRONE ROOM *fades, the blackness disintegrating into a city. No, not just any city—the Jannuari from my patched-together memories.*

AND IT'S SNOWING.

I turn, the cobblestones slick with ice, and the cold that shoots through my bare feet infuses me with euphoria. The earthy aroma of coal and refining minerals coats the air, turning everything a hazy gray. I belong here, in Jannuari. How could I have ever been anywhere else?

The skirt of my pale gray dress is tattered, stained with use and poverty. The thin cotton lets more cold rays wrap around my body as I stand in the street, smiling at a figure running toward me through the snow. Nessa.

"Meira, supper's ready! Your mother sent me to fetch you."

My mother. Something pushes at my mind. . . . I don't think I have a mother.

No, of course I do. I've always had a mother.

"Meira, come on!" Nessa grabs my hand and pulls me up the street. *She's so happy, so healthy, filled with a life of love and safety, her eyes gleaming as snowflakes stick in her hair.*

I lift my skirt in one hand and together we run up the street, passing Winterians tidying up displays in shop windows or hammering horseshoes in a blacksmith's shop. Jobs they should be doing, not like—

They're wrong too. Wrong like my mother. Nessa is even a little wrong, and this city is wrong, though I know it exists.

"He's coming to dinner tonight," Nessa whispers, *her tone seasoned with joy and gossip.*

"Who?"

Nessa laughs, the sound making the air glitter even more. She pulls me up a path to a small two-story cottage and throws open the door, warm firelight falling out into the snow-filled path. Yellow mixes with the gray of Jannuari, warmth meeting snow. It's not a bad warmth, though—it's perfect.

"There she is!" *a voice cries as I step across the threshold. The fire pit on the left holds a bowl of orange coals that heat a cauldron of stew. Conall sits at a wooden table with a small bundle cooing from his arms, a woman behind him resting her hands on his shoulders. His wife? She must be. Garrigan crouches in front of his wife too, along with two little boys who stare in awe while he relates some story that involves mock-stabbing an enemy.*

Behind the table, a small, graceful woman emerges from a back room, locks of white hair curling around a face smudged with flour. "Meira, come! He's almost here," *she says.* Alysson.

Nessa falls into a chair at the table. "Your mother's been cooking all day."

My mother. Alysson is my . . .

"Hurry, everyone! His carriage is pulling up."

A booming voice rolls out behind me. I turn as a man stomps in, dusting snow from his hair. The loose flakes melt into my skin, raising shivers that tingle along my arms. I know him. His dark-blue eyes and gray-speckled beard and white hair pulled back in a tight knot . . .

Alysson is my mother—which means Sir is my father.

Joy chokes me, hot tears pool in my eyes. He's my father. Of course he is—I've always wanted him to be my father.

A swell of pain breaks through my joy and I fall forward, knees cracking onto the wooden floor as thoughts pound against my mind, determined and loud.

I called him Father once and yes, Sir, no, Sir. You are not my father and I am not your daughter and all I ever wanted was for you to look at me. . . .

This isn't right. He exists, I know he exists, but not like this.

"Meira." Sir drops to his knees too, his hands cupping my head and pulling me to look at him. His face is gentle and worried, his forehead wrinkling. "Are you all right?"

He's wrong. He's not supposed to be here . . . something happened to him, something horrible. "I dreamed you died," I whisper.

Sir's worry melts into a smile and he pulls me into him, wrapping his thick arms around my shoulders and letting me rest against his chest. "There's my sweet girl. It was just a dream."

He's cold from the outside air and smells like snow, clean and crisp. The buttons on his shirt pinch my cheek when I press my face into his chest, absorbing the feel of him all around me. This is what love is like. He loves me. He's my father and I'm his daughter and he's all I have, all I'll ever need.

"He's coming!" Alysson cries. "The prince is here!"

Sir eases me into a chair facing the front door. The darkness of the snowstorm beyond the open door looks like a dream from which anything could materialize, and Nessa takes my hand from her chair beside me as a man appears. A sharp blue military uniform covers him, his polished black boots gleaming in the firelight. The snowstorm pushes him to us like it created him, morphed him from the deepest recesses of my mind.

"Thank you for having me," he says, and bows his head, every part of him the proper prince he's always been. Strong, confident face, eyes vibrant and alert and memorizing each person in the room like he wants to know us by heart.

He stops in front of me. Nessa's hand tightens around mine, cutting off the blood to my fingers.

"Meira," Mather says. My name, just once, just those two syllables echoing to me like no other words exist. Just us. Like it should have been.

Explosions. Mather, terrified, screaming my name. Screaming and screaming . . .

I don't love him. I can't love him, so I don't, not anymore. It's too hard to love him.

Mather sits across from me, his eyes never leaving mine. Alysson moves to the fire, shooing away Garrigan and his wife and sons. They join the table, Conall and Garrigan and their wives, and Nessa with her happy family, and me with my happy family.

The front door is still open. Beyond the snowflakes, a flash of white hair makes me spring from the chair and rip my hand from Nessa's.

Alysson ladles stew into bowls. "Meira, sit, please. Dinner has started."

But I can't sit. I can't tear my eyes away from the door, from the snow, from the white hair that's caught in the wind and tangling up around a face—who is that?

Sir touches my arm. "What do you see, my sweet girl?"

He yelled at me when I was small and Mather and I were found giggling in the meeting tent, covered in ink. . . .

No—why would I have been with the prince as a child? I step around the table, the white hair beyond the door drawing me like I'm tethered to it and she's winding me in.

"Meira." Mather leans back in the chair, his fingers trailing down my arm. "What happened?"

It's so safe here. Everything I could possibly want. How could anything bad ever happen? This is perfect, this is right, and I have to tell Mather everything because he is perfect.

"I healed a boy," I hear myself say. I think the white hair outside belongs to Mather's mother, the queen. I've heard she's beautiful. "I matter."

"You do, Meira." Mather stands, his chair sliding across the wood. "Of course you matter. Why?"

He takes my hand but the feel of it, of him, is a sharp, sudden break in the perfect picture around me. "No, I'm wrong for you," I hear myself tell him. "I'm not good enough."

Sir folds his hands on the table and looks up at us. "I only told you that so you wouldn't jeopardize our future. Lies are stronger than truth sometimes."

"Truth?" The familiar pain pulses against my temple, threatening to tear me to pieces if I don't—what? I need to sit down and eat dinner and talk with Mather, tell him why I matter, because this is all I've ever wanted. To be here.

"Meira," a voice calls from outside. The queen is here. Why doesn't anyone invite her in?

I step toward the door, my toes barely cresting the threshold, when Mather grabs my arm. "Where does your magic come from?" he gasps. He looks scared, desperate, his eyes reflecting my own trepidation back at me. He looks so much like Sir. The same strong jaw, the same sapphire eyes, the same emotionless veil. I never noticed it before.

"Magic comes from—" Why am I answering him? He shouldn't ask me about this. I take a step backward, toward the door and the snowstorm. "Magic comes from the Royal Conduits."

Mather's eyebrows tighten. "Conduits? No, Meira." He licks his lips, trying again. "How do you have magic? How is Hannah feeding you magic? You have to tell me."

"I told you," I say. "Only conduits have magic. Hannah isn't giving me anything."

"Meira," Hannah calls to me. I turn my back on the room, on the

warm firelight, on Nessa's giggles and Sir calling me his sweet girl and Mather shouting for me, reaching for me. On everything I've ever wanted, because Hannah needs me, and I have to go to her.

The moment I leave the cottage, heat pulses behind me, a burst of warmth much too strong to have come from the fire pit. I turn as the cottage disintegrates, folding in on itself like it cannot sustain the weight of the night around it. But no, it isn't disintegrating—it's burning, piece by piece, into a small pile of smoldering ash. My mouth hangs slack as shadows of the night rise over the ash, swallowing it into a startlingly pure black void. The city around me follows it, everything folding into itself and vanishing until Jannuari is gone and I'm left standing in a beam of light.

"Meira, I am in control now. Not Angra," Hannah says, her voice urgent like she's fighting to keep us safe.

I shake my head. Angra was in control? Of what? No, I'm safe now, not in Angra's black magic anymore. Hannah is protecting me because he pulled things out of my head. He tried to make me fall apart, but I'm safe now, safe, safe. . . .

Hannah waits behind me, the space around us still filled with dancing snowflakes. Like we're shielded, cupped in invisible arms that will keep the darkness from touching us. Angra can't touch us here. He didn't mean for me to leave the cottage. He wanted me to stay inside, where it was comfortable and I would tell him all my secrets. But I left, and Hannah is using her connection to Winter's conduit to talk to me, like she's been doing all along.

Her connection to Winter's conduit, not the blue stone. There was never any magic in the blue stone. Only the Royal Conduits have magic.

I turn, snow crunching under my feet. Hannah stands with her back to me, her hair flailing in the storm. Explanations whirl around me, but not from her—from me. My mind eases here, in this space between asleep and awake, and as it does information pours into the light, sudden bursts of clarity I never would have seen on my own.

"Angra broke your conduit, but magic is more powerful than even he knows." The words tumble out of me from some delicate area of surrender, a mysterious space in my heart that connects Hannah and me. The magic. It's known the truth all along. "You were desperate when Winter was falling, so you surrendered to your conduit. You let it tell you everything. The truth behind magic, and that if a Royal Conduit is broken in defense of the kingdom, the king or queen of that kingdom becomes the conduit."

This knowledge springs into my head, the magic giving me this last piece that lets me put the rest of the puzzle together. The Royal Conduits are connected to the kingdoms' bloodlines. Magic always needs a host, and with a human host, magic doesn't have the limitations that come with object hosts. Life and pure magic would have been a beautiful combination, like a fire nursed by endless fuel. So if the rulers had let their conduits be broken when they faced the Decay, they would have become their kingdom's conduits. The Decay could have been destroyed with all that power, and the world would have glowed with prosperity.

But conduit magic only works if the bearer acknowledges the magic and chooses to use it, and conduits only give answers when people put aside their selfish will and dare to surrender themselves for the good of their kingdom. It's a magic all about choice, and no one chose to surrender until Hannah.

Hannah shifts in the snow, tipping her head back. "Where is Winter's magic now?"

"You didn't know you were pregnant. And then Angra killed you," I whisper. It's so cold. Cold seeping through me until I'm sure I'm nothing but ice through and through, just a hollow, glassy sculpture. "Angra broke the conduit and killed you so the magic went to the heir. To——"

My mouth freezes and the cold controls me, pushes me into the scene that Hannah tried to show. The night before Jannuari's fall, the study in the palace, the heavy aroma of burning coal hanging all around. Those who would escape Angra's wrath are gathered, Hannah kneeling in front of Alysson, who cradles baby Mather—

In the background. There's something in the corner, something I didn't see before.

"I'm so sorry," Hannah tells Alysson. "You don't have to obey me. You can still choose not to do this."

I step around Hannah and Alysson. I walk past Dendera, Finn, Greer, and Henn. Crystalla and Gregg huddle by the fire pit, alive and holding each other. I walk past Sir, his looming body curving protectively around his wife and the baby.

In the corner of the room, forgotten, sits a bassinet. Mather's bassinet?

No. It's not empty.

A tiny hand shoots up, grasping at the air. Small, fat fingers curl against a plump little palm, two gleaming blue eyes stare with wide curiosity at the stillness around her. Her. A pale pink blanket is wrapped around her small body, the hem folded down and stitched with pink silk thread. The stitching forms snowflakes all around the hem until those snowflakes form a name, the pink silk bending and twisting into five small letters.

"No, my queen," Alysson says. "We will do it; of course we will do it. Winter needs us. We will raise our son as yours."

The name. Those five letters stitched so perfectly.

MEIRA.

27

THE FLOOR OF Angra's throne room gleams in the light from above, letting my reflection stare up at me as I cower on my hands and knees at his feet.

I'm Hannah's daughter.

My eyes flit back and forth, my lungs inhaling and exhaling panic. I can't be Hannah's child, because Mather . . . but Hannah asked Alysson and Sir to say Mather was the prince. Angra knew Hannah's heir escaped that night, so they couldn't just say the child had died—he would never have believed that. They said it was Mather so Angra wouldn't care that Winter's heir was just a boy, not a girl, not a threat even if we got the conduit put back together and the magic returned to it.

But the locket is powerless now, has been powerless since Angra broke it sixteen years ago, because all that power sought a new host. It went into me.

I'm Winter's conduit.

No one knew it was even possible except Hannah, because she let her conduit tell her what needed to be done to save Winter. Her locket needed to be broken in defense of Winter, a sacrifice so its power couldn't be taken away, couldn't be broken or cast off, wasn't limited by an object. This power *is* me, is Winter, is unfettered because it's connected to my life now. . . .

I'm Winter's queen.

I suck in a breath, forcing the air into my body to keep me alive under all of this, a weight heavier than anything I've ever felt.

Sixteen years of everyone keeping this secret. Of Sir training me, treating me like I was some nameless orphan who should be grateful to be free. And Mather . . . no. All this time, his true parents have been right there, until Sir—

There's my sweet girl.

The cottage. Sir hugging me. That wasn't real. It was a cruel trick of Angra's, a horrible toying with my dreams. Everything I want out of life, everything I will never, ever get—a simple, happy family in some cramped little cottage. But Hannah—that was real. That was her attempt to save me from Angra, a desperate ripple of protection urged by her connection to the conduit magic, to her bloodline. My bloodline.

I fall forward, forehead touching the cool obsidian, mouth opening in the beginnings of a sob. Tears stream down my face as I remember Sir's arms around me, the way he held me in Angra's evil dream, completely unafraid of loving me.

But he isn't my father. He's Mather's father. My own father is Winter's dead king, and my mother is Winter's dead queen. She's been using her connection to Winter's conduit to talk to me. Because I—

I'm Winter's conduit. No matter how many times I push those words through my head, they don't make sense.

"Herod!"

Angra's shout, dripping with uncontrolled menace, shakes the palace apart. He'll kill me, destroy me here and now, rend every piece of me into inconsequential bits and scatter them over Winter's desolate land. He'll win.

I fly up, stumble back, not sure where I can go or where I can hide. I can't just die—not this easily. It can't end now, just like that—

Angra throws open a door. "Herod! Bring him, NOW!"

I pause, hands out, chest heaving up and down. Him. Has Mather been captured?

Angra turns back to me as footsteps draw closer from the hall. "Winterians, always getting in the way of greater things," he says, riled into a fantastic desperation. "You may be able to resist me, but there's another way to get you to talk."

Resist.

He didn't hear any of it. He doesn't know. For him, the image of Jannuari must have dissolved once I left the cottage. Hannah used the conduit magic to keep us hidden because she needed to prepare me; she took the risk to give me a fighting chance to save our kingdom.

My chest gets cold again, a small shiver that darts down to my hands.

Footsteps pound into the throne room, shadows falling on two figures. One is Herod, his looming shoulders recognizable anywhere. The other is smaller. Still strong, still big, but—

Herod throws the other man into the beam of light in front of me. He collapses, clothes ripped and stained with blood, body bruised and decorated with cuts and gashes. When he looks up at me, everything else vanishes.

It's Theron.

"Tell me everything," Angra orders, stomping toward me, the black of his staff creating a cloud of shadow around his hand. "Or I'll break every bone in your prince's body."

Theron sits back on his heels. Theron is here. In Spring.

A cut on his forehead trickles blood into his eye, and half of his mouth cocks to one side in a pathetic attempt to look happy to see me, even here. I fall to the ground in front of him, running my hands over his face, his arms, hesitating on his injuries. "How did you get here?"

Theron's smile falls. "I could ask you the same thing."

Angra's staff slams into Theron's head and sends him sprawling onto the floor. Theron lifts up onto his elbows, draws in a calming breath, and looks back at me.

"Don't you want to tell her how you handed yourself over to me? Gallantly tried to sneak into Spring to save her, but ended up in the same situation?" Angra sneers at Theron, but his usual smugness is marred now, his control wavering in the face of my resistance to his magic. "Shall I show your prince how visitors are treated in Abril?"

I surge forward as Herod rushes to me, both of us colliding an arm's length from Theron. "No!" I shout, the word echoing around me. I don't have time for nausea or revulsion or Herod's slow leer as he wraps his arms around my body and grunts when I kick against him.

"Do you know what happened to the last refugees we caught?" Herod's breath brushes my hair, my neck, flowing over my body as he pulls me to him.

Angra steps over Theron and lowers the staff's orb, pressing it against Theron's spine. But Theron doesn't flinch, his eyes on mine, his breathing labored and quick as he gathers determination for whatever might lie ahead. He doesn't know about Angra's Decay—he doesn't know Angra's magic can affect him—

The first rib snaps and Theron cries out, surprise shattering any chance he might have had at remaining stoic. True, unyielding fear washes away the color on his face as he gasps in the silence after the break, his eyes finding mine in a surge of unasked questions. I can't explain anything, though, not as Herod presses his face against my ear, not as the second rib cracks in Theron's chest, an echoing pop of bone grating against bone that makes my own body ache with memory.

"You do, don't you?" Herod continues. "Because we let one of them go, so he could tell you what your fate would be. The one who died—R-16? She was a fighter, just like you. Determined to resist. But they always come around in the end."

The third rib breaks and Theron releases a strangled cry into the floor that makes my heart seize. Angra's eyes flick to mine. He's smiling with a child's delight, his hand twisting around the staff as he continues to break Theron's ribs one by one. I can stop it. I can stop it if I just tell him who I am—

"I'll make your prince watch," Herod whispers.

He made Gregg watch. He kept him chained to a wall in his room while Crystalla was kept in a cage, a doll that Angra made Herod take out and play with at his bidding. Angra showed her a Winterian's place in Spring by having Herod torture her to death in ways a body can't fathom.

Theron groans from the floor as Angra finishes healing the ribs he shattered. Herod finally releases me and I fall on top of Theron like my body can shield him from Angra's magic.

"Stop," I mumble into Theron's shoulder. "Stop. He's

not a part of this. This is between us, Season and Season. This isn't Cordell's war!"

Angra laughs. The sound pulls me up, my mistake ringing in my ears.

"No, you're quite right." He turns to Herod. "Go get 1-2072, 1-3218, and 1-3219. I promised R-19 that you could have them once you're done with—"

"*No!*" My scream tears through the throne room so loud and so desperate I can feel the rocks tremble. All around me, the darkness of the obsidian seeps into my vision, painting everything I see and feel a startling black. Can I use the conduit magic to stop them, this, everything? What can my magic even do? I can only affect Winterians, give them strength or endurance or health—

I think Theron takes me into his arms. I think he whispers something in my ear, but I'm screaming now, lashing out as soldiers come in and haul us up. I can't hear anything beyond the roar of blood in my head, the horrifying image of Herod sneering at me as he turns, pauses, smiles again. Walks down the throne room and leaves through the two heavy doors with such controlled grace. He's going to get Nessa and her brothers. He's going to kill them—

"Take them to Herod's chamber," Angra orders. "If she feels like talking, bring her to me instantly. No matter her state."

I scream again, fingers tearing at the soldiers who drag us away. I will not let Nessa or Conall or Garrigan or myself or *anyone* die like this.

The soldiers don't care. They pin my arms back and carry me up stairs, down halls, weaving through Angra's obsidian palace. Everything is decorated with the same heart-achingly poetic spring-in-darkness motif, colorful etchings of vines and flowers dug into the black rock. The vines wrap around us like the words in Nessa's memory cave.

Someday we will be more than words in the dark.

Bithai had a poem. A beautiful poem like the one Theron wrote. But Winter has no poem, just those words scrawled in the dark and that one sentence, that one desperate plea that shakes through my body with a frantic need.

The soldiers throw open a door in a second-floor hall. A room spreads out before me, a canopy bed against the back corner, wide clear windows along the southern wall, gleaming wooden floors that the soldiers drag me across until we stop by—

A cage. Barely big enough for me to sit up in. They open the door and toss me in and lock it before I can even breathe.

One of the soldiers slips the key onto Herod's desk.

I follow his movements and my attention freezes on the one object I never expected to see again: my chakram. My original chakram, which Herod stole so long ago, sits prominently on his desk like a prized trophy. *Exactly* like a prized trophy, in the same way I'm a trophy too.

So close. My weapon, so close and yet so useless.

I lunge against the cage, the bars groaning where they're

bolted into the floor. Nothing gives, and the soldiers laugh as they march out of the room.

Across from me, the other soldiers chain Theron to the wall. They punch him in the stomach, his body slamming back into the wall with a sickening crack. Then they leave us, shutting the door like they can forget what will happen.

I grip the bars, blinking away a foggy veil of tears as I keep my focus on Theron, locking onto his deep brown eyes and the sparkle behind them, the light that I didn't even realize I'd missed. He stares back at me, the tension in his face unwinding in exhaustion, anger, at seeing me in a cage in Herod's chamber, waiting for that monster to return and slowly torture me. And knowing that for all his training and power in Cordell, Theron has no power here. He's just as close and just as useless as my chakram.

"How did Angra—" Theron starts, one of his hands pressing tenderly on his healed ribs. He shakes his head, closing his eyes in a quick flicker of repulsion. "Never mind. I don't think I want to know."

I draw in a wavering breath, ready to explain, but the words fall flat and lifeless in my throat. "What happened?" is all I can manage.

Theron drops to the floor, the chains leading from his wrists clanking against the wood. Blood trails down his face, fresh and scarlet, dripping onto the collar of his tattered military uniform, Cordell's green and gold caked in red. "Bithai survived," he says.

I open my mouth. *No, I meant what happened to lead us here. What happened to get us so far gone, so far from—*

"Shortly after you fell, Cordell overcame Spring's infantry. They were forced to retreat. They couldn't compete with our conduit; it was the only thing that saved us. But my father refused to retaliate." Theron winces, working out a pain in his shoulder.

I can't grasp what he's saying. I shake my head, drop my face into my hands. The colors from the hall swirl in my memory, Angra's black and pastel-green and pink mixing with the brown and maroon of Herod's chamber. Green vines crawl around me like words in the dark. Memories. Nessa's memories.

Herod is bringing her here. She'll see him kill me.

"My father refused to go after them," Theron continues. "He refused to go after you. He said he wouldn't risk so much for a worthless Season anymore."

I start rocking back and forth. *Herod will kill Nessa too. Will they make Theron watch that? How long will they keep him here before he dies too?*

Theron runs a hand down his face. "Mather nearly killed him. Drew a sword and everything. But my father still wouldn't . . . He's so proud. So selfish. I hate him."

I can't use my conduit magic to get out of this cage. I can't use it to free Theron. I don't even know what it can be used for beyond the basic functions of kingdom life. How can it help me in this situation? What can I do?

"I hate the prejudice. I'm tired of watching my father hoard our power when we could be working *together*, Rhythm and Season, against the true evil in this world. I knew what would make him act. If Spring had me, my father would finally do something about Angra." Theron laughs an empty laugh, his eyes darting around the room. "Starting to rethink my plan now."

That makes me stop. Makes my whirring thoughts stumble against a sudden burst of clarity, and I hear everything he said slowly, his words coming to me through my fog.

He handed himself over to Angra. He let Spring catch him.

I gape across the space between us. "You *wanted* Angra to capture you?"

Theron's eyes jump to mine. Connecting us, just us now. Together. "Yes."

A smile uncurls on my face. It feels so wrong and yet so wonderful, how much I need to smile at him.

Something pounds in the hallway, something like . . . footsteps. Coming closer.

I cling to the bars of the cage. "I'm Hannah's daughter. I'm the queen of Winter," I hear myself say.

Theron frowns and leans forward, his chains rattling. "I—"

The door to the chamber flies open and Herod's dark mass barrels in. He hurls himself at his desk, scrambling through papers and books until he grabs the key and holds it triumphantly in a tight-fisted grip. "I'm going to destroy you," he hisses, eyes burning into mine.

28

SEEING HIM HERE shatters me. He's back too soon. *Too fast, not yet, I need more time—*

Herod stomps toward me, his eyes bloodshot, his hair sticking out around the face of someone scared, frantic. I press against the back corner of the cage. He's mad, Angra's evil driving his need to kill.

And Nessa, Conall, and Garrigan aren't with him.

"Where are they?" I shout. "What did you do to them?"

Herod laughs and stops just above the cage, towering over me. "You just keep fighting," he coos. "Keep pretending you can win. You don't know what my master is. You don't know how futile it is to contest him."

"Don't touch her!" Theron's voice booms out from the wall and he runs to the end of his chains, a tantalizing distance from where Herod stands, bending slowly to the cage's lock.

"Your prince brought an army with him, did he tell you that?" Herod puts the key in the lock but doesn't turn it, waiting for my reaction. "He brought the armies of the world to save you. Bittersweet, don't you think? All that, and he'll still watch you die."

An army? Is that what Theron has been saying?

Noam. He forced Noam to attack Spring. And if Cordell is attacking Spring . . . Autumn will attack with it.

Herod unlocks the door. Theron yanks against the chains, stretches out to Herod, yanks again. I press as far back in the cage as I can, willing myself to be as small and inconsequential as possible. I'm Winter's conduit. I should be able to get out of this, kill him, do something to survive. Winter needs me to survive.

Herod swings the door open and reaches for me in one swift motion. His fingers grab my collar and drag me out, the bars of the cage flying past before I can find purchase and stop myself. Then I'm above the cage, soaring through the air until I smack into something soft, something covered in a quilt of silk squares on a mattress of stale feathers.

Herod's bed.

I scramble back and press into the wall, trying to shove myself to my feet. Herod strides toward me, his face wild, a savage dog cornering his long-hunted prey. His eyes flash with power forced into him from someone else. Angra is here, doing this even more than Herod. Does Herod even exist beyond the things Angra makes him want?

"Do you remember when I first saw you?" Herod whispers. He stops at the edge of the bed, his fingers twirling down the post that holds the canopy above my head. "Years ago. You were a child still, small and fierce."

I stand, grab the opposite post, and start to swing around, propel myself off the bed, but Herod dives, his hands grabbing my thighs and landing me flat out on the silk quilt. As horror shoots through me, Theron shouts from the wall, still pulling uselessly at the chains. Blood drips from his wrists now, jagged tendrils of red falling onto the floor as he pulls and looks at me with such helplessness my heart cracks.

I jerk to Herod, scrambling for any last bits of strength. "You didn't have time to get them, did you? Theron's army interrupted your master's fun?"

"My master has nothing to do with this. He merely makes me"—he pauses and smirks—"unstoppable."

Herod whirls me around so I land on my back with him on top of me, his bulk pressing me into the mattress. I want to believe it's a lie. I want to believe he's still human in there, somewhere, a small flicker of someone who doesn't want to have done the things he's done. But when I look into his eyes, there's nothing. A vast and horrible nothing lined by need and obedience and strength.

He doesn't exist outside of Angra's commands. Maybe he never did.

"I regret that this will be faster than I always imagined,"

Herod whispers, his warm breath cutting my skin like a knife. "But your prince has forced my hand."

I wiggle against him, hands slipping on the quilt. Herod rolls against my movements, pinning me more and more until he grabs one of my wrists and traps my arm above my head. My other arm twists under my back, useless without a plan.

Herod pauses, eyes darting over my face. He wants me to fight him. He wants me to struggle. And everything in me, every part of who I am, wants to fight him too.

This is where my most unbearable nightmare will play out. Moments before the Cordell-Autumn army can save me, Theron so close yet worlds away. A knot of terror locks my throat tight, making me wheeze as I fight down desperate sobs.

Herod shifts, his body pressing more heavily on top of me. Something jabs into my hip, something sharp—

A medal on his jacket. Some military badge of honor that dangles lopsided off the fabric.

A rush of cool, sweet hope turns my sobs into gasps for breath, and I wiggle my arm almost free. Herod takes my motion as more fighting and laughs, pressing my trapped right arm more firmly into the bed. His other hand tangles in my hair, tilting my head and neck into a painful arch.

But the medal is free now, dangling over my hip.

"Looks like I was right," I hiss. "I *will* kill you before this ends."

Herod hesitates and I flip my arm up to rip the medal off his jacket. The fabric tears, giving me a sharp gold pin that glints in the afternoon light from the open windows. I shove it up, the medal folding into my palm as I jam the pin into Herod's left eye.

He screams, lurching off me and cupping his hands over his eye as I fly out from under him and roll off the bed, using the bedpost to propel myself around.

"Meira!" Theron tugs back against his chains, his whole body angling toward the desk where my beautiful weapon sits.

Herod bellows and rips the pin out of his eye, blood running in a morbid tear down his face. He roils with pain and fury, his one good eye locking on me.

I can't get to the desk without diving between Theron and Herod. There are no other weapons near me, no chairs I can break or vases I can throw.

Herod yanks a dagger out of his boot and lunges forward in a wave of rage. I shove off the bed, gain momentum, and drop to my knees, sliding between the wall and Theron, ducking just under his bloody chains. My tattered cotton pants glide across the wood floor until I whip my foot around, catch the edge of the desk, and pull to my feet.

A lump gathers in my throat. My chakram. The one Herod stole months ago, the great curving handle worn smooth from my palm. I grab it off the top of Herod's desk and spin around, body coiled in the effortless motion of the breath before a throw. As I turn, the entire expanse of the world around us freezes, holds, caught between me with my chakram ready and Herod with his knife to Theron's throat. The pause before a fight—

A close-range fight. I choke on a sob at the sudden memory of Mather sparring with me, of Sir refusing to let me go on missions until I got better at it, and now here I am—my life, and Theron's, depends on me killing Herod at close range.

"Drop it," Herod hisses. His left pupil lies sightlessly in a mess of purple and red, his right eye fierce and fuming.

Theron doesn't flinch, just keeps his dark eyes fixed on me. His lip curls and his eyes shine with panic, mouth moving in four small words. *Don't listen to him.*

I keep my chakram up, my body prepared for attack. The fingers of my other hand grope over Herod's desktop. Something else, please, something else to distract him so I can get a clear shot—

At that exact, perfect moment, a siren echoes over Abril, a panicked screech calling all soldiers to their stations and all generals to their posts. Herod's face spasms at the noise but he doesn't move. The siren wails again and he growls, a low bubble telling me his focus isn't entirely here. It's on his king, who is probably using his dark magic to tell his highest-ranking general to get to his post, to leave his toy for later and obey his ruler.

My fingers close over something. An ink jar. Perfect.

I flick my arm out when Herod's attention jerks to the door for one perfect, distracted second, the jar twirling through the air like a black shooting star. Ink trails around it, painting the air between us until it pops against Herod's jaw. He jerks back enough that Theron is able to duck against the wall and rip the knife out of his hand. Herod claws at the air but Theron drops to the ground, darts out of the way, giving me a clear shot at Herod's neck.

The chakram leaves my hand. As it flies I follow it, closing the space between Herod and me until it licks through his neck, the force of my throw making it rebound into my hands as I leap off the floor. The chakram hitting Herod shocks him backward and I'm already soaring toward him, weapon rising above my head. Herod's one good eye blinks up at me, ink dripping down his cheek.

The two of us fall onto the floor, my knees slamming into his stomach. My chakram's worn wooden handle cradles in my palms like it never left as I slide the blade into Herod's skull, the vibration ringing up my arm. It rises, blood trailing the metal. And down again, bone rending.

You are weak, Herod. You don't exist beyond the things you let Angra make you do.

I should be killing Angra, not Herod. Herod is just a pawn. But he doesn't deserve to live.

You are weak.

Meira, stop!

Hannah. Cold sucks my breath away as hands grab my arms.

"Meira!" Theron pulls me back and we collapse in a tangled ball of limbs and tears and blood. He broke the chains with Herod's dagger and pulls me into his arms now, cradling me and stroking my hair and whispering my name over and over, the lull of his voice rocking me away from this horror. Like the rush of morning light that floods a dark room after a night of endless, mindless terror, sending reminders that the world is not a completely awful place. That even screaming children awaken from nightmares.

Theron tightens his hold on me and I realize that I *am* screaming, my voice pinching in strangled sobs. I drop my chakram on the floor and bury my face in Theron's shirt, wanting to splinter into fragments of myself and disintegrate into him. I don't think it's possible for him to hold me any tighter but he does, his arms clasped around me, impenetrable walls enveloping my body as the smell of blood washes over me.

I killed Herod.

"Meira," Theron says again, just my name, like it's all he knows how to say. "Meira."

He kisses my forehead, my hair, keeping my face pressed into his chest and away from the mangled corpse of Herod at our feet. He's dead. He's gone.

Something on the edge of my mind, something distant

and numb, urges me to pull back from Theron. I look up at him until he comes into focus, his dark eyes, the bruises on his face, the dried blood on his forehead. The small shadow of a smile on his lips, still trying to offer comfort in a place so horrible.

"We'll be all right," he says. Us. Together, we'll be all right.

Theron pulls me to my feet, keeping my back to Herod's body. I watch his eyes dart to the bloody corpse behind me. I don't even know what I did to Herod. I don't remember anything but the feel of my chakram, slick with blood.

I'm coated in blood—my pathetic cotton shirt, the torn pants I wore under my armor for Bithai's battle. It's splattered all over my face, my hair, but I can't bring myself to touch it to wipe it off.

"What now?" I close my eyes and draw in a calming breath, focusing on how the air flows into my lungs, fills me up. *Alive. I'm alive.*

And Angra will never be able to use Herod to hurt anyone again.

I don't think what I saw in Sir when he killed people was ease. What I saw was what I'm feeling now—tired and sad and even more connected to the endless strands of life. But not regret. I don't regret killing Herod.

I wish I could tell Sir all of this. I wish I could talk to him about everything.

Theron backs up a step, and when I open my eyes he's

surveying Herod's room. A wardrobe in the corner catches his attention and he marches toward it. The doors swing open, light from the windows spilling over an array of clothes and shoes and weapons.

"What's next," Theron says, "is we join my father's army and free your people."

29

THERE'S NO TIME to find proper battle gear or steal
something from Angra's armory, so we divide the weapons
in Herod's room between us and I take clothes from the
wardrobe. Theron busies himself with strapping knives to
his shins while I peel out of my blood-soaked clothes and
put on Herod's too-big shirt and pants. There's a black
leather vest I tighten around the shirt and a thick belt that
keeps the pants up. It's ridiculous for a battle, far too baggy
and loose and about as protective as running around stark
naked. And it belongs to Herod, which makes my stomach
roll with the same nausea I feel from his blood drying on
my skin.

When my chakram settles in its familiar holster between
my shoulder blades, I'm able to breathe for the first time in
weeks. Like I'm never truly whole without it. Coupled with

the knife and sword I strap to my waist, I'm as prepared for war as I can be.

Theron hefts a sword in one hand, a dagger in the other. "Ready?"

I nod. He approaches the door to Herod's chamber, shifts his weapons, and opens it a crack, surveying the hall beyond. I take one determined step after him, keeping my eyes on Theron's back and the two crisscrossing knives strapped over his spine. Not on the body still in the center of the room, the unmoving mass of darkness and blood that pulls at my mind like an anchor on a boat.

Theron looks back at me. He is an anchor too. Something to hold on to when all other things drag me down.

I nod again. "Let's go."

The hall is empty. No soldiers, no frantic, running servants. It's quiet and desolate, as if we've already won and Spring has fled.

Theron creeps ahead of me, his blades ready, while I slide the chakram into my hand. The farther we get from Herod's room, the more chaos bubbles up. Clumps of uniformed men sprint between rooms, servants bustle down hallways and keep as out of sight as possible. Theron and I duck under wall hangings, hide behind statues and plants, as we weave our way out of the darkness.

After what feels like a lifetime of this hide-and-run through the palace, we reach a narrow servants' staircase, open doors revealing the entryway to the palace at the bottom. We slide down the stairs and pause behind the open door, listening for movement in the hall.

Theron shifts his weapons to one hand and gropes for mine with the other. "We leave the palace," he whispers. "Wherever my father approaches, we run in the opposite direction. Abril's wall will be less patrolled there and we can—"

"Leave Abril," I finish, my voice trembling.

Theron looks back at me, his face dropping like he knows what I'm going to say next. "We will free your people, I promise you. But you're no good to them if you're dead."

I shake my head and pull my hand out of his, heart pumping ice through my veins. I start to protest, tell him I have to go to the Winterians, have to help them because I'm their conduit and it's my duty. I start to tell him again. I'm Winter's queen, all this time. I'm—

But Theron shifts his attention for a beat to the hall, where a stomping group of soldiers files past, into the throne room. The hall quiets in their wake, empty, and he pulls back to me, not seeming to care about anything beyond the way his eyes lock on mine with a gentle intensity.

"I never wanted to be a king." Theron's voice is low and quick, cutting through me with urgency. "I wanted to sit in my library and write until the sun fell from the sky. But you—this—the Winterians, your entire kingdom, gone in a heartbeat—it's made me realize how I would feel if Cordell ever fell like that, if I ever lost something so much a part of me. I want to be someone worthy of my kingdom. I want to be someone worthy of *you*."

My whole body lights up with a wondrous chill that amplifies when Theron slides his hand around the back of my neck. He draws my face up to his and pauses, some of his certainty fading in the realization of what he's doing and how close we are to each other. His fingers curl against the back of my neck and I stare up at him, waiting, unable to move or breathe or think beyond the way his lips part in an exhale, so close to mine.

Then he falls into me, his mouth collapsing over my own. A moan eases out of my throat as I grab at the emotions that fly through my body like flurries of snow in the wind. Fear we'll be caught by Angra's men; ecstasy at the burst of comfort and need that swirls off his lips; and a steady flicker of shock that this isn't at all shocking, that I've been waiting for this to happen all along—our lips and tongues and his fingers pulling my hair, desperation exploding out of us in a few too-short seconds of needing each other.

He pulls back, gasping through a rapid array of emotions before he nods firmly, decisively. "Go to them, but don't die. Primoria needs people like you," he finishes, and dashes into the empty hallway, leading the way to the two large front doors, blades glinting for hidden enemies. My body follows but my mind is stuck on the feel of his lips on mine. Beautiful and equal, gentle and certain, making me cold and warm all at once.

We ease out the doors and slink down the great obsidian steps, not stopping once our feet hit the rolling expanse of Angra's lawn. It's empty here too, all soldiers either guarding Angra inside or busy at the front gate, where the firing of cannons echoes back at us. Theron shoots me a small smile of reassurance before he flies across the lush grass, running and running for cover at the north end of Angra's palace complex. From there, he'll go east, opposite his father's approaching army.

But my path lies southwest.

My feet move before I realize I'm running, the palace complex whooshing past me in a blur of black and green. I leap over the garden Nessa and her brothers have been working in for weeks. The entire area is empty, no soldiers or workers. It's late afternoon now, the sun high and bright, with plenty of light left to force out a few more hours of work. But no one is here, so that must mean they're in the camp, a panicked switch in their daily routine, or—

I won't think about *or*.

Anxiety pushes me faster as I twist out a side gate and fly into Abril.

This part of the city is not so empty. Spring's upper-class citizens prepare their houses, servants and stable hands nailing planks of wood over windows at their masters' orders. They don't care when I run by, don't even flinch in my direction when the blur of white and black flashes past them. I scale the side of a bridge and I'm gone, leaving them to their worries.

The bridge drops me into the lower part of the city. I surge down alleys, leap over piles of trash. The residents of these buildings stay exactly where I've always seen them—huddled behind windows, peeking through doorways, staying out of the way in the hope that life will pass them without too much notice. As if, if they don't acknowledge the approaching battle, it can't hurt them.

One last bend up ahead will put me right in front of the entrance to Abril's work camp. I slow to a walk, holding my breath to keep from gasping for air. It may be empty in this alley, but it's not quiet—noises filter to me from up ahead. Soldiers shout orders at each other, and beyond their mangled barks lies the hum of people in confusion. My people.

The words feel wrong, like they don't belong to me, like I'm not worthy of calling them that. But it doesn't matter what I call them, what they call me. I have the ability to free them, therefore I have the responsibility to free them. That's all that matters now.

That's all that has ever mattered.

I stop parallel to the corner. *One more step, Meira. Just one more.*

I march onto the road, pulling my chakram out so it dangles like a harmless toy from my hands. Five buildings ahead of me, the gate is madness. Spring soldiers on the outside throw blades and fists against the bending, creaking metal, punching back the swell of Winterians who push against the other side. The Winterians cry and scream, flinching against the blows. They're confused, jerked out of their routine of work and forced back into their prison in chaos.

The first soldier drops without a fight. My chakram whizzes across the back of his neck, severing the top of his spine from his skull, and thunks back into my palm as the man collapses on the soldier next to him, pulling attention to me. First the dead man's neighbor, then the man next to him, then every soldier charged with keeping order in the work camp. All eyes are on me, one lone Winterian girl against a whole battalion.

One soldier steps forward, his thick sword dinged with age and use. "Herod's toy escaped," he sneers.

"Herod's toy killed him," I respond, and a satisfying flash of shock takes over his face.

Another voice cracks out over the street. "Meira, run!"

My eyes flick behind the line of soldiers to the gate. Conall presses against the iron, the wire leaving streaks of blood on his cheeks and arms. He's panicked, seeing me on the street. There's a light in his eyes now, a light so different from his usual hatred that I have to be imagining it.

But no—it's hope. He wants me to live.

Angra senses it too. He knows somehow, this hope they all have, and the Spring soldiers fly at the gate in one organized mass, raising all their weapons at the same moment. A strangled moan pops out of my lungs. Angra's dark magic. He's told them to—

They start striking to kill now. Jabbing their blades through the metal, stabbing chests and necks, no longer mere warning blows. I can feel Angra's order pulsing out of their driven bodies: *Slaughter them.*

My chest numbs, and for once I know what it is. Cold, icy cold, darting out to my shoulders and rushing down to my fingers. The conduit's power churns around me, surging in and out of my body like an uncontrollable snowstorm, begging to coat the world in glorious white.

Winter has a conduit now too. And we won't be weak anymore.

I drop my chakram at my feet and shoot my hands out, fingers stretching to the Winterians in front of me. The cold blasts out of me, an eruption of such perfect chill that I wonder if I'm nothing more than a snowstorm now, a great twirling column of flakes. The cold rushes around the Spring soldiers and plunges through the gate, flooding every frail, white-haired body, every pair of wide blue eyes, every bleeding, tired soul with strength, power, energy, healing their bruises and soothing their cuts and making them stronger, stronger, stronger—

The magic pours until every free space in every body is filled with strength. Their eyes shine brighter, their bodies stand straighter, their fists clench tighter. Cold and frost, so much beautiful power that when the icy sensation stops, I'm left gasping in the aftermath of such wonder.

Adrenaline courses through me, blissfully combatting the pull of exhaustion that makes me sway forward under all the power I just exerted.

The Winterians scream, something far beyond their cries of pain and anguish, something breaking out of them in a rush of freedom. The Spring soldiers' attack pauses in the echoing war cry from their prisoners. And the Winterians, their eyes fiery with life, slam forward, breaking open the gate with a frantic determination.

"Attack!" a Spring soldier cries, and charges at me.

I hook my chakram with my boot and kick it into the air, grabbing it and launching it in a great spin of death into the approaching stampede of Spring soldiers. A few fall as my chakram smacks back into my palm, but the soldiers are too close now, a few seconds from colliding with me. I return the chakram to my back and yank out the sword and dagger I stole from Herod, body coiling down. Four seconds. Three . . .

The farthest soldiers go down as one, their legs falling out from under them. The next row glances back, panicked, and falls just as easily, pulled to the ground by the mad hatred of sixteen years of oppression. The Winterians rise up and over the Spring battalion in a deadly wave of destruction, tearing weapons out of hands and turning those weapons on the shocked faces of soldiers who never thought they would lose.

The last row of Spring soldiers reaches me, caught between fear behind them and fear ahead. My dagger jabs into one's stomach, my sword through another's neck. I twirl between the soldiers, my body a machine of slice and stab and duck.

I move around one last dying man, my boots kicking up dust around me, and stop in front of Conall. He's bloody and wild, his white hair streaked with red, his hands clasped around a pair of short knives. Beside him, Garrigan is just as untamed, a beast inside them unleashed, and behind them are the other Winterians.

Arms clamp around my neck in a storm of white and tears. "I knew you'd free us," Nessa breathes.

Conall steps forward, his knives glinting with Spring blood. "We're not free yet. What next, my queen?"

My queen. How does he know?

I pull back from Nessa and stare at them, all of them, every eager face. Every innocent, patient soul, accepting the power from me without question, without hesitation.

And I feel Hannah in me. Her gentle, waiting presence, as connected to the conduit's power as I am. She's in all the Winterians too, connecting us in an inexplicable and marvelous world all our own.

She is my daughter, she whispers to them, a voice so quiet they could mistake it for their own thoughts. *It's going to be all right. I'm sorry I lied to you, but your freedom is so close.*

The hope on the dirt-smudged faces fills me with a different emotion, one that snuffs out any fear of who I am now. Happiness.

"Cordell and Autumn are at Spring's gates, but our freedom is not theirs to win," I shout over the crowd. The next words stick in my throat, building and building alongside all the bubbling anxiety, the years of abuse, the scars and blood and gore. "We are Winter!"

Conall and Garrigan tip their heads back, arms outstretched as they shout to the sky. A battle cry that spreads to every Winterian, their voices creaking, their eyes shining.

"We are Winter!" Nessa echoes, and leaps over the fallen Spring bodies, running up the road with her stolen sword blazing above her head. They follow her, dashing over bodies, waving weapons like banners of victory.

Their strength, conduit-given or not, is invigorating, filling me with my own magic. I want to bask in it forever.

You're so close now, Hannah says.

I fall into line with them, running just as hard, screaming just as loud, lost in the voices and the power and the lives of the Winterians.

WE FOLLOW THE sounds of battle to the square at Abril's front gate and find Spring soldiers sprinting in perfectly lined groups, cannons firing with lethal precision, cranks lifting weapons up and down the walls. Angra's conduit pushes them with a threat that makes every movement deliberate, in line, perfect.

A horn cries out as we surge down the streets leading to the gate. Angra's faultlessly aligned soldiers pivot toward us, snapping out of their conduit stupor. Angra warned them we were coming, but knowing does not a prepared army make.

We raise our weapons, raise our voices, raise our speed. We are one body now. One all-consuming wave of white and filth and sixteen years of death. Angra's men realign themselves to face us, their backs to the gate, more than half of their focus pulled away from Noam's attacking army to us. The one thing Abril in all its war-mindedness never prepared for: a breach *inside* the wall.

We collide with Angra's men, pouring into them like a plague. They return with just as much force, pushing into us with strength pulled from the Decay in Angra's conduit. There are only a few hundred of us and most are no more fighters than the children and elderly who stayed behind. Our advantage of surprise won't hold for long.

I impale a Spring soldier and drop to the ground, pulling his body down beside me to serve as a shield. The square before the gate is nearly the size of Angra's palace grounds, wide and open to allow for ease of movement. Two staircases frame the gate and lead to the walkway above, and a small building leans against the wall on my left. The gatehouse.

A group of Winterian men tackle a charging cluster of Spring soldiers, and I use the chaos to shield myself from other enemies. They fall backward and I get up and run, dashing over bodies, discarded blades, stacks of crates. The iron tang of blood and old weapons hangs in hot, heavy balls of repulsion, smacking into me as I barrel for the thin wooden door of the gatehouse.

I sheath my blades and draw out my chakram before planting a firm kick that sends the door banging into the wall. Inside the gatehouse, two soldiers flip around and, just as quickly, two blades fly through air, small knives that spin with desperate determination for me. I duck and one flies over my shoulder while the other grazes my wrist.

But it's my turn now, so I bite back my wince. I let the chakram go, my blade slicing the soldiers' necks in death-blows before it shoots back to me. As their bodies fall, I jump over them, eyeing the lever in the center of the room. A thick metal rod stretches into the air at an angle, nearly as tall as me, from a hodgepodge of gears. The rod sticks out more to the left than the right, so maybe if I move it to the right . . .

I holster the chakram and throw all my weight into the rod. It groans against my movements, the old iron creaking in angry rebuttal against being opened. I brace my foot on the wall of the gatehouse, pulling and heaving, begging the stupid thing to just give in and release.

A hand slides on the lever over mine. I flinch back, already half reaching for my knife, when Garrigan stops me. Conall stumbles in behind him, a bloody sword in one hand, and moves around me to grab the rod too.

We heave as one, and the crank releases under our collective weight, giving up as if it can feel the impending collapse of its kingdom. It slams into place and beyond the gatehouse, beyond the fight, the massive wall of iron starts to lift into the air, grinding and groaning.

Conall, Garrigan, and I run out of the gatehouse. Winterians and Spring soldiers alike pause, eyeing the lifting gate, analyzing what it means for Abril.

As soon as the gate gets high enough, a wave of men pours through, adding Cordell's green and gold to Spring's black-sun armor and Winter's stark-white hair. Mixed with the Cordellan soldiers are copper-skinned men in maroon and orange that fly between batches of enemies with an exotic grace, slicing through flesh with hair-thin blades and hurling balls that spew toxic smoke. Their heir may be too young to wield her conduit, but Autumn soldiers can still make a sword fight look like a choreographed dance and wield weapons that are just as functional as they are gruesome—like chakrams. As a few spinning metal discs soar into the air, I grin. Sir originally got my chakram from Autumn, and seeing dozens of them shooting all around me now makes me feel even more united in this effort. A Winterian wielding an Autumnian weapon, using Cordellan allegiance to bring Spring crumbling down.

The Winterians roil into a frenzy, adding their brute hatred to Cordell's organized attacks and Autumn's skilled warriors. But Angra has numbers. It makes for a horrifying and mesmerizing fight, black and orange and green and white.

An arrow whizzes past my ear from somewhere on the other side of the square. My eyes find its source and a white-haired man in Cordell's armor slashes through the Spring archer before he's swallowed by a group of black-clad soldiers. Mather? Or maybe Greer or Henn—

I dart around parrying enemies, duck under flying

blades. Angra's men swivel the wall's cannons to focus on the square inside the gate. Their blasts send mounds of earth scattering into the air around me, making it rain rocks and rubble. Blades up, I slash blindly at Spring soldiers where I can as I work my way to that flash of white hair in Cordellan armor. A pair locked in combat swings around me and I twist to narrowly avoid a blade to the head, sliding on my knees in a small patch of grass on the other side of the square, where Abril's slums rise into the sky.

For a breath I pause, scanning the area, muscles tight and waiting, until a blade lunges at me. I spin and catch it, instinct driving me as I see beyond the blade, to the soldier holding it.

Not just a soldier—Angra.

And it isn't just a blade. One hand holds a thin, strong sword, the other grasps his staff, a weapon in its own right.

Angra wears his own version of Spring's armor, but his is fine and gleaming. He pulls back, taking his sword and staff with him, and glares down at me as our men kill each other around us. "All this time," he growls. "I should have felt the magic in you long before you were able to use it."

My fingers turn white on my blades. "You shouldn't have let yourself become corrupted."

Angra growls and rears back. I leap to him, talking as fast as possible, squeezing words into the space between us. "There's a way to defeat it, Angra," I hiss. "The Decay. If you let the other monarchs know, we can vanquish it like they almost did thousands of years ago!"

Angra pauses, blade and staff raised, his eyes narrowing in something like shock. I hold my breath in the roar of adrenaline around me, latching on to the flicker of hope in his face—

But someone shouts my name, a distant warning on the edge of my subconscious. I flinch and Angra strikes, swinging his sword out, his staff close behind. He bats the knife from my hand as I drop, sliding away from the falling metal. He's far more experienced than me and uses my momentum to bring his sword back to meet me halfway, his blade slicing clean through my shoulder.

I groan and fall on my arm, pain searing across my skin. Can I heal myself? Angra doesn't give me time to try. He drops to the ground on top of me, a knee pinning me to the grass between one of his dilapidated slum buildings and the chaotic battle. He swings his face down, blond curls matted with sweat and filth.

"I don't need saving," he spits, and flies back off me, readying for another strike.

Angra comes at me again and I release my sword from my injured right arm to flip backward, watching his blade impale the grass where my head was a heartbeat ago. He slashes and thrusts, not giving me a chance to retaliate, chasing me as I scramble on hands and knees across the lawn to the square. Legs fly out of my way, allies cut down by Angra's swinging, biting weapons, forging a haphazard path through the chaos that allows me to crawl away.

"Meira!" someone screams, but I don't have time to look for who it is.

A Spring soldier runs at us, intent on helping his king. But Angra rounds on him in a flurry of hot anger. "She's *mine!*"

I use that opening to hurl my last weapon. My chakram flies through the debris-heavy air only to smack feebly off Angra's armor. He knocks it out of its spin, sending it skittering over the ground, and turns to me, manic glee streaked over his face.

"That's all you have? Hundreds of years of war, and this is your kingdom's grand finale?"

"No."

The voice rumbles over the lawn, over the world. It floods me from the recesses of Angra's cruel nightmare, when I knelt on the floor of a cottage in Jannuari and Sir held me, rocking me back and forth.

But this isn't a nightmare. This is real, better than anything I dared dream up myself, and as my eyes lock onto him, I don't know how I'll ever be able to breathe again.

Sir is alive.

Angra turns as Sir leaps through the air, two curved knives slicing the wind into fragments and speeding straight for Angra's heart. Only a breath passes before Angra reacts, swinging his staff up to stop one of the blades and his sword to catch the other.

"Meira!" Mather slides to the ground beside me, his arms coming under my shoulders to pull me to my feet. I blink at him, caught in another cruel dream. Mather's here. And Sir—

I stare, trying to get the last image I have of Sir to make sense with what I see now. Bleeding and broken on the ground outside of Bithai; dancing through the air on grunts and thrusts, driving Angra back just as viciously as Angra returns his blows. His body is whole and strong, flying around as his muscles do what they were made to do. He and Angra are matched blade for blade, moving before us through the bloody massacre of war.

My fingers dig into Mather's arm, my heart freezing.

"Sir?" I breathe.

The tension in my chest loosens. It doesn't matter who I am now, queen or not, because Sir's here. Sir's alive. And he'll be able to help me through this.

When I look at Mather, he nods. "You healed him, Meira. Everyone thought he was dead, but when he awoke after the battle, he told us you healed him. A fluke in conduit magic that somehow you harnessed," Mather whispers.

I grab onto his words and try to fit them into the gaping puzzle around me. What I remember most about Sir's death is my desperation, my thoughtless need, pure and strong, for him to live. Maybe that was a type of surrender—opening myself up to anything, everything, that could save him. An unconscious decision, like when I healed the boy.

Mather reads the distance in my eyes, my swelling exuberance. He bows his head. "My queen."

That pulls me back to the present, roaring and horrible. To Mather, a broken look in his eyes.

"You know?" I gasp on the words and feel everything else come crashing down on me. All of Mather's worries and concerns and strain, how he wanted so badly to be enough in a station where he never would be. And now—none of that matters, because it isn't him anymore.

Mather bobs his head again. Around us the battle rages on, but in that one moment of looking at each other, I can't tell if he's relieved or scared. All I can feel is his strength, the determined way he looks at me, a soldier to his ruler. He'll hold on as long as I need him to.

The locket half still sits around his neck, a physical reminder of the lie of his life. My eyes lock on it before swinging away, a rush of adrenaline pushing through me as I look back at Angra and Sir trapped in a flurry of swords. Angra's conduit dances through the air and Sir's focus follows it, his gaze hungry and desperate.

A weight drops in my stomach. Sir needs to know what it really is, what he's really fighting. The way he looks at Angra's staff, like he wants to obliterate it into a million pieces—that cannot happen. Angra's conduit *cannot* be broken, the magic allowed to link with him in an endless feed for the Decay.

A blade comes out of nothing, the cannon debris making the air a dark and dangerous place. I scream and shove Mather down, buckling under the sword as the Spring soldier continues his swipe through the air. Mather turns, throws me his blade, and I grab it midair before barreling headfirst into the soldier's stomach. We fall, rolling down a slight incline in a fit of darkness and dirt as my sword slides home into the soldier's gut.

A series of screams. Names shouted in rapid order, panicked screeches that make me pivot in the dirt.

"Mather, grab it!"

"William—"

"MATHER!"

I struggle to my feet, eyes flashing over the space now between me, Mather, Sir. A swell of horror pulses in me and I'm frozen, watching it all happen.

Sir knocks Angra's staff from his hands. It flies through the air, flipping end over end to land in a clatter at Mather's feet. Sir lunges away from Angra as he reaches out to Mather, something horrible and terrified exploding out of him like nothing I've ever seen. Panic pushes up my throat, tasting like the iron tang of blood.

Mather picks up the staff.

"Break it!" Sir's voice is strangled. He swipes at Angra, knocking him to the ground. "Destroy it!"

"I will kill you!" Angra screams, scrambling against the dirt. He flies up and Sir tackles him next to Mather's feet.

One of Sir's curved knives slams into Angra's shoulder, pinning him to the earth with Sir hovering a breath above him.

Mather looks at me. There's that determined severity again, some great pull of desperation. He'll protect me. He'll keep me safe. He can still do this one thing, even if he isn't who he always thought he was.

He raises the staff over his head. Angra's conduit. The Decay that overtook the land, the hideous, unstoppable evil that came to Angra, joined with him and has been gaining strength from his corrupt magic use. Mather's arms tighten against the coming impact as he pulls the staff through the air, a slow and painful draw.

Dismay overcomes me, so palpable it rushes in molten rivers through my body as all the last lingering pieces click and I fly forward, scrambling toward Mather.

"Mather, no!" I shout. "*Stop!*"

But he doesn't hear me. He doesn't know, doesn't even think about it. No one did. No one would have thought the answer was so simple, the power so close.

The staff cracks against the earth in a glass-shattering burst. Darkness explodes out of it, a storm unleashed, a funnel of smoke that erupts in a shaft of black. In the chaos, the surrounding battle halts, the wind whipping into screams, desperate fingers of sound that plunge through the crowd of watching soldiers. The column of black launches up into the sky where thick clouds have gathered, twirling around and around in a vortex that will destroy us all.

I throw my arms around Mather and pull him back from the shattered staff, the embodiment of all that has held us captive for so long. We collapse on the ground, my arms around his shoulders, his eyes twisted in confusion. Around us, everyone has stopped. Spring, Cordellan, Autumnian, Winterian—everyone casts aside their fighting to gape in unabashed wonder.

Everyone except Angra. His eyes meet mine, barely two steps from where I cling to Mather. The hilt of the knife sticks up in the gap between Angra's breastplate and arm piece; blood runs from a gash through his cheek. But his eyes flash, the pale green depths reflecting the whirring gale. The expansion of magic in the Royal Conduits that even he didn't know about until he saw me, until he pieced together my use of the magic without the locket and realized what I am now. The magic and Decay that are locked in his conduit will join with him, feed into him, become one. He will be able to use his magic for evil at an unstoppable rate—without a staff or an object conduit, because he will *become* the magic's conduit, and the Decay will grow more powerful than anyone can control.

The column of black sucks into a thin line and holds, waiting, ticking through time. On a great gust of wind it explodes, slamming into the ground and unfolding over us with a powerful burst of air and debris. Mather throws himself on top of me, and we bury our faces in each other as the force tosses rocks through the air.

It's over. Just like that. No final explosion, no departing scream of death. Just nothing, like it was never anything more than the shattered ball of glass and metal at Mather's feet.

I push away from Mather, but I know what I'll see before my eyes find it. The magic in me whispers it in the deepest, most open parts of my mind, a quiet nudge of knowledge.

Sir sits back on his heels, staring with wide eyes at the empty splotch of dirt under him. His knife still sits in the earth, poised vertically against the gentle current of wind.

But Angra is gone.

31

THE WORLD IS wrong, tilted off balance, and when I stand on shaky legs I fall forward, scrambling in the air.

Sir catches me. He cradles me against his chest, his strong arms wrapping around me so tightly I know it must be a dream, and I expect him to call me his sweet girl and for Alysson to be just behind us, serving dinner to Nessa and her family.

But Sir is real. He is here. He is alive. And when I push back from him, look up at his face, the world stops tilting quite so much.

His lips part. "It's over."

My eyes fall behind him, to the empty expanse of dirt where Angra's body was. Like the staff breaking destroyed him. Like it was just that easy.

Everyone thinks it was. Everyone including the Spring

soldiers, who dropped their weapons at the disappearance of their king and magic, now cowering in reluctant surrender while their enemies rejoice. Green and gold and maroon and white bodies dance around the square, cheering at the cloudy sky.

I close my eyes, breathe in, focusing on the air flowing in and out of my lungs, on Sir's arms around my shoulders. I focus beyond him, on the sound of the Winterians' pure and shameless happiness turning this miserable city into a paradise just for a moment.

"Meira."

I open my eyes to see Sir staring down at me, his face locked in an expression I've never seen on him before. It takes me a moment to realize it's admiration.

"We decided long ago that I would be the one to tell you. The others who escaped, I mean," he whispers. "I don't know how Angra found out. I should have—"

My body goes cold, the swirling conduit-magic now awakened and wild. I inhale, trembling as I put a hand on Sir's arm. "No." I shake my head. "It was Hannah's secret to tell, not yours."

Sir frowns. "Hannah?"

I shrug, not sure how I can explain this, but Sir shakes it away. He takes a step backward and drops to his knees as he lifts a fist up to me. Dangling out of that fist is a silver chain.

"My queen" is all he says.

I flinch, hating the fear that blossoms at the title. I don't want him to call me that, but the way he looks up at me is something I've wanted all my life. Like he sees me, truly sees me, no matter how I am. Covered in blood and dirt and dust, glowing with the potential of a renewed kingdom.

Like he sees all the sacrifices he's made and doesn't regret a single one.

I reach for the locket but another hand beats me there. My fingers pause, outstretched in the dusty air, lingering over Mather's hand as he takes the locket from his father.

Mather unclasps the other half and slides it off his neck. He holds both halves out to me, his jewel-blue eyes glistening gray under the overcast sky. "Yours, my queen," he says. His hands shake and he runs his tongue over his lips. Everything about him is strong, unwavering, but the look in his eyes speaks of a deeper fear. Fear of unbecoming, fear of all his many, many responsibilities shifting onto someone else's shoulders.

I lift my hand. A hundred things push at me, a hundred different ways I want to apologize or grovel or cry. I'm sorry it's me. I'm sorry his whole life was created to keep me safe, his entire existence shattered around this one simple lie. I'm sorry we had to grow up so abruptly. I'm sorry for everything.

But I don't say any of that. I take the locket pieces from his hand, keeping my eyes on his, my mouth open like maybe, just maybe, I'll find the right words.

Mather exhales when the locket leaves his skin. He rises, standing with the weight of all that has happened. His lips twitch into the pale beginnings of a smile but he stays there, suspended between happiness and shock.

"I am yours to command, my queen," he whispers, and bows his head.

I place my palm on his cheek before I even realize I've moved, the cut on my shoulder making me cringe.

I wish we wouldn't hurt. Not now. Not after all this.

Numbness shoots up my hand and my eyes widen. I didn't mean to call on the magic, but it's alive now, awakened, and the numbness climbs, grows, and surges from my palm into Mather's cheek.

He gasps. My whole body goes cold, icy and brilliant, and a new light shines in Mather's eyes. It chases away his exhaustion and fear, filling him with the same strength that filled the other Winterians. Nothing definite. Just a small ray to keep him going, to keep his uncertainty at bay until he finds the will to face it.

Is he relieved to have the burden of being king gone? Or is he just afraid?

Mather steps back, pulling out of my hand, and slides to the ground, mimicking Sir's stance. Behind them, the cheering has dissipated into reverent awe, and every Winterian slowly slides to the ground. Their heads bow, their white hair smudged brown and red and black. My breathing tightens, and I can't decide whether I want them to stop or not. They look so happy. So whole. And I can't break that happiness, no matter how terrifying it is that I'm the reason they're bowing. Me, the orphaned soldier-girl.

I spot Dendera near the gate with Henn beside her as they kneel, both of them locked in an embrace that's tight and intimate and makes me nearly intoxicated with happiness. Greer and Finn lean on each other, a bloody gash through Finn's left leg. Conall, and Garrigan, and Nessa, and even Deborah—everyone is happy, and here, and safe.

And Theron. Behind them all, Theron lingers beyond the gate, a contingent of his father's battle-bruised men around him. His eyes meet mine across the expanse between us and he smiles, a slow, deliberate smile that echoes the reverence of this moment. He bows his head, mimicking the Cordellans, the Autumnians, absorbing the awe and wonder of a kingdom that isn't theirs. All of them smiling under the relief that came when Angra's body vanished.

Maybe Angra did die. Maybe the Decay disintegrated and ripped him down with it. So many maybes. So many years of thinking maybe they'll come, maybe they'll save us, maybe we'll see our kingdom whole again someday.

I bend down to Mather and Sir and put one hand on each of their shoulders. They look up at me, tears making them look morbidly happy.

I exhale and smile. "Let's go home."

With Angra gone, the other three work camps fall easily. Spring dissolves into a panicked chaos without its king, which makes our merged army's job even easier as we move through the kingdom, fighting off the soldiers who hold the other Winterians captive. Any exhaustion or fear or pain the Winterians felt in the camps is snuffed out beneath the roaring joy we bring when we save them. It's something I never get tired of, seeing their faces alight with the knowledge that they are free.

Two weeks pass, two weeks filled with freeing the other three camps, tending to the wounds of my people, slowly feeding nutrients back into them. The Autumn army departs once the last work camp is free, but Cordell stays, a choice I try not to question. Theron is quick to offer food and supplies from his army, and I take what he gives before Noam can say anything to the contrary. The Winterians see a unified front, soldiers and food and medicine, not a queen who until a few weeks ago had no idea who she was, or a king who a few months ago wanted to dominate their land rather than save them. I will do everything I can to keep it that way, long enough for permanent healing to settle into their bodies and minds.

The permanent healing starts the moment we see Jannuari.

Winter's capital sits just inside the border, a few hours' ride from Spring. The vibrant cherry trees and emerald grass of Spring fade to Winter's fields of white perfection, unbroken rolling hills of snow and frozen clusters of icy, ivory trees. The change is instant, sweeping over me in a rush of . . . right. This is right. The chill, the frozen forests, the way everything is white—the sky, the ground, the air. This is home.

But it's Jannuari we all wait for with breathless excitement. Jannuari, our lost capital, a city I've only ever seen in crafted memories. The deeper we plunge into Winter, the more my chest tightens, until I fear I'll turn solid from anticipation long before we reach our destination.

The other Winterians see Jannuari first, the hazy outline of a city in the distance. They alert me with a cry of excitement and burst free from the ranks of Cordell's army with renewed vigor. Hundreds of feet pound in sudden delight over the empty fields, the vibrations shaking the whole world to bits.

Jannuari sits ahead of me under a snowless gray sky. Towns lie around the main bulk of the city, its wall shattered, rocks torn into a lumpy, uneven perimeter on the horizon. Within it a few towers still stand, their determined fingers reaching up to the sky like nothing's wrong, like they have been just waiting for us to come back.

You didn't kill us, Angra, and we will rise again.

I gallop alongside the other Winterians but pull my horse to a stop, a great war beast borrowed from Cordell's army. The Winterians continue running, too caught in their exuberance to notice I've stopped. My horse dances nervously on the old snow caked on the field, Winter's pale grass popping through the thin layer of ice beneath his hooves.

Sir pulls up alongside me, both of us sending clouds of frosty breath into the air.

"It'll need rebuilding. And we'll need to barter more rations from Cordell," he says.

A cold wind pushes through the white cotton shirt I borrowed from Theron. We're already indebted to him and his father more than we could ever repay—and the thought that we'll need even more makes my stomach pinch with dread. I know what Noam will want for all he's given: access to the Klaryns, to Winter, in an attempt to find the chasm of magic. Maybe that's why he hasn't stopped Theron from providing us with supplies. Maybe that's why he hasn't returned to Cordell yet, why he's let his army linger around us like guards standing watch over an investment.

Whatever his reason, we need him and what he offers, and until he tries to collect, I can't worry about it. Too much.

"I know."

"But it'll be good for them." Sir shifts on his saddle, one hand relaxing on the reins. "It'll be good. Rebuild the city as they heal. They need this."

I nod. We all need this. We need to fix something, work through it with our bare hands and feel the life flow back into our veins. To do something true and brilliant and right.

Sir looks sidelong at me, turned away enough that I can't see his expression. "You're just like her."

I search his face. "Hannah?"

He nods. "Every moment of your life."

Cold twinges through me. His way of telling me I can do this. I can bring our kingdom together again, lead them on to a better future.

Whatever that future holds, Angra resides there too.

I swallow, catching my lower lip between my teeth as I inhale the cold, cold air. We've been so busy with the happiness of freeing the other work camps, of traveling to Winter, that I haven't wanted to ruin the joy. It's so fragile, this joy, and a part of me doesn't want to say anything, doesn't want to draw attention to bad things until we need to.

But not telling Sir could make it worse when the time does come. If it comes. If my suspicions are right, if Angra isn't dead and his threat not over and everything we fought for still only an illusion of true peace.

"I don't think Angra died," I whisper, a sad sound on the chill air. "And his magic . . . it's worse than we thought. Much worse."

Sir doesn't say anything, and for a moment I think maybe my voice got sucked away on the wind. I look at him and he wears that same impenetrable expression he got when I returned from Lynia with the locket half. Scared and determined, like he's staring down the future and doesn't have room to fear the past.

I touch the locket at my neck. It's whole now. Whole and empty, powerless, but touching it gives me a strange calm. Just like that lapis lazuli stone. Just like hope. The Winterians around me think the power is now safely back in the locket—they think all the times I used it were what Mather told me, a fluke. A desperate surge brought on by how far we had fallen. It doesn't occur to them that the magic could be anywhere else now, and I'm not sure I want to correct them.

Not just them, though—Cordell too. Noam especially.

"One thing at a time," Sir says. His eyes meet mine, showing me how tired he is, how scared. "We'll handle the future one thing at a time."

I start to nod when horses gallop through the crowd of still-running Winterians and canter to a halt beside us. Theron and Noam shiver in their saddles, eyes darting between Jannuari, Sir, and me. Noam at least tries to look dignified in his coldness while Theron wraps his arms around himself and lets his teeth clack together like hooves on the plain. Mather pulls his horse between mine and Theron's, an eyebrow lifted as he assesses our nearly frozen foreign guests.

"Tell me there's a cloak shop somewhere in there," Theron says, a shiver making him twitch awkwardly on his horse.

Mather laughs, a sharp and beautiful sound that I haven't heard in years. He's been smiling a little more each day, that beautiful, full-face smile that makes everything around him light up. "Poor Cordellan prince. Can't handle a little chill?"

"A *little* chill?" Theron squeaks. He motions at the army, the Cordellans looking just as frozen and uncomfortable as their leaders. "We're going to have nothing but soldier-icicles by the end of this. My father sneezed earlier and it froze in midair!"

I giggle from my horse and Theron glances at me. The look in his eyes shifts from lighthearted laughter to something deeper, something lingering from our anxious kiss in the halls of Angra's palace.

Mather adjusts himself on his horse between us, his jaw setting. I tear my eyes away from Theron as a slow grin spreads across my face, and I want to laugh at the absurdity of this situation. Normal problems. Normal worries about suitors. It's what Sir wanted all along, wasn't it? And after everything . . . normal problems feel wonderful.

Noam grunts on the other side of his son but doesn't say anything. Whether it's because he has nothing to say or his lips have frozen shut, I can't tell. We've yet to discuss the marriage arrangement, whether a Rhythm still wants to ally his son with a Season, or if Winter's growing debt to Cordell is enough of a connection. He started to ask me a few days ago, when we were resting between raids on work camps. Noam stretched out his hand to shake mine and when our skin touched, I saw again the vibrant image of him kneeling at his wife's bedside. A connection that comes from the fact that I'm a conduit myself—a connection the other Royal Conduit–bearers must not be aware of, except for Angra, and only because he used the Decay. Noam must think I'm just a weak, unstable queen who trembles when she touches him.

I think he needs to believe that, though. It's better if he underestimates me, if he has no idea about my true power. An extra boost in Winter's favor when he does decide to collect on all he's given us.

"If you're done bickering about the chill," Sir cuts in, "I believe we have introductions to make."

He meets my eyes, beams, and kicks his horse to a gallop, hooves tearing up clumps of melted snow as he darts between the running Winterians. Theron and Noam plunge after him, weaving in and out of my running white-haired people toward a city many of us don't remember. Only Mather lingers, his exhales releasing bursts of icy clouds between us, his eyes on me as I watch everyone around us.

"I'm sorry," I exhale.

Mather's horse dances on the snow, disturbed by our tension. I peel my gaze away from the running horde to meet Mather's sapphire eyes for more than a passing glance. It's the longest either of us has looked at each other since the battle in Abril, and the gaze is heavy with apology.

He snorts air out his nose in a soft, incredulous laugh. "Don't apologize. You didn't do anything wrong." His focus sweeps over the city ahead of us. "At all."

"I know, I just—" I stop short, and Mather pivots back to me.

"I know," he echoes, and the smile he gives me is genuine. He shifts again, tightening the reins in his hands. "If either of us should feel bad, it's me. William told us the truth after you were captured, and all I could think was: You're the one who has the responsibility now. I'm free."

Mather keeps his gaze firmly on the horizon as he talks, and if I hadn't been looking at him, I might've accepted his lighthearted tone, his jovial manner. But I watch his face as he speaks, watch the way his eyes narrow, his lips pull into a thin line. There's far too much truth in what he says. *I'm free.*

Maybe it's not a freedom he wants.

"When I was in Cordell," I start, "and I had to play the part of their future queen, I pretended I was—" My words catch and I chuckle. "I pretended I was you."

My confession hangs in the air, a whispered strand of words that hovers in the falling flakes of snow. Mather smiles at me through it, some of his tension softening before he drops his head in a small bow.

"My queen," he says in response. He kicks his horse into a gallop that sends them both launching into the running horde, another body racing for Jannuari's wall.

I watch him go, my chest unwinding. We're really here. Jannuari. A city I've seen only in memories and dreams, its cobblestone streets, its cottages. The way snow falls constantly, an ever-present rain of perfect, unique flakes. It needs to snow. It needs to always snow.

Something wet tingles my nose. I look up, my mouth opening in a true, pure grin. Snowflakes fall now, steady and strong, pouring down all the way to Jannuari. Covering us as we should be covered—in winter. Breathtaking, frozen, perfect winter.

I urge my horse into a gallop, the steady beating of his hooves chasing after the others toward Jannuari, a place of snow and light.

Your city.

Hannah's voice fills my senses, pulls up from the conduit magic that resides in me. She could talk to me all along, it appears, but didn't want to risk revealing what I am to Angra, which is why she never stopped us from looking for the locket halves. It was all a cover to protect Winter's line, and the dreams and visions were meant to ease me into conduits and magic, being linked to her in a way I never thought possible. My mother. I still have trouble adjusting to having a mother at all. I'm not sure where it fits in this new world.

Our city, I amend. *We wouldn't even be alive if it weren't for you.*

A knot of sadness forms in my head, Hannah's regret and pain. *But you will succeed where I failed.* She pauses, and I can feel a wave of her remorse in the silence. *I wanted to tell you. So many times, I wanted to speak to you. I couldn't risk you realizing who you are before you were old enough to use your magic, and if*

Angra found out what you are when you were still too young . . . She pauses, gasps. *Our kingdom would have been lost forever.*

I know, I say. It's all I can say. Today isn't a day for tearful apologies. Today is a day for inhaling the cold, snowy air, watching the Winterians as I gallop through them, seeing their smiling, radiant faces.

I spot Nessa up ahead, laughing and throwing snowballs at Conall. I see Dendera on her own horse, racing Henn to the wall. Happy and free, like they always should have been. People in the light, not just words in the dark.

It doesn't feel real. I've tried so long and so hard to be just Meira, but who I am isn't as simple as *just* anything. It's like this snowstorm over Jannuari—one flake falls, twisting down through the empty sky. One frozen speck of snow. Then another, and another, and before I know it the roads will be covered in dozens of distinct flakes. All these little pieces combining to create one giant, volatile snowstorm, something beautiful and dangerous and epic.

I'm Hannah's daughter. I'm Winter's conduit. I'm a warrior, a soldier, a lady, a queen, and most of all, as I plunge across the snowfield toward Jannuari's silent ruin, I'm Meira.

And no matter what Angra might try to do, he will not stop me from washing away the ashes of this kingdom's past and filling our lives with the glorious icy peace of snow.

ACKNOWLEDGMENTS

I'M NOT EVEN sure where to begin with this fantastically intimidating thing. "Write your acknowledgments
page," they said. "It'll be fun." And yes, it would be fun,
except I keep needing crying breaks, because this book is
so many things all at once and so many people have come
in and out of it and . . .

Oh geez. WATERWORKS.

First and most obviously of all, thanks are due to my
severely epic agent, Mackenzie Brady. She is the kind of
awesome where everything she says is at once brilliant and
infuriating in how right she is. *Snow Like Ashes* owes much
of its greatness to this woman, and without her I'd be lost.

To my editor, Kristin Rens, whose excitement for *Snow
Like Ashes* took my breath away from day one. I still have a
hard time wrapping my brain around the fact that someone

else loves my weird little world as much as I do, and has put so much time and effort into molding it. Kristin and all the people at Balzer + Bray are glorious, shining examples of publishing chivalry and might. Additionally, thanks are owed to Jeff Huang, who gave me the severely epic chakram along with severely epic giddiness. You, Sir, are wonderful.

To my ever-supportive, ever-positive, ever-forever husband (I will never get tired of calling you that!), Kelson. Being with you is the culmination of a lifelong dream every day.

To my writer friends who cheer me on, lift me up, and, when they have to, drag me back to earth in the most gentle and loving ways possible: Jenn "JR" Johansson (because double dates are more fun when our husbands listen to us yell at each other in the kitchen); Natalie Whipple (my cross-country-road-trip fairy godmother); Renee Collins (peachy good times!); Kasie West (the only person I'll make Junior Mint cupcakes for); Candice Kennington (I will never stop loving Courant); Michelle D. Argyle (*Cinders* breaks my heart on a daily basis); Jillian Schmidt (Sophie and M are next); Kathryn Rose (you are the Holy Grail of friends); Laura Elliot (I love you so much it hurts a little); Samantha Verant (who, to me at least, is a French princess); Nikki Raasch (blood is thicker than ink); Nikki Wang (for making my first piece of fanart ever—you are glorious); the YA Valentines and the OneFours (debuting with you was an honor); and all the other critique partners, writing groups, Twitter friends, bloggers, and various writer types who have made me laugh, given me advice, and kept me going in this crazy world of ours.

To my parents, Doug and Mary Jo, whose pride and excitement remind me why I'm so lucky to be their daughter. To my sister, Melinda—I wish everyone could have a sister as entertaining and lovable as you, and I will try my hardest to get someone to make *Snow Like Ashes* into a movie. To my grandfather Don, who makes me proud to be a Raasch. To my grandmother Dottie, who is no longer with us, but if she was, I know she'd be making all kinds of *Snow Like Ashes*-themed quilts. To my fantastically varied and endearing family—Lisa, Eddie, Mike, Grandma Connie, Debbie, Dan, Aunt Brenda—and all my cousins who grow up way too fast—Suzanne, Lillian, William, Brady, Hunter, Lauren, Luke, Delaney, Garrett, Krissy (and Wyatt), Brandi, and of course, Kayla the Librarian (love you, Older Cousin!).

To all the teachers and friends who have been so excited, so supportive, and so family-like that my eyes get all misty—Kim, Bob, Kayla, Jay, Kelly, and Katelyn; Janet Ross; Terri Thompson; Matt Langston (you will be in every one of my books); Ali (I will love you forever for being the first person who cried over this book) and Ashley (Three Musketeers for life!); Jennifer, Allie, Sarah Black, Diana, Sarah Kucharski, and Lauren (you guys made college worthwhile); and Stevie (the fancy-insole-add-on to the running-shoe-sale of my life).

To all those people . . . THANK YOU. For tolerating my weird writer behavior, for encouraging the crazy publishing ambitions of a twelve-year-old, for being so, so excited for me when those crazy publishing ambitions came true eleven years later. *Snow Like Ashes* may be the fulfillment of a lifelong goal, but having friends and family as amazing as each and every one of you is an even greater gift.

To properly thank all the people who helped shape this book in one way or another would take a novel in and of itself, so all I can do now is reach out and throw my arms around every single one of you. Yes, you too, who are reading my acknowledgments page and shaking your head in that half-concerned, half-amused way. The reason this book is anything now is because of YOU, magnificent YOU, for picking it up, for giving it a chance, for letting my bizarre world become part of your bizarre world.

You are better than any conduit.

The Epic Reads team sat down with Sara Raasch to ask her a few questions about *SNOW LIKE ASHES*

Snow Like Ashes kicks off an epic YA fantasy series—and one that made us fall in love with the genre. It feels like we owe a lot to Meira! What made you want to write her story?

Meira has been my wish-fulfillment character since I was a preteen. She saw me through middle school, high school, and college, the character who embodied everything I wanted to be—loyal, confident, stubborn, and above all, self-assured. Once I started seriously pursuing publishing, I knew this book had to be my debut. So I rewrote it, keeping all the pieces that had seen me through the hardest times, and I was thrilled when it sold. I love that I can share Meira's story with the world and help encourage other teens who might also want to be like Meira but haven't found their voice yet.

At the start of the book, Meira has feelings for her best friend, Winter's would-be king. No spoilers, but her story gets a bit of a twist in the final act. We're here for the ride regardless of where it takes us, but when it comes to romance, what's your favorite trope?

My favorite trope can be summed up in one couple: Zutara! Even though they weren't endgame, Zuko and Katara from *Avatar: The Last Airbender* are my always and forever couple obsession. Enemies to vaguely tolerated allies to begrudgingly supportive friends to lovers? SIGN ME UP.

If you had to pick one scene in this book, which would you say was your favorite to write?

I love chapter 26! Dream sequences are always so fun—getting to weave symbolic visions alongside brutal emotional truths—and this one is the pinnacle of a lot of the book's arcs. It was so satisfying to write!

One of the reasons that we love fantasy worlds is that they afford us an escape to places filled with magic, adventure, and almost limitless possibilities. If you found yourself in the world of *Snow Like Ashes*, which of your kingdoms would you want to live in?

I'd love to live in the Autumn Kingdom! Who doesn't love autumn weather, amiright? Perfectly crisp, not too humid, NO ALLERGIES; plus, the smell of fallen leaves everywhere. And pumpkin everything! Give me Autumn forever, please.

And for all the readers with worlds in their own imaginations, we have to ask: When you set out to build a fantasy world, where do you start?

Each fantasy world for me begins with a nugget of an idea. Whether that's a question, a theme, an object, et cetera—no matter what it is, I take that nugget and extrapolate details from it. What would people who live in a country like this look like? Sound like? What would they eat? How would they interact with other countries? What kind of seasons would they have? The list of questions is endless, and I spend way too much time going through them with my own projects! But if you just start asking questions, pretty soon, you'll find yourself with a solid fantasy world.

Read on for a sneak peek at

ICE LIKE FIRE

Meira

DENDERA TAKES US to a square that opens mere paces from the Tadil Mine. The buildings here stand whole and clean, paths swept clear of debris, cottages repaired. The families of the miners already deep in the Tadil pack the square along with Cordellan soldiers, most bouncing from foot to foot in an effort to keep warm. An open-air tent caps the entrance to the square, our first stop as we file in alongside tables littered with maps and calculations.

Sir and Alysson bow their heads in quiet discussion within the tent. Their focus shifts to me, a genuine smile crossing Alysson's face, a sweep of analysis passing over Sir's. They're just as sharply dressed as Nessa and Dendera in their gowns—while traditional Winterian clothing for women consists of pleated, ivory, floor-length dresses, most of the men wear blue tunics and pants under lengths of white fabric that wrap in an X pattern around their torsos. It's still strange to me to see Sir dressed in anything other than his battle gear, but he doesn't even have a dagger at his hip. The threat is gone, our enemy dead.

"My queen." Sir bows his head. My skin bristles at my title on his lips, one more thing I have yet to grow accustomed to. Sir, calling me "my queen." Sir, my general. Sir, Mather's father.

His name seizes me.

Mather, back in Jannuari, training the Winterian army. Mather, who hasn't really talked to me since we sat on our horses side-by-side outside of Jannuari, before I fully took up the responsibilities of being queen, and he fully surrendered everything he thought he once was.

I'd hoped he just needed time to adjust—but it's been three months since he's said more than "Yes, my queen," to me. I have no idea how to go about bridging the distance between us—I just keep telling myself, maybe foolishly, that when he's ready, he'll talk to me again.

Or maybe it has less to do with him no longer being king and more to do with Theron, who, even though our engagement has been dissolved, is still a permanent fixture in my life. For now, it's easier not to think about Mather. To fake the mask, force the smile, and cover up the awfulness underneath.

I wish I didn't have to force it away—I wish none of us had to, and we were all strong enough to deal with the things that have happened to us.

A tingle of chill blossoms in my chest. Sparking and wild, icy and alive, and I stifle a sigh at what it signifies.

When Angra conquered my kingdom sixteen years ago, he did so by breaking our Royal Conduit. And when a conduit is broken in defense of a kingdom, the ruler of that kingdom becomes the conduit themselves. Their body, their life force—it all merges with the magic. No one knows this, save for me, Angra, and the woman whose death turned me into Winter's conduit: my mother.

You can *help them deal with what happened,* Hannah prods. Since the magic *is* me, unlimited within my body, she's able to speak to me, even after her death.

I'm not forcing healing on them, I say, withering at the thought. I know the magic could heal their physical wounds—but emotional? I can't—

I didn't mean that, Hannah says. *You can show them that they have a future. That Winter is capable of surviving.*

My tension relaxes. *Okay,* I manage.

The crowd stills as Sir leads me out of the tent. Twenty workers are already deep in the mine, as every opening has gone the same way—they go in, I stay up top and use my magic to fill them with inhuman agility and endurance. Magic only works over short distances—I couldn't use it on the miners if I was in Jannuari. But here, they're only in the tunnels just ahead.

"Whenever you're ready, my queen," Sir says. If he senses

3

how much I hate these mine openings, he doesn't say anything, just steps away with his arms behind his back.

I grind my jaw and try to ignore everything else—Hannah, Sir, all the eyes on me, the heavy quiet that falls.

My magic used to be glorious. When we were trapped in Spring and it reared up and saved us; when we first returned to Winter and I wasn't sure how to help everyone, and it came flooding out of me to bring snow and fill my people with vitality. When I had no idea what I wanted or how to do anything, I was grateful for the way the magic always just *knew*.

But now I realize that if I wanted to stop it from pouring out of me, surging through the earth, and filling the miners with strength and endurance, I couldn't. That's what scares me most about these times—I can *feel* how boundless the magic is. It sparks and swirls up, and I know, deep in the throbbing pit of my heart, that my body would give out long before the magic would even consider stopping.

I've tried to harness the streams of iciness that whirl through my chest and turn every vein into crystallized snow. But reason clogs my certainty, knowing that my people need the very magic I'm trying to stifle, and before I can will myself to control it, it's done whatever it wanted to do.

Like right now, the magic pours into the miners before I'm able to breathe. I stand in its wake, trembling, eyes snapping open to look on the expectant faces of the crowd. They can't see it or sense it, unless I channel it into them.

No one knows how empty I feel, like a holster for arrows, existing only to hold a greater weapon.

I tried to tell Sir about this—and immediately choked it back when Noam came in the room. If Noam finds out that all he needs to do is have an enemy break his Royal Conduit and he would *become* his own conduit, he wouldn't have to find the chasm. He'd be all-powerful, filled with magic.

And he wouldn't need to pretend to care about Winter anymore.

I turn, hungry for a diversion. The crowd takes that as my dismissal and softly applauds.

"Speak to them," Sir urges when I move for the tent.

I curve my arms around myself. "I've given the same speech every time we've opened a mine. They've heard it all before—rebirth, progression, hope."

"They expect it." Sir doesn't yield, and when I take another step toward the tent, he grabs my arm. "My queen. You're forgetting your position."

If only, I think, then immediately regret it. I don't want to forget who I am now.

I just wish I could be both this *and* myself.

Alysson and Dendera stand quietly behind Sir; Conall and Garrigan wait a few paces off to the side; Theron made it here and converses with a few of his men. This normalcy makes it easier to notice how out of place Nessa suddenly looks next to her brothers. Her shoulders angle forward, but her attention is pinned on an alley to my right.

I shake out of Sir's grip and nod in Nessa's direction as I stride forward.

"They're back," she whispers when I reach her. Her eyes cut to the alley, and I can see from this angle that Finn and Greer stand at the edge of the light, motionless until my attention locks onto them.

Finn bobs his head and they move toward the main tent as if they've been in Gaos all along. They left Jannuari with us but split off soon after, creeping away before any Cordellans could realize that the queen's Winterian council went from five members to three.

Sir guides me to the tent as if afraid I'll refuse to do that too. But I push ahead of him, crowding around the table in the center with Alysson and Dendera. We all try to maintain a relaxed air, nothing out of the ordinary, nothing to draw attention. But my anxiety splits into frayed strands that loop more tightly around my lungs with every passing second.

"What did you find?" Sir is the first to speak, his tone low.

Finn and Greer push against the table, sweat streaking through smudges of dirt on their faces. I cross my arms. Such a normal thing—the queen's advisors returning from a mission. But I can't get the gnawing in my head to agree.

I should have gone on this trip to retrieve information for the monarch—I shouldn't be the monarch herself.

Finn opens his sack and pulls out a bundle while Greer removes one from his waist. "Stopped in Spring first," Finn says, his attention on the table. Only Conall, Garrigan, and Nessa look out of the tent, watching the Cordellans for any sign of movement toward us. "The early reports that the Cordellans received were correct—no sign of Angra. Spring has transformed into a military state, run by a handful of his remaining generals. No magic, though, and no warmongering."

Relief fights to sputter through me, but I hold it back. Just because Spring is silent doesn't mean everything is fine—if Angra survived the battle in Abril and wanted to keep his survival a secret, he'd be a fool to stay in Spring.

And since we haven't heard a word from him since the battle, if he is alive . . . he definitely doesn't want anyone to know.

"We passed through Autumn on our way to Summer—both are unchanged," Finn continues. "Autumn was gracious, and Summer didn't even realize we were there, which made poking around for rumors of Angra easier. Yakim and Ventralli, on the other hand . . ."

I jolt closer to the table. "They found you?"

Greer nods. "Word spread of two Winterians in the kingdom. Luckily when we said we were there on behalf of our queen, they seemed to soften toward us—but they didn't let us out of their sight until we left their borders. Both Yakim and Ventralli sent gifts for you."

He nudges the bundles toward me. I pick up the first one and pull back the matted cloth to reveal a book, a thick volume bound in leather with black lettering embossed on the cover.

"*The Effective Implementation of Tax Laws Under Queen Giselle?*" I read. The Yakimian queen sent me a book about tax laws she enacted?

Finn shrugs. "She wanted to give us more, but we told her we hadn't the resources to carry it all. She invites you to her kingdom. They both did, actually."

That makes me pick up the other package. This one unrolls, spreading over the table to reveal a tapestry, multicolored threads weaving together to form a scene of Winter's snowy fields overtaking Spring's green-and-floral forest.

"The Ventrallan queen had that created," Finn notes. "To congratulate you on your victory."

I trace a finger down the twirl of silver thread that separates Winter from Spring. "We were in Ventralli and Yakim before Angra fell, gathering supplies and other such things, and people saw us, and never once did the royal families care. Why now?"

Greer's age deepens in the way his wrinkles crease, his body slouches. "Cordell has its hands in two Seasons now—Autumn and Winter. With such a strong foothold here, they'd be able to take Spring easily too, if Noam chose to do so. Summer has trade agreements with Yakim, but no formal alliance. The other Rhythms know Noam is seeking the magic chasm, and they fear his ambitions.

They're testing Winter's allegiance to Cordell, to see if they can unseat Noam."

"They were both most adamant that you visit them," Finn adds. "Queen Giselle told us you are always welcome. Queen Raelyn said the same of Ventralli—she seems to be the one speaking for the king, though he was just as eager to meet you."

I shake my head. "Did any of those kingdoms show signs of . . . him?"

I can't say his name. Can't force myself to feel it grating on my tongue.

"No, my queen," Greer replies. "There was no sign of Angra. We didn't go to Paisly—the trip through their mountains is treacherous, and after the attitudes we observed in Ventralli and Yakim, we didn't think it necessary."

"Why?"

"Because Paisly is a Rhythm too—they wouldn't host an ousted Season king. Yakim and Ventralli were barely willing to host *us*. I don't think . . ." Greer pauses. "My queen, I don't think Angra is in Primoria."

The way he says that makes me shut my eyes. When I first suggested that someone search the world for Angra, everyone thought I was being overly cautious. He vanished after the battle in Abril, but most believe that the magic disintegrated him—not that he escaped.

"He's dead," Sir says. "He is no longer a threat we should concern ourselves with."

I stare at him, drained. He—and the rest of my Winterian council—still believes Angra was defeated, even after I told them that his Royal Conduit had been overtaken by the Decay, a dark magic created thousands of years ago, before the Royal Conduits were made. Then everyone had small conduits, but when they slowly began to use the magic for evil, that negative use birthed the Decay. With the creation of the Royal Conduits and the purge of all smaller conduits, the Decay weakened, but it didn't die—it fed on Angra's power until Mather broke Spring's staff.

If Angra is alive, he could be like me, a conduit himself, unburdened by the limitations of his object-conduit. And the Decay could be . . . endless.

But if Angra is alive, why would he be hidden away? Why wouldn't he have swept through the world, enslaving us all? Maybe that's what makes Sir so certain he's dead.

Everyone watches me, even Conall, Garrigan, and Nessa. My eyes shift past them and open wide. One second, no one watched the Cordellans for one second—

"Trouble?"

A Cordellan soldier ducks into the tent, flanked by three others. The moment their armored frames fill the space, my council yanks to attention, casting off any pretense of ease.

I growl deep in my throat as Theron enters the tent too.

"I'm sure they're discussing how best to proceed with the Tadil's spoils," Theron guesses, moving to stand beside me.

He tips his head at his men. "No trouble here."

The soldiers hesitate, clearly unconvinced, but Theron is their prince. They back out of the tent as Theron tucks his hand around my waist. The chill of magic palpitates through me, only marred now—I shouldn't need someone from another land to sweep to my rescue. Especially to fend off the very men who are supposed to be protecting us.

"Thank you for interceding, Prince Theron," Sir offers.

Theron bobs his head. "No need to thank me. You should be allowed to gather in your own kingdom without Cordellan interference."

I cock an eyebrow at him. "Don't let your father hear you say that."

That makes Theron tighten his grip on me, drawing me closer in a protective lurch. "My father hears whatever he wants to hear," he says. "What were you discussing, though?"

Sir steps closer. My eyes flick to the side, noting Finn and Greer striding down the road, most likely heading to freshen up so as not to appear travel worn.

"We were discussing only—"

But whatever lie Sir might have been about to tell proves unnecessary. Theron unwinds himself from me and snatches the tapestry from the table.

"Ventralli?" he asks. "Why do you have this?"

Of course he would know where the tapestry is from. His mother was the aunt of the current Ventrallan king—Theron's room in Bithai is stuffed with paintings, masks, and other treasures from his Ventrallan side.

I glance at Sir, who holds my gaze. The same emotion coats everyone else—Dendera watches me, Alysson grips the edge of the table. All waiting for my response.

All wanting me to lie.

Finn and Greer's journey was supposed to be secret, one frail act of Winter in the face of Cordell's occupation. Proof that we could do something, *be* something, on our own.

But lying to Theron . . .

Sir's jaw tightens when I hang silent for a beat too long. "The rubble of Gaos," he says. "We found it in the buildings."

I don't realize until the words leave his lips that Theron might find out the truth anyway—if Giselle and Raelyn welcomed Finn and Greer, news will spread. Noam will eventually hear that his Rhythm brethren had Winterian visitors.

I choke, but the lie has been told. Backtracking now would only look worse—wouldn't it? I can't very well ask Sir's opinion on this—besides, he's the one who lied. Maybe . . . it's okay.

No. It isn't okay. But I don't know how a queen would make this okay.

"It's beautiful." Theron runs his fingers down the threads. "A Winter–Spring battle?"

He looks at me, expectant.

I actually manage a chuckle. "You're asking me? You're the one with Ventrallan blood."

Theron cocks a grin. "Ah, but I'd hoped some of me had rubbed off on you by now."

My cheeks heat, egged on by the group of my advisors still watching us, by the way Theron straightens, tilting his head to me. I can't tell if he knows Sir lied—all I can see is the look he gets whenever something artistic is around, a softening at his edges. Seeing him like this is such a nice change from his recent tension, balancing on the edge of fear and memories, that I almost miss where else I've seen it before.

I jolt with realization. It's exactly how he looked at me on the fields outside of Gaos, and every time he wants to kiss me—like I'm a work of art he's trying to interpret.

My heart thumps so loudly I'm sure he can hear. If we were standing in his room, he the prince of Cordell, myself a soldier of Winter, I would have swooned without another thought.

But I look around the tent, at Sir, Dendera, Alysson. Even Conall, Garrigan, and Nessa. They all look at me with similar gazes—like they've only ever known me as the queen of Winter, a figure owed reverence and worship.

I'm not a work of art or even worthy of their reverence. I'm someone who just helped lie to one of her closest friends.

This is what Winter needs. This is who Winter needs me to be.
I hate who I am now.

ALL'S FAIR IN LOVE AND . . .

Don't miss any of these exclusive Epic Reads Editions!

EpicReads.com

JOIN THE

Epic Reads
COMMUNITY